THE VALLEY
AND THE FLOOD

THE VALLEY
AND THE FLOOD

REBECCA MAHONEY

RAZORBILL

Author's note on content: *The Valley and the Flood* contains depictions of anxiety and post-traumatic stress disorder, including several scenes of panic attacks and a brief description of violent intrusive thoughts.

RAZORBILL

An imprint of Penguin Random House LLC, New York

First published in the United States of America by Razorbill,
an imprint of Penguin Random House LLC, 2021

Copyright © 2021 by Rebecca Mahoney

RAZORBILL & colophon are registered trademarks of Penguin Random House LLC.

Visit us online at penguinrandomhouse.com.

LIBRARY OF CONGRESS CATALOGING-IN-PUBLICATION DATA
Names: Mahoney, Rebecca, author.
Title: The valley and the flood / Rebecca Mahoney.
Description: New York : Razorbill, 2020. | Audience: Ages 12+.
Summary: "When Rose Colter hears a voicemail from her own phone playing on her car radio, she follows the broadcast to the small town of Lotus Valley, where she discovers that she's the prophesied bringer of a catastrophic flood"—Provided by publisher.
Identifiers: LCCN 2020020594 | ISBN 9780593114353 (hardcover)
ISBN 9780593114360 (ebook)
Subjects: CYAC: Supernatural—Fiction. | Prophecies—Fiction.
Post-traumatic stress disorder—Fiction. | Grief—Fiction.
Classification: LCC PZ7.1.M34675 Val 2020 | DDC [Fic]—dc23
LC record available at https://lccn.loc.gov/2020020594

Printed in the United States of America

1 3 5 7 9 10 8 6 4 2

Design by Rebecca Aidlin

Text set in Adobe Garamond Pro

To Grandma, the greatest lover of stories I will ever know:

here's mine.

DECEMBER 27, NOW

NOTE TO SELF: the local time is 11:46 p.m., and there are three hundred and thirty-two miles between Las Vegas, Nevada, and San Diego, California.

The drive is long and hot, snarling through hills and canyons and pockets of nothing. In the daytime, there is life, the smell of rubber and pavement and the sound of traffic. But it is dark now. It is quiet. And this late hour, in this empty place, does not belong to you.

The GPS is below you, a bright pop against the night. It calculates four hours and thirty-one minutes for your drive home.

But you are not going home yet.

One

THE SIREN

MY TAILLIGHTS CUT a path down the desert road, flickering with every blink of my hazards. I slide sideways in the driver's seat until my feet touch pavement, and I look past my trunk, past the steady rhythm of the lights, past where I can see anything at all. But it doesn't look like anyone else is coming.

And of course they aren't. It's been two hours since I merged onto the 15. It's been twenty minutes since I drove down an unfamiliar exit, following signs for a gas station—which, if it even exists, is still not close enough to see. The only sign of life out here is a radio tower, miles away, blinking its own rhythm back at me. And the people at my destination aren't expecting me.

It's all of the things that a driver, alone in the middle of the night, isn't supposed to do. And most of it was on purpose.

I reach across the dashboard past the radio, blaring the only all-night station I can still get from Vegas, and I unlatch the glove compartment. My hand stays with the door as it descends, ready to close it again the moment I see headlights approaching. But I don't have that kind of luck.

My laugh comes out as a breath as my fingers find what they're looking for, just past the car manual and under a pile of napkins: the smooth, cold screen of my phone. It's like the setup to a joke my stepfather would tell. *I thought we were supposed to be the ones hiding your phone, Rosie.* That's what he'd probably say, if he knew about any of this.

It sits flat in my palm, screen blank. I haven't heard it once since I left Las Vegas. It should be safe to check.

No bars. No signal. That would be why.

"Okay," I whisper to the lit screen in my hand. "No sudden moves."

It doesn't have anything to say to that. Which is what I appreciate about inanimate objects: no back talk. But this time, I'd really like its word.

I leave the door open behind me as I follow the path of my hazards. The phone is an arm's length away like a scout, and I watch the top corner of the screen for a signal. The way ahead flickers in and out, and I stop only at the very edge, where the road back to Nevada extends into the dark. For a second, a bar pops into view. It doesn't last.

It lasts long enough, though. The phone buzzes once.

My arm jerks back hard, without my permission, and the phone lands facedown on the road.

The sound is dramatic enough that for one wildly hopeful second, I think it must be broken. But when I pick it up, the screen is still lit through a spiderweb of cracks. Like I said, I don't have that kind of luck.

Two missed calls.

Two voicemails.

And still, zero bars.

Behind me, back in the car, the easy-listening jazz fades away, and a soft voice filters through the rolled-down windows. *We hope you're still with us, Las Vegas*, the announcer murmurs. *You're listening to KLVZ. And don't you even think of going to bed, because we'll be here all night.*

"And so," I say to the dark ribbon of pavement, "will I."

A shiver of static cuts the signal, and when my head snaps toward it, I can see how far I've strayed down the road. I backtrack carefully, as if my footsteps might stir something that the radio hasn't, and I slide my fingers under the hood to pop the latch. I've never fixed Stanley without my mother here before, but maybe the problem will be obvious.

The problem is not obvious. The only thing that's *obvious* is that Stanley won't be starting up again anytime soon. He lets out a little hiss and a puff of steam, and that's about the only answer I get from him.

"Oh, baby," I say. "What did I do to you?"

Stanley the Sedan, who has all the sparkle and stamina of his eighth-grade-history-teacher namesake, has never tolerated long drives under the desert sun. Though up until twenty minutes ago, the desert nights suited him just fine.

I shiver. It's hard to imagine the desert sun now. My thin T-shirt might as well be paper against the wind. I had a sweatshirt at some point, but when I checked my bag a few minutes ago, I didn't see it. Still in Vegas, if I had to guess.

Behind me, the breeze picks up. And something rustles.

I look, though I know there's no one there. Even if there were, the most expensive thing I own is right here, the gently smoking

Volvo that no one in their right mind would steal. But I climb into the driver's seat and lock the doors.

The radio signal wavers, first to static, then to the kind of thready hum that aspires to static. "Oh, come on," I mutter, nudging the knob left, to the low, low stations. But despite the radio's promise, it doesn't look like it's going to be here all night.

This is how we die. That's what my best friend, Gaby, would say, were she here.

"This isn't how we die," I murmur to the passenger's seat.

This is absolutely *how we die*, Gaby would respond. *Desert, middle of the night, waiting for some stranger to give us a lift? We are super getting murdered. Be on the lookout for Rose Colter and Gabrielle Summer, last seen in the back seat of an unmarked van.*

Were Gaby actually sitting next to me, I might remind her that I've been listening to her compendium of scary stories and urban legends since we were five. In all the interesting stories, *we* would be the monsters.

I balance my phone on my palm, weighing my options, the silence of the desert versus the two missed calls sitting in my voicemail. Carefully, I hit play. One thing I know for sure now: if someone's calling you in the middle of the night, it's not to say hi.

Rosie? My mother's voice comes through first. She sounds tense, tired—but not like anything is wrong. I've gotten good at telling the difference. *Can you call me tomorrow, even for a few minutes? Dan and I wanted to check when you'd be home.*

There's a pause. In the silence, I think I can hear one of my brother Sammy's cartoons.

If—if you change your mind, I can drive over right away, she says. *I already told Kathy I might have to take some time off, so.* She leaves the thought unfinished. *Give Jon and Flora a hug for me. I love you.*

I flinch. I know she loves me, obviously. But she never used to say it so much.

The message comes to an end, and the voice changes from Mom's sleepy contralto to Flora Summer's voice, wavering like a tuning bowstring. Even in the best circumstances, she never sounds entirely sure of herself, like every sentence comes with a hidden question mark. Gaby used to say that her mom held conversations like she was trying to walk and talk and check for snipers all at once.

Rosie? Flora says. *I—I know you're probably driving. But if you get this, I wanted to tell you that you can come back, even if it's late. We have more than enough room for both of you here, so . . .*

She clears her throat, hard. *Please call me. I want you both to be part of this.* And the message ends there.

I don't notice until that moment that my fist has been clenched the entire time.

I wasn't being totally truthful before. I don't think you need to be *that* truthful when the only person you're talking to is yourself. And I didn't say anything *un*true: I did want the road to myself, and my car wouldn't have survived a daytime drive. But there's only one reason why I'm here, one reason why I left Vegas just before midnight, four days before I was supposed to: to get out as quickly as possible.

I lose track of the phone for a second after the message ends. The second lasts long enough that the first saved message begins to play.

Rose—

I jam my thumb against the cracked screen hard enough that for a second I think I've deleted the message instead of stopping it. But I didn't. I didn't. I stare at Gaby's name long enough to convince myself of that.

Over the blood pounding in my ears, I hear myself descend into nauseous laughter. It might have solved some of my problems if I *had* deleted it.

Fingers still shaking, I delete my mother's message, and then Flora Summer's. I leave Gaby's right where it is, and I tuck the phone back into the glove compartment.

And then it's quiet again. Just me and the desert.

THIS FAR AWAY from the cities, with all the different patterns of light and distance, the night sky ripples like water. This time last year, that was what I would have been here for: to spread a blanket across the dirt and watch the stars scrape against the edges of the universe.

Last year, Gaby would have been here. And let's be honest, we'd be driving already. She'd hack into some rancher's Wi-Fi and find some engine repair how-to. She used to brag that she had as many talents as there were videos on YouTube. My own talents are a bit less practical.

I close my eyes and tilt my head back. I'm not sure how long I stay like that. Or how long the noise goes on without me noticing.

. . . re?

I sit up, dead straight. But it's as quiet as it was before.

Until I hear it again.

Ro . . . are . . .

I open the glove compartment, but the cracked screen of my phone is black. It's not until I hear the crackle of static that I remember the radio.

It's still at the low, low station I left it at before, but this broadcast is coming from somewhere else. The sound is uneven, unclear. But I'm close.

Very gently, I turn the knob clockwise, but even that's too much. The static is worse now. Out of the corner of my eye, the radio tower blinks. And I wonder.

Ro . . . are . . . ere?

I breathe in, slowly, to steady my hand. And I give the knob the slightest flick to the left.

The sound is crystal clear this time. Clear enough that before the voice speaks again, I hear her shaky inhale.

Rose? Gaby says. *Are you there?*

I hear the next word form in the back of her throat. But I can't make it out, I never can. I hear muffled words behind her, definitely male. And the call ends as it always does: with a swish of air.

And then it begins to play again.

Rose, are you there? Rose, are you there? Rose—

All of a sudden, there's hard, heavy breaths, drowning out the message. Mine. I jump out of the car, sure that I'm going to be sick, but before I get the chance, I catch sight of it again. East of the road. The tower, its light blinking in time with the cadence of Gaby's voice.

Rose, are you there? Rose, are you there?

I'm not sure if I make a real decision. It's an instinct almost as old as I am: go to Gaby.

I packed light. All I've got to carry is my backpack—and I do, wrenching it out of the trunk and onto my shoulders. I'm already moving forward as I turn, but I double back, reach in through the window of the car to snatch my phone from the glove compartment and my keys from the ignition.

The tower's still visible, still blinking. Not too far away.

I turn the broadcast off. But I can still hear the echo, looping through the back of my brain: *Rose, are you there? Rose, are you there?*

Three hundred and sixty-one days ago, that voicemail, time-stamped 1:05 a.m., was waiting for me when I woke up. One single short voicemail from Gaby, just minutes before she left the New Year's Eve party at Ariella Kaplan's cabin. I wasn't there. And she wasn't expecting me.

That wouldn't have been so unusual. Despite what people thought, we didn't do *everything* together. As long as I had known her, Gaby had always had more. More friends, more energy, more willingness to try whatever. She was brave. She was fun.

She was killed three hundred and sixty-one days ago, in the early hours of the morning, at the corner of Sutton and Chamblys.

I leave the road. And as I start to run, my car, the broadcast, and the rest of the world fall away.

Two

THE SPOILER ALERT

I DON'T SEE the blinking light anymore.

The sun is above the horizon now, angled straight into my eyes. Everything ahead is a blazing blur. But I haven't changed direction. This should be the right way.

I pull my water out of my bag. The sun's not unbearable, not yet, and there's a lingering chill I can't shake. But the dry desert air has started to coat my tongue, and a very well-trained part of my brain is asking when I last had anything to drink. That's the sort of thing I've gotten good at. Losing your best friend means relearning the basics of staying upright, until you're better at it than most people.

It's funny. Just last year I would have said I knew *more* about death than most people. Gaby and I were, after all, founding members of the Thorn Brook Elementary Dead Dads Club. But Gaby's father died while she was waiting to be born. Mine, when I was two. We knew a lot less than we thought we did.

Like I said: It was more impulse than decision, leaving my car back there. But terrible decisions are still decisions.

For the first time since I left the car, I stop. I glance over my shoulder to where the road probably is. And I make a cold, hard assessment. I don't know where I am. I've lost sight of where I'm going. And Gaby Summer is dead.

Despite the steadily rising heat, the hairs on my arms stand up. Whether in my mouth or in my head, the words always feel wrong. They're *not* wrong, though. It's the one thing I know for sure.

It was a closed casket funeral. If it were me and not her, Gaby would have needed to see. But I never needed proof. I knew before I officially knew.

So. Note to self: Here are a few more things you know for sure. It was late when you heard that broadcast. You weren't exactly in the clearest state of mind when you left Vegas. And most importantly, Gaby's cell phone no longer works. The only one with that message is you. Anything else is paranoia.

Hypervigilance. That's what my therapist, Maurice, had said the first time I tried to use the *p* word.

Hyper-what now? I'd said.

That sense you're describing, like you're constantly scanning for threats? he'd said. *Hypervigilance.*

Oh? I'd said. *That still sounds like paranoia to me.*

Not really. He'd smiled one of those deceptively placid smiles. *Not the way you mean it, at least.*

English is Maurice's third language. So naturally, he understands it better than any native speaker I know. He listens to every part of a word: the meaning, the nuance, and the stuff that goes unsaid.

But hypervigilance, to me, has always been a physical thing: tight shoulders, tension headaches, that potential energy too deep in my rib cage to unfurl. Sometimes it's just a feeling, a shift in the air that washes the world into an uneasy gray. It isn't hearing broadcasts that couldn't possibly exist.

The early morning haze lifts. And gradually, up ahead, shapes start to form: dark and boxy cutouts against the sunlight, and behind them, the thin black line of the tower.

I'm a lot closer than I thought.

A bit farther and the shapes start to form into neat rows of houses, little villas of reds and oranges and angular bricks. The kind of desert houses that try too hard to be desert houses. The closer I get, the more I see, lined up at the edge of a thin wrought-iron fence, and behind them, violently green grass and the edge of a spiraling street.

It's late enough that I should see people. I should at least *hear* them. But there's no movement. And it's as quiet as it ever was.

I slide my backpack off my shoulder and toss it over the fence.

It lands with a soft *thwump*. Not quite soft enough to go undetected. But nothing changes. The air stirs a little, curling the grass in on itself. And that's about all the response I get.

So I go ahead and vault the fence, too.

I touch down on the grass, right into someone's backyard. There's a big picture window facing me head-on, curtains trailing at the edges like it's a screen and I'm the movie. I don't seem to have an audience. From what I can see, the house is fully furnished and totally empty. Walking quickly, I round the corner and step out onto the street.

Places like this aren't totally unheard of in the sprawl of the Mojave Desert. My stepfather has a thing for abandoned places—I've heard all about housing developments built in the middle of nowhere, finished and polished and never filled. But I've never seen a place so dead look so . . . cared for. The paint seems fresh. The windows are spotless. The grass is similar enough from house to house that I'd think it was fake if I hadn't touched it myself. There's a sign facedown in one of the driveways, and I carefully wedge my shoe under it to flip it over.

A drawing of a '50s housewife-type grins up at me, teeth glinting in the sunlight. LETHE RIDGE LUXURY HOMES, the text proclaims. WE'VE BEEN WAITING FOR YOU!

I laugh darkly. "Sounds like a threat, bro."

I use the broadcast tower's spire for reference as I curve through cul-de-sacs and dead ends, and I spend more time doubling back than moving forward. There's no way to get anywhere in this place without cutting across someone's lawn, but I decide to stick to the street.

That turns out to be a good move on my part when, with a hiss and a sputter, every sprinkler in the neighborhood starts running.

"Sprinklers," I say out loud. Maybe if I reason with my stomach, it'll find its way back down my throat. "They're sprinklers."

"Mmm," hums a voice from behind me. "Like clockwork."

I spin around. And behind me, where I was walking just seconds ago, there's a girl lying on her back in the road.

She doesn't notice me stumble back a step. Or if she notices, she doesn't care. She stays sprawled on the ground, her eyes still closed.

I squint down at her. She's even whiter than I am, if that's possible—way too white to be sunbathing in the middle of the street. But she stretches out a bit farther, taking in more and more of the light. The pavement must be getting hot. She doesn't seem too bothered.

"Um," I say. "Are you okay?"

"What?" she says, eyes still closed. "Oh. Right. You know those times when you just can't get warm?"

I try not to stare. That doesn't work. "Not really."

"Well." She sits up, shaking her loose blonde curls. "All in good time."

I get a better look at her face now: round, pretty. Probably my age. And still not looking at me.

Carefully, I ease my water bottle out of my backpack's side pocket and take a few steps toward her. "Here."

She opens her eyes, but she still doesn't look at me. She takes in the water bottle instead. "No thank you," she says.

"Come on," I say. "Desert 101: hydrate. And, you know, watch out for snakes."

Finally, she smiles. Crooked with a little squint, like that was unforgivably nerdy but she'll allow it. It's so similar to how Gaby would have looked at me that for a second I forget what we're doing.

"Well," the girl says, extending her hand. "How can I say no, then?"

I close the distance between us and hold it out to her. Our fingers brush as she takes the bottle.

And suddenly she's looking right at me.

Her eyes widen a little. She looks me up and down. And then she says, "What brings you here?"

Without realizing it, I've taken a step back again. "Car trouble."

"I see," she says. "You walked all this way?" I make a small, affirmative noise in the back of my throat. "You'll be going to Gibson Repairs from here. Theresa will take care of you. And I think you'll be grateful for the quick turnaround."

"Th-thank you," I say. "Is that close to the broadcast tower?"

Her eyes narrow, just a fraction. "Same road. Eight blocks down Morningside Drive. Why?"

"Point of reference," I say.

She nods at that. "I can walk you there, if you think you'll get lost."

"No, that's fine," I say quickly. "But thank you for the offer."

I turn away and start walking, but behind me, I hear her climb to her feet, her heels clicking against the blacktop. "Would you like a reading, then? In exchange for the water."

"What?" I turn, my feet still moving. She misspoke, maybe, or I misheard her. "Um, no. You can keep it."

"You can't get something for nothing," she says. "Didn't anyone ever tell you that?"

"It's really fine," I say. "I don't need anything."

"I don't mean to tell you your business, Rose," she says. "But it looks like you need quite a lot."

I stop dead. When I turn back, she's looking at me with a mild, unassuming frown.

"Did I give you my name?" I say slowly.

She brushes past that. "What do you want to know?" she says. "Let's see . . ." She hums and tilts her head to the side. "You want to know if it's going to get worse, right?"

I lean hard on my back foot. Lately, when I hear something that doesn't make sense, it means that I missed the context, that my mind's been wandering. It's not wandering now.

"Okay," I say. "I don't know what you're talking about, so—"

"Or would you like to know what's going to happen to Nick Lansbury?" she says. "*He's* certainly on your mind, isn't he?"

There's a weight on the curve of my throat. Sudden. Heavy. Normal these days, whenever I hear that name. But it's a name she couldn't possibly know.

"Who are you?" It's hard to speak, like there's a wall in my lungs.

"Okay, okay, I get it." She waves a hand. "Not everyone wants to get personal, I understand. Something else, then."

"Where did you hear that name?" I want it to sound threatening. Instead I sound like I'm underwater. "What do you—"

"Just a moment now." She looks me up and down, and her impassive face flickers with something too brief to see. The hot, dry breeze starts to build. And something decisive shifts behind her eyes.

"You will find a window that is not a window," she says. "You will find a thing as old as the desert and twice as lonely. You will find exactly what you're looking for."

Behind me, something slams. A window shutter snapped open in the wind—it raps against the side of its house twice, then shivers to a halt. My eyes are off the girl for a second, maybe two.

But by the time I turn back, there is no girl. Just me. And when I listen for the click of her heels, all I hear are sprinklers.

I start walking. Carefully at first, conscious of every noise I make and every move in the corner of my eye. And then I tear through Lethe Ridge in a flat-out run. This time I don't care whose lawn I'm on.

I don't slow down, even when the spinning cul-de-sacs give way to a straighter, wider road, even when the identical houses start to thin and I can see glimpses of the small city beyond them. I barely stop to read the sign that marks the end of the Lethe Ridge housing development.

CITY LIMITS, it says. LOTUS VALLEY.

ENJOY YOUR STAY!

Three

THE ROAD

MORNINGSIDE DRIVE, AS far as I can see, runs the length of Lotus Valley. But it's not much busier than the empty streets I left behind in Lethe Ridge.

But at least there are signs of life. There's the odd car headed out to the desert. The Sweet as Pie Diner, from my glimpse through the windows, could actually be described as crowded. I walk past a row of abandoned stores papered from the roof to the dirt with fluttering, yellowed campaign signs, advertising MARGUERITE WILLIAMS: YOUR FRIEND, YOUR ADVOCATE, YOUR MAYOR!

I don't see any for her opponent. There are a few older signs, reading WHAT DO YOU YEARN FOR? There's a number at the bottom, but no name or company, just the symbol of a bird, and in little letters, COMMISSIONS OPEN.

I'm halfway through town before I encounter another person.

I force a smile as we approach each other. It's usually a good way to trick my fight-or-flight reflex into shutting off. But then we lock eyes. And he's the one who goes pale.

"God," he says, and there's something bone-tired in his voice. "Already?"

"Sorry?" I say. But he only shakes his head.

I pass seven more people on my way to Gibson Repairs. One young man in a business suit takes a look at me and *runs* in the direction he came. But for the most part, their reactions are similar to the first. Muted. Uneasy.

Most don't try to speak to me. But there's this ambient muttering in the air. *"Should we call someone?"* I hear a person hiss, and when I turn, I see a woman grab her companion's arm and jerk her along. Farther down the road, someone steps forward, as if to say something, but they're pulled aside by quick hands and a sharp whisper.

I walk faster.

The tower looms ahead, shimmering in the pavement's heat. I look away from it to the painted sign of Gibson Repairs, coming up on the right. I need to focus. I need to have my car. Because whatever it is I'm going to do next, I need to be sure I have a way to get out.

I step to the edge of the garage. Someone was just here—one of the wrenches on the wall is gently swinging. But they're not here now.

I decide to wait. And then I decide against that. Fear has a way of casting the world in a different light. Distortions, warped fun house mirrors of reality that make the world seem more dire and threatening than it actually is.

The unease in this town—there's a better than average possibility that it's all in my head. And I've decided on one rule, these past few months: don't get lost in your own head.

"Excuse me?" I try to channel my mother's phone voice. "Hello?"

Business doesn't seem great for Theresa today—there's no one here but me, no car except for the garage's tow truck. The girl in Lethe Ridge said she was the best in town. Though that was the only thing she said that made sense, so maybe I should have checked Yelp.

It's quiet enough that I can almost hear a *click* in my blood, the valves of adrenaline uncapping. I square my shoulders, drive my feet more firmly into the concrete, send every signal I can to my body that there's nothing to be afraid of. Hypervigilance or not, I need my car back.

"Hello?" I say again. Then, quieter, "You wanna maybe put a bell out here or—"

"Gibson Repairs," says a voice, right over my shoulder. "What can I do for you?"

I whirl around, and I find myself nose-to-nose with Theresa herself. She doesn't look the slightest bit fazed. The only response I get is a level, flat stare—from one eye, at least. The other eye is strapped into a leathery black eye-patch.

"Um," I manage. "I called for someone, but—"

Her eye widens a little with recognition, and she reaches into each ear and pops out a pair of earbuds. "Roadwork," she says. She sets aside a small, battered CD player. "Hell on my migraines."

She moves in a circle around me. Despite her combat boots, laced all the way up to the knee, her footsteps are barely audible. "Who are you?"

"Nobody." It comes out before I can blink.

Theresa doesn't miss a beat, either. "Well, then. What brings you here, Ms. Nobody?"

Something in the way she says it makes me hesitate. It's not the same uneasiness I've sensed from those people I passed in the street. It's closer to curiosity.

"My . . . car broke down a couple of miles from the 15," I finally say. "Near the state line. I was hoping I could get it towed here."

"Near the state line?" She hums, impressed. "Which side?"

"California," I say.

"Your feet must be pretty tired, then," she says. "You're in Nevada."

I almost laugh. The idea was to get *out* of Nevada. "I know it's a lot to ask, but I don't have AAA or anything, and was told you were the person to see—"

"You remember which exit?" she says. "You could show me, if we went there?"

"I . . ." Slowly, I nod. "Yeah?"

"Then it's not a lot to ask." She jerks her head toward the tow truck parked to the side. "Let's go."

I go to take a breath as I follow her to the looming, rusted-red pickup. It stops somewhere past my throat.

I swallow, like that'll push my insides back into place. "Weird question, but . . . I don't suppose you'd let me drive?"

"You suppose right." Theresa laughs. "There a problem, Ms. Nobody?"

"No, no problem." Two minutes into the conversation, and that's the first lie I've had to tell. That's pretty good these days. "I don't like being a passenger, that's all."

"You and me both, sister," she says, swinging my door open like it's a chariot. It creaks and shudders before it stills. Waiting.

I can feel the sticky-warm breeze from the garage door behind me, and the soles of my feet *itch* to run through it. But if I want an escape route, this is the way to get it.

I let my backpack slide to my feet as Theresa swings herself into the driver's seat next to me. "Just curious, though," she says as she starts the truck. "Who told you I was the person to see?"

I swallow hard, blink harder, try to breathe past the lump in my chest. Somehow I manage words. They even sound calm. "I didn't catch her name. My age, blonde?"

"Ohh," Theresa says, with dry recognition. "What an honor."

I watch the road, at first. It doesn't help. I try to channel the buzz under my skin anywhere else: I tap a beat against the door with my fingers, and when that's too noticeable, I jiggle my foot instead. I've hated the passenger's seat since I was fifteen, when I got my learner's permit and realized how many things could go wrong. Even under normal circumstances, I wouldn't like this. But my circumstances haven't been normal for a while now.

I fish out my phone. If I'm going to spend this ride in a haze of nerves, I might as well get this part over with, too.

New message to: Mom.

hey, sorry I missed you last night. gonna stay with Flora till new year's—is that okay?

That one wasn't too bad. But now for the tricky part.

New message to: Flora Summer.

sorry I missed your call, I type with shaking fingers, *phone was off. I think I'm actually going to stay home for new year's. sorry this was last minute—parents wanted me here.*

There. Easy. My heart's pounding so hard I might throw up, but when isn't it?

Then my phone shivers in my hand. Someone's texting me back.

New message from: Mom.

Of course that's okay. That was the plan, wasn't it?

Maybe she won't realize anything's wrong. Until I have to tell her about the repair shop charge that's about to hit my never-used, for-emergencies-only credit card.

I start typing a response—except my phone vibrates again. *New message from: Flora Summer.* Shit.

Call me?

Dammit, Flora. This is why Gaby muted you on Twitter.

at movie, can't talk right now, I type. *email you later?*

And then, to Mom: *oh yeah, just wanted to make sure you knew!*

I start to slide my phone back into my pocket, but it buzzes twice in quick succession. If not for Theresa sitting next to me, I might scream.

"You're pretty popular," Theresa says.

"Something like that," I mutter as I look back at the phone.

How are Flora and Jon doing?

And right below that, from Flora: *I hope we can talk about this. You're very important to me. You and Nick both.*

Biting the inside of my lip, I type back, hard enough that I hope I'll punch through the cracked screen: *I know. and I'll be back in Vegas soon, so I'll see you then.*

I hit send. And then I take a closer look at the screen. *Shit.* I sent that to my mother instead of Flora. Shit, shit, shit, shit.

hahaha sorry!! I type, the autocorrect covering for my shaking fingers. *wrong person! was supposed to meet a friend, turns out they're out of town. and Flora and Jon are doing okay.*

I hold my breath. *Mom is typing*, the phone tells me. "Mom is typing" for about a minute longer than I can stand. Then, finally:

You're so in demand. Give everyone my love.

I exhale, and I send Flora's message to the correct person. This time, there's no quick reply. And I start to slide the phone back in my pocket.

Except it buzzes, one last time.

New message from: Nick L.

hey, colter. can we talk?

Vaguely, I feel the hairs on my arms stand on end. I delete the message. But before I put away my phone, I flip through my contacts and delete his entry, too. I didn't know I still had him in there. Almost a year, and there are still pieces of him I haven't tucked away. Like broken glass waiting on a bare foot.

I watch the road after all.

I DON'T GET my first clear look at the town of Lotus Valley until we head back, my car shuddering and bouncing on the tow hook. There's a steep incline just west of the Lethe Ridge housing development, plateauing into a high overlook, but otherwise, the land is flat as far as I can see. Under the afternoon sun, the broadcast tower looks quiet and unlit.

I shift in my seat and make a point to uncurl my fists. Theresa's been unusually quiet since we picked up the car. That was more than fine with me for the first few miles, but it's starting to make me more nervous.

"So is the valley nearby?" I ask.

"Huh?" She doesn't look at me. "Ah. No. There's no valley."

"Oh. Okay." I pause. "Lotuses, then?"

"Nope," she says.

"Makes sense," I say as sincerely as I know how.

We make another turn, and the tower passes back into my field of vision. I swallow. I've got my car now. Which means the detour is over.

"Could we turn on the radio?" I say. "I—I like the music. When I drive."

Convincing. A flawless normal human impression. But I'm not sure the question warrants the stare I get in return.

I decide to keep my mouth shut until we get back to the garage.

Theresa swings her long legs out of the truck and strides to the back to unhook Stanley. I follow with a lot more scrambling. "Um," I say. "About the payment—"

"Pay me when I'm done. It's not like you're going anywhere." She snorts. "Might take a couple of days, though. You're not in a hurry, are you?"

On one hand, there won't be a credit card charge from the middle of nowhere, dated when I was supposed to be with Flora. But there's a shift in the air, a pressure that I know doesn't exist outside my head. For a little while, at least, I'm trapped.

"I guess not," I mumble.

Theresa doesn't say anything at first, and for a minute, I think we're done. But as I start to turn away, she says, "You asked about the radio."

Something in her tone stops me short. It's kind of like how that blonde girl sounded, right after I handed her the water. That same sudden interest.

"Y-yeah," I say.

"Well," she says. "Sorry to disappoint. But we don't get any signals here."

I heard what she said. But I must have misunderstood.

"Nothing?" My voice sounds admirably steady. "I found your local station, though—while I was out on the highway?"

"Our local station," Theresa repeats. I nod. And she smirks. "Then you must have been having a pretty good dream, Ms. Nobody. We haven't had a local station since 1973."

I say something back to her. At least, I hear myself do it—a thank-you, or an apology, or both at the same time. And when I turn back to Morningside Drive, I try to walk like running hasn't crossed my mind.

I haven't slept a full night since I got to Flora's. I didn't leave Vegas in the clearest state of mind. And most importantly, the only existing recording of that voicemail is on my phone.

And yet I know what I heard. I'm sure. And lately it takes a lot for me to be sure.

"Need a ride?" someone calls from over my shoulder.

It doesn't sound like Theresa, but it must have been—it came from the garage. "What?" I say as I turn back.

Theresa's not there. Neither is the garage.

I inhale sharply. The sound echoes down the pavement. Morningside Drive is gone. Lotus Valley is gone. I'm standing in the middle of an empty stretch of road, in the kind of dark stillness you only find in the earliest hours of morning. I'm surrounded by flat, burnt-yellow grass. And the only light to be found is the line of streetlights, few and far between.

"Theresa?" I try, pointlessly. But the only response I get is a low rumble, far in the distance.

I take a few uneasy steps, conscious of any movement behind me. And at the end of my sightline, something starts to take shape. Something tall and gnarled, climbing straight out of the middle of the road. An ancient oak tree.

This isn't Morningside Drive in Lotus Valley. This is miles away, just outside San Diego, at the corner of Sutton Avenue and Chamblys Road.

I take another step. The branches of the tree become sharper, more defined. The rumble is louder now, lower. So low that my skin ripples into goose bumps just listening.

Another sound breaks through—louder, higher, closer. Then a light, faint at first but growing steadily brighter.

And inches from my toes, the screech of brakes.

My back foot turns wrong as I try to run, and I hit the pavement backward, palms first. The streetlights around me burst open. And when I blink, it's midafternoon, and I'm sprawled in the middle of the street, nose-to-nose with the grille of a car. The driver leaps out, and the first thing I see is the insignia on his shirt: LOTUS VALLEY SHERIFF'S DEPARTMENT.

I twist around, and Morningside Drive whirls overhead. I blink hard. And it stays right where it is.

Four

THE APPOINTMENT

THERE ARE BITS of pavement stuck to my skin, dug into little divots. I run my palm under the water until the skin isn't flecked with black anymore, and then I peel back my sleeve where my forearm hit the street. The fabric isn't torn, but underneath my arm is scraped up to the elbow. Nice to know this fifteen-dollar shirt is more resilient than I am.

I glance back up at the mirror, at my dark, ringed eyes and the dirt streaked across my clothes. But my reflection isn't looking back out at me. She's looking down at her scraped, angry-red palms.

And she's wearing different clothes.

I jerk back from the mirror. But so does my reflection this time. She blinks back at me, startled, wearing my clothes again. I lift my hand—clean and unscratched—to wave. And she doesn't miss a beat.

Post-traumatic stress disorder. The full name doesn't sound that bad. Reasonable, even. The kind of thing that can be fixed with yoga, or a massage, or some good, solid Me Time.

It's when you boil it down to its acronym that things get tricky. Four little letters and subtext for miles.

I don't use those four letters. What happened, happened to Gaby. Just because she's not around to feel the fallout doesn't mean I have any right to it.

But I do know what's happening to me.

In the most basic and recognizable ways it is cold, hard physiology. A body hardwired to sense danger in a quick movement, or in someone standing too close, or in a series of obstacles between you and the way out. But there's specificity to each sensation. The hot cement in your chest, the wild and reeling beats of your heart, the dizzy spin of the world. You never have to reach far to remember the worst moment of your life. Your body remembers for you. It remembers with every cell.

But my body can remember all it wants. My brain isn't going back there with it. For everything I've felt over the past year, I've never felt anything I would describe as a flashback. This thing that's happening to me, it hasn't been controllable, not yet. But by now it should be predictable.

Then again. When I shut my eyes, I still see last night, in the Summers' narrow kitchen. I still see Nick, standing in the center of my vision, smiling that smile. After what happened— after what *almost* happened—maybe I can't expect predictable anymore.

He's certainly on your mind, isn't he? That was what that girl had said.

I squeeze my eyes shut and press my nails once, light but insistent, into my palms. Not what I need to be thinking about. Not now, not ever.

Easing my phone out of my pocket, I pull up my text messages and flip back to when my therapist texted me his number and charitably pretended he hadn't already given it to me five times. *In case anything comes up,* it says. Every one of those five times I nodded, smiled, and silently resolved that if anything came up, I'd handle it myself.

I shove my phone back into my jeans. I've read all about flashbacks, what they're like. Disjointed, impressionistic, almost physical. They're not literal time travel. Not like that road. Not like the mirror, just now.

I know my diagnosis. I'm not sure this is part of it.

There's another knock on the door. "Miss?"

"Yes!" I say, stepping back from the sink. "Just a second!"

I turn to grab a paper towel. And I pause. Opposite me, blemishing the wall of the perfectly clean, perfectly orderly bathroom, there's a boarded window.

You will find a window that is not a window. The girl had said that, too.

I open the door and step back out into the lobby. And I have about two seconds to get my bearings before the deputy sheriff's wide, concerned eyes are inches from mine.

"You're sure you're all right, miss?" he says. I don't think he's moved since I went into the bathroom. Guess it's a slow day on the Lotus Valley, Nevada, crime beat.

"Very sure," I say. "I really appreciate you letting me clean up here, but I should be heading out now, so—"

"And I'll get you on your way as soon as possible!" he says. "If you could just step into my office over there, we can get started on your statement—"

"Am—" I blink. "Am I in trouble?"

"Oh! No! Of course not!" he says quickly. "I'm citing myself."

"For what?" I say.

"Reckless driving, of course," he says.

I blink. "You're serious."

"I injured a pedestrian," he says with a firm nod.

I go for a straight face. It's hard to tell how successful I am. If Gaby were here, we'd be leaving this station with money for new clothes, fresh coffee, and emotional distress. For a second, I'm tempted.

"Listen, Deputy—" It comes out sharper than I intend. The deputy, whether he meant to or not, is firmly situated between me and the front door.

"Oh, please," he says, oblivious. "Call me Jay!"

"Deputy Jay," I continue, raising my voice a little. Someone in the foyer keeps ringing the front desk bell. "I wasn't paying attention, and I wandered into the road. I don't think this is really—"

"And it may well be unnecessary, miss," he says earnestly, seemingly unbothered by the now-constant ringing over his shoulder. "But with the sheriff out of town, I have to make sure all of this is aboveboard. Does that make sense?"

I gesture to the front desk and ask, "Shouldn't somebody—"

"Think of it this way," he says, as if he didn't hear me. "Say your parents are on vacation, and you break your mother's vase—"

"Jay," someone calls from the foyer.

He finally turns away from me. The relief is short-lived. Standing on the other side of the front desk is a blonde girl in a polka-dot dress, finishing off the last swig of my water bottle.

The girl from the Lethe Ridge housing development smiles at

the deputy. "Why don't you let me get our guest settled?"

"Cassie?" he says, blinking. "What are you—"

Then he turns back to me, slowly. His smile fades as his eyes lock with mine. And the blood drains from his face.

He's looking at me with understanding. Which is funny, because I couldn't be more lost.

"Well." He clears his throat as he backs away, never taking his eyes off me. "If that's the case, I've got quite the stack of paperwork to finish, so you'll let me know if you need anything, Cassie?"

"Don't I always." She wiggles her fingers in a wave. "Bye, Jay."

And he *bolts*. I hear a door slam shut down the hall. Which leaves me and the girl.

I know I'm staring. I don't think she cares. She looks down at her watch with a light frown. "Hmm. A few minutes behind schedule. But all things considered, not bad."

Despite my best efforts, I keep staring. I was holding out hope that she was another one of those mirages this town seemed to have in spades. But she looks pretty solid to me.

Finally, I do the one thing I can think of. I grab my backpack from where I left it on the floor, I swing it onto my shoulder, and I start toward the door.

"Where do you think you're going?" Cassie says.

"He said I was done here," I toss over my shoulder.

"Not right now you're not," she says. "That's not the proper order, first of all."

It's just weird enough to stop me. "For what?"

"*Any* of it," she says, maddeningly patient. "Like I was saying, we're more or less on schedule. Let's not lose our heads."

"What do you *want*?" I snap, whirling to face her.

She looks mildly confused. "Right at this moment? A strawberry milk shake."

"Why are you following me?" I say.

"Strictly speaking, I've only just started following you," Cassie says. As I take another step toward the door, she adds, "But, for one, you're not going to make it far in this town on your own. And, more immediately, you're about to waste your time. You can't get in that way. It's locked."

"What is?" I say.

She tosses my empty water bottle into the recycling bin. "You know what. The old broadcast studio."

Now she's got my attention. I freeze. "How did you—"

"You're going to need permission. And the keys. Both of which you'd get from the sheriff," Cassie says. "So why don't you slow down and come with me? The studio isn't going anywhere. And without your car, neither are you."

I can feel the door behind me. But she's right. I'm not going to get far on my own. And maybe the wrong direction is better than none.

"Okay," I say.

"There now," she says with a smile, like she wants to make sure I already regret this. "Right this way, then. You'll like the interns. They're not originally from here, either."

"Does that mean they make sense?" I say flatly.

Cassie tilts her head, as if considering it. "They certainly like to tell me so."

I follow her deeper into the building. As the hallway narrows, it also opens up: floor-length windows overlook two courtyards, studded with cacti and ferns. The walls are covered with pictures of ceremonies and events and fairs. The building has a lot in common with Deputy Jay: so bright and friendly it doesn't look real.

Before long, I can hear someone's voice around the corner. They're speaking Spanish. Very bad Spanish.

"Okay," says a different voice in English. "That means 'Your monkey is on the table.'"

"Oh," says the first voice, also in English now. "And if I used *usted*, what would it mean?"

"'Your monkey is on the table,'" says the second voice. "Respectfully."

The two boys behind the desk are my age, maybe younger. The boy on the right is quarterback-handsome, with broad shoulders, olive skin, and expressive brown eyes peeking out from his shaggy black hair. The boy on the left is his physical opposite: small and thin and boy band–cute, with neat chestnut hair and bright blue eyes lined with dark shadows. He's pale enough that he might disappear into the white-blue wallpaper in the right lighting. When he reaches over to adjust something across the desk, I can see the outline of his wrist bones.

Without missing a beat, Tall, Dark, and Handsome turns to us. "I want to state for the record that I know three languages."

"You know two," says the other.

"I know English, Farsi, and Klingon," says the first boy.

"You will never use Klingon," says the second.

"Don't be so sure," the first boy says. "I know some great pick-up lines."

I turn to Cassie. "I thought they were going to make sense."

"As you'll recall," Cassie says, "I didn't say either way."

"Sorry." The smaller kid flashes a grin. "Is there something we can help you with?"

"Rose needs an appointment with the sheriff when she's back," Cassie says.

"Of course! At your service, Rose." Tall, Dark, and Handsome jumps up and shakes my hand. "Felix Sohrabi. And this is Allie—"

"Alex," his partner interrupts smoothly. "Alex Harper."

"How many times—" Felix demonstratively cuts himself off, as if he needs a steadying breath. "We can't just *rhyme*, Allie—"

"Appointment, you said?" says Alex, drowning him out. "Let me pull up her calendar."

Felix peers over Alex's shoulder. "You could do tomorrow at twelve thirty, right after she gets back?"

"That's her lunch," Alex says.

"Then what's the problem?" Felix says. "Because I seem to remember some very pointed comments to me this week about being able to work while you eat—"

Alex waves a hand at him, eyes still on the screen. "There's a four fifteen?"

"Sure, if you want to give her five minutes." Felix thinks on that for a moment, then looks up at me. "Do you need more than five minutes?"

Alex looks up at Cassie. "Is this urgent?"

"Mm . . ." Cassie hesitates. "Why don't you tell me?"

Slowly, I see that same sense of understanding cross Alex Harper's face. He hides it better than Deputy Jay did. But it's there nonetheless.

"Ms. . . ." he says, turning to me.

"Colter," I say, my throat suddenly dry.

"Ms. Colter," he says. "Could you stay exactly where you are, just for a second? Try not to move."

It's a simple enough request. I almost say no, if only out of sheer frustration. But something in Alex's voice keeps me still.

He moves to the edge of his seat and cranes his neck, as if looking just past me. And though his expression doesn't change, his eyes widen.

"Felix," he says, with the kind of excruciating, deliberate calm that I know by heart at this point. "Call Ms. Jones. Tell her that she needs to get back here as soon as she can. We're starting."

Felix looks like he's about to ask—until he gets a good look at Alex's face. And in the next second, he's on the phone.

With a slightly shaking hand, Alex pulls out a Post-it note and slides it across the table to me. "Could you write down your number for us? We'll have more information soon." He pauses. "And if you could listen for that call . . ."

There's blood thundering in my ears as I scrawl my number. Behind the desk, Felix hands the phone to Alex.

"Should we call Mayor Williams?" Alex says, his voice low.

"Don't bother," Felix mutters. "She'll know soon enough."

It takes a moment for me to realize that Cassie is guiding me away from the desk.

"Come on," she says.

I look over my shoulder at her. "What's going on?"

"Right at this very moment?" She shrugs. "We just got some time to kill. And I still want that milk shake."

———

THE BELL RINGS as Cassie sweeps into the Sweet as Pie Diner, and in one smooth motion, every head in the place pops up.

There wasn't much conversation to begin with—as packed as it is, everyone in the place seems to be dining alone—but when I step past Cassie and into their full view, the clinking forks stop. A few gazes widen as they sweep across me. This time, I'm sure it's not my imagination.

A waitress in a peach uniform eyes us from behind the counter. "Cassie," she says slowly.

"It's okay." Cassie's own voice is firm, calm. "We'll take a corner booth, please."

"Cassandra." A man in a tan suit stands up from his chair— my fingers twitch as it scrapes across the floor. "You know better than anyone—"

"I've made it very clear where I stand." Cassie chirps. But there's a chill in her voice. "I'm sorry if that disappoints any of you."

A mutter runs through the diner like a current. Four others stand from their tables, swinging their coats over their shoulders as they make for the door.

"Fellas," says the waitress flatly.

The men freeze by the door. And then, sheepishly, dig wallets from their pockets and double back to the tables. "Sorry, Adrienne," one mutters as he passes.

"Who raised those boys, I don't know," Adrienne says. "Corner booth, you said?"

She leads us to a table in the glow of the neon sign, which casts the menus in a shade of icy blue. I almost don't follow. Gaby wouldn't have followed.

But Gaby also used to say that I'd give up a kidney if it was the polite thing to do. And Gaby was, as usual, excruciatingly right.

I slide into the vinyl bench with my back to the wall. The diner's long, like a train car, with one front entrance, one back. Not the worst odds, if I can get to them.

I settle out of sight of the other patrons. And slowly, I hear forks begin to clink again.

"What can I get you?" Adrienne asks.

"The usual, please—with whipped cream and two cherries." Cassie turns to me. "Do you want any pie? You *have* to try the blueberry mint. My treat."

"No," I say to my lap. "Thank you."

"Let's order a slice anyway," she says to Adrienne. "I'll eat it if she doesn't."

With a curt nod, Adrienne disappears toward the kitchen.

As I glance up, Cassie flashes a thin smile. "Now. Why don't you start by telling me what you brought with you?"

"What I . . ." Instinctively, I look over at my backpack on the bench next to me. "You're looking at it."

"What followed you here, then?" she says, unfazed.

"*Nothing*," I say. "I came here alone."

"You really didn't notice anything?" she asks. "Anything strange or different."

"Who was that kid back at the sheriff's office?" I say. "Because you didn't bring me to him to talk about an appointment."

"Rose," Cassie says, "it's not like I want to pressure you or anything, but I'd really appreciate it if you could focus."

"What is going *on*?" I say. "Why is everyone acting like they know what I'm doing here?"

"Because we know what you're doing here." Cassie narrows her eyes. "You're serious. You really didn't notice anything, did you?"

Now I'm the one who ignores the question. "Who are you? Where did you hear the name Nick Lansbury?"

She opens her mouth to respond, but before she can get there, Adrienne swings by with the strawberry milk shake and the slice of pie. Cassie looks away long enough to nod and smile, and as she pulls the glass toward herself, she slides the plate toward me.

"I think we might be talking past each other here," she says with a contrite smile.

I don't return the gesture. But I nod.

"So why don't you answer a few of my questions first?" she says. "And then I'll tell you as much as I know."

"Why do you have to ask?" I say. "Seems like you know everything about me."

"Nobody knows everything about anyone," she says with a dismissive wave of her hand. "Now. You said your car broke down on the highway. You didn't wait with it. Why?"

I shrug as nonchalantly as I know how. "I saw the blinking light on the broadcast tower. Figured there must be a town here to go with it."

"And that's why you want to go to the station so badly?" she asks, stirring her milk shake. "To thank it in person?"

I flush. Yeah, that's fair. "I heard something. On the radio," I say. "A message no one but me should have. I'd like to know what it's doing on a station that closed up shop fifty years ago."

If she has questions about that, she hides it well. She nods thoughtfully. "And you're sure you came here alone?"

"Of course I'm sure," I say. "You *saw* me, right after I got into town."

She takes a long sip from her straw. "And what is it you don't want to get worse?"

"I'm sorry?" I say.

"When I met you this morning," she says, "you were worried that something was getting worse. What, exactly?"

"What does that have to do with anything?"

She slides the straw out of her glass and runs it across her tongue. "Curiosity."

The weird thing is, I want to tell her. Just to see what it sounds like here, in a place where it wouldn't change how everyone's already looking at me. But my own parents don't know. It doesn't seem fair that some stranger should know first.

"Migraine," I say. "Had it since this morning. Is it my turn yet?"

"By all means," Cassie says. "But why don't I start by answering your other questions?"

I wait, but she doesn't speak at first. She twirls her straw. "You asked about Alex Harper," she finally says. "It's like I said. He's not from around here. His father brought him here when he was a very small, very ill child. He heard that the warm, dry air would help his lungs. He found a . . . different kind of treatment.

"And I did bring you to him to book an appointment, by the way," she adds. "He's a very good intern. Very perceptive. He always knows exactly how urgent something is going to be."

She starts looping one of her cherry stems into a knot. "And as for who *I* am," she says, "my name is Cassandra Cyrene, and I'm the third-most accurate prophet in Lotus Valley."

"Prophet?" I'm not sure I should be laughing. But once I start, I can't stop. "Okay. So you're psychic?"

"People ask questions. I find them answers." She raises an eyebrow at me. "May I ask what's so funny?"

"There's, um," I say, my voice still shaking with laughter. "Rankings?"

"I missed second by that much, too," Cassie says, holding her thumb and index finger centimeters apart. "If not for John Jonas and that drought."

I'm still smiling, even through the chill settling in my stomach. Theresa Gibson said that Cassie's recommendation was an honor. The waitress said Cassie's name like she was waiting for instructions. "Don't sell yourself short," I say. "That deputy did what you said without even asking."

"Oh. That?" she says. "That's not really because of me. That's because the prophecy that's about to come true is one of mine."

The diner feels as if it's gone quieter than before. I lower my voice. "How can you be so sure? Sounds like you've been wrong before."

For the first time, she looks annoyed. "If you're asking *why* I'm only third, it's because I miss the big picture, from time to time. Sometimes I see so much that I make too many assumptions about what I *didn't* see. But I've never been *wrong* wrong. Now, would you like me to answer your question, or would you like to be snide?"

It should be ridiculous. But I don't have Gaby here to tell me not to apologize. I sit back against the bench. "I'm listening."

As weak as the apology is, she seems satisfied. "Have you lived near the desert long?"

"My whole life," I say.

"So do you ever get the sense that you're not alone out here?" Cassie asks. "Is this really the first time you've heard something on these empty stretches of road that couldn't possibly exist?"

"I'm not sure I understand," I say slowly. "You're talking about—"

"I'm talking about living things, like you or me. Things living out of the corners of our eyes, flitting in and out of the gaps in time. Things that exist separate from us. For the most part."

She scrapes up the last drops of milk shake with her straw. "I don't know that you can lump them all together. Some communicate, some don't. Some have shape, some look different from person to person—and some of them can't be seen at all, except by the right people. Some of them want to be left alone. And some of them need us to survive, for better or for worse. They've only got one thing in common. When there's a shift in the world that can't be undone—from the greatest cataclysm to the smallest broken promise—that's one of them, being born.

"Where you're from, you might call them a feeling in the air, or an unexplained noise, or someone walking across your grave. Here, we call them our neighbors. The oldest of them was born right here, where this town was built. And now they're coming home."

She levels her gaze across the table at me. I stare back blankly. "Still doesn't ring a bell? Then how about this. If you ask any person in this diner, they'd tell you that the most notable things about our town are as follows: The yearly quilting competition.

The blueberry mint pie. And the massive flood that is set to wipe us off the map in three and a half days' time. What do you know about that?"

I almost start laughing again. But she looks as serious as I've seen her so far.

"Three days as in New Year's Day?" I start to reach for my phone. "But the weather says—"

"I know what the weather says." She leans back. "I'd like to hear what you have to say."

"Well, if it's not going to rain, then how—"

"I have no idea how," Cassie says. "But I think you do."

What eventually comes out of my mouth isn't so much a laugh as a nervous giggle. "How the hell would I know?"

Cassie's lips curve a little, and she makes a twirling motion with her finger. "Turn around."

I turn, deliberately, so she knows I'm humoring her. And behind me, as far as I can see, stretches the flat, burnt-yellow grass of Sutton Avenue.

I whip around to face front. Cassie's still there, pooled in the icy-blue light of the Sweet as Pie Diner. Behind me I can hear mumbled orders, forks hitting plates, something sizzling from the kitchen. But when I venture another look over my shoulder, Sutton Avenue hasn't moved.

It's not there. It can't be. But when I breathe in, my lungs fill up with cool, damp air that can't possibly exist. And my body starts to remember again. All on its own.

"Now," Cassie says, pushing the slice of pie onto my place mat. "Let's talk about what followed you here."

Five

THE FINISH AND THE START

"ON AN UNREMARKABLE day, a teenage girl crosses the city limits of Lotus Valley and sets off a chain of events she can't reverse.

"The girl herself isn't the problem. Visitors aren't completely unknown to this town. But this stranger brings on her heels an ancient visitor, a visitor wrapped in loneliness and hunger. And its reach is vast, as long as the desert itself. It will take time to catch up in its entirety. But its arrival, in the early hours of New Year's Day—it's inevitable."

I balance the takeout container on my knees and shift my weight against the hard steps of Sweet as Pie's back entrance. Through the slats of the wood, the shadows look like they're swimming. But when I blink hard and look closer, they're still.

"Then what?" I ask. "That's the whole prophecy?"

"Well . . ." Cassie takes a long sip from her to-go cup. "What came next is *one* version of events. The idea is to alter that. At least, that's the hope."

"But why three days?" I say. "I'm already here."

"The way I've always pictured it," Cassie says, "it's like a hurricane. So tremendous that you start getting the wind and rain long before the worst of it comes. Think of that but bigger."

"But it's a living thing," I say. "Like your neighbors."

"Not like the ones you'll meet here." I must look nervous, because Cassie's lips twitch when she looks at me. "I'm sure you've gathered that this place is different than where you're from. Lotus Valley draws an interesting crowd. Strange things, for one. But strange people, too. We don't always mesh. But we have an understanding."

"Which is?" I say.

"That none of us could be anywhere else." Cassie's smile goes grim. "Something about this place draws you in. For us, and for the neighbors. Maybe you feel it, too."

Strange, I think, my heart sinking an inch. Great. I think of Gaby's voice, calling for me across the desert. Was Lotus Valley drawing me in, too?

"But the thing that followed you here . . ." I can hear Cassie swallow. "Ms. Jones, the sheriff, she's combed through our town archives. Records, oral histories, anything the neighbors were willing to tell us. There was an ocean here once, thousands of years ago. And when life on Earth shifted, when that ocean dried up, something fathomlessly powerful was born.

"And this is where this thing is different from the rest of them," Cassie continues. "Usually when the neighbors have such a strong interest in us—in humanity—it's because we had a hand in creating them, intentionally or not. The death of an ocean couldn't have had less to do with us. But through the ages, it's us they've followed. Filled their currents, which once held waves and water and life, with our stories."

It should sound ridiculous. Impossible. But the air of Sutton Avenue is still swimming through my lungs.

"Why?" I ask.

"That's what we're still trying to figure out," Cassie says. "Why they followed us at all. What changed. But it explains what you've seen today, doesn't it? We've been calling it a flood because it's the closest word in our vocabulary for what I saw. But they're a different kind of ocean now. An ocean of memory."

"So . . ." I wrap my arms across myself. "How does a flood of memories destroy an entire town?"

Cassie glances down, but not before I see something in her gaze cloud over. "No one's experienced this thing for decades. Not even our neighbors. It's possible that along the way, something changed. All I know is that what I saw wasn't here for our stories. They were here to swallow us whole."

I cross my arms tight. "So what happens at the end of your prophecy?"

An odd expression freezes on her face. But slowly it melts into her serene smile. "Well. Let's not overwhelm you more than we already have."

Her phone buzzes, and whatever's on the screen catches her full attention—the sudden, powerful shiver that passes through me goes unnoticed. As she taps out what sounds like a novel-length response, I reach my plastic fork into the container and slice off the tip of the blueberry mint pie.

"I told you. Nectar of the gods," Cassie says. When I glance up, she's pocketed her phone already. "You're going to get much further in this town if you start trusting me, Rose."

I smile weakly. "And do you trust me?"

She smiles back, though her eyes narrow. "Ask again later."

"So you can't tell by looking at me?" I ask. Her eyes narrow some more, but I'm being sincere this time. Mostly.

"That's the trouble with prophecy," she says slowly. "You never know what comes before. But whether I trust you or not, my plan is still the same. How about you?"

I drive the fork into the crust and give it a twist. "I need to see that radio station."

"I can arrange that," she says.

"And I need to know how that message was playing," I say. "Do you think one of your neighbors had anything to do with it?"

"Don't know," Cassie says. "But we could figure it out, if you work with me."

I already regret this. But. "Then I guess I'm working with you."

Her smile goes a little crooked again, like it did when I offered her the water this morning. "Don't sound too excited."

And then, weirdly enough, I laugh. "It's not you, exactly. It's— I have post-traumatic stress disorder. There's not a whole lot that I trust right now."

Wow. I said it. I said it like it was *easy*. It's not until the seconds after that it feels like I've thrown a Molotov cocktail into the conversation.

Cassie doesn't react like I did, though. She inclines her head in a half nod. "Then I'll do my best to be trustworthy," she says. "If that's enough."

"Yeah," I manage as my heart starts to slow. "That's plenty."

I cheated, though. I told her one truth to avoid another. I need to see that station. And then, if I can, I am getting out of this town.

"Anyway," Cassie says, breezing on, "that was Alex texting. The sheriff's going to be back very late. She says you should get a full night's sleep and see her tomorrow morning."

It doesn't occur to me until just then that I could really use that. I smother a yawn.

"I'm sorry to drag her back from her trip," I say, if only because it seems polite.

"Oh, don't be." Cassie smiles thinly. "She was looking for you. She goes out there every year, every day from Christmas to New Year's. Trying to find you before you find us."

Catching the look on my face, she shrugs. "On the bright side, she doesn't have to look anymore. Come on. I'll show you where you're staying."

"I passed the motel on my way here," I say, gathering up my things from the steps.

"Oh, you won't be in the motel." Cassie gently dislodges the backpack from my shoulder and slides it over her own. At the look on my face, her own darkens. "Trust me. You're not going to want to stay in town. And if at all possible, try not to talk to anyone without Sheriff Jones or me there, okay? You never know where someone stands."

She'd said something like that to those men in the diner, too. And if I really have brought something terrible, where *they* stand makes complete sense.

It's where Cassie stands that I don't get.

"Don't worry," she says. "It's a little unorthodox, but you'll have a lot of space. Now—"

She doesn't finish. Her head moves a little to the left, and her eyes widen, as if catching something over my shoulder. Taking my hand, she tugs me around a corner and into a little walkway between two buildings.

My head whips back to the road, at whatever it was she saw. The red town car squealing up to a halt along the diner's back parking lot doesn't look like cause for concern. But until we hear the door open, close, and the click of heeled footsteps up the diner's stairs, Cassie's completely still.

"We'll take the back way." She still sounds cheerful, if much, much quieter now. "Come on."

"What was that?" I hiss.

"Don't worry about it," Cassie says. That could refer to any of the four or five worrisome things that just happened, but. Sure.

Cassie's back stays turned as I follow her—she doesn't try any further conversation. And without her laser focus on me, I can think.

Three days until this town will, supposedly, cease to exist. And I'm not sure Theresa would consider that a good reason for a rush job on my car. I walked to the highway once, I guess I could do it again—see if I could flag someone down. My phone is in my pocket, still about 30 percent charged. But calling my mother, explaining to her why I'm here, would be a bell I couldn't unring. That's the nuclear option.

But I'll worry about that when I get there. The station comes first. That message comes first.

Whether Cassie can see the future or not, one thing is true either way. New Year's Day will be one year to the day since Gaby ceased to exist, too.

And Cassie has no way of knowing that.

———

NOTE TO SELF: If someone tells you that you're going to stay somewhere "unorthodox," ask, no matter how distracted you are. Because if you don't, you're going to spend the night in a strong contender for Creepiest Place in Town.

Cassie was right, though. I definitely have space. The model house in the Lethe Ridge housing development is bigger than anything I'll ever own. Bigger than anything I'll ever rent, probably. If I get into Stanford, I'll be paying off student loans until I die.

I push the door shut behind me, and it glides back into the door jamb with the lightest *click*. A dark, symmetrical room sprawls out ahead of me, all reds and oranges and angular shadows.

I hit the lights. The shadows retreat through the polished floorboards. But aside from that, not much changes.

I move quickly and quietly, flicking every switch from the cheery yellow kitchen to the wood-paneled home office, opening door after door. With every switch flipped, I look over my shoulder again. Sutton Avenue's not there. Or it hasn't caught up to me yet.

The deepest breath I can take keeps inching farther and farther up my throat. Which is funny, because I didn't think I was afraid of the dark. But it's hard to keep track of all the things I'm afraid of now. I'm going to have to start a list.

From the end of the hallway, I have a good view of every room. So I slow down, and I take a look.

I survey the bedrooms: one with a kid-size bed and light-up

crayons on the walls, and one with the same blue-striped sheets that all my rich friends seem to have in their guest rooms. But if I'm going to play house for a couple of days, I might as well sleep in the master bedroom.

I turn to the door behind me. And it's closed.

I stop short. My bag's already halfway off my shoulder, but I push it back slowly. I opened this door, I think. I should have opened all of them.

Did I, though? This room is at the very end of the hallway, so it should have been the last one I checked, but I have no memory of seeing it.

With unsteady fingers, I gently push it open. The lights are still off. When I flick the switch, I look closely this time. I check the walk-in closet, the bathroom suite. But it's just me.

Me, and anything that followed me in.

"You don't know that," I whisper to myself. But I do, don't I? I can dismiss Sutton Avenue as a product of my imagination. I can dismiss what Cassie said, if I try hard enough. But Alex Harper looked behind me, and he saw something, too.

And besides. Hypervigilance has given me what must be the worst superpower ever: somehow these days, I can feel when someone's moving behind me, even when they don't make a sound. Like the air itself is shifting.

I thought it was just the unease. But these past few hours, I've become steadily aware of something stirring, just over my shoulder. I feel it even now. With my back to a wall.

I make a quick mental list. One front door, heavy, triple-locked. One back door, sliding glass, an open fishbowl view for anyone who wants to look—but as locked as I can get it. No attic. No basement. And not many places to hide.

I backtrack to the living room and crawl onto the couch, watching the hallway behind me in the reflection of the TV. And for the first time since I left my car last night, everything is still.

The couch cushions are stiff, and I can feel every beat of my pulse pounding against them. Through my ribs, through my back, through my head. Before last May, I don't remember being that aware of the motions of my heartbeat. Now everything I do, from the way I stand to the position I sleep in, feels like an effort to contain it.

And besides. Times like these, when I'm just sitting here, can be the worst of any of it. I waste half of my day wishing things would be this quiet, and when it finally comes, it doesn't feel that peaceful. It feels like waiting.

I uncurl my clenched fingers and pull my shoulders down and back. I try to clear my mind and breathe, like Maurice taught me.

I make it about two minutes.

"Shit." I dig through my pocket until I unearth my sad, cracked phone, and I scroll through my voicemails. I was hoping never to listen to this again. But okay, universe. Fine.

Very gently, I tap Gaby's name. And I let it happen.

There are little details that the radio broadcast missed. I knew that, of course. For the first two weeks, I must have listened to her voicemail every day.

I half expect it to end differently here, in this empty neighborhood, in this symmetrical house. It's almost a disappointment when nothing's changed at all.

Rose? Are you there? And then a boy's voice behind her, asking her a question, and a little rustle, as if Gaby turns toward him. And this is when she hangs up.

As always, the boy's words are hard to make out. But I know what he's asking. I've known for months.

Need a ride?

Gaby and I had a scary amount in common. Our dead fathers. Our iron-willed mothers. Our grandmothers growing up just minutes apart without ever meeting, and our stepfathers sliding into our lives before we knew much else. And for all our personalities could be different—Gaby was outgoing, outspoken, thrived on debate—in that moment, it didn't matter. When you're alone, and tired, and stranded, and a boy offers you a ride, you say yes, because you don't know how he's going to react to no.

To be fair, I don't think Gaby was afraid of what would happen when she got into his car. I think she just didn't like him.

My phone buzzes in my hands, a pinpoint hit to my startle reflex. It takes a second to hold the text steady enough to read.

Let me know if you need anything—Cassie

An ellipsis pops up. Then another text.

Or if you're just bored, I guess.

I laugh shakily, tap out a *will do*. And before I put my phone down, I add Cassie Cyrene to my contacts.

I should sleep. That seems like the most sensible idea. But as many nights as I've spent lying awake, wishing my upstairs neighbors would shut the entire hell up, I think I've actually found somewhere that's *too* quiet.

I try the remote, not expecting anything. But it flips on to a woman's smiling face.

The background shivers behind her, like movement trying to

break through. The words are garbled, the feed jerky and unnatural, like a stream that's still buffering.

I change the channel. This one's playing smoothly, but it's hard to tell until I turn up the volume to hear the soft, trancelike soundtrack. The image of the dusk-lit playground looks still, at first, but when I look closer, I can see the swing rocking gently, on its own.

White words swim into view: *What do you yearn for?*

Unnerved, I flip forward again.

You might say, "But, Joe, they don't understand our 'human laws,'" booms the man on camera, finger-quoting the last two words. *I say, they can learn! If you've got a neighbor-related property dispute—*

Pulling a face, I flip forward one more time. But it looks like all I've got for channels is this public access hellscape—I'm back to the smiling woman from the start, her blonde waves just so, her teeth glinting as brightly as her pearls. This time, the signal comes through:

Some will tell you I'm questioning our values. She walks toward the camera down the length of a storefront. *I'm here to tell you: I believe in Lotus Valley. I believe in the values it was built on.*

Her smile still hasn't shifted. But lines form around her mouth, thinning her cheeks. *What I do* not *believe in? Prioritizing the comfort of our neighbors over the safety of our citizens. Prioritizing ideals over human residents like you. It's your turn to be prioritized, Lotus Valley. I don't stand for some academic idea of our town. I stand for reality. I stand for you.*

And next time someone tells you I'd like to change what we are, feel free to tell them: They're right. Because when you love something, you change it for the better.

The woman disappears, and a message takes her place. REELECT

MARGUERITE WILLIAMS: YOUR FRIEND, YOUR ADVOCATE, YOUR MAYOR!

The text fades, and at length, so does the music. And gradually, the screen transitions into what looks like the slow pan of a camera down a sunlit, empty Morningside Drive. NEXT PROGRAMMING: EIGHT A.M., reads a card at the bottom of the screen.

The camera curls down a side road into a neighborhood dotted with trim, vibrant green grass. It languidly loops into a cul-de-sac. And there's a sudden, inexplicable jolt through me.

My heart's still reeling even after I hit the power button. It's not unusual for my overtired, overtaxed, hypervigilant brain to jump at something I haven't consciously registered. But it'd be nice, once in a while, if it could tell me what it was so scared of.

The residual light and static fade from the screen, and only my own reflection, my blank, tired stare, is left for company.

And I sit up. I had left the master bedroom door wide open before. But in the reflection over my shoulder, it stands just slightly ajar.

Before I can turn around, the house starts to shake.

Whatever it is, it's *loud*, loud enough that my hands immediately clamp down over my ears. For a long, earth-rocking moment, it's hard to distinguish anything but a pulsing *thump, thump, thump*. I almost don't recognize it as music.

Someone is playing music down the street. *Blasting* music, actually.

Someone else is here.

Like I said. There is a front door made of heavy wood. There is a back door made of sliding glass. There are windows I could probably fit through, closets I could duck inside. But very few places to hide.

And besides. I want to know what's coming.

I take a breath, hold it. And I ease open the front door. Even over the music, every creak of the wood echoes.

I should be looking at the front steps. Except they aren't there anymore. And neither is the Lethe Ridge housing development.

Before I can think better of it, I'm through the entryway and across the porch.

A chipped set of stone steps leads me down to a street that couldn't look less like Lethe Ridge—an asymmetrical suburbia worn around the edges. There's trees, and grass, and one lit house, and its windows rattle with the beat of the music. It doesn't take me long to recognize it. I've been to enough parties at Marin Levinson's house that I would have recognized it from the sound system alone.

Marin graduated last year. She went to Sarah Lawrence, and her parents still live in San Diego. I'm going to take a wild guess that they didn't buy an identical house in Middle of Nowhere, Nevada.

My heart flutters. But I take a long, controlled breath, and I focus. Whatever this is, it isn't new anymore. Panicking isn't going to help. But getting a good look around might.

I turn in a slow circle as I walk. The houses around me, even the one I just came from, look darker and flatter than Marin's. Like someone etched every loving detail into re-creating the Levinson house and didn't save any effort for the rest. Still, I watch those dull, lifeless doors closely as I pass them.

By the time I make it to the bottom of Marin's steps, my lungs feel tight and shallow. The lowest notes of the music rattle the pit of my stomach.

I should run. Never mind that there's nowhere to go.

I start to climb the front steps instead. Except I don't get the chance.

The door swings open hard enough that it hits the side of the house and bounces back to the girl halfway through it. Her head snaps to the sound, and she grabs it with a sharp punch of an exhale, pushing it off her as she stumbles through. She hits the railing and grabs on with both hands, breathing hard as she bends over double. Her blank stare, fixed on the steps, goes right through me.

"Oh," I breathe. Because even with her hair covering her face, it's not hard to recognize myself. Me, over seven months ago.

MAY 24, SEVEN MONTHS AGO

NOTE TO SELF: these things have no sense of timing.

This was never going to be easy. You thought it'd be, at least, straightforward. But this isn't the five stages of grief people keep telling you about. This has no sequence. It resists scheduling. It will come when it will come, and it will come at Marin Levinson's graduation party, surrounded by people you know, with the longest year of your life still ahead of you.

But first, some answers to questions you may have. Yes, this is happening. Yes, Marin Levinson's earth-shaking sound system is to blame, although that's not for you to know yet. Right now it's just you and the slow-growing awareness that whatever this is, it isn't stopping. It's tight, tight in your chest and lungs all at once, and it burns like sprinting down a long, cold road.

You're taking sips of water, like you can wash this down. But your heart starts clawing like an animal, too wild and too *fast* to be exertion. You weren't doing anything. You were just *standing here*.

There's a wet shock down your thigh, and it takes a good second to realize that you've spilled your drink down the front of your dress. No one's noticed. No one's noticed you for a while now. Gaby was the one who babysat you at these kinds of things. They're not doing it on purpose. It's been months, and you seem okay. And that's good. You didn't want them watching you. You're fine. You're supposed to be fine.

You go for another breath. It catches hard and short in the back of your throat. You're dying. You're dying, and you're not even going to say anything about it. The bass pounds away, hijacking your pulse, reeling and shivering and squeezing and *clawing*—

You wrap your arms around your ribs like that'll hold your insides in, you drag the air in and out of your narrow throat, but someone laughs, and someone else screams, Marin Levinson's sound system keeps *pound, pound, pounding* at you from your feet up. And when you can't stop it, you try to outrun it instead. Distance doesn't help. It's just as fast as you are.

You hit the railing of Marin's front porch with both hands, but you're not done. You keep going, down the stairs and down the street. You don't remember where you parked, it doesn't matter where you parked, nothing matters more than running as fast as you can.

At the end of the cul-de-sac, the sidewalk dips and flings you to the pavement. The gravel bites into your palms. The wind, unseasonably warm, hits you like a wave. With every gasp of your breath, a little more color seeps back into the world. Exactly five seconds pass.

And this is when you finally think to wonder what you're doing.

You push yourself back to your knees, and you stare down at your hands, watching the beads of blood swell through the skin.

THE VALLEY AND THE FLOOD

The air's still warm. But for some reason your teeth keep chattering.

"What the hell . . ." It comes out in a huff of air. It's then that you notice how sore your chest is, how scratched your throat feels. Slowly, you stand up, look around. But if anyone heard you, no one's coming out to look. The only movement is the rippling of the trees in the middle of the cul-de-sac.

You *should* get it now. You have everything you need to piece together what's been happening, slowly, these past few months. But nobody saw you leave. And if no one's here to ask if you're okay, there's no one to think up an answer for.

But you'll catch up. Gaby's gone. What else do you have if not time to think?

Six

THE SPLIT SCREEN

FACT NUMBER ONE: I'm sitting in my car, parked along the cul-de-sac down the street from Marin Levinson's house.

Fact number two: I'm also standing in front of my car, directly in the headlights, watching myself through the windshield.

But other than that, everything's fine.

I lift a hand—carefully at first, and then right in May 24 Rose Colter's face. She looks straight through it. But to be fair, she's looking through pretty much everything.

"Neat trick," I say softly. She doesn't hear that, either.

I keep looking at her, this living, breathing aftermath of my first panic attack. She doesn't look like how I remember feeling. She's fished her—my—flannel shirt out of the back seat, and she's blasting heat from the front vents. I know, I remember, that she's waiting until she feels steady enough to drive. But other than the occasional, subtle shiver, her face is still, placid. Distracted, maybe. But normal.

It's not cold—I can still feel that unseasonable warmth through the memory, or the flashback, or whatever this is—but I shiver, too. Sometimes, when it gets bad, I have this disconnect. Like everything's gone quiet and muffled, like I've stepped outside my own trembling mess of nerves and sound to try to get a good look at myself.

To *literally* step outside myself, though—that's a little different. But it's also a little easier to look at myself and know, for once, exactly how I'm feeling.

She takes the car out of park, and I jerk back onto the curb, unsure if this place can hurt me, but not willing to test it. But she drives past me—down the street, round the corner, out of sight.

Marin Levinson's neighborhood doesn't disappear with her.

I turn in a slow circle. The path from Marin's house to where I'm standing has gone from black-and-white to full color: from the sidewalks, to the houses that surrounded me, to the tiny dots of blood on the pavement where my hands hit the ground. In the cul-de-sac, the trees have started rippling gently, gray shadows slowly defining into individual leaves.

It's Marin's house that looks flat and lifeless now. The colors and lights have dimmed, and as my car ventures farther down the street, the thump of the bass gets quieter. As my taillights turn the corner and disappear, the music stops. Like now that I'm gone, the party has ceased to exist.

Sliding my phone out of my pocket, I turn on the camera and take a long look at myself. My face white in the streetlights, whiter still next to my dark auburn hair. My shoulders straight, drawn up to my full gangly height—*lanky*, Gaby would want me to say, because supposedly that sounds sexier. My brown eyes big and dark. The image, splintered in the cracked screen, shakes with my hand. But I look as normal as I did that night, sitting in that car.

At least this answers one question I've had all these months. If I looked like this the entire party, it makes sense that no one came out to check on me.

I pull up my text messages and flip back to the one Maurice sent the day I left. *In case anything comes up.* And his number.

I tap the number with my finger. It isn't until it starts ringing that I realize I didn't plan any further than this.

It rings again, which means it's officially too late to hang up. It's going to look weirder if I do. He has my number, I gave it to him during that first appointment—it won't exactly be hard for him to figure out it was me.

Maybe it'll go to voicemail. He told me it almost always goes to voicemail. But even then I still have to tell him *something*. And not about Flashback Theater in 3D. Or that I ruined my visit with Flora. Or that I might soon be responsible for the destruction of an entire town.

Rescheduling. I'll tell him I need to push back a week. And then I'll sound like I don't *need* to see him the second I get back.

So I'm completely prepared. For everything except the possibility that he'll pick up.

"Hello?" he says.

"Oh, shit," I blurt out.

"Rose?" he says.

And I immediately hang up.

The phone sits flat in the palm of my hand. It's silent for a few beats. And then it rings.

I suck in a deep breath through my teeth, and I pick it up.

"Hi, Maurice," I say.

"Hello, Rose?" Maurice sounds totally, enviably even. "I think I just missed a call from you?"

Oh my God. That was way more generous than I deserved.

"Um. Yes. Sorry," I say. "I was going to leave a message. I thought you had a separate work phone."

"That's right," he says.

"You're checking your work phone at midnight?" I say.

"It was next to me." I can hear the jovial shrug. "I was awake anyway." Probably at his desk, learning a fourth language. God-damnit, Maurice.

"You know," I say, "there's this thing called work-life balance—"

"And I'll be sure to look into it," he says. "Something on your mind?"

I straighten. Mild as it sounds, that's as direct as I've ever heard him. I can waste time all I want in our appointments. But if I'm going so far as to call him, he's going to know something's up.

I think. It's not like I know a lot about him personally. His office is in a first-floor apartment, facing the street. He takes clients in French, English, and three dialects of Arabic. When I ask if he had a nice week, he always says that he did, in a way that suggests we're stopping there. He has two framed paintings of cities behind his chair. The first is Paris. When I asked about the second, he told me it was Algiers.

And he's a ridiculously, frustratingly kind person. Kind in a way I've never doubted.

So. What's on my mind.

I laugh. "Can I have an easier question?"

"Okay," he says. "What would help, then?"

I start tapping my feet in a rhythm. The beat echoes. "What helps other people, when they call you?"

"Sometimes it helps to just talk," he says.

"Hard pass," I say, smiling despite myself. "What else?"

I can hear him mulling it over. "Well . . . I'm not sure how to put this, but oftentimes what people are looking for is a . . . I'm trying to think of a better phrase than *reality check*."

"*Reality check* is an excellent phrase," I say. "But you're probably not talking about the 'blue just isn't your color' type."

"Blue is everyone's color," he says very seriously.

This time, I laugh for real.

"So you mean, like . . ." I rub my thumb against the inside of my palm. But the cuts I'm thinking about are long gone. "If someone's seeing things?"

"Could be like that," he says. If he reads anything into the question, it doesn't show. "Or maybe they see what's there just fine, but they don't know how to interpret it."

Somehow, sitting on a street I know is hundreds of miles away, watching a night from seven months ago—it feels about ten times more surreal now, talking to someone so unrelentingly grounded. But I know what he's saying. Everything I've ever asked him, since that first appointment, has been some form of "Is this happening or not?"

I swallow, hard. "You get texts, right?"

"I do," he says.

"So . . ." I stare into the floodlights of the house across the street until it hurts my eyes. "If I texted you a picture, right now, could you describe what's in it without asking any questions?"

There's a beat of silence. And this is the one thing that annoys me about him. No matter what I say, he never seems that surprised.

"And that'd help?" he says.

"Yeah. I think it would." It's my turn to pause. "I'm going to hang up now."

"You can always call back later if you want to talk." After some consideration, he adds, "Maybe not later *tonight*."

"Sure, yeah," I say. "Sorry again."

"Not at all. Take care, Rose."

I hang up. And for a second, I consider not taking the picture. But maybe this *will* help.

I angle my phone's camera straight down the middle of the street, I take the shot, and I text him the picture. No context.

An ellipsis pops up on his side of the screen. He's typing.

Cul-de-sac with three trees in the middle, says the text. The same thing I see.

But when I look up again, that cul-de-sac is gone. I'm in the middle of the street, but a street back in the Lethe Ridge housing development. That ever-present stirring over my shoulder feels farther away now, like whoever it was took a big step back. And Marin's neighborhood isn't there.

But if my reality check saw it, too, then there we are.

The phone buzzes again. Maurice sent another text. *Why?*

I shake my head as I text back. *I said no questions.* ☺

I read his message again. And this time, it lands. *Cul-de-sac.* There had been a cul-de-sac on the public access channel when I had that little jolt of panic, back at the house. Somewhere in the back of my mind, I saw that and thought of Marin's neighborhood. It's the kind of logic leap that hypervigilance is so good at. But I didn't consciously connect the dots.

So how did this thing—this flood—recognize what I didn't?

I close out my messages and go back to my home screen. It's midnight. If I'm going to trust Cassie, that means that in exactly three days, whatever I've brought to this town will be here.

And it suddenly feels much easier to believe her.

Before I delete the picture from my phone, I take one last look at it, broken into three parts by the cracked screen. I wonder how Maurice would react if I told him where I'd taken that picture—*when* I'd taken it. As far as he knows, that's where the story started: that first panic attack, this street. Everything before that, I sketched in fuzzier terms. I told him how normal it all was. I lost my best friend, sure. But everything else was normal.

Maurice is very good at his job. If he doesn't believe what I'm telling him, it doesn't show. And if he wonders what I'm not saying, that doesn't show, either.

He's not wrong to wonder. I've told him a lot. I haven't told him everything.

Seven

THE FIRST DAY

FOR THE FIRST time in months, my phone doesn't wake me up.

Not for lack of trying. The only time I keep it on silent these days is in class. If someone calls, texts, whatever—I want to know right away.

But I wake up to silence. The only thing moving in the empty model bedroom is the light through the blinds, shifting upward. And when I check my phone for the time, I see two new texts. The first is from my little brother, Sammy. The second is a number I don't know.

Coming to pick you up, be there in 20 min—Alex Harper

I pull up Sammy's text as I wiggle into my jeans. *Hi, Rosie*, I read as I jam a clean shirt over my head. *Is it warm where you are? It is cold today but Mom says it will not snow. Dad says to tell you to call tonight if you have time. Please write back. Bye.*

I allow myself a second to smile before I shove a granola bar into my mouth. Getting Sammy to practice writing has been like pulling teeth, so much that his teacher gave him a project recently: to write, just once a day, about whatever he wants, and to show it to one of us. So every day, he texts me.

Sammy is seven. I used to think he was too young to notice me flinch every time my phone buzzed. Now I can't help but wonder if he's trying to fix something.

The doorbell rings, and I hurriedly swing my backpack over my shoulder and bolt for the door. But the person waiting for me on the other side isn't Alex Harper.

"Well, now." A middle-aged woman stands on the porch, her sweater set matching her eyes, her teeth matching her pearls. There's something intensely familiar about the lines at the crease of her mouth, thinning her cheeks. "I suppose a welcome is in order?"

"Oh," I say involuntarily, because I remember now. I saw this woman last night, on the public access channel.

"Aren't you lovely," she chirps. "My daughter has always wanted to grow her hair out past her shoulders. She's got that beautiful wave you have, too. How do you keep it from tangling?"

My brain stutters, bypassing the *what are you doing at my house* and the *I guess it's not my house but still* that are on the tip of my tongue. Somehow what I say is "Coconut oil twice a week."

"How nice." Her lips widen. "But you look so tired. Were you not comfortable here? You know, I love this neighborhood. I have since it was built. I was on the planning board, I remember when this was an empty bit of desert. Twenty of the houses sold before we broke ground!"

I smile, nod, and let her keep going. But as the lines around her mouth deepen, I shift my weight to my back foot, still resting safely inside the house. She's fully blocking the door now.

THE VALLEY AND THE FLOOD

"And do you want to know what happened?" the woman says. I finally notice that her smile never reaches her eyes. "None of these houses ever filled. No one wants to live in a half-empty community, as it turns out. Most of the buyers left town, dear. Because of you."

Neither of us speaks for a long moment. Her stare, directed at me, never wavers.

Finally, she thrusts out an arm and an open palm. "Marguerite Williams. Mayor of Lotus Valley."

For a long moment, all I can do is stare down at her steady, outstretched hand. Then, gingerly, I shake it.

"Rose," I offer quietly.

"Oh, good. You're polite at least," she says. "Don't look so worried. We're just going to talk. That's okay, isn't it?"

"Do I have a choice?" It's out of my mouth before I can think twice. But lucky for me, she laughs.

"Not too polite, I see," she says. "But that's good. That's smart. Polite doesn't mean you have to let people walk all over you. I think you can relate to why I'm here, then."

I wouldn't go *that* far. But remembering that election ad last night, I think I have an idea. "If by that, you mean you want me gone . . ." She smiles. That's a yes. ". . . then to be honest, I don't understand why there are people who disagree with you."

She laughs, high and humorless. "We *do* understand each other. But I can't force you to leave, much as I'd like to. It's not that simple, even I know that. There's a force older than the rule of law. Do you know what that is?"

She doesn't wait for me to answer. She barely waits for the question to sink in. "Hospitality. It's what this town was built on: a shelter from the storms of the world, or so I keep hearing. We even enshrined it into our charter not too long ago: to never turn away a soul in need, unless our every effort to help them has failed.

"But by the time we've made our efforts with what you've brought, my dear," she says, "it could be too late for us. Do you understand?"

I swallow. My mouth is as dry as my throat. "If that's true," I say, "then I think you can ignore your charter."

But she doesn't smile this time. "If," she repeats, low. "So you don't believe it?"

I start to tell her no. The truth slips out instead. "I don't know what I believe."

I could take that sympathetic purse of her mouth as genuine. But I think I'd be wrong.

"If you're hearing me," she says, "and I think you are, we don't need to bother with that charter, you and I. We can solve this little problem by close of business."

"Meaning what?" I say.

"You haven't spoken to the sheriff yet," she says. I can't stop the little shake of my head. "She'll be along soon, I imagine. We're both meant to talk to you today, we could agree on that much. And she'll try to convince you that something *can* be done. She'll tell you that what you brought was always meant to return. That it's our responsibility to help. No matter what that means for us. Are we still understanding each other, Rose?"

"I—I think we are."

"Good," Mayor Williams says. "Because you'll see how easy it is to get swept into the romance of this town, its purpose. I had my own regrettable dabblings long ago. All I ask is that you remember this. The sheriff has the means to stop this tragedy. She just chooses not to."

She smiles beatifically. And she never for a second looks away. "But if you told Sheriff Jones you wanted rid of it, she'd have no choice."

It sounds simple enough. But the way she says it sends a chill through me.

"And if I just left?" I say.

"I'm afraid that's not one of the choices, dear." Something in her smile hardens. "You've heard, haven't you? There's a pull to Lotus Valley. Like an ocean's current, drawing us in. And this flood feels that more keenly than anyone. Now that you've led them here—they won't simply turn back and follow you out. You may be intriguing to them, but this town is more intriguing by far.

"And besides," she says, "it found you out there. It chose to follow you. If you left without resolving this, who's to say it wouldn't find you again someday?"

Sutton Avenue isn't here. I can't see it, anyway. But when I breathe in, I feel the cold, clammy air.

She's trying to scare me. But I know she's right. I could go on not believing Cassie. I could discount half the things I've seen here. I could leave this place and try to trust that I didn't destroy it.

But something *is* following me. I can't deny that anymore. And once it's finished here, it could follow me home. To Mom, and Dan, and Sammy.

There's a long, loud rush of blood through my ears. Loud

enough that I don't hear the music until the car careens around the corner.

TONIGHT, I'M GONNA HAVE MYSELF
A REAL GOOD TIME
I FEEL ALIIII-I-I-IIIIIVE

As the beat-up Dodge screeches in front of the house, I turn back to Mayor Williams. "I want it gone," I murmur.

She slides a business card into my hand and whispers, "Talk to Sheriff Jones. Hear her out, by all means. But more importantly, see her methods. Ensure that you have the resolve."

"I have the resolve," I shoot back. "There's something I need to do. But I'll call you after."

I didn't know how hollow that smile was until right this second, when her face lights up.

"You've got yourself a deal," she says.

The passenger's door sails open, nearly flattening the mailbox. And I tuck the business card into my pocket and out of sight.

"Rose?" Alex Harper from the sheriff's office calls out. Even from across the lawn, I see the furrow in his pale, delicate features. "Is everything okay?"

Mayor Williams has a beauty queen's wave. "Just introducing myself."

The furrow deepens, but the tone remains the same. "I was asking Rose, ma'am."

The mayor lets out a single startled laugh, leaning forward to peer past Alex. "And how are you, Felix? Feeling good about your decision?"

Over Alex's shoulder, I can make out Felix Sohrabi's queasy

smile in the driver's seat. "As good as I feel about any of my decisions, Ms. W."

"Don't let me keep you." The mayor makes a show of stepping out of my path. And as I walk past, I feel a light brush against my shoulder. "But don't forget."

I can see her in the rearview mirror as I slide into the back seat. I don't think she moves once as we pull away.

For a long moment, I forget to be anxious about Felix's driving. But I get there eventually.

"Are you okay?" Alex asks. It takes me a second to remember that he's asking about the mayor, not about my fingernails curling into the shredded back seat.

"Fine," I say. "She wanted to talk." They both make little noises of assent, and we lapse back into silence.

"Thanks for the ride?" I add.

"Oh, you know, yeah," Felix says.

We make our way out of the housing development and toward the city, and I drum my fingers against my kneecaps and concentrate on breathing. Felix is, to put it mildly, not a careful driver. No one's on the road, though, so it should be fine. That's what I keep telling myself.

"You can't talk to her like that," Felix finally mumbles.

"Like what," Alex says, crisply enough that it's clear he already knows what.

"Allie"—Felix lets out a long, controlled breath—"we have to be civil to her if we want her to—"

"She's a hypocrite," Alex interrupts quietly.

"Did you hear me say she wasn't?" Felix says.

"I'm not going to let her—"

"I don't see you *letting* her do anything," Felix says.

Alex only raises his voice a little. But I have the feeling that for him, this is a shout. "I'm not going to let her spin me as some *victim* for her—"

The word cuts off in a little half-suppressed cough. And Felix, with the intensity of someone who's had to say this more than once, blurts out, "Will you please use your inhaler?"

"I'm good," Alex says. "Thank you."

"What, are you self-conscious?" Felix turns to look at me. "Rose, could you look away for about ten seconds?"

"Felix," Alex says, now through his teeth. "Watch the road, please?"

"There's no shame in it," Felix says. "I mean, look at this car, it's practically a biohazard—"

Alex's sigh doesn't sound particularly short of breath. "I've been dealing with asthma at least four times longer than I've been dealing with you. Trust me, if I can't breathe, you'll be the first—"

I shift in my seat, and catching sight of me out of the corner of his eye, Alex stills. "Sorry," he mumbles, glancing over his shoulder.

"Yeah." Felix flashes a wobbly grin. "And sorry about the . . . welcome."

"No," I say, more of a laugh than a word. "It's fine. It's actually . . . kind of a relief, to see what you were all being so weird about."

Felix grimaces. "In our defense, if you had her for freshman history, you'd be weird, too."

I wince. "Ouch."

"Thank you for your support in this difficult time," Felix says, startling a more genuine laugh out of me. Another awkward beat. "So. You're the mysterious stranger, huh?"

I wiggle my fingers in a weak wave. "Yo."

"I expected someone more . . ." Felix takes a hand off the wheel to make a vague gesture. "Ominous?"

"You've, ah," I say, "been very nice for someone who knows what I'm doing here."

"Listen," Felix says, sailing past a stop sign, "we aren't from Lotus Valley originally. I've been here for two years, and I still don't understand half the stuff that comes out of people's mouths. Do I get this whole prophecy thing? No. Do I have questions? Boy, do I ever. Am I going to go along with it? Signs point to yes."

"Taking things in stride is one thing," I say slowly. "But how many people agree with your mayor?"

Felix and Alex exchange a quick look. "It's . . ." Alex says. "Maybe about fifty-fifty."

"Ouch," I say again, much quieter this time.

"Tends to fall along age lines, too," Felix says. "People under thirty-five, especially kids our age, are more likely to support Ms. Jones, while older residents are more likely to support Ms. Williams." He throws an exasperated look over his shoulder. "Typical, right? We're the ones who'll be living here for the next seventy years, and yet the octogenarians want to leave us with the worst resident-neighbor relations possible."

"They're good people. Most of them are." Alex looks at me through the overhead mirror. I don't miss the shadow that passes over his expression. "And not all of them want what the mayor wants."

"She has to be careful," Felix agrees. "It's not like the neighbors vote or anything, but they're still her constituents. Technically."

"And not all of her supporters feel the same way," Alex says. "Some of them agree with her that the neighbors have been allowed too much leeway. Some of them are fine with them as long as they keep quiet and stay out of the way. And some of them are—well. Some of them are just worried about what would happen if we tried to overturn the charter."

"Mostly because there were some decidedly scary characters *negotiating* that charter," Felix says with a shudder. "There are things her supporters agree on, though. Wanting you gone, for one."

I smile weakly. "That's one way to unite the people."

Alex's smile is apologetic. "You should be careful who you talk to. There are people who might feel differently if they knew everything. There are people who might even benefit from you being here."

"Benefit how?" I ask.

Alex shifts in his seat. "Ms. Jones didn't say."

Felix snorts. "How totally unlike our dear sheriff."

"Don't start," Alex says.

Felix raises his hands defensively. Not the best thing to do when you're driving. But before I can say anything, he puts them back on the wheel. "So, okay," he says over his shoulder to me. "Apparently she and Cassie knew the whole time that the flood was meant to roll in on New Year's Day, but not which year? I get keeping that quiet from the town. You don't want to panic people, or whatever. But it would have been cool if la capitana gave her *interns* a heads-up."

"How long have you been interning for her?" I ask.

"Seven months," Felix says.

"Seven years," Alex says at the same time.

I blink. Alex doesn't look old enough to be interning *now*.

"Seven—" I take a minute to lower my voice. "You started interning when you were eight?"

"Nine," Alex says. "And I wasn't really *interning*, just running errands for Ms. Jones."

"Still," I say. "Did you, like, go to career day and never look back?"

"It just worked out that way." Alex tugs absently on his seat belt. "She would have had to keep an eye on me, anyway—"

Felix looks at him. It doesn't look like he's *warning* him, I guess, but he looks serious—which is warning enough.

"We should be there in ten minutes," Alex finally says.

He hesitates, his head already half turned away. "Rose," he says. "We told you before to be careful what you tell people. But Mayor Williams . . . you should always assume that she already knows."

I blink. "Why would she know?"

"She claims she can't do it anymore," Felix says quickly. "But she could have just been saying that for the election . . ."

"When she was younger," Alex picks up, "she was good enough that even now, she's still considered the most accurate prophet in Lotus Valley."

I watch them for a moment. Maybe I'm missing something. "Does that mean she's better than Cassie?"

Felix snorts. "Don't let Cassie hear you say that."

"But if she *is*," I press on, "then what if she's seen what's coming?"

"Well," Felix says, "that's why Ms. Jones believes she really lost her abilities. She says Williams isn't a bad person. And if she's seen something that could help, she'd tell us, no matter how much she disagreed with us."

"Then again," Alex says, quietly enough that it might be to himself, "Ms. Jones sees the best in people."

They both watch the road, and I stare at the back of their heads for a long moment, waiting for them to elaborate. But they exchange a quick, uneasy glance, and they stop talking.

"You can turn the music back on," I say.

Felix flashes a smug smile as he fires up the stereo. "See? Everyone loves Queen."

"Drive the car, Felix," Alex replies.

WITHOUT A CONVERSATION to distract me, I find myself watching the tower instead, growing closer and closer. I rub at my thigh, the friction of my palm creating a simmering heat around Mayor Williams's business card in my pocket.

The building we pull up to doesn't look like a radio station—it's pretty clearly a school. It's cut in the same clean, angular lines as the houses of Lethe Ridge and is as polished as if it was built yesterday. And yet rising straight up from the center is a radio tower that, supposedly, hasn't been used since 1973.

"Ah," Alex says. It's almost too quiet to be heard, but Felix's head snaps toward him.

"What is it?" he says, barely a question.

"Nothing," Alex says.

Felix puts the car in park, still watching Alex. His hand twitches off the wheel, gets halfway to reaching the passenger's seat, but at the last moment, he drops it to the center console instead. "It's okay," he says haltingly. "We're not going inside."

I don't have time to wonder about it. Because it's then that I notice the woman standing in the shadow of the building; early thirties, in a sundress and a crisp orange blazer, with a twist-out that falls a few inches above her shoulders and bright blush contoured across her high, dark cheekbones. She holds a closed parasol at her side, tapping it in an aimless rhythm on the ground. She looks like she's stepped out of a Fashion Week candid. And there's no question as to who she is.

"Hi there." The sheriff smiles without showing her teeth. "Rose, I take it?"

For lack of anything more intelligent to do, I nod.

"Christie Jones," she says. "Now, why don't you follow me inside? We're already running on Felix-time this morning, so we should get right to it."

"We were driving carefully," Felix says.

"We were not," Alex says.

Sheriff Jones motions for me to follow her. "If we wait for them to stop bickering, we'll be here until the heat death of the universe."

I catch Felix's and Alex's gazes flickering from each other to the two of us as the doors swing closed behind me, and I have a brief second to connect the dots. *We're not going inside*, Felix told Alex. But apparently, I am.

We step inside the front hallway and into the school. A series of windows dot the hallway, flooding long swatches with late-morning light that doesn't reach the shadows in between. Sheriff Jones steps around the sunlight as she walks.

"You're not exactly what I expected," she says.

"Everyone keeps saying that," I mumble. My shadow curves along the wall as I pass a window.

She throws her head back and laughs, a bright, clear sound. "I just figured you'd be—I don't know. More imposing? But I guess you really are a kid, aren't you?"

"Well . . ." I fall a few steps farther behind. "Sorry?"

"Do you know how much time I've spent looking for you in the past five years?" she says, her voice still light. "Or more to the point, do you know how much of my life I'll spend apologizing to my wife's parents when this is over? All this time we've been telling them we can't spend the holidays with them because I'm allergic to their cats."

"Sheriff Jones—" I start.

"Christie, please," she says. "Formalities give me hives. So Maggie Williams talked to you already, huh?"

"How did you know that?" I say. I thought the mayor was the psychic one. Honestly, if they're *all* psychic, I'm leaving.

"A good guess. You've got that post–Maggie Williams look on your face," she says. "She must have been excited that she got to you first, before I *got in your head*." She dips her tone and waggles her fingers, her eyes fluttering into a devastating eye roll. I like her, despite myself. Gaby would be obsessed with her.

"She was," I confirm, smiling a little.

"And are you considering her offer?" Sheriff Jones says, just as casually.

My stomach drops. I don't mean for it to show on my face,

but it must, because she grins. "It's okay. You don't have to tell me what you discussed with her if you don't want to. We're here to talk, that's all."

"I understand that," I say. "But why are we *here* here?"

"This is where you wanted to be, right?" she says. "I was told you wanted to see the old radio station."

"Well," I say. "Can I be honest?"

"Please," she says.

"I understand the mayor's position," I say. My voice only wavers a little. "I don't understand yours."

She glances over her shoulder at me. "You're a little young to be cynical."

"If it were me, I wouldn't want to lose my home. I don't think that's cynical," I say.

She hums thoughtfully. "If it makes you feel any better, I'm not meeting you out of the goodness of my heart. My position couldn't be more practical. The neighbors—they're my constituents, too. And if I owe you the benefit of the doubt, I owe it to whatever you've brought, too."

I pause. The ever-present movement over my shoulder has stilled since I greeted Christie Jones. Like they're standing at a distance, waiting to see what happens.

"She says you can get rid of it." I say it so quietly, I almost don't hear it myself.

She's still smiling. But her eyes go sharp.

"Well," she says. "First things first. Why don't you answer your own question for me. Why are you here?"

I keep smiling, though my back straightens. "What happened to the benefit of the doubt?"

"You're looking at it," she says.

"I mean . . ." I say. "You know my car broke down on—"

"You're clearly very smart, Rose. So I think you know that's not what I meant," Christie says. "Why were you on the road? Traveling somewhere?"

My phone shivers in my pocket. Flora Summer, maybe, checking in on me. She hasn't heard from me in a day, after all. Clearly I must be dead.

My stomach drops. Maybe not the best idea to joke about the *d* word when it comes to Flora, even in my head.

"Home from somewhere," I finally manage. "I was visiting a family friend in Vegas."

"Awfully late to be driving," she says.

"My AC's busted. Has been for a year." Under her stare, I find myself adding, "And I left earlier than I was supposed to."

She nods approvingly. "Something happen?"

For a second I almost see it, like it's burned on my retinas: that slouched figure standing in the center of the Summers' kitchen. There's a sick, sudden drop when I blink, like I've slipped under the floor. The thought of him in that kitchen, looking through their fridge, pouring himself drinks, still prickles like a long, fresh scrape. Gaby's parents moved after she died, that house wasn't hers, that kitchen wasn't hers. But it's yet another thing Nick would get to see and she wouldn't.

I shouldn't have left Flora alone with him. But maybe that's an irrational thought. It's not like I left her in a car with him.

I squeeze my eyes tighter, then open them again. I'm in Lotus Valley Elementary School. Not the kitchen. Not Vegas. Not with him.

"Someone else showed up," I say. "Someone I wasn't expecting. And I didn't want to be in the same house with him, so . . . I left."

"So that was the end of it?" she asks. "This person showed up, and you left?"

I laugh. "I think you're underestimating how much I dislike this person."

She suddenly looks very serious, glancing back at me. "Did he hurt you?"

It's a jolt I feel down to the bones. I've known Christie Jones about five minutes. I didn't expect her to look at me the same way Gaby did once, almost two years ago.

Rose. Tell me what he did.

The echo of it trips me up for a second. Long enough that I'm sure she doesn't miss it.

"Not . . ." I swallow. "Not me. Specifically."

She watches me for a moment longer. But eventually, she lets that pass.

"So you left this family friend, drove into the desert," she says, "and then what?"

I remember that look that May 24 Rose Colter had on her face last night: distracted, maybe, but outwardly calm. I'm pretty sure that's exactly how I look now. But Christie doesn't trust it. She's right not to.

"Well," I finally say, "there was some walking thrown in there."

"Ah, yes. The broadcast." She glances into the classroom behind her. "I don't think you said whose voice it was you heard."

"I don't think I mentioned it to you at all," I say slowly.

She shrugs. "I'd very much like to trust you, Rose. But I don't think I ever promised that we'd trust you without question, did I?"

I suddenly realize that everything I told Cassie yesterday, Sheriff Jones knows by now. My pulse goes loud and fast in my ears.

"Besides," she says, "I think the feeling is mutual, isn't it?"

"Meaning what?" I snap back.

"Meaning you don't trust me," she says.

"Would *you*?" I make myself take a deep, shaky breath. "I get what you've been saying. And I can believe that in this town, you're more used to weird shit than most. But if what's following me is half as scary as you keep implying, I have to be honest. Mayor Williams says you could stop this if you wanted to. And I don't understand why you wouldn't."

She chews on that for a long moment. Finally, slowly, she sets her parasol against the wall. "Should I explain it to you, then?"

There's a kind of shift in the air. My foot slides back through the dust.

Her smile softens a little. But the line of her shoulders is still taut. "I suppose this answers two questions at once really," she muses. "How you can get rid of it, if that's what you want—and why I'd rather not."

Her purposeful stride slows as she approaches the windows. As her hand reaches for the blinds, she looks over her shoulder and smiles.

"Try to keep your voice down," she says. "He startles easy."

She yanks the cord, and the low angle of the sun fills the room with a burst of light and long shadows. Only, her shadow seems to be a little longer than it should be. A lot longer.

Long enough that it splits in two.

Those two shadows split into twos, on and on until they stretch wall to wall, floor to ceiling, writhing and swarming around the fixed point of her legs. They shiver silently at the base of her feet. She glances down at them, patient but firm. And at length, their movements begin to slow, smooth out. By the time she looks back to me, they're drifting gently back and forth like kelp on an ocean floor.

Christie Jones, surrounded by a thousand shadows, turns back to me. "You see," she says. "You're not the only one being followed."

Eight

THE LONG SHADOW

NOTE TO SELF: As catchy as it is to say, fight or flight are not the only two options available to you. There is, according to Maurice, door number three: freeze. It's simple enough. You stand there with your mouth open and do nothing.

Well. I don't do *nothing*.

"What the hell is *that*?" I blurt out.

Christie's brow creases. "You're one to talk."

"Oh God, sorry," I say automatically. At least my hindbrain is still trying to be polite. "It's—I'm—How are you doing that?"

"Me? I'm not doing anything," she says. "Aside from my damn impressive 5K and my, frankly, superhuman mac-and-cheese recipe, I'm pretty normal as far as people go. This"—she gestures to the room, packed to the walls with inky black shadows—"is Rudy."

"Rudy," I say faintly.

"It started as a joke," she says with a shrug. "But he's never had the words to tell me his name, and I'm not sure he *has* a language to begin with. So it stuck."

We've been calling it a flood, Cassie had said, *because it's the closest word in our vocabulary for what I saw.* I wonder if they ever had a name. I wonder if anyone else ever knew it.

Christie eyes me for a moment. "You don't seem that surprised."

"I have a good poker face," I say faintly.

"You don't have to be so polite." She swings her arms behind her back, clasping her hands. The shadows don't move with her. "This is new to you. I get that. If you have something to ask, ask."

"Okay . . ." Carefully, to test it, I move my foot into the classroom without touching the floor. The shadows ripple for a moment, as if unsure what to do. Then the tangle of his limbs recedes, creating a bare spot of floor right before my toes.

I laugh and slowly transfer my weight into the circle. Thanks, Rudy.

"So I'm guessing you'd like to start with how," Christie says.

"And how long," I say.

"Ten years," she says.

"Ten—" I swallow the rest of the sentence. "Where did he come from?"

Part of him disconnects from the floor and reaches up—off the ground, the limb rounds out, turns solid and three-dimensional—and comes to rest on her shoulder. She scratches at the underside, and his whole body shivers with delight. When he withdraws, satisfied, the limb flattens and slides to the linoleum, melting back into the maze of shadow.

"Well," she says. "Not all of us get a prophecy to give us the heads-up. By the time I noticed him, he was already there."

I shift from foot to foot. Out of the corner of my eye I can see Rudy slide farther back, giving me a little more space. "Were you scared?"

"No more than I already was at the time." She eyes me, her face impassive. "I was far away from home back then. Far away from everyone who cared about me, with someone I shouldn't have trusted as much as I did.

"Cassie must have told you that for all the differences between our neighbors, there's one thing that unites them. They're born from change—sometimes good, sometimes bad, but always irreversible. But it doesn't have to be an earth-shattering change. Sometimes it's just in that moment a relationship drops all pretenses. Becomes as ugly as it always was, deep down."

She smiles and shrugs. "I'm Lotus Valley born and bred. Some of us go our whole lives without seeing a neighbor up close, let alone have a hand in creating one, but you're always a little ready for it, you know? So when I stepped out of my building back then and my shadow filled a whole block, it felt like the logical conclusion."

There's a sharp crunch. I flinch, Christie doesn't. Out of the corner of my eye, I see that Rudy appears to be chewing up a takeout container from the trash. So I guess those were mouths.

"Rudy," Christie says, mildly chiding. "Gross."

He curls around her ankles, chastened.

"I couldn't understand him," she says. "Or make him understand me. But there's one more thing our neighbors have in common. Like any living thing, there's always going to be something they need to survive. And like we need food and light and water to live? Rudy seemed to *need* to protect me.

"He wasn't violent with my boyfriend, at first. I think he just wanted to scare him." Christie's smile drops, and for a moment, I see myself in that car last night, blank-faced and shivering. "Sometimes I think Rudy learned that violence *from* him. Because when my boyfriend escalated, so did Rudy."

For a moment, Rudy looks bigger. One of his arms crosses in front of the window, casting the room into brief but total shadow. "I don't know if I was afraid before," Christie says. "But I was then."

"What changed?" I ask slowly.

Catching the look on my face, she laughs. "Believe it or not, I don't know much more than you do about things like Rudy. I don't know if they think or feel like we do, or have a sense of right and wrong. For all I know, Rudy wouldn't have thought much of anything about taking a life. Lotus Valley and the people here, we don't have any special insight into them, exactly. They're from everywhere, just like we are. They want different things, just like we do. But the only thing we really have in common is that we're drawn, in the end, to the same little town."

She's thoughtful for a moment. "I know it's not my fault he exists. But he came from me. So I wanted him to be something good.

"So I left that boyfriend, and that town. And maybe we both felt this place pulling us home, but it was more than that. I felt like whatever we were capable of together, we'd find it here. And on that road I could feel us both getting softer. He liked the car engine. He liked stealing fries out of my bag. And by the fourth motel, I stopped worrying that he was going to hurt someone. When I told him to stop, or calm down, he'd listen."

She chews on her lower lip. "And he still listens, for the

most part. But if there's a threat that's beyond my capability to handle . . . it doesn't leave him much choice."

"And you never tried to get rid of him?" I say it softly, like there's any way Rudy might not hear.

She pauses. "Maggie Williams told you about our charter here."

"To never turn away a soul in need," I say.

"We didn't have that charter when I was growing up," she says. "There was this understanding, like we didn't have a choice but to try to get along. And not everyone here is like Cassie, you know? Some of us don't know yet what our particular strangeness is. My family's been here for so long, we've forgotten what drew us to Lotus Valley in the first place.

"I did wonder at first how to make Rudy leave." She smiles down at the floor. "But welcoming him in—getting to understand him, and understand what we could be if we built something together—it's the most rewarding thing I've ever done."

I hope I'm subtle enough as I take a long, slow breath in.

"And is it always rewarding?" I say.

"Well," she says. "If you were to ask Alex, he might have a less rosy view than I do."

"Your intern Alex?" My next question comes a little slower. "What happened to him?"

That careful blankness smooths out her face again. "Sometimes the neighbors are born from something natural, like the flood. Sometimes, like Rudy, they exist because of human actions. Those neighbors—they take a stronger interest in us than others." There's a beat. "And just like Rudy was fixated on me, the neighbor that came to Alex was only interested in him. But unlike Rudy, he wasn't there for anything good. And we couldn't understand why. Not in time to make a difference."

She doesn't elaborate. I swallow down a sudden tightness in my chest. Not only at the thought of what might have happened to Alex. But at the question of why this ages-old force of nature considered me so particularly interesting.

Christie's eyes flicker briefly to the walls, where the shadows have started to fill the boundaries of the room. "I believe these things have a right to be here. Maybe more right than we do. But that doesn't mean Maggie Williams is wrong. Intentionally or not, some of them *can* be dangerous. And if they can't live with us, then I can't allow them to stay. And Rudy—well. He's got a big appetite."

"He . . . eats them?" I say, a little queasily.

Christie smiles humorlessly. "Let me put it this way. When Rudy first came to me, he had fifty arms. I counted. About a dozen good meals later? I can't count anymore."

He trills a little, weaving a long limb in and out of the space between her feet. It's almost cute. But I can see the way he puffs himself up, just a little, in response to her words. In anticipation. His arms, many more than fifty, visibly twitch.

This, at the sheriff's feet, is the fate that awaits my unwanted guest.

Well. I guess that's up to me.

The soft, thoughtful lilt of Christie's voice hardens, as if she knows what I'm thinking. "You're going to hear a lot about what you should be doing. You don't have to agree with me, or with anyone. But this is what I can tell you for sure: Rudy's never gone against anything as big as what's following you. I don't think he stands a chance. This flood isn't part of you the way Rudy is part of me, but they *are* following you. If there's a fight, you may be in harm's way. The way I see it, the best option we have is to talk to them—figure out why they're here, try to convince them to stop. And that's where you come in."

I laugh queasily. "To do what, exactly?"

"Something older than humanity itself took an interest in you," she says. "That's not random. There's something this flood needs to survive, too. Figure out what that is, and maybe you can communicate with them. They may not listen to you the way Rudy listens to me. But there's a good chance no one's tried to understand this thing in a long time.

"And on that note," she says, "let's talk about why *you're* here."

"Me?" I say. "I don't—"

"It's okay. You're here because of that broadcast, you've made no secret of that," she says, handing me her business card. "Two birds, one stone, honey. This building wasn't always the elementary school, you know. You're standing in what used to be the offices of Lotus Valley Community Radio."

"All this," I start. "What's—"

"—the catch?" she drawls. "To get to the broadcast studio, you'll need to use the basement stairs. I've asked someone I trust to wait there with the keys. And once you connect with her, wherever you go in this town, she goes with you. If you're not with her, you're with Felix or Alex, and even then, you tell her what you're doing."

"So you're giving me a chaperone," I say.

"Like I said"—she shrugs—"trust is earned."

I almost don't ask the next question. "Okay, so—say I do talk to them. Say I try to understand them. What if there's nothing to understand? What if dangerous is all they are?"

The tendrils of the shadow start to curl. She, on the other hand, looks very still. "Rudy can help us clear this town in hours if we have to. I taught him to deal with stragglers, how to direct traffic. Hell, I even taught him how to pack a suitcase. I'm prepared to give you as much time as I possibly can. Focus on what you can do before it gets to that point. And try not to worry about what happens after that. That's my job."

She moves on, a little too quickly. "Oh, and Rose? I don't need to know what you and the mayor talked about. I'm sure she gave you a lot to consider as well. Whatever you decide, could you tell us by the end of the day? I hate to rush you, but, you know."

She tugs the blinds closed, and as the light recedes, so do the shadows. As she slings her parasol over her shoulder, I say, "I can do that."

She hesitates, a half smile on her face. "Remember, basement stairs. Don't get lost now."

Her footsteps move briskly down the hall, steadily fading. I hear a faint *thump* that must be the front doors. Then, once again, it's quiet.

I breathe out, and it echoes.

I glance over my shoulder, but the darkened classroom is all there is. No street. No neighborhood. No scene from my past.

For a second, I imagine a life of this flood following me. Maybe, like Rudy, they'll slip into the boundaries of my shadow, waiting until the moment I lower a parasol. Maybe they'll follow me a few paces back, like they are now. Slipping in and out of Sutton Avenue every time I look over my shoulder.

Unless this town isn't enough to satisfy them. Unless we leave here, the two of us, and they just keep destroying.

I don't want to understand them. I want Rudy to swallow them whole.

I should have told Christie Jones my mind is already made up. That it was a question of when we could get them off me, not if. But I think of the way she smiled at Rudy. And a little reluctantly, I slide her business card into my pocket, next to the mayor's.

Stepping into the hallway, I face away from the double doors, deeper into the school. I've always loved abandoned buildings. It was the one reason I could put up with Gaby's insatiable horror movie obsession—I liked looking at the sets. I liked putting those places back together in my mind, imagining what had been there before. Gaby thought I was missing the point, but she tolerated it.

It's different to see an empty place that should be full. Like reality itself doesn't quite fit together. Like this school *is* full, and I just can't see it.

And I choose this moment, right now, to remember Felix's words to Alex when he dropped me off. *It's okay. We're not going inside.*

The hairs on my arms stand up. I think it's nerves, at first. But then I realize it's getting colder. A harsh, artificial kind of cold, like central air on full blast. I don't *think* the air is on; I don't hear the telltale hum. The only sound is a soft kind of wheezing, hitching in and out, like the wind through a window somewhere.

I'm halfway around the corner before I realize what the sound is. It's not the wind. It's someone crying.

And before I think to turn back, I see that the tile under my feet has turned to carpet.

I look up. Ahead of me is a different hallway, dim and narrow. The long windows of the school are gone. I'm not *in* the school anymore. But I know exactly where I am.

A couple of feet away there's a door, slightly open, nothing visible but a sliver of pale light. And beyond it, I can hear muffled sobs.

"Ohh boy," I whisper.

Air rattles through the vents above me, and my skin prickles with a wave of goose bumps. I get the hint. I'm supposed to go in.

There's no reason to be afraid, I remind myself. I know exactly what's ahead.

"It's actually back here," someone calls from over my shoulder— a voice that doesn't belong in this memory.

I whip around, and the bright and empty school hallway twirls back into place. In front of me, between two classrooms, is a heavy gray door labeled in all caps: BASEMENT. And standing directly next to it is my chaperone.

"Morning." Cassie the prophet jingles a set of keys between her fingers. "Sleep well?"

Nine

THIS IS A PUBLIC SERVICE ANNOUNCEMENT

THE BASEMENT DOOR opens with a little *pop*, as if we've punctured a seal, revealing a set of narrow, wooden steps.

Cassie lets out a low whistle. Even from a few feet behind her, I get a hint of cool, musty air. "We should throw a rock," she says. "See when it hits the bottom. Got any rocks?"

"Sorry," I say. "I'm fresh out."

With a glance back at me, she finally notices I'm staring. "Something on your mind, Rose?"

"No." Maybe. I drag in a breath. "You're the sheriff's trusted chaperone?"

Her eyes narrow. "I'm very trustworthy."

"Does she have any staff above the age of eighteen?" I say. "Is this some kind of work-study thing?"

"I never thought of that. Do you think she'd give me college credit?" When I don't smile, she sighs and lets her own drop. "Do your parents ever tell you 'don't drink, unless it's in the house'?"

"My parents stopped at 'don't drink,'" I say.

"It's not like we're out there chasing down criminals, is the thing," Cassie says. "Crime in Lotus Valley has held at a record low for the state of Nevada since Josephine Martin shoplifted three pairs of shoes five years ago. Ninety percent of the time, the city council meetings are about zoning and property lines and setting up the tent layout for Quiltfest.

"It's just that sometimes Lotus Valley needs . . . a special kind of supervision. And why not bring in a couple civically minded young people to help with the legwork a couple of hours a week?"

She takes a breath. "That's what Ms. Jones would say if you asked her. The truth is, she thinks we're safer here, where she can keep an eye on us."

"Safer?" I say.

"Some of us are a little bit stranger than most," Cassie says. "And sometimes that means the neighbors . . . notice us a little bit more."

An artificial chill skims my shoulders. But when I glance behind me, the hall is just the hall. No door standing slightly ajar. No muffled sobs.

I move toward the basement door. But midstep, I stop dead.

There's a humming. Not a hum of central air like before. Someone—a very low-voiced someone, from somewhere very far down—is humming a tune.

"Do you hear that?" I say softly.

"Hm?" Cassie tilts her head toward the door, listening. Then she laughs. "Oh, that? Don't worry. It's always done that."

Oh, well. I guess it's fine, then.

My phone shudders in my pocket. Maybe it's Sammy, practicing his composition homework again. Or Flora, because I didn't text her back earlier today.

Somewhere down those stairs someone broadcast Gaby's voice.

In a couple of hours, I'll be calling the mayor, finishing this. But this comes first.

We step through the doorway and make our way down, into the underbelly of Lotus Valley Elementary.

"It might not be that bad," Cassie says.

"Hm?" I say, without looking at her.

"You know how you can go through your whole life afraid of a place and then find out there was no good reason all along?" Cassie says. "Happens to me all the time. Just last week I had to make a trip to my grandfather's storage unit. That place's given me the creeps since I was four."

"And it was fine?" I say.

"Oh, no, I never made it there. I was lost in those hallways for hours," Cassie says. "I'm all for security, but some things are just *excessive*, right? But anyway, the point is, I may never actually find those photos I needed, but at least I know what I'm up against."

"I don't know if that was the message you wanted," I say.

"Life's messy that way," she says with a dismissive gesture. "Oh, watch your step. That one's rotted."

I move carefully over the next stair. "Why would they put the broadcast studio in the basement?"

"You know public radio," Cassie says. "Real bad boys."

I miss that she's joking at first. It sounds believable by Lotus Valley standards.

"It's soundproofing, Rose," she laughs. "Lotus Valley used to be under four different flight paths. Down here, they only have to worry about what's underground."

"What's underground?" I ask.

"What *isn't* underground," she says.

The air in my lungs feels stale. The humming thrums under my feet, gently shaking the wood of the stairs. "Why did they stop broadcasting?"

"This was a dangerous place to be back then," Cassie says. "I hear it just stopped one day. No explanation. They played a message from their sponsor, then — static. That was it. And no one wanted to come pack up their things."

"If I were you . . ." My voice echoes. I have no way of knowing, but I feel like we're halfway down the stairs. "I wouldn't volunteer to be the first."

"Better the devil you know," Cassie says.

"Better the basement than the flood?" I say. "You don't know either of them."

"Maybe," she says. "But this was my school. That recording studio's been down here all my life, under my feet. Some meetings are just inevitable."

One of the patchy overhead lights catches something on the wall. A poster, emblazoned with a faded blue logo at the top. Cassie is the first to draw closer. But then she slowly, as if I won't notice, takes a step back.

Over her shoulder, I read:

LOTUS VALLEY COMMUNITY RADIO REMINDS YOU OF THE FOLLOWING:

DON'T LOOK AT HER.

DON'T SPEAK TO HER.

PRETEND SHE ISN'T THERE.

WE THANK YOU FOR YOUR COOPERATION.

"Don't worry too much about that," Cassie says. But her voice has gone noticeably higher.

"And yet I'm still worried," I say slowly.

"She's not here much anymore," Cassie says. "She went legitimate, a while back. Has a much more reputable office now, in the center of town. But that doesn't mean nothing's moved in in her place."

As if to prove her point, the humming jumps an octave.

"Her?" I say. "Legitimate?"

"You've seen the commercials by now, haven't you?" Cassie says. "*What do you yearn for?* When we negotiated the charter, she represented the neighbors. She was the best communicator of them, so we didn't have much of a choice. But people came to respect her. And I think working with us, she saw an opportunity. She rebranded herself. Takes commissions in exchange for personal mementos and raw meat. The sheriff's office checks in to make sure she's not hurting anyone, but if she behaves, she's left alone. Some people've already forgotten what she was. But it wasn't that long ago."

I hear Cassie swallow. "Ms. Jones . . . for all that she's been through, she's an optimistic person. Thinks every problem comes down to a failure to communicate. But not every neighbor comes to Lotus Valley for sanctuary or for connection. Some of them come for a hunting ground. And this was hers."

I glance over at her. But Cassie's eyes are on the stairs, down in the dark. "They say she was born when the first lie was told. And she lies every time she opens her mouth. She'd hide here, calling to us. Calling in other people's voices. We named her the Mockingbird."

There's a vague, cold feeling circling the pit of my stomach. "She does commissions of . . . voices?"

"People you long to hear," Cassie says faintly. "Gets good business actually. I don't know why anyone would risk it. But Ms. Jones always says she never really hunted us for need. She feeds off the fear and anger and pain of the people who hear her, not off the people themselves. She hunted because she was bored."

The humming, little by little, grows louder. Cassie looks distant for a moment. When she does speak, it's quieter. "Can you talk to me?"

I laugh. I shouldn't feel *better* because she's scared. But at least she's reacting like a person, finally. "I'm talking to you right now."

"Tell me a story, then," she says. "Anything. Tell me about the road."

"Weird that you don't want that humming to be the last thing you hear," I say dryly.

"Oh, no." She looks distant for a second. "This isn't how I die."

It catches me off guard. For a beat, the humming is all there is. And suddenly, I realize what she'd asked of me a second ago.

I play dumb anyway. "What road?"

"I saw you, you know. Well, I've seen you a couple of times now, but this was the first. Almost . . . three years ago now, before I knew who you were. Just you, standing in the middle of this empty road," she says. "There's usually more detail than that. But if I'm seeing it, even the little things are something big."

It would be easy, right now, to tell her that I don't know. That I've stood in the middle of countless roads, and I can't be expected to remember them all. But she knows I know.

"There's this girl," I begin. Ahead of us, the hallway narrows. "Ariella Kaplan. Her grandparents have a cabin outside of the city that they never use anymore. So naturally the entire school is up there every other weekend.

"A couple of miles from the cabin, you turn onto Sutton Avenue. And the woods get *thick*—really thick." I'd forgotten that until just now. In my memories there's nothing past the boundaries of the road. Even yesterday, in that vision, Sutton Avenue looked the same way it looks in my mind: clear, flat. I never remember most of the trees. Just the one.

"Right where Sutton meets Chamblys Road, there's this huge oak tree. Older than anything alive. I guess they didn't want to tear it down." There's nothing to see, ahead or behind us. Nothing to remind me that I'm standing here in the present—nowhere else. "They built the road around it. And everyone knows it's there. Everyone knows about the tree. And still."

Cassie makes a small, understanding sound. It echoes.

"If you're coming from the city, it's better. If you swerve, you swerve onto the grass. But if you're coming from the cabin, Chamblys runs across the edge of this retention pond. Pretty shallow. Just not shallow enough." I take a breath. I count off, so I remember to breathe deep. "I heard they were talking about filling it. I don't know why it's easier to fill a pond than to cut down one tree."

Up ahead, I can see the stairs smooth out into solid floor. Two steps above the landing, I falter. At some point in the past few minutes, the humming had stopped.

"We should stop talking," I say.

"Agreed," Cassie breathes. If anything's there, we want to hear it coming.

The hall ahead is quiet. Cold. I slide my hand along the wall

THE VALLEY AND THE FLOOD

until I feel the light switch, but it doesn't help much. The shadowed gaps between the overhead lights feel impossibly long.

The posters are more frequent now, reminding us every couple of feet:

DON'T LOOK AT HER.

DON'T SPEAK TO HER.

PRETEND SHE'S NOT THERE.

IN FACT, PRETEND YOU NEVER SAW THIS.

IF YOU STOPPED TO READ THIS, WELL THEN, YOU'RE NOT PAYING ATTENTION, ARE YOU?

Just up ahead, there's an open door, and beyond it, the hallway opens into a wider space. As we move closer, there's one more sign, facing us: QUIET PLEASE. BROADCAST IN PROGRESS.

"I don't suppose you already know what's in there?" I ask.

"If I did," she says, "I would have saved us the trip."

I try to sigh, though I can't quite get enough air. "Convenient."

I go first. Cassie looks perfectly happy with that—she hovers by the doorway as I hit the lights. Half of them flicker on, fluttering on and off with a rapid *click-click-click*, but it's enough to give me a better look at the broadcasting studio.

The equipment is pale with dust. The microphone, placed triumphantly in the center of the small desk, looks just as abandoned as the rest of it. There's certainly no sign that someone might have been speaking into it just two nights ago.

There's just one device that looks clean: a small, boxy tape deck, hooked into the console by a tangled mass of wiring.

"Look at this." Cassie hits the eject button. The top gently pops open, revealing a tiny gray cassette tape.

I take a step closer. It looks noticeably darker than the rest of the machinery. Newer, though not by much. And I'm not an AV expert, but just going by the sheer number of wires, someone had to try really hard to get whatever's on that tape to broadcast.

"I don't think that belongs there," I say.

"Maybe they recorded one of their shows," Cassie says, inspecting the cassette before she slides it back in. "Here, listen."

She hits play, and the recording starts mid-sentence. I only need that half a sentence to know what it is. I only need one syllable.

. . . ere?

I've heard her voice so many times in the past few days, you'd think it would've lost its edge by now. But hearing it here, wound around that little gray cassette tape, it's different. And the world runs as cold as it did almost a year ago, when I heard those words for the first time.

Rose, are you there? Rose, are you there? Rose, are you there?

I step closer. Maybe not step. I lunge, I grab for that little dust-less box. Cassie catches my hands in midair.

"Wait," she says.

I mean to say, *Let go.* What comes out is "Shut it off."

"Rose, wait a second—"

"Shut it off!" The last word comes out high enough, frantic enough, that for a second I stop. I haven't heard myself sound like that before. Not out loud.

"*Listen* to me." Cassie spins me around by the shoulders and holds me there, looks me in the eyes until I look back at her. "It's that message, isn't it? The one you said no one else should have?"

Suddenly, I'm out of words. I nod.

"Then give me a moment," she says. "I haven't heard your

message, but I can tell you for sure that it's not what I'm hearing right now."

She moves away from me then, leans over the tape deck with both palms on the surface of the desk. Her hair is hiding her face, but as she listens to the loop, she's gone very still.

Rose, are you there? Rose—

The words start mangling, like the tape's caught on something, and Gaby's voice distorts until the words are meaningless pops and gasps. I jerk back and away, my body moving quicker than my brain. And then I see it painted on the opposite wall.

I think it's another poster, at first. But this isn't a message from our friends at Lotus Valley Community Radio. This is painted right into the concrete: thick, fresh capital letters from floor to ceiling. And those towering words pop in and out of view with the flickering overhead light.

HERE COMES THE FLOOD.

MAY 30, SEVEN MONTHS AGO

NOTE TO SELF: Sammy doesn't know what *insomnia* means. He repeats it because he heard you say it once. But for Sammy, *insomnia* means that his big sister is binge-watching Korean dramas again.

It's a thick, humid night, hotter still with your brother's weight against your side. You move the laptop off your legs to catch every bit of breeze from the ceiling fan, and you spot little scrapes across your kneecaps. You've got a few on your palms, too, right where they caught the pavement.

It hasn't happened again since the party. Maybe if you don't think about it, it won't happen again. But that doesn't stop the sour, sick feeling that's curled into your stomach since.

Sammy watches, rapt, as the therapist leans forward onto his elbows. *When you remember the earthquake,* he intones, *do you feel as if you're reliving it?*

Jae-hyun flashes a wide, fake grin. *Not at all,* he says.

There's a musical cue like a person leaning their entire weight on a piano. Sammy laughs. Your laugh comes slower.

You lean forward and tap the spacebar to pause. At Sammy's little noise of protest, you say, "Water. I'll be right back."

All the windows are still open: in the living room, the kitchen, the hallway. It doesn't help with the heat. It just leaves you feeling like the walls aren't walls, like the apartment is bleeding into the outside world. You leave the lights off as you walk. You can see everything going on out there. They can't see you.

You love that show. You love watching it with Sammy even more. So you should feel better than you do now. You shouldn't feel the heat and Sammy's fidgeting and every snatch of a voice outside ricocheting off the insides of your chest.

Do you feel as if you're reliving it?

Note to self: Don't think about Marin's party. Even if you can't *stop* thinking about it. How it feels whenever you think of that voicemail. What you're feeling right now. Like the air in your lungs is damp and cold. Like the floor is gone, and you're just tumbling through negative space.

What you're feeling has a name. Or, to be more precise, four letters.

"Oh," you whisper through your fingers. "Oh, shit."

So. Now that we're all on the same page. Let's begin.

Ten

THE FAILURE TO COMMUNICATE

THE GUTS OF the cassette are tangled in the belly of the tape player somewhere. It's not torn, but it will be if we try to take it out. We leave it where it is.

We do, however, find the little circular goldenrod sticker on the bottom left of the tape player. As identifying features go, it's not very specific. Unless, of course, you do odd jobs for a small town sheriff's department on afternoons and weekends. Alex takes one look at it and identifies it as a price marker from Paul's Pawn and Loan.

Alex has one more thing, too. The phone number for a respected member of the community who can imitate the voice of any lost loved one you desire.

Or, more precisely, for her booking agent.

Mockingbird Productions, chirps a distant voice through the phone. *What do you yearn for?*

Paul's Pawn and Loan is a quiet storefront in an empty strip mall, with a collection so mismatched it has to be deliberate. Paul himself is a short, owlish man who moves slowly and blinks even slower. "I haven't seen you before," he says to me, leaning in a little as he squints.

I'm from that one cataclysmic prophecy, maybe you've heard of me seems like a longer conversation than we'd like to have right now. "I'm visiting," I say, cradling the tape player in my arms.

He turns creakily. "And you two work for the sheriff?"

"Felix Sohrabi," Felix says. "And this is Alli—"

"Alex Harper," Alex says quickly, dipping the phone just below his ear. He's on hold. He's been on hold for the past five minutes. "I know this is a strange request, but if you could tell us anything about the person who bought this—"

"It's no trouble," Paul says with a serene smile. "Anything for Christie Jones. Could you hand that here, miss?"

I keep it steady as I place it into his hands. "There's a cassette caught inside," I mumble to the counter. "Please be careful with it." With a slow nod, he disappears behind the back curtain, leaving the four of us standing on the shop floor.

Well, three. Cassie waits outside, her back to the window, perfectly still as she watches the strip mall parking lot.

"I'm telling you," Felix says. It sounds halfhearted. "People aren't going to take us seriously if our names rhyme."

"I was here first," Alex says mildly. "Change your own name."

"I don't have any good nicknames," Felix says.

Alex doesn't hesitate. "The Sohrabinator."

Felix stares in silence for a good twenty seconds. "Holy shit," he says softly.

Alex turns his attention back to his phone, currently spitting out a tinny, staticky sound.

"This is ridiculous," Felix suddenly blurts out. "You don't have to talk to her."

"Would you like to, then?" Alex snaps back. I notice then that his knuckles are white around the edges of his phone. "I'm still on hold."

Felix falters. And slowly, he turns his attention back to the shelves.

Faintly, I hear a voice with a questioning lilt, and Alex jerks up straight. "Yes, I'm still here. Did you—"

The woman's voice cuts him off. Even without hearing the words, I pick up on the perky chirp in her tone. "Three tomorrow," Alex mumbles. "That's the earliest you could—I think you know what the situa—"

The voice interrupts again. Whatever explanation she gives, Alex looks less than impressed. "Yes, I understand," he says. "Yes, I know where. Thank you."

"She can't take us until tomorrow?" Felix says, before Alex can completely hang up.

"Her staff would like us to remember that this is a busy time of year," Alex says wearily.

"She's messing with us," Felix says.

"She is," Alex says. "But there's nothing we can do about that."

It goes quiet after that. It leaves me without much to do but stare at the counter and try to ignore the rustling behind me as Felix sifts through one of the shelves of merchandise. His fidgeting is, at least, preferable to the echo of that tape still ringing in my ears.

I glance over my shoulder to the window. Cassie told me there was no way we could have heard the same thing on that tape. But she never did tell me what it was she heard.

Suddenly, there's a loud crackle behind me, and a grainy mechanical voice bellows, *YOU'RE BREAKIN' MY NECK.*

I whip around so fast, I have to catch myself on the counter. Felix rocks back on his heels, sheepishly holding out a plastic, grimacing waiter figurine.

"It's a pepper grinder," he says, giving the head another half twist.

Alex crosses the store, stony-faced, and places it back on the shelf.

Through the window, Cassie winds one of her curls around her index finger, catching my attention. Back to Alex and Felix, I ask, "Is she okay?"

"I . . . um. Couldn't say," Alex mumbles. "We don't really . . ."

"Know her that well," Felix finishes.

"She doesn't work with you?" I say.

Alex blinks. "They didn't tell you?"

"Are you surprised?" Felix says. To me, he adds, "Cassie's, um. The boss's foster kid, sort of."

"Ms. Jones took Cassie in when she was thirteen," Alex says. "We don't know the circumstances, but . . ."

"It's complicated," Felix says.

"Sounds about right," I mumble. Asking your intern to chaperone the harbinger of destruction is one thing, but asking your sort-of kid?

"But who knows." Felix shrugs. "Ms. Jones is the queen of need-to-know."

"Because most of the time we don't need to know," Alex says mildly.

Felix throws his head back and groans. "Don't start."

"I just don't think we should criticize her for—"

"I'm not criticizing her!" Felix says. "I'm allowed to ask questions."

"So *ask* her," Alex says.

"Really." Felix snorts. "Here's just a few questions I'm still waiting for answers on. Can Rudy really stage-manage an evacuation? What do I tell my family? *When* do I tell my family? Why three days?"

"Believe me," Alex mutters, "that last one makes sense up close."

I glance at Alex. And I remember how he looked at me when I met him yesterday. Or more precisely, how he looked *past* me.

"Can you see all of them?" I say. "The neighbors."

"Depends. Some don't try to hide," he says. "Or care if you see them. Others do. And some of them are just too big or too strange for comprehension. And for things like that, I see more than most people can. I still don't know whether it's just something I can *do*, or if they're just . . . more inclined to show themselves to me."

"Oh." My voice wavers a little. "And, um, you can see this one right now?"

"I have to try. And right now I'm not exactly trying," Alex admits. "But even the biggest one I've seen before, it was still recognizable as a *thing*. What's behind you is just . . . total darkness. Like the world ends right where you're standing. And if what I'm seeing is just the tip of the storm, then I can believe it'd take three days to get here."

We go quiet for a second, and I remember what Christie Jones said: *If you were to ask Alex, he might have a less rosy view than I do.*

"What did yours look like?" I ask softly.

Alex's eyes widen a little. He doesn't ask whether or not the sheriff told me. But he looks a bit surprised that she did.

"Seeing them . . . it's not something I was born with," he says slowly. "And I never saw that one, either. I thought I was sick, just like everyone else did. I mean, I'd *been* sick since I was little, so everyone always assumed it'd get worse someday. At least, that's what they said when they thought I wasn't listening."

He paused. "My dad heard about Lotus Valley from someone in my pulmonologist's waiting room. Said the dry air would be good for my lungs and that we'd be happy here. I still have no idea why he took life advice from a stranger. Maybe he was just relieved to hear someone say it would get better, instead of talking to him like my life was already over."

His shoulders jerk upward, like he's suppressing a shiver. "Ms. Jones came to our house that first night. She wasn't sheriff yet, and she'd only recently come back to town herself. She just kind of saw us and knew. I don't know what she said to my father. But she came down the hall, into my room, and she shut the door. And then she looked up about eight feet, smiled, and said 'Let's get this off you, shall we?'

"And . . . I don't remember anything after that. I know Rudy must have killed it, in the end, Ms. Jones has never told me the details. But I didn't start seeing them until months after that. I think being so close to one for so long kind of of—opened something."

His pale lips twitch. "I wasn't the only person attacked that year. Or even that month. But I think it's different when it's a kid. And this wasn't just an attack. It clung to me, fed off me, for *months.* But on the other hand, Rudy saved me. It wasn't the first time a neighbor had intervened for a human. But it was the first time a lot of people realized that neighbors can be killed.

"It brought a lot of things to the surface," Alex says. "Things that had been simmering a long time. And the town was of two minds. They were scared of what the neighbors were capable of, but they couldn't reject them completely, knowing that one of them had the power to protect us. That's how you end up with a town where Maggie Williams is mayor and Ms. Jones is sheriff. They can't decide, even now."

He smiles. But it's bitter. "Ms. Jones kept reaching out to me after that. Maggie Williams thinks that's when she 'got in my head.' But she never told me how to feel. She just knew, even before I told her what I'd started to see, that my world was going to be different now. And she knew I'd need to hear that different doesn't mean dangerous."

"Oh." It's a full second before I realize that's inadequate. "Sorry."

He shakes his head quickly. "I'm telling you this so you know where I'm coming from. You didn't invite this in. No one ever does."

"Except me," Felix says.

"Felix's time with the sheriff isn't so much an internship as a Scared Straight program," Alex says dryly.

"But *in my defense,*" Felix says, ignoring the warning groan from Alex, "my parents are scientists! I was raised to ask questions! If you're going to plunk me in the middle of nowhere and tell me my neighbors are ageless eldritch beings, you can't expect me not to go see for myself!"

"You yelled that you didn't believe in them," Alex says.

"I was trying to get them to show themselves!" Felix says. Back to me, he adds, "But on the bright side, when one of them followed me to Natalie Meyer's sweet sixteen, Alex literally broke in to rescue me. So, worth it."

"And if you'd listened to me when I asked you to come to the sheriff's office," Alex says, "I wouldn't have had to."

"I didn't know you yet!" Felix says. "I thought you were hitting on me!"

"I told you there was something attached to your back," Alex says.

"I don't know how y'all flirt here!" Felix says.

I smile and duck my head. It's kind of Alex to say I didn't ask for this. But he doesn't know that.

"So sorry to keep you waiting." Paul emerges, as if in slow motion, from behind the curtains. "Quite a few records to sift through. Got some receipts here, if you'd like them."

"Did you find anything?" I ask as Alex takes the bundle of receipts from Paul's hands.

"It's certainly from my stock," he says with a nod. "And it was in my inventory until about two weeks ago."

"Do you remember who bought it?" I say.

"No one did, young lady," Paul says. "I have no record of selling this."

"Someone . . ." I stop, uncurl my fists. Not now. Breathe normally.

"I'm afraid shoplifting happens," Paul says with a slow, unconcerned smile. "I must have been in the back."

"Then let's look at the security tapes," Felix says.

"Felix," Alex mutters. "Do you see any cameras in here?"

"Good heavens," Paul says. "Why would I need such a thing?"

"I mean," Felix says, "I don't mean to tell you how to run your business, but—"

I wave him off. "And the cassette?"

Paul turns to me. His expression stays neutral, but the movement is deliberate. If I had to guess, he's starting to think about who I might be. "It wasn't sold with the tape deck, if that's what you're asking. I check all such merchandise for any personal items that might have been . . . left behind."

Breathe normally, I remind myself again. But I think we're past that point.

Alex bundles up the tape deck and cassette into his bag. "Thank you, sir. Sorry we have to take this again."

"Not to worry, young man." Paul waves a hand lazily. "If I didn't miss it the first time, I won't miss it now."

Alex heads for the door first, nudging Felix in the same direction. I turn to follow, but a hand lands on my shoulder from behind.

"It's you. Isn't it?" Paul smiles, slow and grave. "I should have known."

"I—" I have to swallow hard to wet the back of my throat. In the late afternoon sun, the glass windows of Paul's Pawn and Loan look transparent, wide open to the rest of Lotus Valley. And anything else that's watching.

"I'm sorry," I blurt out. And I turn and leave as fast as I can without running.

The light outside glints hard off the pavement, and I duck my head, rummaging through my backpack for my sunglasses. But by the time I raise it, the sunlight isn't there.

Neither is the pavement. The parking lot is gone, replaced by the long, dark hallway of my apartment. All the windows stand open, hot sticky air and distant noise bleeding in from the outside, the city open and watching. And distantly, I hear that same dull, shivery roar.

It could be any night ever. Except I know exactly what night it is.

I scramble back, and my foot hits something behind me, throwing off my balance. My heel is backed into the edge of the sidewalk where it meets the blazing bright pavement. And when I look up again, Felix is about two feet away, staring.

"You all right?" he asks.

"Yeah." I manage a laugh. "I tripped."

I want to say I don't know where that came from. But faintly, I do. Just for a moment, I felt the same as I did then, right? Like walls weren't enough to protect me.

Somehow, this thing is following my triggers better than I am.

When I get my bearings, I see that Cassie's moved away from the outside wall of the store. She's standing at the other end of the parking lot now, a hand cupped over her mouth as she mutters into the phone.

"You're not liste—" She pauses. I hear her take a breath. "Yes, I know. But that's not what's—Yes. Okay. Whatever you want."

She hangs up and turns to us in one fluid motion.

"Is everything okay?" Alex asks.

"Felix," she says, her eyes not quite focused on any of us. "Could you give Rose a ride back to Lethe Ridge?"

"I could use the walk actually," I say, slow but automatic. It's only five. We should be using every second we have. "Cassie, I don't think—"

"Hang on, hang on," Felix says. "Rose should be with us, right?"

"Ms. Jones says the most helpful place for her to be is at that house." If it's possible to shrug aggressively, that's what Cassie does. "And she's got a decision to make, besides."

I blink. Right. That's what I agreed to—that by the end of the day, I decide what I want to do.

The others are looking at me. And I hope my answer isn't written on my face: that for all I've seen today, I haven't found a single scrap of evidence that this thing following me can be reasoned with. Or that I could do something that Rudy can't.

For the first time since I've met him, Felix's easy, sunny smile darkens. "Then let's get going," he says. "Alex?"

Alex, on the other hand, hovers. "Do *you* need a ride, Cassie?" he asks, partially to his feet.

"You know what?" The soft, round lines of her face are uncharacteristically rigid. "I could use the walk, too."

Felix crosses the parking lot to the car in long strides, but Alex hesitates before following. "Whatever you decide . . . it's up to you," Alex says slowly. It takes me a second to recognize that he's talking to me. "I know you must want it gone. But you have time, Rose. It's a terrifying thing to think, but this flood followed you for a reason. If you don't try to understand why, that stays with you. Trust me."

I rub at my pocket as he disappears into the car. And the business cards of Maggie Williams and Christie Jones crinkle together.

"He doesn't like me that much," Cassie says with a tight laugh as they drive out of the lot. "Felix, that is. He doesn't think I'm telling him everything."

I tread lightly. I'm pretty good at reading people, I think. But right now, I'm at a loss. "I'm sure he's just stressed," I say.

"Oh, I don't blame him," Cassie says. "He's right."

I hold very still and leave a wide open space for her to elaborate. At length, she finally makes eye contact with me.

"I know what you've been seeing, Rose," she says.

My foot, of its own accord, slides back. I don't know if she notices this, but she laughs. "Not *specifically*," she says. "I trade in the future. I always thought that's why I never see the flood completely, in all those visions. A creature that pulls past into present—makes sense that we'd be like oil and water, right?"

Cassie rubs at her arms. "There are things we've hidden from this town. We never told them it would be New Year's Day. We took town records, all the encounters with this thing, all the things people see, and locked them in Ms. Jones's office. She's always been adamant that they can't know what to expect. That the temptation would be too great."

"Temptation?" I say.

Her smile twitches into a thin line. "Not everyone considers the past an enemy, Rose."

My brain feels sluggish after so many nights of short, fragmented sleep. But it doesn't take me long to wrap my head around what she's getting at. That tape, that cassette player didn't get to the basement on its own. Somebody paid the Mockingbird to say those words. Recorded it. Hooked it up in that basement. Set it to broadcast.

"Think about it," Cassie says. "Why are you here, Rose? Would you have led the flood here no matter what? You didn't feel the pull of Lotus Valley until you heard that broadcast, did you?"

"So you're saying," I say faintly, "that whoever made that tape was trying to make sure the prophecy would happen."

"I'm saying they were *instrumental* in making it happen. And in all my visions, I never saw that," Cassie says. "If I missed something that important, there might be even more we don't know. If whoever made that tape has information we don't? We need to find them, fast."

"If only a few people know what this thing can do," I say, "you must have some idea who'd want to—"

"There's no way they would have done this," Cassie says shortly. "I already told you—"

There's a long, tense beat. She tilts her head into the low afternoon sun and sighs. "Oh," she says quietly. "Sorry. We didn't have that conversation yet, did we?"

She's already backing away. Despite the heat, her jacket is buttoned shut. "Like you said," she calls, "the list of people who know what's coming is a small one. And Ms. Jones thinks she knows exactly where to start—with the only two people I told before I told her. My parents."

I don't see her expression before she looks away, but I think she's smiling. "Big decision tonight, Rose. I'd tell you what you'll do. But where's the fun in that?"

Eleven

THE LANGUAGE OF MEMORY

MY BROTHER, SAMMY, is his mother's son. In case I didn't know that before—and I kind of guessed—people make sure to tell us at least once a week. He's got the little nose, the round face, the way she squints when she doesn't buy a word you're saying.

But when Sammy and my stepfather open their mouths at the same time, you get exactly where Dan's genes went.

"Hold on, hold on." I laugh, readjusting the phone. "One at a time."

The volume of Sammy's voice goes from seven to eleven, like he's grabbed the phone. "Are you going to make us millionaires in Las Vegas, Rosie?"

"Did Dad tell you that?" I ask.

There's a rustle—Dan taking the phone back, I think. "I would never." He pauses. "But he's got this wacky idea that once you hit the jackpot, you're going to buy him an Xbox."

"Xbox!" Sammy echoes, his voice already distant, like he's started sprinting laps around the couch again. People always ask,

coming over for the first time, why we've got little crop circles burned into the carpet.

My mother shifts closer to the phone with a sigh. "Rosie," she says, "you left me outnumbered."

Over the phone, I hear the telltale sound of a little foot catching on the edge of the carpet, and the *thud* of someone falling face-first. There's a brief silence. Then a slowly building wail.

"Well," says Dan, over the sound of my brother's screams, "that was bound to happen sometime."

"It's almost like it was inevitable from the second you said *Xbox*," Mom says, her grin audible.

"And that's my cue to exit." He grunts, like he's scooped Sammy up from the floor. "Come on, Road Runner. Bed."

"*No!*" Sammy wails.

"A compelling argument," Dan says solemnly. Into the phone, he says, "Rosie, give Flora and Jon a hug for me. And call anytime. We miss you."

Something in my chest curls, and I fidget. "Miss you, too," I say.

"Love you, Freckles," he says, with a smooching sound so loud I have to pull the phone away from my ear. "Sleep well."

My smile spreads despite itself. Dan has always called me Freckles. My father's family has always called me Beanstalk. I like Dan's better.

The sound quality sharpens as Mom takes me off speakerphone. She lets out an exaggerated sigh, and I laugh. And then, for a second, we're quiet.

My hand's still quivering. It has been since the long, hot walk back to Lethe Ridge. Toward the end of Morningside Drive, someone had leaned out of his car. *What gives you the right?* he'd yelled at me.

It's a fair question.

I should make some excuse to hang up. If it gets much later, I might not get Mayor Williams on the phone.

But then Mom asks, "How's Flora?"

Flora. As if my nerves needed more adrenaline to process. "She went to bed early," I say quickly. The question wasn't *Can I talk to Flora?* but it would have been.

"Mm." A pause. "And how are you?"

I glance around at the sharp angles and long shadows of the model house. "Fine."

"Rosie." Even from the other end of the phone, I know her mouth is sort of twisted off to the side. "I know you want to be there for the Summers. And I'm so proud of you that you made this trip. But this is going to be hard for you. Anniversaries always are."

"I don't need Flora to comfort me, Mom," I say, through the sudden tightness in my throat.

"You might need *someone* to," she says. "And Flora loves you very much, but I don't think she can right now."

I can't think of anything to say that wouldn't give me away. This balancing act is hard enough already: before I called the house, I spent about ten minutes reassuring Flora via text that I'm fine, I'm not mad, I just can't call right now. I'm sorry, Gaby. I was always a little horrified at how easily you could lie to your mother.

"Did you tell Sammy I won't be there on Thursday?" I ask.

"He already knows," she says.

"He's been talking about counting down with me, to the new year." I twist the hem of my shirt around my fingers. If all goes well, I'll be out of Lotus Valley tomorrow. But as for where I go after that . . . "I just thought—"

"He's seven years old! He'll be in bed by nine thirty." She's laughing, but the unease still comes through. "What's this about?"

"Nothing." Obviously not nothing. I take a breath. "This is hard for you, too, Mom."

"What is?"

Me. But I'm not going to go there. "This trip. I know you weren't sure about it."

She sighs. "Rosie, this has to be about what's going to help you. And if this trip is what helps, I promise I won't worry."

For a second, even with all this distance between us, she feels so close it's excruciating. I could tell her right now why I left, what happened in that kitchen. She could tell me that it was okay, that it wasn't as bad as it felt in that moment. She would tell me that even if she didn't mean it.

My phone has been a necessary evil this past year. But at least I don't have to look her in the eye right now. "Yeah," I say. "It's helping."

"Okay." Her smile is audible. "Then consider me not worried."

I smile back. The muscles in my jaw feel tight, and the stiffness bleeds down to my shoulders. I stretch my head to the side. "I'll be home in a few days, and we can—"

It's only then, tilting my head to the side, that I see her there. Just a few feet away, in the mouth of the darkened kitchen. Gaby.

We lock eyes. At least I think we do, at first. But she's looking past me, at something that doesn't exist in this time. She curls in on herself, cupping a hand over her mouth, and whispers into her cell phone. Her favorite maxi dress flutters in a breeze I don't feel.

That day before the funeral, I tore Gaby's closet apart looking for that dress. *It was her favorite*, I said. *She called it her mystical beach goddess dress*, I said. I said all this in front of Flora as we looked for a dress to bury her in. But it wasn't in her closet anymore. She was wearing it that night. She was wearing it.

Rose? Are you there?

Behind her, there's a voice, low and indistinct. She glances over her shoulder. And then she's gone.

"I'm actually gonna go," I say. "I'm a little tired."

"It's only eight." I can hear her chewing on her lip. "Everything okay?"

"I'm fine." My fingers feel numb around the phone. Even my toes are tingling. "Long day. Can I text you tomorrow?"

"Of course you can. Just . . ." She falters. "You can leave anytime you want. You know that, don't you?"

"Of course," I echo. The words sound far away from me. "Good night, Mom."

My hand drops away from my ear before she finishes saying it back. And I end the call.

Silence falls like a slab of concrete.

Gently, I lower my dangling foot to the carpet, pushing myself off the couch without looking away from the spot where the living room meets the kitchen. The light ends at the point where the ceiling slopes. I can't see anything past it.

"Gaby." I swallow, wetting my throat. "Gaby?"

Somewhere in the darkened kitchen, someone beats a rhythm. *Tap, tap, tap.*

The living room crumbles at the edges. The kitchen tugs like some gravitational anomaly, pulling me into its center. My toes curl into the carpet just shy of the entryway.

I slide my hand around the corner and hit the lights.

The knob of the kitchen sink has been nudged a little to the left, just enough to let the droplets find a rhythm. *Tap, tap, tap. Tap, tap, tap.*

My exhale comes out as a laugh as I step into the kitchen. "If you have to result to half-assed haunted house tricks, I think you might be running out of—"

But then I cross the entryway and get an unobstructed view of the room. Sitting by the sink, just barely balanced on the countertop, is a small paring knife.

The handle wobbles a little, as if someone only just let it go, but it doesn't fall. Its movements even out, its blurred lines sharpen. It goes still. It plays dead.

"So . . . what," I say "You want to go there, too?"

They don't respond. But if they have ears, they're going to listen.

"You know, the sheriff thinks you can't hate a shark for being a shark," I say. "She thinks this is just your nature. Is it? Or are you having fun?"

The lights flicker twice, three times. But I'm shouting over my own fear now. If something's happening, that's good. It means they can hear me.

"You understand me, then." My voice keeps rising. "So how about you use your words, because I'm not impressed with the smoke and mirrors show anymore. Tell me why you followed me here. Tell me what you want. *Talk to me.*"

Then a quiet, familiar voice to my left says, "Okay."

And there she is. Leaning against the doorframe, watching me steadily, unblinking. That mystical beach goddess maxi dress whipping in a breeze from another time. Nearly every inch of her is Gaby. But when I meet her eyes, I know better.

"You're not Gaby," I say.

She shakes her head gently.

I take a deep, shuddering breath. The room feels cool and damp and vast, like the air at the edge of the ocean. "Then I'd rather you pick another face, if that's all right with you," I say. "Not hers."

Her head tilts a little to the side. Her face remains Gaby.

"Okay," I say. "So what do I call you, then? Because Rudy's already taken. Got a nickname, maybe? What do the other ancient, unknowable somethings call you?"

Her head slowly rights itself, her eyes unblinking.

"Okay," I say quietly. "The Flood it is. Closest word in our vocabulary, I hear."

Her eyes don't leave mine. She looks whole. Three dimensional. But the longer I look at her, the more I see a paper doll. A flat, inanimate face at the edge of a closed curtain. And somewhere in that moment, I remember to be scared.

"Do you understand me?" I cringe. I sound so small.

She nods.

I swallow. "Then answer the question. Why are you doing this?"

She inclines her head at something past me. I look where she's looking, at the now-still paring knife behind me.

"And your point is what?" I say. "That you know everything?

Then you know nothing happened. That I *left* before anything could happen."

It's then that her expression changes. She narrows her eyes. "No."

"It's true," I say, with more force.

"*No*," she says, her own voice rising, and with a sound remarkably like annoyance, she points at the back of the kitchen.

I look behind me. Over my shoulder is the dusty, empty classroom of Lotus Valley Elementary School, and in the center is Christie Jones, smiling affectionately at the massive shadow spreading from her feet.

"*But he's never had the words to tell me his name,*" she says.

There's another flicker of the lights, and the scene collapses on itself, leaving only the kitchen.

I turn back to Gaby—to the Flood. Her face has turned to stone.

"I don't understand," I say slowly. "Is this . . . how you talk? Through images?"

"Memory," she says softly. Gaby's voice handles the word gently, reverently. But that softness is gone with a flicker of her gaze.

"Memories, then," I say. "*My* memories?"

She nods.

I let out a sigh of a laugh. "I don't know if you've heard, but . . . post-traumatic stress disorder. Memory is my problem. I mean, of course you've heard. You know everything."

I don't think she understands what I'm saying. She's looking at me, but her stare is focused somewhere far away. In the distance, I hear that sound again. That low, shivery roar.

"What's that noise?" I say. "I keep hearing it."

In the harsh light of the kitchen, Gaby's eyes look black and endless. "The beginning," she says.

I don't ask. I don't want to know.

"Okay. Christie Jones says you came to me because there's something you need from me." I cross my arms tight across my chest. "But I don't know what you're trying to say, unless you'd like to drive home that life's sucked for the past year."

She shakes her head.

"No?" I say.

"No," she echoes. And for a second, she does look like Gaby—like that look Gaby used to get when I picked at plot holes in her favorite movies. "Listen," she says. "Remember. Understand."

"Listen . . . to what you're showing me?" I ask. She nods. "Sure, but I can't *stop* remembering it, that's my entire . . ." I get the Gaby look again, and I stop. "Okay. Understand. So . . . I look at what you're showing me. I remember it. And then I understand . . ."

There's a surge of air from behind her shoulders, like an exhale. I remember, a little late, that this is not a person. This is a lure at the end of a hook.

Just like the voice on that cassette. Broadcasting into the desert. Knowing I would come.

I've started shivering. I hear it in my voice before I think to look at my fingers. "I listen," I say slowly. "I remember. And then I understand what I've brought to this town."

She nods. No emotion. Like I asked if she wants cream in her coffee.

"This is your home. The place you were born," I say. "You're really going to destroy it?"

Another cool nod.

I look at her empty face. I don't see anything familiar. I don't see anything human. I don't see my best friend, even in this thing that's wearing her likeness.

But I do see something alive. Something that chose me, even if I can't understand why. Christie and Alex said the Flood is following me for a reason. That I would regret not learning what it was.

I don't think I want to know the reason.

But I don't think I want Rudy to kill the Flood, either.

"Can you tell me why?" I say softly.

There's a creak at the far end of the bedroom wing. And then, almost inaudibly, soft, desperate sobs. The same I heard just hours ago at Lotus Valley Elementary School.

I jerk back instinctually. And that's when I realize that my bare feet are no longer touching tile. I look down, then up again. And my world tilts sharply. Straight into the upstairs wing of the Summers' old house.

"That's not an answer." I say But the Flood is already gone.

Central air drifts across my shoulders and fills the hall with a sputtering artificial chill. My jeans feel cool against my legs as I take a step. In the back of my mind, I can almost feel the nice black skirt I was wearing that day, brushing my ankles. That skirt was so soft. I wish I'd worn something I hated that day. At least then I wouldn't mind never wearing it again.

Gaby always liked me in black. She liked that it made my red hair look redder. But I don't think that was how she meant for me to wear it.

"It's already happened," I whisper. This day is over, done, already survived. Keep going. Keep breathing.

I move toward the sobs, remembering how my cheap heels wobbled in the carpet. I leave the hall lamp off, as I did then. There's light coming through the door up ahead.

I raise my hand to knock. I'm not sure if the hesitation that follows is mine now, or mine then.

But eventually, I do knock. I do call out to her.

"Flora?"

JANUARY 5, ELEVEN MONTHS AGO

NOTE TO SELF: There are days you never leave. Days of new rules you never meant to carry forward. But they stick, don't they? They stick to the bottoms of your feet and the curves of your shadow.

Maybe it would have happened one way or the other, you and Flora. Knowing you and knowing her, it probably would have. But in reality, it happened like this, with you standing in the Summers' hallway. You weren't trying to be helpful. You weren't trying to be there for anyone. You were just trying to find a second alone.

Gaby's house is bigger in her absence. Longer. Stretched taut and quiet. And you were all running late, which she would have *loved*. You can almost hear it. *My one and only funeral, and none of you assholes can tie a tie?*

So with your mother and Dan fussing at Jon's collar and Sammy fiddling with the edges of the carpet, you duck upstairs. You hadn't noticed Flora wasn't with the rest of them.

You don't think to wonder where she is until you see the lights on in the master bedroom. Then you hear the crying.

The air shifts upward and the lights flicker as the AC kicks on. You could go back downstairs. She hasn't heard you. She'd never know you were there.

She's on her knees by the foot of the bed, a piece of paper curled into her fist. Her hands rest by her sides; she doesn't bury her face in them like you do. She doesn't swallow her gasps, like Mom did in the years after your father died. Her mouth is wide open. She doesn't care who knows.

Flora's always been like that. When she's upset, Gaby knew it, you knew it, the cashier at Trader Joe's knew it. You can't help but wonder if that's why she reacts so big: because she wants people to know. Maurice will tell you later that that's not a bad thing, wanting people to know. You're not a better person for suffering alone. No one's going to give you a prize for the best poker face. If they did, you'd have won a long time ago.

Later, you're going to be ashamed of how long it takes you to say something. But eventually, you do.

"Flora?"

She jerks the crumpled paper closer to her chest as she turns. Her breath hitches. Her lip keeps trembling.

"I can't do it," she whispers.

Carefully, you lower yourself to your knees in front of her, and you take the crumpled piece of paper as it's offered. You smooth it out against the soft black skirt you'll never wear again. And you catch the first few lines of a reading from the book of Ecclesiastes.

"I c-can't get up there." Her teeth are chattering.

"You don't have to read it." Your voice is low. "You don't have to do anything."

"But it's already *planned*," she says, more firmly now. "And we're already late, and I just don't have time to call Judy—"

"Judy?" you ask.

Flora's breath shudders as she speaks. "The venue coordinator."

You laugh. God. There are venue coordinators for funerals.

Flora knows what you mean, though. Her lips even twitch. "There are so many *steps*, Rose. You have to wait for the congregation to sit, you have to finish the reading, you have to sit at the back of the altar until the cantor tells you to go—"

"Or what?" You can't even sound angry. Just puzzled that Judy's been given the slightest say. "She's *your* daughter."

Her face crumples again. "Please, Rose. I can't. I can't, please . . ."

The piece of paper trembles as your legs do, and you take in the words, line by line.

There are days you never leave. Days that change the makeup of the ground. And while you are looking at that paper, she will look at you, for the first time, like someone different. Not her daughter's friend. Not a child. But someone strong enough to get through this. Strong enough to carry her with you. She will never stop looking at you like that.

And maybe that's not true. Maybe you don't want to get through today. Maybe you've never wanted anything less.

You'll do it anyway.

Under the full force of that stare, it's not hard to tuck your own grief away. To put it somewhere safe. To tie it tight like a boat on a dock.

But there's something you don't know yet about pain: it flourishes with or without you. You push it back, and nothing changes. All you've done is make it harder to reach.

"It's fine," you say. And it even sounds fine. "Okay, Flora, it's fine. I'll do it."

She pitches forward against your chest with a muffled wail. And you rest your hands, gently, against her back.

"Shhh," you say, more breath than word. "It's okay. Shhh."

Almost since you were old enough to listen, people have spilled the contents of their hearts into your arms. Mom says it's your eyes—big, brown, understanding. Your father's. But listening was one thing. You always hoped you sounded like someone who knew what to say.

But you understand now. Knowing what to say is easy. Think of what you want to hear most in this world—what you would never let yourself ask for—and tell them.

And then later, when you're alone, say it to yourself.

Twelve

THE SECOND DAY

I DON'T SLEEP much that night.

I try, for a while. But after a few hours I move to the living room couch. I can't relax unless I can see both doors. Throughout the night, I keep looking at them. The front door made of heavy wood. The back door of sliding glass over my shoulder, within tantalizing reach.

Around three a.m., I finally call Sheriff Jones. She answers so quickly the phone must have been in her hand.

It's a short, delirious conversation: she tells me that I'm making the right choice, that she'll ensure I don't regret it, that she'll help as best she can, and that I should rest until the morning. I ask if I should call Maggie Williams. She tells me she'll figure it out soon enough.

I fall into an uneasy doze by the window, snapping awake at every little sound.

I don't know what I'm expecting Mayor Williams to do, exactly. I don't know what she *can* do. And if she can still see the future, maybe she already saw what I was going to choose. All I know is that for the past few hours, I've heard the voice of that man, yelling from his car.

What gives you the right?

I don't know what gives me the right, exactly. But this isn't some nameless something anymore. Whatever they want, they're trying to tell me. And maybe it's Alex's words still ringing in my ear. But I think I should try to listen.

And since our conversation, that stirring over my shoulder—the feeling I've come to recognize as the Flood—feels a little closer. I wonder if that's a good sign or a bad one.

As the light spreads across the pavement, my phone buzzes with a text. I pick it up, heart hammering. But it's not Mom, or Flora.

Rose, it's Christie Jones. I'm heading out for an interview, should be back by late afternoon. Felix is picking you up.

I start to respond but pause when I see she's typing something else. Eventually, my phone buzzes.

Can you check on Cassie when you get to the station?

I laugh softly. Sounds like that conversation didn't go well. *Sure, but I've only known her a day?*

She likes you, Christie types back.

She seems really sure her parents didn't do this, I type.

The response comes a few minutes later. *See, this is why she likes you.*

I toss the phone to the couch cushions and try to close my eyes a little longer. I don't sleep very deeply. But when I open the door to wait outside, there's a note, in a flowy feminine hand, sitting on the doormat:

Have it your way.

I spend the rest of my wait on the front steps, watching the road.

Felix pulls up eventually, looking as tired as I feel. So at least we're in the same place emotionally.

His stare sharpens a little when I get closer, though, and I can feel him watching me as I offload my bag into the back seat. I manage a weary smile as I wave.

He takes a breath, and I tense. But he doesn't ask why I'm giving the Flood a chance, or if I considered the mayor's offer, or any of what I'm expecting to hear.

"Are you okay?"

For a long, blank second, all I can do is stare. It's been a while since anyone asked me that.

"What?" I say.

"Sorry." His eyes get wider. "You've got kind of a . . ." He indicates his face with a circular gesture, which is both impossibly vague and immediately understandable.

"It's fine," I say quickly.

"I mean, if you say so," he says. "But if there's anything I can do . . ."

I give him a look across the hood of the car. And then I swallow. "Can I drive?"

He blinks. But he doesn't ask. He tosses me the keys, and he starts to walk around to the passenger's side.

I take a second to adjust the seat, the mirrors, I slide the keys into the ignition. And it unties a knot I'd forgotten was there.

Felix, buckling his seat belt, smiles at me. "What'd you do about the mayor?"

I smile queasily back. "Blew her off."

He nods, long and serious. "Power move."

I snort. "And you guys? What'd you find?"

"In terms of actual information?" Felix says. He doesn't elaborate, but his grimace says it all. "Not to worry, though. Allie has a Plan."

"Oh," I say. "Good. What?"

"Well, first of all, we're detouring a little," he says. "Head to Gibson Repairs, and we'll go to the station from there."

Reflexively, I glance at the dashboard panel, and he quickly adds, "Not for me, don't worry. You'll see when we get there."

And as we pull up next to the garage, I still don't get it. It's not until I get a closer look at the strip mall across the street that I realize where we are: sitting exactly opposite Paul's Pawn and Loan.

Theresa herself is leaning against the garage when we pull up, and as Felix rolls his window down, she unceremoniously thrusts a piece of paper into his hand. "It's not a complete list or anything," she says. "I do work from time to time, you know."

Felix unfolds the paper, and I catch a lengthy list of names. "No, this is perfect," he says. "And the people you've seen more than once are at the top?"

"I can follow simple directions, Felix," she drawls. "You gonna tell me what this is about, or do I have to get it outta Christie at the next bowling night?"

Felix squints. "You do bowling nights?"

"Mind your business." Theresa glances over him to me, and smirks. "Watch out for that one. She's already driven one car into the ground this week."

"Bye, Ms. Gibson," Felix singsongs, rolling up the window.

I wave as we pull away, already distracted by the list in Felix's hand. "What is that?"

"Pawn shop customers. Anyone she's seen coming and going," Felix says, sliding the list into his jacket pocket. "Theresa's good friends with the boss. We knew she wouldn't ask many questions."

It gets quiet after that, aside from Felix telling me when and where to turn. We don't say much as I park the car in front of the sheriff's department, and the only sounds as we walk across the threshold are the swish of the door and my own mumbled "thank you" as Felix holds it for me. But headed down the hall to Felix's and Alex's cubicles, it's not long before I hear shuffling paper and the click of a keyboard.

As we round the corner, I catch sight of the source—the blur of Alex Harper, making a beeline from the computer to the printer. The lines of his body language say "chipper." The deep purple smudges under his eyes say "sleep-deprived and over-caffeinated." But when he sees me, he smiles.

"You changed your mind," he says.

I laugh nervously. "You don't know that. Maybe I always planned to stay." Judging by the look that passes between the two of them, they doubt that.

I think it's the first time in months, aside from Maurice, I've been seen through. I'm not entirely sure how to feel about that.

"You owe me lunch," Alex says, shuffling his printouts.

"Wh—" Felix chokes a little. "You were serious?"

"*Felix*," I say with a slow smile. I shouldn't find this funny. But it's not like he was wrong. "You bet against me?"

"I thought we were—" Felix looks back and forth between us. "I didn't mean—"

Alex throws his head back and laughs—the first I've heard from him so far. It's a bright, rolling sound that lights him from the inside out. Felix ducks his head. And right before he does, I see him flush red.

Oh, I think. So that's how it is.

Felix clears his throat, still a little pink. "Are you done?" At Alex's arched eyebrow, he adds, "With the receipts."

"Almost," Alex says. "Give me the list from Theresa."

"Maybe if you asked nicely—" Felix starts, even as Alex leans forward and plucks the list from his hand.

I move closer. The receipts from last night are on Alex's desk, divided into neat piles. "These are from the pawn shop?"

"From the last three months," Alex says. "Deputy Jay took the other half. We obviously can't find who stole the tape deck, but between the receipts and the names from Theresa, we can get a good idea of who the regulars are and try to get a sense of where they stand on—you, I guess. And with any luck, we'll figure out who made that tape. And hope that they know more about this flood than we do."

"I don't get it." Felix shakes his head. "Who says you get to choose what part of the past comes knocking? Imagine reliving middle school for the rest of your life. What the fuck."

"Don't have to tell me," I mumble in agreement.

Sighing, Felix reaches for one of Alex's receipt piles. Alex slaps his hand away.

"Ow!" Felix says.

"I have a system," Alex mumbles.

I eye them, dubious. "You really think they shopped there before?"

"Must have. Paul may move at the speed of a shambling corpse, but you still can't spend too much time fumbling around," Felix says. "If you're going to steal something, you need to know where it is before you walk in."

"Speaking of which," I say. "Do you have any coffee here, or . . ."

Alex grins. "Kitchen's back down the hall and to the right."

I push back the chair. "Be right back."

I don't have to go far before it gets quiet. We must be the only ones here right now. I got lucky, I guess—I still haven't decided how much I want to tell Christie Jones about last night. Maybe she already knows. She's got a prophet under her roof.

Finally, I settle into a shadowed corner opposite a row of cubicles. I still do want that coffee. But first I think I should try this again.

I go still and I listen. Nothing answers—just the high-pitched whine of silence. But distantly, unless I'm imagining it, there's this hollow sound, like the air at the edge of a sheer drop.

This is why we stayed, I remind the unease settling into my stomach. There's no point to my being here if I don't keep talking to them.

"Are you here?" I whisper. But the air barely shifts.

Until a voice behind me asks, "How's that working for you?"

Someday soon, Cassie Cyrene is going to catch my elbow with her face. I'm not saying I'll like it, or that she'll deserve it. But it's going to happen nonetheless.

I spin around with a laugh that's mostly a wheeze. Cassie sits calmly against the wall, her legs folded to the side, her gingham skirt flat.

"You remember the part where I have post-traumatic stress disorder, right?" I say. It still feels unearned in my mouth. But there's a thrill to it, too. They don't know me. I can say it as many times as I want, and nothing will change.

"Sorry," she says. "I forget that not everyone can see where they're going."

I can't be entirely sure, but I think I was just on the receiving end of a prophet burn.

"So . . ." I smile, shrug. "Guess we'll be working together after all."

The grim line of her mouth spills into a real smile. "No kidding."

"You could have told me," I say.

"I've been told not to rob people of the journey," Cassie says airily. At my raised eyebrows, she concedes, "It wouldn't do you any good if you were here just because I told you it was meant to be. Also, you wouldn't have believed me."

I snort. Fair enough. "Ms. Jones, um, went to the interview?"

Cassie eyes me impassively. I don't get around to asking before she answers. "We're not family. Not in any kind of official sense. They let me live in their house—she and her wife, Sandy. They let me eat their food and read their books. Sandy takes me thrifting once in a while. But on paper? As far as my school knows, I 'grew up early.'"

She shrugs. "I'm the one who wanted it that way, so I shouldn't be surprised when I don't get special treatment. But I know what I'm talking about, even if I didn't foresee it. She should get that by now."

I let out a slow breath. "So you *didn't* foresee it." When she narrows her eyes, I add quickly, "You just seem really sure."

She eyes me for a long moment, as if to make sure I'm not doubting her. "No one can be a hundred percent sure of everything. Not even me," she says. "I see a *lot*, you know. Maybe even more than Maggie Williams did, in her prime. But I see moments. Fine details. Not context. And it means I jump to the wrong conclusions, sometimes.

"So when I told my parents what was coming, I don't know what they decided to do with that information," she says. "And I'll admit, there's something they'd give almost anything to relive. But they have a better reason not to. At least, I like to think so."

I wait for her to keep going. And when she catches me looking, her cheeks flush. "I'd prefer not to say why."

I don't know how to react. But I know what Gaby would have said. "Want to talk about literally anything else?"

She uncrosses her arms with a sigh. "I'm not sure *how* anymore."

"Then let's make it a game," I say. That's what Gaby did whenever we had a transfer student, or a new kid sitting with us at lunch. "You ask anything you want, and I ask anything I want. Only rule is, nothing heavy. No big life stuff. The more insignificant, the better."

I think I catch a smile as she sweeps past me. "My favorite color is green."

"Okay, new rule," I call after her. "You can't foresee the questions."

As we round the corner at the end of the hall, I hear the churn of the printer again, and I've barely taken a step toward their cubicles when Alex slides a stack of warm sheets of paper into my hands, exuding pure, wired triumph.

Cassie slides around me and peers over at the packet. "Oh, this looks good. We'll be making a few unexpected stops, though."

Alex looks unfazed. "You can pencil those in, if you want."

"Oh, I didn't see who they'd be," Cassie chirps. "Just that they'd be unexpected."

"Have you been back there this *entire time*?" Felix hisses as Cassie brushes past me to pick up her own packet.

"Don't worry." Cassie smiles over her shoulder. "Your singing voice is very nice."

Masking a snort, I finally look down at the result of Alex's hours of work. Names and addresses: John Jonas. Jessica Graham. Loreen Murphy. The last on the list is just an address: Lotus Valley Central Caverns.

There's a sheet below it, a printed, clearly standard survey: how long have you lived here, are you married or single, please rate this list of priorities from most important to least. Handwritten at the bottom, however, are two very different questions:

What is your happiest memory?

What would you give to live it one more time?

I pick it up to take a closer look and catch one more sheet underneath. This one is just locations. Hospital, attic stairs. Lotus Valley Public Library, southwest corner. The corner of Morningside and Jacobs (*midafternoon only!* adds a scribbled parenthetical). There's a question on here, too. But only one.

Are you familiar with the entity that was born here?

But I've barely finished reading that sheet when Alex plucks it out of my hand. Carefully, like he's trying not to draw attention. And when I catch his eye, he shakes his head.

"This is the survey?" Felix asks, oblivious.

"Ms. Jones's suggestion," Alex says. And though he sounds calm and even enough, he hunches a little as he tucks the last sheet of paper nonchalantly into his back pocket. "We're going to act like we're conducting a survey on the Flood's presence in Lotus Valley, see if anyone tips their hand. Though I don't know if everyone will talk to us. Maggie's supporters especially."

There's a damp, heavy chill curling into the base of my lungs. That buzzing click of the adrenaline valves switching on. But for all the anxiety I'm feeling right now, uncertainty doesn't follow. Because I still hear it in the back of my head. *What gives you the right?*

I think whether they support me, want me gone, or believe that I've brought them a gift, one thing will be true. I don't think we'll have any trouble getting Lotus Valley to tell us what they think of me.

JULY 3, FIVE MONTHS AGO

NOTE TO SELF: Like anything, this is a skill that can be learned. And if nothing else, you're good at homework. Maurice made you a photocopy of the diagnostic criteria. He wants you to look at these words and know that you're allowed to feel them. Those pages are heavy with ink now, with underlines and asterisks and notes. You know what's yours. You know what isn't.

But don't make the mistake of thinking you know everything.

Let's back up now to this crisp, hot afternoon at the thrift store, down the street from your North Park apartment. You're not looking for anything. You don't need anything. But there's nothing like buying a jacket for the price of a sandwich. And it's reliably still, in a way home rarely is—no clatter of dishes or footsteps, no cartoons blaring. No one comes here.

Usually. Tomorrow is a holiday. You might have remembered that otherwise. But in the whirling mass of adrenaline and summer haze, your sense of time was the first thing to go.

You don't see if they come in together, but it's unlikely that a group of nine strangers formed a flash mob to ruin your fucking day. By the time you look, they are thoroughly and overwhelmingly *everywhere*. A pair of boys by the entrance. A man rifles through the hangers, metal against metal, plastic against plastic. A cluster of women decide, consciously or not, that whatever rack they want is the one behind you. You slip from aisle to aisle. They trail you, their laughter high and sharp.

Hypervigilance. You know that it makes sounds louder, it makes proximity nearer, and that when your world narrows, the exit is all there is. But when a woman parks her stroller by the next rack, hems you into that stretch of aisle, you forget every bit of diagnostic criteria you've ever learned.

This is what it would be like to have your thoughts blasted apart by dynamite. You have the actions, even the order—move around the women, move around the boys, move out the door. You can't string them together. They're too much. It's pounding, through your chest and to your fingers, you're trapped, you're trapped, you're *trapped*.

To them, what happens next looks like nothing. If it looks like nothing to the people who love you, it most certainly looks like nothing to these strangers. It flickers through your mind almost too quick to register, a thought with definition and color in a sea of whirling white.

Push her.

Then the stroller shifts, leaves an opening, and you jump for it. Once you have momentum, the rest snaps into place: a quick and rigid smile to the cashier, a polite mumble to the boys at the door, and a slow breath out as you tumble into the summer heat. In, out. In, out. Like you're supposed to do.

It's a little funny now. You imagine Gaby wrinkling her nose at you—*You tried to push a baby?* You should savor these moments while you have them, these days. Those moments before you overthink.

Because note to self: It will hit you. It always does. It will settle on you in hour three of the long night to come: those words burnt into your brain, the itch of potential energy in your hands. There's a word for that feeling. Something you've never felt for people who've earned it, let alone nine loud and harmless strangers.

Rage.

Thirteen

THE BRINGER OF CALAMITY

I ALWAYS THOUGHT I knew the desert. The nights were my time out here—with the Astronomy Club, with my family, with Gaby, looking for faint stars and little forgotten civilizations.

I'm squinting in my sunglasses as we cross the terrace from the station to the parking lot, the light bouncing off the pavement and right back into my face. "Where did we park?"

"Right down that way." Felix is smirking at me. Which I'm not sure I appreciate.

I'm still half-turned to him as I reach the bottom of the steps. So I completely miss the person I'm about to bowl over.

"Oh!" I stumble back, laughing to cover the quick punch of adrenaline. "I'm sorry, I didn't—"

But in a way I'm beginning to recognize now, the scene has changed.

I blink. The person two inches from my face blinks back at me. It's a woman with a short black bob and thin penciled eyebrows, a stranger. It's what's around her that I recognize. The racks, the

'80s wallpaper, the warm dusty smell of the Second Time's the Charm thrift shop. And the stroller resting under her light grip.

In real life, though, she was looking at a sweater. She wasn't looking at me with blank, unblinking eyes.

She wasn't soaking wet, either.

I flinch. But the shop twists away like a curtain, up and out of existence. I'm back at the steps of the terrace, but one thing stays the same: someone's standing in front of me, staring.

Not for long, though. His hands go slack, the flyer he's holding drifting to the ground like a paper airplane, and he straight-up bolts across the parking lot without a single glance back.

I can hear Cassie calling out to me, but the others are still a few steps behind. It gives me a second to catch my breath.

"Rose?" Cassie says again. I hear the sound of footsteps quickening behind me, the others catching up. "What was that?"

I can still see the man's retreating back, shimmering in the desert haze. "I'm not sure."

"And what is *that*," Felix says, nodding to the flyer. I stoop to the pavement, pick it up, and unfurl it.

TO ALL LOTUS VALLEY CITIZENS:

The mayor's office requests your presence and participation at an emergency town hall meeting this evening, eight p.m., to vote on the best course of action regarding the dangerous interloper and bringer of calamity, Ms. Rose Colter. Further information on the imminent threat will be available on channel three.

GO ARMADILLOS!

The flyer concludes with a loopy, feminine signature—one I recognize from the note on my door this morning.

"A vote," I mutter. "She's gonna *vote me out*?"

"Well," Alex says, his voice a little queasy. "Not you, exactly."

Right. Of course. It's not just me they want gone, is it?

Felix tilts the poster to the side, as if that'll help. "She knows the Armadillos' season ended in November, right?"

"It's not funny," Cassie says quietly. I turn to her, halfway to saying that I get to decide if it's funny—until I catch the look on her face and clamp my mouth shut. It's my flood, but it's her home.

Felix falls into step alongside me as we cross the parking lot, and there's a beat after he leans in. "Do you wanna drive?"

My head snaps toward him. He looks a little embarrassed, maybe. But dead serious. "What?"

He shrugs, his blush creeping down his neck. "It seemed to help, before."

"I . . ." For a long moment, all I can do is gape. "We're on a schedule. It's just gonna slow us down if you have to direct me, right?"

"Okay, but . . ." His brow furrows. "You're sure?"

Not long after I started with Maurice, I told him how every week, no matter how diligently I expected it, it would startle me, every time, when he opened the door. I said it to laugh at myself, to joke about how jumpy I was. And then I noticed, a few weeks later, just how lightly he eased the door off the jamb. It slipped into our routine so matter-of-factly, I didn't see it at first.

It felt a little like this feels, right now.

"Thank you." I smile and jerk my head away. "I'm sure."

———

"ARE YOU SURPRISED?" Christie Jones's voice filters in through a dull crackle.

I lean closer to the center console, where the phone rests in Alex's outstretched palm. "More surprised that it's so civil."

"Civil is the only way they're going to do it," Christie says. "Thanks to the charter, Maggie either needs Rose's consent, *my* consent to use Rudy, or to prove that we've exhausted all peaceful avenues. So without any of that? All she can do is try to suspend the charter. She's always wanted me to use Rudy to keep the neighbors in line. And if the town votes to let him loose on the Flood, that's precedent she can use next time she'd like to drive a 'danger' out of town."

"And then there might not *be* any town to protect." Alex's outburst is vehement enough that he nearly drops the phone.

"Yes, Alex," Christie says. "We agree on that."

He flushes. Felix absently pats at his arm.

"In any case," Christie says. "I'm listening to that 'further information on channel three' now . . ."

There's a *swish* through the speaker as Christie holds the phone up to Maggie Williams's tinny voice on the TV. ". . . and what of the evacuation?" she's saying. "Sheriff Christie Jones would like you to believe that her creature can assist. Now, we are *all*, of course, grateful for his assistance in the Harper incident. But do we feel confident, Lotus Valley, that he will not turn that same violence on us? Because I, your mayor—I'm not sure I do."

Harper incident. I glance at Alex up front, but he's studiously watching the road.

Another *swish* as Christie comes back on the line. ". . . so it's safe to say the campaign has already begun."

"So she trusts Rudy to take on the Flood," I say, "but not to help with the evacuation?"

"It's not trust, exactly." Christie's voice goes dark. "She doesn't think Rudy's capable of anything but violence. But she doesn't see an issue with using that violence for her own ends, either." There's a beat. "You're talking to the pawn shop customers today?"

Alex makes a noise of assent. I think, for a second, of that *other* other list in his pocket.

"And you're . . ." She clears her throat. "Sure about the Mockingbird? Jay said he could go later."

Alex draws his shoulders a little straighter. "She's more likely to talk to me."

"All right." She doesn't sound happy, but she doesn't argue, either. "Well. I know you're thinking about who stole that tape deck. But it's just as important that you charm the living hell out of these people. Listen to their hopes, their worries, their wildest show business dreams, whatever makes them think twice before voting tonight. Be courteous, be quick, be vague. Felix, I swear to God, if you criticize anyone's baking—"

Felix sighs all the way around the tight corner. *"Once!"*

Christie ignores him. "And remember that Maggie has a lot of friends," she says. "Whatever you do today, assume it's going to get back to her."

"If she hasn't already foreseen it," Felix says.

Next to me, Cassie shifts, but she doesn't say a word, or turn away from the window. She's been trying her best, these last five minutes, to pretend this conversation isn't happening.

"Don't get hung up on that," Christie says. "I'll be back this afternoon, but until then, Jay's nearby." There's a pause. "Is Cassie there?"

I half turn, too nervous to look at her dead-on. She doesn't even flinch. Alex is the one who finally has to say, "She is."

There's another, longer beat, and it's quiet enough that I can hear the five of us breathing out of sync. "We'll talk later, Cass."

Christie's name vanishes from the screen as she disconnects the call.

"Does she not want us to see the Mockingbird?" I ask.

Alex chews on that for a moment. "Ms. Jones doesn't like me alone with her."

"Isn't that a good thing?" Felix drawls. "You always wanted the two of us to agree on something."

"I work for the sheriff's office," Alex says. "She's a respected citizen. I can't just *avoid* her."

In the quiet that follows, I turn my attention back to the list of names in my hand. "So," I say. "Our first stop is this . . . John Jonas?"

And that's enough to finally get Cassie's attention.

"Please, no," she groans.

"He bought something," Alex says with a shrug.

"Apparently an . . . antique bassinet," Felix reads off the receipt. "You know, like a weirdo."

Cassie wrinkles her nose. "What does he need an antique bassinet for? He lives alone with his begonias."

Felix grins. "I'm sensing a lack of respect for Lotus Valley's second-most accurate prophet."

"He's a clown," Cassie says dryly.

"Must suck that he's got a place on you in the rankings, too," I say.

"Wow. Okay," Cassie says. "I lost the fourth-grade spelling bee on *nebula*. Did you want to rub that in, too?"

I duck my head, laughing. At least I distracted her for a second.

It was bad enough to think that somewhere among these names was the person who brought me here. Now I also need to convince them that I can fix this.

Even though I haven't convinced myself.

"What's wrong," comes Cassie's voice from my right. Not quite a question. Rarely a question, with her.

Any number of answers could be correct. The weightless, sliding sensation of a car that's not under my control. The distant line of the highway out of the corner of my eye, all those exits open in theory but closed to me. That voice asking what gives me the right to take chances with a home that isn't mine.

"Is this my decision to make?" I ask quietly.

Cassie doesn't need clarification. But a little wrinkle appears in her nose, like the question makes no sense to her nonetheless. "If it makes you feel any better," she says, "it was inevitable."

And we ride in uneasy silence to our first stop.

Fourteen

THE PREVIEW OF COMING ATTRACTIONS

"SO HEY," FELIX says. "Thanks for the heads-up."

John Jonas, second-most accurate prophet in Lotus Valley, blinks like a cat. "I'm not sure what you mean, Felix."

"You predicted every meal my father cooked last week," Felix says. "I'm just saying, you could have been paying a *little* closer attention to the ETA of our cataclysmic prophecy."

"The whims of fate are unpredictable." John smiles slowly. "So, too, is the third eye."

The apartment regards us as John does: sleepily observant. There's a mirror on each side, elongating the walls, and the curtains hang open, fluttering with every whir of the ceiling fan. But the feel of the place sharpens when my eyes fall back on the door. There are four sets of locks, each heavier and more forbidding than the last.

"There's such a thing as too much knowledge," John says, following my eyes. "I'd see anyone coming, of course. I always do."

I glance back at him. The way Cassie looked at me that first time, the way Mayor Williams looked at me, the way he's looking at me now—in some ways they couldn't be more different, but they all have that one thing in common: the recognition.

He *looks* harmless. But on Theresa's list of pawn shop customers, he's easily the most frequent visitor.

"Rose Colter," he says, like he's feeling it out.

I try to smile. "Hi."

"You'll make the right decision," he says. "You might not be able to imagine it now. But you wouldn't have been happy at Stanford. UC San Diego is the far better fit."

I blink. That's not where I saw that sentence going. "Hang on. I'm getting into both?"

"What happened to not fair?" Felix says.

"This is the only time I'll talk to her," he says, slightly wounded. "I won't get to tell her later."

"Wait, wait," I say. "This is for real, right? Because Cassie says she gets things wrong sometimes."

"Yes, Rose," Cassie says with a sigh, "thank you for bringing that up here and now."

"John is never wrong," Alex says. "Or hasn't been before."

"But you're still ranked under Mayor Williams?" I say.

"John's prophecies are more accurate," Cassie says. "But his predictions have always been decidedly small scale."

"Jealousy is unbecoming, Cassandra," John says.

Cassie's expression darkens. "One drought," she mutters. "Anyone can predict a drought. The *weatherman* could predict a drought."

"And many did," John singsongs. "You, as I recall, did not."

Alex, in his own impressive display of foresight, puts out an arm just as Cassie steps forward. "Anyway," he says, "that short survey . . ."

"Ah, yes," John says. "But I'm already planning to vote in favor of Ms. Colter. Anything to understand the Great Sea."

The *Great* Sea. Hope they didn't hear that. Don't want to give them an ego on top of everything else.

"Then," Alex says slowly, gesturing to the TV, "why do you have Maggie Williams on?"

John regards the low drone of the TV with a sleepy nod. "Don't you find it sort of soothing?"

Alex tactfully doesn't answer. But John smiles anyway.

"Don't be too hard on Maggie," he says. "She struggles with her gift."

"She's never struggled with anything in her life," Cassie says darkly.

"You know better than that, Cassandra," John says. "Haven't you ever regretted what you've seen? Maggie came to me once, when she was younger. She told me she saw a future where her prophecies controlled this town, from the laws passed to the decisions we made day to day. She asked me if that meant it would really happen."

Cassie's expression flickers but doesn't lighten. "I didn't know that."

"What did you tell her?" Alex asks.

"I told her that she was the most gifted young prophet I knew," John says, "and that if she saw it, then it would likely come to pass. She never asked me about it again. But when she claimed, years later, that she lost the sight, I wondered if she was trying, the only way she knew how, to stop what she knew would come."

In the beat of silence that follows, I think of Mayor Williams: her sweater set, her pearls, her beatific smile. A future where she controls this town seems like something she'd kill for. But maybe that's not always how she was.

I don't know if what John and Cassie have is something you can wish away. But with enough time and practice, you can bury just about any part of yourself. No matter how big.

"Look at me, chattering away." John laughs. "You have questions, don't you? Ask."

"Right." Alex digs for his survey. "The first question is, what is your happiest memory?"

"Happiest? My," John muses. "Next week I'm going to have a particularly good cup of tea."

"Memory," Cassie grits out. "Mem-o-ry."

"Cassie," Alex warns. But then thinks about it further. "But yes, a past thing. A past thing is better."

"It's all the same, isn't it?" John says. "The premonition came on a Tuesday last year. So isn't it both past and future?"

"Oh," I say, in sudden realization. "That's not going to work."

"Why?" Felix says.

"The next question is 'What would you give to live it again?'" I say.

There's a collection of quiet, rueful noises around the semicircle. John watches us thoughtfully.

"I think I see the problem here," he says.

"I think there are actually multiple problems," Felix says. But John shakes his head.

"You're not on the same page," he says. "None of you are. If you can't communicate with one another, how can you hope to communicate with me, let alone the Great Sea?"

"How many people do you know who can communicate with you?" Cassie says.

"I'm going to give you something," John says. "One prophecy, free of charge."

"Um." I raise my hand. "Were the others not free?"

"Ah, no," he says, perfectly serene. "Those ones were just for fun."

Cassie's eyes glaze over. I think she's still listening. But I also think she's slipped into some kind of rage fugue state.

John settles back in his chair, tilts his neck slowly from side to side. "The abandoned multiplex," he says. "That's where you should go next." Alex frowns, glancing down at his list, but John laughs and shakes his head. "It's no one you planned to talk to. No one's talked to them for quite some time. But if you don't go there next, you will not be successful today."

"So we *will* be successful?" Felix says.

"Who is it?" Alex asks at the same time.

"I'm afraid both those answers are out of my reach," John says. "All I know is that this path grants you your best chance. Perhaps your only chance."

I start to look at the others. But before I can, Cassie says, "I'm fine with that."

Alex scribbles on his schedule without looking down. "Thanks, John."

We mutter thank-yous and goodbyes as we shuffle to the door, which John accepts with a gracious incline of his head. As I slip out last, he gestures to me, "Ah, Ms. Colter, when you find the

Great Sea, do treat them gently, yes? You never know someone else's story."

I smile and duck through the door before he can see the shiver that works its way through me.

"I'm kind of surprised, Cassie," Felix says as we make our way to the stairs. "That you're taking John's advice, I mean."

Cassie looks at him sideways. "I'm petty," she says, "I'm not stupid. I said it before, didn't I? John's prophecies may be trivial. But even I know that they're never wrong."

THE ABANDONED MULTIPLEX sits tucked between two restaurants on a busy corner of Morningside Drive. But when you step off the block and into the entryway, it's easy to forget that. Like in the middle of this lively downtown chaos, there's a pocket of airless space.

Wordlessly, Cassie offers her purse, and Alex pulls out a keyring, squinting at the color-coded caps.

"Do you guys have keys to the entire city?" I ask.

"Just the public buildings," Alex says. "Sometimes Ms. Jones brings me to check on the places that need a . . . closer eye. But we've never been here before."

"You've heard a lot about the neighbors by now," Cassie says, "but you haven't seen many, have you? That's because they're happy enough to leave us alone if we leave them alone. You avoid the right parts of town, you can go weeks without seeing one at all." For a moment, she watches Alex, sorting through the keys. "And there are particular places you shouldn't go at all, whether you want to see them or not."

"Unless you're Felix," Alex mumbles, most of his attention still on his task.

Felix sputters. "Again! The child of scientists here! If you hand me a list of places I shouldn't go, what do you expect me to do?"

"I mean," I say, "probably not go there."

Alex smiles, just a little, and it untwists something in my stomach. He's been quieter than usual since I saw that list in his hands.

I watch his face a little more closely as I ask, "But the multiplex isn't one of those places?"

I think I see recognition on his face. Then he finds the right key, and it's gone.

"No," he says, sliding it into the lock. "If it was dangerous, Ms. Jones would have told me."

That's the exact moment that Alex withdraws the keys and pushes at the door. It unsticks with a *snap* and creaks slowly open. The air rushes out with a little sigh. Then it stills.

It's darker than dark in there. Dark like nothing within our atmosphere should be.

Felix takes a huge gulp of an inhale. "I'll go first," he says. But Alex is already slipping past him, braced against the chill of the hallway. Cursing, Felix bolts after him.

Cassie turns to me with a wry smile. "Shall we?"

So we do.

My eyes adjust slowly. And as they do, I catch the ticket booth looming ahead, broad strokes of light fixtures framing the sides like peacock tail feathers. I can just imagine it: bombastic splashes of light against dark carpet and dark paint. But I don't think this place has been lit in a long time.

I sidle up next to Cassie and whisper, "Are we really going to find someone here?"

Cassie shrugs. But even in the dark, I see a brief, rare flicker of uncertainty.

From up ahead, Alex clears his throat and points at the darkened door. "Let's try theater one."

I glance to the right as I follow, through the double doors. I know from the sign outside that there are only four screens. But in the dark, the theater stretches on and on.

There's light filtering through the emergency exits. By it, a stream of dust cascades from ceiling to floor. The screen looms above, framed by the scalloped edges of the curtain. Something about a dark screen always looks like waiting.

Alex clears his throat. "If there's anybody here," he calls, "could we ask for five minutes of your time?"

There's no response to that. For a second, I think I see a dark, fuzzy shape, hovering at the edge of the curtain. But I blink hard, and the image clears.

My imagination, maybe. I hope.

"John Jonas sent us?" Felix adds hopefully.

At the silence that follows, Cassie attempts a smile. "We want to talk to them, Felix, not scare them off."

"Let's try theater two," Alex says. And even he sounds uneasy at this point

We turn around. The good news is, I'm no longer at the back of the line. The bad news is, I'm at the front.

I take a breath. I've been telling myself these past few months, whenever that nameless panic crept in, that the worst thing that could happen to me has already happened. Now I think I was tempting fate.

I reach for the doorknob. Something gets there first.

Something black and thick and solid stretches across the doors like rope.

I jerk back, nearly taking myself and Cassie to the floor. Something slithers along the walls, laced into brambles across the door.

From the front of the theater, by the darkened screen, there's the sound of something slithering. And it whispers, low.

"*Talk.*"

Fifteen

THE FEATURE PRESENTATION

"COME ON. COME *on*." Felix thrusts his phone above his head, waving it. But there's as little signal here as there was on the desert road, and Felix realizes that quickly. "Help!" he bellows. "Someone help!"

"What's happening?" I turn to Cassie.

"I don't know," Cassie says. Her eyes are wide, darting. It's deeply unnerving, seeing her thrown off. "I didn't see this."

"I'm trying the other door," Felix says over his shoulder, already halfway across the theater.

"*Felix*," Alex says, "get away from there."

"And do what?" Felix reaches out, rattles the doorknob. "I'm not just going to stand here while we—"

But then Felix stumbles back, one hand fully recoiled, the other gripping his wrist. When he speaks again, it's quieter, higher. "Guys," he says, "something bit me."

Through the dark, I can barely make out the web barring our way: solid, dark strokes branching into thinner spindles. They

THE VALLEY AND THE FLOOD

look almost like tree branches. But they're vibrating just slightly. Pulsing with potential energy.

"Is that you?" I say slowly.

And the web, piece by piece, shivers like the limbs of the spider Dan killed in the bathroom a couple of weeks ago. I'm starting to wish he were here.

"*Talk*," it whispers.

This isn't the Flood. For the first time, the thought doesn't come as a relief.

Felix grips Alex's arm. "Say something," he whispers.

Alex twitches, startled back into the moment, and clears his throat. "Ex-excuse me," he manages. "We're . . . sorry to bother you. But if I could ask you a few questions—"

"What are you doing?" Felix hisses. "Convince them to let us out!"

"Not yet," Alex says softly.

"What do you mean, not yet?" Felix says.

"What if they know something about the Flood?" Alex says.

There's a low-level buzz now, rattling the seats around us, rising steadily in pitch. "*Talk*," they say. "*Talk, talk, TALK!*"

"We'd like to," Alex says, his patience just barely steadying his voice. "But if we could just ask a few questions—"

"*NO!*" The buzz turns high and crackling, a shriek of a roar. "*YOU! TALK!*"

It takes a few seconds for the room to still. My fingers, curling around the back of a chair, feel just as unsteady.

"Alex," I say, never looking away from the door. "Was that what the list was for? Were you going to interview the neighbors, too?"

He whips around, stricken. "I didn't know about this place," he says. "If I had, I never would have brought you h—"

"Hang on," Felix interrupts. "You were going to do *what?*"

Alex stands a little straighter. But even in the dark, I see his face flush. "They live here, too," he says. "They know more about the Flood than we do. I was just going to ask around a little. I wouldn't have gone anywhere dangerous."

"But you *were* going to go alone," Felix says.

"I never said—" Alex starts.

"You don't have to!" Felix throws his hands in the air. "If you wanted us along, you wouldn't have hidden it from us!"

Alex takes an audible deep breath. "They're more likely to talk to me," he says, "if I'm by myself."

"Right," Felix says, "because they're buttering you up *before they eat you.*"

"Guys, stop," Cassie says.

"You know what, no," Felix says. "I'm not going to let this—"

"Look at them," Cassie says, a little more emphatically. "They're listening."

I glance back at her, and then at the thing blocking our path. They look less solid at the edges now, like their grip on the door has loosened somewhat. Not enough that we could force our way through, maybe. But I think she's right. They're listening.

"We should figure out what they want," Alex says.

"They told us what they want," Cassie says. "Right?"

A low, shivery hum fills the room. Like approval.

"Okay, so, talk," Felix says. "Talk about what?"

Cassie blinks. "I didn't say I knew *that.*"

We stand there, glancing from each other to the walls. Felix slumps against a chair, all the fight gone out of him for the time being, and Alex's gaze drops to the ground. I wonder, at first, if our captors will get impatient with us. But they seem perfectly content to wait us out.

"Rose . . ." When I look to Felix, he's chewing on his lip. "You said, 'Is that you?' Who were you talking to?"

"Oh." I said that, didn't I? "I'm . . ."

"You spoke to them," Cassie says. I glance over my shoulder. There's something—hungry about the way she's looking at me. "The Flood."

"I—" There's no reason to deny it now. She already knows. "I did. Last night. But it was more of a—I mean—I didn't really learn anything. We just—talked. Or I tried, anyway."

"You could've told us," Felix says. Before Alex gets the chance to glare at him, he quickly adds, "Sorry. I just mean, we want to help, y'know? But if you don't say anything—"

"I know," I say. My chest is burning, like I'm embarrassed. But I don't think that's it. "It's not that I don't trust you. Or that I don't *want* to say anything. It's more like I can't?"

I pause, ready to let that be explanation enough. But the more I say, the more the web of shadows blocking our way seem to—calm down. They look almost smaller now. Like a puffed-up cat slowly realizing that you aren't here for a fight.

"My dad died when I was pretty young?" I say. I don't know why I make it a question. "So it was . . . difficult, for my mom. She hid it well, and she did a great job for me, but I always had this sense like I didn't want to be another problem. And even when things got better, and when she met my stepfather, I guess it was a habit by then. The only one I really talked to was . . ."

They're still watching, still listening—my new friends and the shadows around us. But there's no way I'm going there.

I clear my throat, hard. "So I still don't. I never know where to start."

Felix and Alex glance to each other. But Cassie's gaze hasn't wavered.

"What did they say?" she asks.

"I don't know," I say. There's a little ripple in the air, a shiver running through each of those dark branches. "I think they wanted to tell me something, but I didn't understand it. But I asked if they planned to destroy this place. And they said yes."

Felix laughs, just barely loud enough that I can hear the panic. When he speaks, it's quiet. "Guys. Let's give this up."

Cassie's outline quivers. But Alex speaks first. "We've talked about this."

"And now we're talking about it again," Felix says. "We're not getting those votes tonight. And even if we do, you heard Rose. They're not going to stop."

"We'll keep trying," I say.

"That's not enough for me," Felix bites out. "My entire family lives here. And they won't leave without me. I've asked."

Alex's eyes soften a little. "You don't *have* to stay, Felix."

Felix looks away, his shoulders hunched. "I'm not leaving without you, either. And I'm guessing you won't."

Alex doesn't answer right away. I wonder if Felix can see what I can—that his resolve is there, fastened into place as firm as he can make it. But that maybe, just a little, he wishes that it wasn't.

"You know I have to do this," Alex says.

Felix drags a hand through his hair with a choked laugh. "You don't have anything to make up for! You were a child! You asked for help! That's what you were supposed to do!"

"I do." Alex's voice is still firm. But he looks far younger than he did just a second ago. "I was the one who made it the way it was."

Felix opens and closes his fists, like he'd like nothing more in the world than to shake sense into Alex. But his voice is quiet. Gentle. "How do you figure that?"

Alex doesn't answer right away. His gaze, still a little lost, shifts to me. Maybe because I'm in the same boat now. Or because it's easier than looking at Felix.

"I was sick long before my neighbor ever found me," he says. "Complications from my asthma, mostly. Rarely anything serious. But enough that it feels like my whole childhood was doctor's offices and emergency rooms.

"And this particular time—well, I didn't make the connection then," he continues. "I guess there's no way I could have, until I was older. And it was such a little thing. It shouldn't have bothered me as much as it did. But I was maybe six or seven years old and getting discharged from the hospital after my usual winter pneumonia. And the nurse said something like . . . I don't remember exactly what it was."

I nod as he pauses. Though it seems pretty clear to me that he remembers it word for word. At length, he presses on. "She said, 'You're becoming quite the regular, aren't you? It's a good thing your father can take time off work.'"

Alex swallows. "It's amazing, the things people say to sick kids. Like they're doing it intentionally."

"She didn't know what she was talking about," Felix says.

Alex's face softens. "I know that *now*. But back then, it flipped a switch I couldn't turn off. I started noticing all the little sacrifices Dad made. I started looking at the bills. We were learning about symbiotic relationships in science class that year. I learned that a parasite is something that feeds off other animals to survive. So that's why I looked at him one night and thought, What if I'm a parasite?

"And . . ." He shrugs helplessly. "That neighbor came to me that year and took the form of a parasite. That can't be a coincidence, right? It had to have been born from what I was feeling."

I can tell two things from the look on Felix's face: that he'd forgive anything Alex ever did, and that he understands, maybe because of this, that Alex might not believe what he wants to say right now. So I step in.

"You couldn't have controlled what you were feeling. Especially when someone forced their own feelings onto you," I say. "My th—Someone I know says it's hard to admit that you didn't have control over something. But he says it's really freeing to finally accept."

I can tell that argument doesn't fully land—I can see it on Alex's face. This is the same person who told me I didn't ask for this. I wonder if it would be hypocritical of me to remind him of that.

"I know it wasn't my fault. Or Ms. Jones's," he says. "I just . . . want to be able to do something about it next time."

"You have," Felix says. "Over and over, for so many people. Me included. And you don't have to stay here just because you feel—"

"No." Alex shakes his head. "It's not *all* because of that."

"What do you mean?" Felix says.

"I know this doesn't make sense," Alex says, "but just evacuating isn't enough."

"I get that you think that," Felix says. "I want to understand. But I don't."

"You would if you could see it." He barely shifts. But I can tell he's talking to Cassie now. "It's going to be really bad, isn't it? If we can't stop it."

I turn to face her. She's not looking at me, or at Alex. When she speaks, she sounds far away. Like a voice at the bottom of a well.

"If we can't stop it," she says, "it's more than just the end of this town. And if the Flood fully crosses our border? Then what I saw is inevitable."

I take a breath, and it fills my lungs with that same cold, humid air that I'm beginning to recognize. Every one of us is still, hanging on Cassie's words. And so is the Flood.

By then I notice the low rumbling sound by the door, slowly building. As I turn my head toward it, I feel a weight shift, slide from my shoulders and vanish. I think the Flood has moved back, just a little. But they're not my first priority this time.

"Rose," Felix hisses as I make my way across the theater, but all common sense aside, I'm not afraid. I've been a cat person since I could speak. I know that sound. The branches are purring.

"Is it okay if I ask you a question now?" I say softly, moving closer. The rumbling grows louder. "You wanted us to talk. Were you asking us to talk to one another?"

I lift my hand and hold it out to one branch, close enough to feel the static between us but not quite there. In the dim light, the branch shifts, unknots itself, and reaches back. And I feel soft fur and a cold nose slip between my outstretched fingers.

The branches burst apart and scatter.

I hear a scream behind me—Cassie. She's got one of the creatures draped around her neck, nuzzling her face. Soon they're swarming me, too, like sleek black party streamers weaving between my limbs.

"Rose, what the hell is—" Felix gasps as one slips down the back of his jacket.

"They didn't just want us to talk." Alex lifts his hand wonderingly to one that's draped across his shoulders like a feather boa. It tilts its little head into his touch. "They wanted us to have a conversation?"

"Every neighbor feeds off something, right?" I watch a few sail and crisscross overhead. I realize then that I'm smiling. Wider than I'm used to, these days. "And I figure they can't have had a lot to eat these past few years."

There's a chorus of deeply aggrieved huffs and a volley of whispers overhead.

"Street."

"Noise."

"Television."

"No."

"More."

"Than."

"Snacks."

"They're very welcome," Cassie says, standing stiffly. "Maybe they could show their appreciation a little farther away?"

There's a high, rolling sound, like laughter, and they sail into the air again, collecting against the walls on either side of us. One tries to settle into my arms, but another, with a little huff, pulls it along to join the rest.

"Well?" a little voice says.

"Ask," another chimes. Now that they're speaking above whispers, I can hear that their voices are distinct, theatrical—one word is a brassy mid-Atlantic drawl, the next has a Brooklyn lilt.

Felix, mouth agape, nudges Alex again. Alex dives for the folded piece of paper in his pocket. "Ah. Um. Are you familiar with the entity that was born here?"

This time, they're definitely laughing. And again, their answers come in clipped, individual words, volleying all around us, each voice different from the last.

"We."

"Are."

"But."

"Children."

"To."

"Them."

I shiver. I knew, didn't I? I can feel it every time they're near, how many lifetimes they've lived. "But you've heard of them."

A low hum. "Stories."

"Whispers."

"Memory."

Cassie watches them, eyes wide and wary. When she speaks again, her voice is determinedly, rigidly polite. "Is there anything you know that would help us? Please. We don't—we don't have much time."

There's low, indistinct chatter, like they're talking among themselves. This time, the answer takes much longer to come.

"Listen."

"Remember."

"Understand."

Felix shifts behind me, leaning in to Alex. "Do you know what that means?"

"I do," I say without looking. My own voice sounds very far away from me.

I can feel their eyes on me, how badly they want to ask. But the next thing Felix says is, "Then what else?"

"I don't know." Alex scans his list of questions again, like something there will help.

"I think I do," I say softly. We're interviewing them not just as neighbors, but as citizens of Lotus Valley. So we should ask them what we're asking everyone else.

I take a step back, so I can see both sides of the swarm. "What's your happiest memory?" I call.

They don't know what to do with that, at first. But then they dissipate, collecting by the ceiling overhead, then darting to the screen. Some of them form shapes against the backdrop: two people, chattering indistinctly. Others fill the first row of the audience, whispering, laughing. A crowd, watching a movie.

And I think I recognize those distinct, theatrical voices now. They're not voices, exactly. They're bits of dialogue.

There's a little sound that echoes. Something like a sigh.

"With."

"Every."

"New."

"Word's."

"Creation."

"One."

"Of.

"Us."

"Lives."

"So each of you was born from the invention of a new word," Alex asks.

"And if conversation feeds you," I say, "this theater must have been all you needed." There's a trill of approval. "And those memories, what would you give to live them one more time?"

This time, there's no question of what they form: a slowly rotating orb, patterned with vague shapes of continents.

"The world," I say softly. "Okay. That's fair."

We didn't learn anything that we didn't know before. But I glance at the piece of paper in Alex's hands, those forbidden areas of town. And they feel a little less foreboding than they did just a few minutes ago.

They live here. Just like everyone else.

"Alex," I say, "I think you're right about talking to the neighbors. And I think you should take us with you."

Somehow, I don't think it needed to be said. When he looks back at me, he breaks into one of those rare smiles. Like he already knew.

To the theater, he says, "Thank you for your time."

They swarm us again before they scatter, to the ceiling and to the corners.

"Good."

"Luck."

Their rustling, eventually, goes still. And when Felix tries the door, it's open.

"Sweet dancing Christmas." He sighs, slumping headfirst into the frame. "I'm gonna kill John Jonas."

"I liked them," Alex says mildly.

Felix shoots him a soft, indiscernible look. "Of course you did."

I smile at their retreating backs. Half of me does want to drive back across town to introduce John Jonas to a few projectiles. But I guess he was right. We're communicating now.

Alex and Felix are the first to head through the door, and I'm close behind them. But then I see Cassie out of the corner of my eye.

"Cassie?" I say.

"Hmm?" she says brightly. "Go on ahead. We're a little behind schedule, by my estimation."

But I don't move. With our company gone, I suddenly remember what she said.

"'It's inevitable,'" I echo slowly. "What's inevitable?"

"The tides," she says. "The death of our sun. The questionable quality of the avocados in the Jacobs Street Market. Take your pick."

"Cassie," I say. She still doesn't look at me. "You never told me what happens at the end of your prophecy."

"The future is a variable, Rose," she says to her feet. "It can change. It changes all the time, without our knowing. When a prophecy doesn't come to pass, it doesn't mean the prophet was *wrong*. It just means we as a species took an unexpected turn somewhere."

Her voice shrinks. "Sometimes it doesn't matter how many

turns you take. Sometimes a thousand different things could change, and every single one of them leads you to the same place. And if we don't stop that flood from coming—there's only one way this is going to end."

I reach for her arm—not sure what I'm going to do with it, exactly. She sidesteps me and starts to walk.

"Let's go," she says to the hallway.

"Cassie—" I try again, but she keeps at that same clipped pace. And without conscious thought, I remember something she said yesterday, halfway down those basement stairs at Lotus Valley Elementary.

This isn't how I die.

But I don't just remember it. Someone whispers it in the dark behind me, too.

The skin on the back of my neck prickles, and I take a breath. "Something you'd like to say?" I ask.

Behind me, I hear the silver sound of jingling keys and a cleared throat. Then the voice.

"Need a ride?"

The air thickens as I spin around. The world behind me is no longer the darkened movie theater but a porch decked out with tea lights, a warm, bright island in a sea of trees. And at the top, grinning down at me, Nick Lansbury tugs at his key chain like a baited hook.

And that ever-present distant roar—it's gotten louder.

I understand panic now. I understand it well enough that it doesn't carry me away like it used to. This isn't Nick. Nick has never in his life been so still. The Nick at the top of the stairs regards me in that same placid, watchful way as Gaby did last night.

"Okay . . ." I run out of breath halfway through the word. I take in a gulp of cool, damp air. It's misting rain, here in the memory. I can see droplets of it clinging to Nick's hair. "You want me to learn your language? Then I'll guess. Are you trying to tell me that she's right?"

Without blinking, the Flood nods.

One step forward for our communication, I guess.

I glance behind us, into the endless stretch of Sutton Avenue. I know I'm not really here. I catch those little differences from reality: the bare grass, devoid of trees, and the starless sky. But if not for the click of Cassie's heels still echoing from the present, I might've forgotten where I was.

"Do you know what she means," I say, "when she says you're going to do something terrible?"

Another nod is my answer. This isn't Nick. But I shiver. This might be as close as I ever get to an admission of guilt from him.

"I don't know what you want," I breathe. "But if you're still trying to tell me, maybe you think I can give it to you. I'll keep trying to understand. So just—don't stop talking."

The road doesn't disappear when I turn. But I follow the sound of Cassie's footsteps until it does.

Sixteen

THE INTERMISSION

"IT'S BEEN YEARS. Many of your lifetimes, I'd say."

The figures overhead, perched on the library roof at the southwestern point of town, look about fifteen feet tall in the light of the sun. But it's hard to say. They're only visible from a certain angle, and it's impossible, somehow, to look at them directly.

But however hard they are to look at, they're strangely easy to talk to.

"We are surprised," another says. "We knew your flood to be a gentle soul. We heard rumors over time of a change. But we did not give them much weight."

"Perhaps you might ask one of your own kind," another chimes in politely. "They went to live among you. You've seen much more of them than we, surely."

Cassie clears her throat. She's not quite hiding behind me, but she's close. "Humans don't all know one another."

I scribble *Live among us?* in my running list of notes, right below their collective happiest memory: a lengthy, lurid description of an ant climbing a cactus.

"Thank you," I say. "That helps."

"We wish you peace, child," one says softly. The hairs at the back of my neck prickle.

"You might tell your kind to visit more often," another says. "It's become quiet, this place."

"You kidnapped fifteen people from this spot in the seventies alone," Felix says.

There's a pause. Then, in a perfect imitation of Cassie, the sound of a throat clearing. "Our thoughts on humanity have evolved."

"Oh," Felix says faintly. "Neat."

"HOW DID YOU *not see this?"*

"I'm not a gumball machine!" Cassie says hotly. "You don't put in a quarter and get a—Rose!"

I barely start to peer around the doorframe before Cassie yanks me back. Seconds later, a casserole dish sails out of the house and shatters onto the front walkway. Casserole included.

"Mrs. Graham?" Alex, huddled at the other side of the front door next to Felix, somehow manages politeness and urgency as the same time.

"Get her off my property, Harper!" Mrs. Graham howls back. "Or I'll call the law!"

There's a pause. I think Mrs. Graham realizes, at the same time we do, that we're technically the law.

And make no mistake, Mayor Williams chirps on the blaring TV. *We must find common ground.*

"You first," I mutter.

Mrs. Graham recovers first. "I'm counting to five!"

"Mrs. Graham," Alex starts, "if this isn't a good time—"

A mermaid lamp sails through the door, shattering just past the Pyrex-and-noodle carnage by the steps. Felix, lips pursed, nods.

"Let's just run," he says. By the time it's fully out of his mouth, he's already moving.

"*Felix!*" Alex hisses, with a cursory grab at empty air.

"Let's just run!" Felix calls faintly, already halfway across the lawn.

"YOU'RE SERIOUS," FELIX says.

Lotus Valley High Student Council President Natalie Meyer grimaces, tugging one perfectly tight curl. It's then that I remember where I heard her name before: the girl whose sweet sixteen Alex broke into to save Felix from his own curiosity. We're currently clustered on her lawn, fanning ourselves against the boiling heat and watching her glance back at the house, where her father stands in the open doorway with crossed arms.

"Dad understands there were extenuating circumstances," Natalie says in her sweet, high voice. "But Alex still broke a window. He'd feel better if we had this conversation outside, away from anything fragile."

"Felix." Alex has flushed a deep, dangerous red. Whether it's the heat or the embarrassment, I'm not sure. "Just let it go."

"He's the one who should let it go!" Felix shoots back. Alex makes a valiant effort to sink into the earth's core. "I almost got the whole party *eaten*. If he blames anyone, he should blame me."

Natalie glances back at her father questioningly. He seems to think about that for a moment. And then he shrugs his massive shoulders.

Natalie, turning back to us, brightens. "Dad says we all make mistakes."

ACE MARTIN, PTA president and high school band teacher, tells me right off the bat that he'll be voting against me.

"It's not what you think," he explains. "I don't have a problem with the neighbors. I used to be fascinated with 'em, really. My best friend growing up had one living under his house, scratching at his floorboards all night." He chuckles. "I was scared to death. But I wanted to see them more than anything."

I take a sip of the coffee he insisted on ordering me. "You never did?"

"All I ever saw under there was dirt and mice," he says. And for a moment, he's quiet. "I guess I always figured that if I knew what they were, what they wanted, that they wouldn't scare me anymore. It was Maggie Williams who told me that I didn't have to look. That I could live how I wanted, regardless of what they were doing down there. I don't know if I can tell you how freeing that was."

I hesitate before I ask. "Did Mayor Williams stop looking, too?"

Ace answers with the same easy magnanimity as before. But something in the air undeniably shifts.

"She says she gave that future-business up. And I believe her. But if she can see what's coming, and she chooses not to . . . it'd be a tough pill to swallow. But I'd understand." Something in his face darkens. "There's not a lot you get to choose out here."

"ARE YOU FAMILIAR with the entity that was born here?"

An impossible stillness falls over the stairwell of Lotus Valley Memorial Hospital. I ease myself around the corner to get a better look, Felix's hand fluttering nervously above my shoulder. There's a figure up ahead, bent nearly in half. In the dark, it looks massive, sketchy. Its eyes, more than half the size of its face, are a deep, solid black.

Quietly, almost inaudibly, it giggles.

"They will come," it whispers. "And we will feed."

Alex clears his throat. When he speaks next, his voice is nearly a squeak. "Can I put that down as a yes?"

"OF COURSE I'M voting for you, man." Felix's friend Miles barely pauses his rep, hoisting himself above the pull-up bar. "Armadillo pride, right?"

"Aw, dude." Felix looks genuinely touched. "I'm just a reserve player."

Miles drops to the floor to clap his shoulder. "Armadillos don't know the difference between starter and reserve, man. I read that somewhere."

I take a deep breath through my nose. Felix on the other hand is all but welling up.

"You should know you're not voting for *me* specifically," Felix says, his voice choked.

"But close enough," Cassie says with a beatific smile. Miles flushes a little redder.

"You're all coming to the scrimmage Friday, right?" he says. "You can come, too, new girl."

It takes me a second to realize he's serious. "Um," I say. "I might be destroying your town Thursday."

Miles blinks, unfazed. "Right," he says. "But what are you doing after?"

IF YOU'D ASKED me to picture Mayor Williams's personal assistant, I would have imagined the same pearls, sweater set, and smile. But Loreen Murphy is a twentysomething with a patterned undercut, a GENDER? I HARDLY KNOW HER T-shirt, and a resting boredom face that twists into a grimace as we work our way through the survey.

"Ugh." Loreen full-body shudders. "These answers are private, right?"

They don't strike me as the kind of person who'd summon an ages-old being upon their home. Loreen seems moderately allergic to public displays of sincerity—to the point where they're almost too embarrassed to call a weekend with their late grandparents their happiest memory. The person who made that tape is a true believer, I think. Someone who's completely convinced that whatever the Flood has to offer is worth all this.

But I pay close attention nonetheless. According to Theresa's list, Loreen is one of the most frequent customers of Paul's Pawn and Loan, just below John Jonas.

They probably shop there ironically. But still.

There's a sudden blaring sound as a van whizzes by outside, outfitted with loudspeakers. I catch Maggie Williams's face screen-printed on the side, beaming at me.

The time is now, a cheery voice booms. *The time to take the safety of our town into our own hands. The time to bring this chapter of Lotus Valley to an end. Vote YES tonight. For more information . . .*

Loreen grimaces as the voice fades around the corner. "*Ugh*," they say again, with feeling. "I hate how my voice sounds recorded."

"If it helps," I say delicately, "I didn't recognize you."

"Thanks." Loreen brightens a bit. "Sorry. Jobs, right?"

I realize, belatedly, that voting yes actually means voting no—no to the Flood, at least. "So you don't agree with her?"

"Don't have an opinion," Loreen says with a shrug. "It's not like I want to lose my house or anything, but there's no proof that's gonna happen except for Cassie's prophecy. No offense."

"None taken," Cassie says.

"And your being here isn't all bad." Loreen smirks at me. "It's been a while since I've seen Williams so pissed."

I smile for real this time. "I'm surprised she didn't come tell me so."

"Not her style," Loreen says. "She'll go after you tonight, with all her cronies behind her. And until then, she's gonna let you look twice around every corner."

They say it casually, but there's a grim set to their mouth.

Maybe that's why Cassie asks.

"Do you really think her abilities are gone?" she says.

Loreen considers us for a moment. Then defiantly, they lift their chin.

"She says she can't do it at all anymore. I think that's probably bullshit," Loreen says. "But one thing's true either way. Even if she *can* look, she won't."

"So you think—" I start.

"Yup." Loreen grins humorlessly. "We're on our own."

SANDY ALVAREZ, CHRISTIE'S wife, is a five-foot Cuban woman with tight curls and a round, welcoming face. Our detour to her home isn't planned, and yet when we walk in, she's already making pastelitos. Which I guess proves that you don't have to be Cassie to see the future.

"Guava and cream cheese," she says, handing me one. "It's a shame I couldn't make my chicken version. Cassie doesn't eat cilantro."

"It tastes like soap," Cassie says. Sandy shoots a long-suffering look my way.

It's midafternoon, and we've crossed off all but one place from our list. But we've got an hour to kill before the last item:

Lotus Valley Central Caverns, three p.m. Our appointment with the Mockingbird.

And so Felix, with a pointed look at Alex's slumped shoulders, suggested we catch our breath. We've been at the table for about ten minutes before I notice Alex sunken into the living room couch, head tipped back, eyes closed. So his plan to "just sit down for a minute" is going great.

Sandy ducks out after ten minutes to finish packing the evacuation bag, and Cassie hesitates, then trails after her. Leaving Felix and me to load up on a new round of pastelitos at the kitchen table.

"Tired?" he asks.

"Nah," I say, which is a blatant lie. "You?"

"Aces," he says.

I snort into my hands.

After a beat, Felix frowns. "Nothing from the boss yet," he says, looking down at his blank phone screen. "You think she's right about Cassie's parents?"

"I only know what Cassie thinks. Which is no." I'm more worried about what's in front of us now: the pages of notes each of us took today. "And if it's not . . . what do we do with all this?"

"Not for us to figure out," Felix says with a shrug. "Not for me, anyway. My internship's over in less than a year. And until then, my only job is to do what Jones tells me to do."

I watch him across the table. "You don't like her, do you?"

"I like her just fine. It's just . . ." He sighs. "Did she tell you she was at design school, before Rudy?"

"No," I say. "But that doesn't sound like any of my business."

"I mean, it was . . . a bad time from what I know," he says. "But it's not like you have to give up on something you *want* because something bad happened to you."

"Or her priorities changed?" I say, completely perplexed. "It seems like this job matters to her."

Felix struggles with his words for a moment. And finally, he mutters, "I know. I just don't know if *Alex* knows that."

And just like that, the conversation changes to a language I can understand.

"He doesn't *need* to go today," Felix says. "He won't admit it, but the Mockingbird tormented him, when he was a kid. He shouldn't—"

"You don't think this matters to him, too?" I say. "He knows what happened before wasn't his fault. And he's good at this job."

"Well, of course he's good at it," Felix blusters. "But there's other things he'd be good at. There are *safer* things he'd be good at."

"Listen," I say flatly. "There's nothing less cute than a guy who thinks he knows what's best for you. If you really like him, you should think about trusting him first."

Felix's eyes go wide. Then wider. I can see the blood creeping up his neck and into his cheeks. And I realize my mistake.

"Oh." I laugh nervously. "You never actually—I assumed—"

He shoots me a long, tortured stare.

I venture quietly, "Was it a secret?"

"Oh," Felix says. "Oh no, it's obvious, isn't it?"

"No!" I say quickly.

"Do you think he can tell?" he hisses.

"I don't really . . ." I make a vague gesture. "You know, my best friend used to call this my soap opera senses?" He doesn't seem to find that as charming as Gaby did. "He probably can't tell. I don't think so? I'm not sure."

"Those were three different answers!" Felix's eyes go saucer-wide. "Please don't tell him."

"I won't, I swear," I say.

"It'll make things weird," he says. "I mean, he wouldn't make it weird, *I'd* make it weird—"

"Felix." My hand hovers over his arm, careful not to crowd him. "I'm not going to say anything."

He takes a breath and looks me dead in the eye. "Promise anyway. Please. I just—I don't want him to feel like he has to—"

I hold his gaze until I hope he can see that I'm serious. "Not a word. I promise."

Cassie ducks into the living room, snatches a roll of packing tape, and vanishes back into the master bedroom. And the movement draws my eye just past Felix, to the edge of the kitchen counter. Where a paring knife sits balanced on the edge.

A wave of cold washes over me. It's possible that was there before, and I just didn't notice. Or the Flood is reminding me that we're not here to sit around and eat pastelitos.

When Gaby and I were thirteen, she dragged me door to door with her, handing out flyers for her babysitting business. *You look trustworthy*, Gaby had said, laughing. *I don't.*

I forgot for a few hours, didn't I? I'd started thinking like it was Gaby and me, walking from house to house. I almost had fun.

"Felix." I sound just like I always do—at least to myself. But he snaps to attention. "When something bad happens to someone. You don't think that might . . . set them down a different path?"

"Well . . . of course it might," he says with a shrug. "I just don't like to see someone choose a path because they think it's all they deserve."

We go quiet after that. Felix draws my notes to him, and I watch him for a while, flipping through page after page of Lotus Valley's fondest memories. If I look at him, I don't look at what's behind him.

And like that, we count the minutes until our appointment.

Seventeen

THE MOCKINGBIRD

I RUN A little water onto my hands, then push it through my hair, root to tip. It feels as windblown and coarse as it did a second ago, but now it's wet. So that did accomplish something.

I lean in to study my face. This past year, no matter how I felt, it helped a little to know that I was pulled-together on the outside. I don't know that I could say that now. My skin looks pale under the freckles. My face looks bruised from the lack of sleep. When I look at myself, my own brown eyes stare back, dark and unfocused.

Cupping some more water in my hands, I splash it on my face, too. And as I turn, I just barely see that my reflection stays where it is. She's looking down at her hands. At scrapes and bits of pavement.

"I *know*," I mutter. I get it. Break's over.

Down the hall, I hear the rustle of footsteps, the hiss of whispers. Felix's is too low to hear. Alex's is impossible not to.

"You don't get it," he's hissing. "You haven't *tried* to get it."

Felix mumbles something in return, his voice wavering, placating. Alex barely lets him finish. "It's bad enough that *they* treat me like glass—"

They drift out of earshot, Alex's next words tight and inaudible. I wait until they're well down the hall before I open the door.

I pick up my notes and backpack on the way out front, almost running into Sandy in the hall. She brushes off my apologies, her soft face pursing. "I can come along, honey," she says. "That old bat doesn't bother me."

I try to smile. Of course she can see through me. She's used to *Cassie.*

"We'll be fine," I say. "But thank you."

I step out onto the porch, narrowly avoiding Alex as he barrels through the door behind me. I'm not sure he notices me there. Felix trails behind him, defeat in every step.

"What did you do," I say.

"I just . . ." Felix says. "Offered. Suggested? That he could stay with Sandy while we—"

I blink. "Felix."

"I know," he says.

"You don't!" I hiss. "What did I just *say?*"

"He's exhausted!" he says.

"We're all exhausted." We both jump—neither of us saw Cassie slide out of the house behind him. "The Mockingbird's been taking clients for years now without issue. We'll be fine, as long as we follow the rules."

"Wonder if that's what Lotus Valley Community Radio thought," Felix mutters.

"I'm not saying she's reformed," Cassie says with a shrug. "But hunting got old, after so long. This is how she has her fun now."

Felix doesn't look convinced. "You don't like her, either."

Cassie flushes. But she tilts her chin higher, like that'll disguise it. "That's a personal preference," she says. Then she deposits the paper bag she's carrying into Felix's hands and follows Alex to the car.

I nod to the bag as we move to follow. "What's that?"

Felix wrinkles his nose. "Tribute." And he leaves it there.

He barely says a word the entire twenty-minute drive. Alex, next to him, is even quieter. For lack of a rock to hide under until the awkwardness blows over, Cassie and I restart the game in the back seat.

"Favorite soda," I ask.

"Seltzer," Cassie says.

"Oh, girl," I mutter. If I ever make it back here, I'm bringing her a Mexican Coke.

Cassie shoots me that crooked smile. "Worst subject in school?"

"English," I say. "Which is the only language I speak, so you can understand how embarrassing that is for me."

Felix, in the front seat, snorts. So at least I've accomplished something this afternoon.

I turn back to Cassie, still grinning. "Weirdest thing on your five-year plan?"

That was always Gaby's favorite question. And I thought it'd be particularly good for Cassie. But her face goes oddly frozen.

At length, she blinks, nodding to the street corner up ahead. "We're here," she says.

As we pull over, my phone buzzes with an incoming text. I've heard it enough in the past few days that the jolt doesn't hit me quite as hard this time.

How's it going? asks Christie Jones.

Not great, Christie.

We leave the car in a bank parking lot—"*Tow me*," Felix mutters wearily—and duck through a narrow alleyway. I would have missed the little door, if not for the panel next to it, and the neatly handwritten sign.

PLEASE ENTER YOUR CONFIRMATION NUMBER.

Felix would clearly rather not. But he keys a number into the panel.

There's a click. When Felix tugs the door, something gives with a *pop* that I feel down to my bones. And the door jolts open with a rush of cold air.

Alex takes a step forward, and Felix holds up a hand and quickly says, "I'll go first."

"You don't know where you're going," Alex says. But as Felix's stare lingers on him, he sighs, rearranging his tone into something gentler. "It'll be fine."

He all but vanishes as he steps into the dark of the stairwell. Cassie moves from my side and follows close behind, with Felix and me to bringing up the rear.

We leave the door open, but it's hard to tell—the blackness falls in like a curtain.

The ceiling opens up as we step in, and when I breathe, a rush of cool, heavy air fills my lungs. I don't get a sense until we're fully enveloped of just how vast the space is. By the light of our phones, the cavern walls look marbled, shaped by time, and maybe by the ocean that used to rush through it. Next to those walls, the staircase looks jarringly man-made.

I watch the corners of my vision as closely as I can, even as I take Felix's elbow and pull him toward me.

"Don't tell him how to feel." The words are barely a breath. Kind of hard to have a private conversation on an almost silent staircase. "Just be there."

"I thought I was supposed to leave him alone," Felix mutters.

"I'm talking about something *different*," I hiss. "Listen. I don't know what he went through with the Mockingbird. But I can tell he's terrified. And it's okay that you're scared for him. But don't make him comfort you."

He flinches, and I'm pretty sure I should have shut up about ten words back. But the next move I see from him is a nod.

Felix shakes my hand off as he slips around Cassie, and then all I see the rest of the way down is his back. I can't hear whether or not he says anything to Alex, but I can see their shoulders, nearly touching.

I think of the distant look in Cassie's eyes, back at the movie theater. And I take my own advice. Sometimes people are counting on you to notice when something's wrong.

Closing the distance between us, I slip my arm into the crook of her elbow.

She glances over, frowning slightly. "What's that for?"

I shrug. "Best to stick together."

I can feel Cassie's eyes on me, but I keep my gaze ahead. And after a moment, she starts to talk.

"It wasn't as bad for me as it was for Alex," she says softly. "But she likes the loners. And I wasn't a nice kid. I told my classmates' futures without their permission. So no one really talked to me. Just her."

I wait for her to elaborate. But as usual, she breezes on. "I was in fifth grade when she went legitimate. I hoped I'd never hear her voice again. But I already knew it was a foregone conclusion."

"Well." I shrug. "We're here to *change* some foregone conclusions, aren't we?"

Out of the corner of my eye, I see her smile. There I go again. Giving really pretty comfort I can't seem to apply to myself.

At the very least, I'm not scared—at least, not as scared as I should be. These past few months, I haven't been able to shake the feeling that something is dogging my footsteps. But whether it's something in my head or something waiting at the end of this hall, it's the same difference. If I get caught, I get caught. Either way, I get to stop running.

We reach the bottom of the stairs.

The cavern feels a lot like the Flood. Far too vast to see fully, but every time I breathe in, I feel all the years behind it, all the shifts of time and earth that created it. We draw ourselves into a tighter formation, listening. The air barely registers our presence. But something tells me we've been noticed all the same.

There's another sign, in those same neatly printed letters.

PLEASE MAKE YOURSELVES COMFORTABLE.

And a little lamp clicks on, revealing a couch, two armchairs, and a water cooler, all as incongruously modern as the staircase. There's a little rectangle of white propped up behind it like a tiny film set, a halfhearted illusion of a wall. A waiting room, right in the middle of the cavern.

Alex lets out a high, involuntary sound, not quite a laugh. Felix glances away sharply, as if he's intruding, and I have a sudden, fierce memory of Gaby's face the first time she saw me cry. How flat-out terrified she looked. How angry she got when I looked up and saw her and laughed until I choked. I forgot she used to think I had my shit together, too.

Sometimes in my head, I soften her edges too much. I forget her learning curves and her missteps and how she couldn't watch her mouth, even for a second. I don't have to soften anything. Thinking of that dumbstruck, slack-jawed face, I love her so much I can barely breathe.

I catch Felix's eye and jerk my head toward Alex, exasperated. And somehow I keep from screaming into my sleeve when he goes for the awkward shoulder pat.

Carefully, I sink onto the couch.

Felix settles on one of the arms next to me, and Cassie hovers on my other side. Alex stays standing. And we count down the seconds until three p.m.

The feeling of the room shifts slowly. It's a familiar sensation now. Like standing at the edge of a wave, bearing down.

I breathe in deep until it fills my chest. I'm used to the Flood's presence now. This doesn't seem that different. But something about it feels—smaller.

The lights dim, and the cavern ahead crumbles into the gathering dark. We stand, move forward. And something stirs.

"Welcome, dear customer," calls my mother's voice. "What do you yearn for?"

I start to move. It's not intentional, it just *happens*. But there's an arm, firm and unyielding, in my path. Cassie's.

A chill climbs up the floors and into my blood. I look to Cassie, who's closest to me. As dark as it is, I see enough of her face to feel very sure that it wasn't my mother she just heard.

And it's like my feet leave the ground. Like I've come unhooked, and I'm spinning.

"Hi there," I say hoarsely. "Big fan."

She chuckles, a low, rolling sound that could never be Mom's. "You're a clever one, aren't you? I like the clever ones."

Strange how my body's still standing here untouched, like my insides aren't collapsing in on themselves. I wonder if the others can feel it, too—the vacuum around me, the gaping black hole. I knew this already, knew it wasn't Gaby on that tape, but now here it is, undeniable, in front of me. It wasn't Gaby. It was never Gaby. Gaby is nowhere. She's nowhere. She's nowhere.

I can feel Alex looking at me. Then, softly, he says, "Hello again."

I still can't see her. But I feel her attention, unmistakably, shift to Alex. "Little one," she says, with something like fondness. "Sheila should have told me it was you. She's not a very good assistant. As appetizing as she smells."

Her focus narrows on him. It seems strange to say that for sure when I can't see her, and yet I have no doubt.

"He's here for work," I say. "Not for you."

"Is that so?" That brief softness in her voice—Mom's voice—is gone. "You should be careful with him. Something already took a bite. You can't bleed into the water and hope the sharks stay away."

I hear shuffling. Felix has shouldered his way in front of Alex.

The room shivers with her hum. "Are you still that scared of me, little one?"

Alex's breath hitches on the inhale. But when I glance back at him, he's drawn himself taller.

"Yes," he says, his voice small but firm. "But as of this week, I've seen scarier."

The darkness ahead stills. Out of the corner of my eye, I can see Felix gaping at him. If we survive this, I'm going to tell him that he's not nearly as subtle as he thinks he is.

"All right," she says, imitating his careful cadence. "You know how this goes. Payment first, and then we talk."

Felix has started to look queasy. But he grabs the paper bag.

"Brave boy," she croons. "On that cement block, right there. That's right."

Very carefully, Felix shakes out the contents of the bag and unwraps it from butcher paper, and my stomach does a flip—it's meat. Bloody rare. There's a sharp tug, like a pull of the current, and it vanishes into the dark ahead.

I try very hard not to listen too closely to the wet smack of each swallow.

"I certainly hope there isn't a problem," she says between chews. "I run a legitimate business, as your sheriff well knows."

"You know why we're here," Cassie says. We all feel the Mockingbird's attention shift to her, and despite the wobble in her voice, she presses on. "And yet you made us wait a full—"

"You know, you're all being terribly dramatic about this whole business," the Mockingbird drawls. "You have another day before your prophecy comes to pass, don't you? The days before a disaster are a busy time in my line of work. Your poor planning is no reason to cut in line."

"Then we'll make this quick," Alex says. "This is about one of your customers."

There's a short, intrigued silence. "My clients expect confidentiality. I can't hope to create a safe space here if I hand their most trusted secrets to the law."

"Safe space," Felix says flatly.

"*Emotionally* safe," the Mockingbird allows. "And how am I to remember every commission?"

"I think you'd remember," Alex says. Polite as ever. But the sharp certainty makes me look.

"How's that, dear?" the Mockingbird says.

"This was a specialty order," Alex says. "Your premium package."

I've never *felt* someone smile before. But it's unmistakable. "I'm sure I don't know what you're talking about."

"It sounds like you care about your business," I say before I lose my nerve. "I'm sure you'll be disappointed to lose it."

"The destruction of buildings means nothing to me, clever one," the Mockingbird says. "This town will continue, one way or another. It always has."

"And do you think it's *just* the town above that's at risk?" I say.

"Meaning what?" says the Mockingbird.

"Oh!" Cassie, catching my glance, blinks her big blue eyes. "Gosh, this is awkward. This isn't public information, but since small businesses are so important to Sheriff Jones, we'll make an exception."

"This isn't going to be an ordinary flood," I say. "It's the ocean that dried up here all those years ago coming back home. The ocean that must have formed these caverns. And I don't know, Cassie. What do you think is going to happen to this place when it floods?"

"Good question," Cassie says. "It's embarrassing, but I don't always see *everything*."

"She's only third-most accurate in town," I say in a stage whisper.

The Mockingbird's voice is low when she speaks again. "You're bluffing."

"I wish I was," I say. "Now. I'm here because of a broadcast that couldn't possibly exist. The voice of someone I lost. Was what I heard your 'premium package'?"

There's a long, cold pause. And then somewhere ahead, a slow breath in.

"How clumsy of me," she says. Her tone is light. But the temperature drops. "But let's look on the bright side. I can point you in the right direction. And perhaps you can do the same for me."

"I'm not sure I can," I say.

"Don't be so modest, dear," she says. "After all these years, you've brought my old friend back."

Eighteen

THE QUESTION

I **LOOK OVER** my shoulder. It's an unconscious gesture now. Even when there's nothing there, even when it's just the present and nothing more, I never forget what's coming.

"If I'd known," I say brightly, "I would have come down a lot sooner, let you kids get caught up."

The Mockingbird lets out an agreeable hum. "Has anyone ever told you, my clever thing, that you say very little for a creature that talks so much?"

I let out a burst of air, half a laugh and half an exhale. "Ouch," I say. "Do you take requests? Because that one would have been perfect in my third-grade teacher's voice."

Her confusion is like a physical sensation. There's a shift in the atmosphere, from puzzlement to understanding. "Oh. It's not my voice that changes, dear," she says. "It's your perception. The same is true for many that you call the neighbors—we may exceed your limited comprehension, but you do your best to catch up. Sometimes, that means how you see us, or how you hear us, says more about you than it does about what we really are. When

I hear myself speak, I sound only like myself. But you hear who you most long to hear."

"Most of the time," Alex says.

Her sigh moves the hair off my shoulders. "I told you, it's not on purpose. It doesn't sound like anything to me."

"What doesn't?" I ask.

I can feel her considering me. It raises the hair on my arms. "We're not all the same, you know," she says. "We don't always speak the same language. That was my friend and me—your flood. Their words were not words. More like little wrinkles in the fabric of time. Our existences are long ones, theirs even longer than mine. I thought learning the language of my friend would be a fun way to pass the time."

"So your premium package," I say, "is you speaking in the language of the Flood?"

She laughs, a short, dismissive sound. "It's a fascinating thing, human perception. When I speak in the language of my friend, I hear my own words. But it's the language of memory, after all. And that's what you hear: your own memories. And to each listener, even the words are different."

There's a stirring at my shoulders, the pressure of someone drawing closer. The Flood, listening. I wonder if they recognize her.

"I always thought they were very sweet," she hummed. "I'm not a dreamer. But I like the way dreamers think."

"A dreamer," I echo. "I wouldn't have thought that."

"No." There's an edge to her voice now. "Not for a long time now."

"Do you know what changed?" Cassie asks. She's speaking to the Mockingbird, but her eyes are on me.

She pauses. "If we are born from humanity's actions," she says slowly, "then we are tied to humanity forever. I was born when the first lie was told—and whether I'm feeding on your fear, or confusion, or rage, one way or another I seem to need you to survive. That wasn't my friend. They were born of nature, of water and energy, creation and destruction. They shouldn't have needed you. But they wanted to be with you nonetheless. They decided, when their life as the ocean ended, that they wanted to be something different. Something gentler. They saw you, this different kind of life than the water they once held, and they wanted to become something that could live alongside you. They wanted to fill their currents with your short, turbulent lives. Your pain and joy. Your stories.

"But they never considered that all of you are as capable of destruction as they once were," she says.

"You think watching *us* changed them," I say.

"Why wouldn't it? You do such terrible things." Her voice shivers in my bones. "A hunter has to hunt. That's its nature. But you don't *have* to cause pain. You choose to. They wanted to become an ocean of memory. But what happens when those memories are as chaotic and ruinous as a storm? What does that ocean become?"

I flinch. Her voice has gradually shifted from Mom's. The last word is unmistakably Nick Lansbury's voice.

I wonder if you *really* hear what you want to hear, listening to her. I can't think of any scenario where I'd want to hear Nick.

"Prophet," she says. "This end you've foretold—you're certain it's my friend?"

At Cassie's nod, she sighs. "They never intended to return here.

THE VALLEY AND THE FLOOD

They always believed that if they did, they'd become what they once were. If they've come back to Lotus Valley now knowing what could come to pass, then they truly have changed."

"They didn't choose to come back," I say. "They were drawn here—*I* was drawn here by the message you recorded. Someone made sure that this would happen. That's why we have to find them."

"And I wish I could help," the Mockingbird says. "But they were a drop-in. Stole someone else's confirmation number. If you don't respect the rules, you don't respect me, that's what I always say. But they were an excellent tipper, and so few spring for the premium package. No good deed, I suppose."

"What did this person look like?" Alex asks.

"Don't remember," the Mockingbird singsongs.

"I find that hard to believe," Alex says.

"I'm afraid you all look the same to me," she says. "I prefer to know what's in the soul before I look to silly things like appearance."

"Ah," Felix says. "Yeah. We humans like to . . . take things slower."

"But," the Mockingbird says, "they said there was a person they had to meet again, no matter what—that this recording of my voice would help. They thought we had that in common. We don't, of course. Desperation doesn't become anyone."

"You think they were desperate?" Alex asks.

"To send that message out into the world?" the Mockingbird says. "Can you imagine how many times they would have had to listen to it? They planned to draw you in with the voice of your memory, clever one, but to them, it sounded like a memory of their own. I've been told that's a rather . . . painful experience for you."

Her attention shifts to me again, like an icy breeze. "All that money, all that time, just to reach you. I wonder why that is."

"Why don't you tell me?" It's sharper than I intend. Or maybe I do intend it.

"I simply recorded a tape," she says. "You should have seen to your own unpleasantness, if you didn't want to be drawn in."

"Meaning what?" I say.

"I can't presume to know." There's a rhythmic tap, like a clicking tongue. "But I've always thought the memory you hear is one that haunts you. If you had nothing to regret, I'd have no power over you."

Now that sounds like Nick. Like harm just happens, and she's got nothing to do with it. Maybe that's why it slips out.

"Must be nice," I say, "to be totally blameless."

Something in the air turns, like that warm, heavy shift before a storm. "It's hard to understand, I suppose," she says. "Perhaps this will make it clear."

The next words that come out of her mouth aren't Nick anymore.

"Rose. Tell me what he did."

It's not just Gaby's voice. It's *Gaby*. Sincere. Direct.

It's not like talking to the Flood. I don't see Gaby. But I'm *there* all the same, back in that moment almost two years ago. I can hear how I responded.

He didn't do *anything*, I'd said, which wasn't true. But it was a stupid, thoughtless thing. Nothing meant to hurt anyone. Nothing worth telling.

(A lie isn't a lie if the truth gets things needlessly complicated. Gaby knew that's how my brain worked, and she fought it. She wanted to hear everything I thought, even if it was complicated, even if it was ugly.)

I just don't like him, I'd added. That was true. Except not liking him wasn't the important part. Not liking him didn't keep her out of his car.

"You see now," the Mockingbird croons. "That regret. That's your poison."

There's a *click* in my blood, valves of adrenaline shuttling open. *Not now.* I've had badly timed panic attacks before, but this'd take the fucking cake. I look down at my feet, to the dirt of the cavern floor—*Ground yourself, remember where you are, you're here, you're not there, you're here.*

And then my vision clears. And a laugh punches out of me.

It's pavement. It's *pavement.* I'm standing on Sutton Avenue, the Flood's version with its bare treeless grass and its starless sky.

The landscape shifts, half present and half past. I can see Cassie, Alex, and Felix, their faces white against the dark. But even here, in the present, that light, misting rain is falling. It floats through us, touching nothing.

The color in the room drains, shifting the cavern's lamps to pale shades of gray. The air whirls, spinning us right into another memory. But I don't recognize this. I don't recognize the living room, or the two adults on the couch.

I recognize the girl opposite them, though. Younger than I know her now.

It's *Cassie.*

You know we can't, one of the adults—the woman—is saying.

Her face is crumpling. *You must have known when you—*

Why are you saying this? Cassie must be twelve, thirteen here. Behind her wide blue eyes, something splinters. *It's not like I wanted this to—*

But the scene changes again. A bedroom and a young boy, curled facedown into his pillow, his body shaking with quiet sobs. Around him, the outline of something massive, not quite visible. Something latched around his shoulders.

I don't see his face. But I hear Alex breathe, "That's me."

It's then that I look over at the three of them. And one look at their faces tells me they're seeing this, too.

The scene flips again. Felix crouched in a darkened room, on the floor behind an overturned table. His arm is wrapped around a crying girl—Natalie Meyer, from earlier. *It'll be okay*, he's whispering soothingly, but there's terror in his eyes. *It's here for me.*

"My, my," the Mockingbird says, her voice dancing with a dangerous lightness. "That's not supposed to happen."

"What is this?" Felix says. The Flood flickers from one scene to the other, almost too fast to register: me, Cassie, Alex, Felix, me again, me *again*.

But the Mockingbird's attention is still on me. "Why don't you tell us? My friend is following your lead."

"I . . ." The words hitch. My lungs are already squeezed tight. "I don't—"

"Take a breath and think, my dear," she says. "Haven't you noticed a pattern to what you've seen?"

Somewhere in the midst of the panic, what she's saying clicks. There *is* a pattern. I noticed it that first night, when I saw a neighborhood that looked like Marin's on TV, and the Flood showed me her party. I thought the Flood was recognizing my triggers before I did. I assumed it was deliberate. But what if they *are* following my lead?

"Do you understand now? What you see will always connect back, one way or the other, to what you're feeling. And whatever you see, my friend is experiencing it with you," the Mockingbird says. "There's something each of us need to survive. But memories are more than sustenance for my friend: they're comfort and sorrow, the truths they hold, the answers to their questions. You gave them an answer out there, whether you know it or not. Something about that answer changed things, for both of you. And you brought that answer here. Together."

My fingers lock against my upper arms, into the fabric of my sleeves. But the chill is somewhere deeper. Somewhere that can't be reached or warmed.

I thought we collided out there in the desert, two forces disconnected from gravity and spinning through empty space. I thought, I hoped, the Flood saw me in that car, saw someone who felt as alone as they did.

But they saw me leave Flora's the other night, didn't they? Long before the desert, they saw me in that kitchen. What almost happened. What I almost couldn't stop myself from doing.

And if they feel what I feel now, did they feel what I felt in that moment, too?

"You didn't create this storm, my dear," the Mockingbird says soothingly. "It's been building long before they met you. You're not the first my friend has followed, and you won't be the last. But all those memories, all that pain—they can't carry it anymore. And like recognized like, when they found you out there. You have quite the storm within you, too."

"Rose." Alex doesn't touch me, but I feel his hand hovering. "Rose, look at me."

Startled, I jerk toward him, and I look at his eyes, dark and wide in his pale face. I follow the path of his stare around me, over my shoulder . . .

. . . and into the Summers' kitchen. Not the one back in San Diego, the one that practically raised me on Flora's brownies and Gaby's sushi experiments. The kitchen of their new Vegas condo, long and narrow like a hallway. And I'm looking right down the barrel of Nick Lansbury's lopsided grin.

My thoughts are miles apart and hard to grasp, but there's one clear realization I can cling to: this doesn't stop until I calm down.

It's okay, I think wildly. I clutch at my hair until I remember to stop. *Fingers uncurled. Arms by your sides, shoulders back. It's okay. You're okay. It's okay, it's okay, it's okay.*

It's not exactly the Maurice-approved method. But it's enough that when I look back a few moments later, the kitchen is gone.

When I can finally speak again, I ask her, "What was that?" My voice is wildly shaking. "It's never been other people's memories before."

"I don't know, either," the Mockingbird says softly. "I wonder if that's how this starts."

"What do you mean?" Felix says.

"Their focus shifted," the Mockingbird says. "From the girl to all of us. Maybe that's what it will look like when they arrive. This entire town's history, bearing down upon us."

I keep breathing, careful not to think this through more than

I have to. If I think about that kitchen—about what the Flood must have felt from me, maybe still feels now—I don't know if I can keep us calm.

At length, the Mockingbird sighs. "Listen. Rose, was it? To be perfectly frank, I hadn't planned to do anything about this. If my friend wants to destroy this place, well, that's their prerogative. But I confess, you've got me fascinated. I'd like to see what comes of this conversation of yours."

"There's no *conversation*," I say. "They won't even tell me why this is happening."

"There's nothing I can do about that." She chuckles. "Except, perhaps, suggest that you get going. You have, at my estimate, a little more than a day."

"You're their friend." I'm begging suddenly. "You can tell them to stop."

"I wish that I could. Truly." And I think she actually does. "But there's only one voice that can reach them now. And if you can't speak the same language, you'll need to find some other way to communicate."

Her gaze shifts back to Alex. "Are you sure I can't tempt you to stay, little one? I'll keep you safe. However it goes."

His stare hardens for a moment. Then, grabbing Felix's hand, he tugs them both toward the stairs. "Thank you for your time, Mockingbird," he says.

I nudge Cassie to go first, and I start to follow. But there's a small shift behind me.

"Do you know," she says quietly, "what that boy hears when I speak?"

I don't quite look back, but I stop.

"Me. Just me, speaking." There's a strange, sad sound. "Such a rare thing for my kind, to be known by one of you."

The sound of her voice fades, leaving only a *swish* and pull, like a moving current. And slowly, finally, my eyes begin to adjust to the darkness of the cavern, enough that I can see all the way to the back. And there's nothing there.

I wait another moment, just in case. But she's long gone.

AUGUST 14, FOUR MONTHS AGO

NOTE TO SELF: Flora collects tragedies. She doesn't lead with *hello* anymore—she says, "*Two kids died in an ATV crash in Sacramento,*" or "*A little boy drowned in La Jolla.*" She dives into the tragedies of the day, sorts out the knives to the heart. And then she takes them straight to you.

It's a Saturday when she calls about this one. By now, this is normal. You don't think anything of picking up.

"Rose," she says, breathless. "A man down the street was taken into psychiatric care this morning."

The last thing you want to add to your day is the sadness of someone you'll never meet. But too tired to make an excuse, you nod through it. Mmhmm, Suzanne saw the whole thing. Mmhmm, Hector heard it on his police scanner. Yes, it was a volunteer firefighter—popular, well-liked, commendations from the city just last year—home with a wife and a newborn. Yes, the wife called the ambulance. Said she was scared he'd "do something."

Her voice drops on those last two words. And you, without meaning to, sit straighter.

"Do something?" you echo.

"To himself, Suzanne thinks. Said he wouldn't hurt his family. Wouldn't mean to, anyway." She heaves a giant shuddering sigh. "Irresponsible, don't you think? Bringing a baby into that situation. He had to have known he wasn't well."

Wasn't well.

You will talk for fifteen more minutes. You will hang up. And you will think about this for months.

"What's an intrusive thought?" you'll ask Maurice later that week.

It'll catch him off-guard. He'll say, "Why do you ask?" instead of just answering you. He's usually so careful about his questions, of coming too close without invitation.

You will tell him it's something you read. And that's true. You read it at the three a.m. point of an all-night Google spiral. You'll know what it is. You'll know the definition in your sleep by then. You'll want to hear it in his words.

His definition won't be different. Unwelcome, involuntary words and images, over and over to the point of obsession.

(Like you can't dig it out. Like every effort to untangle wraps it tighter and tighter.)

But then he'll look at you and smile. And he'll say, "It happens to everyone."

"Everyone," you'll say, dubious.

"If I told you right now not to think of a polar bear," he'll say, "what else would you think of but a polar bear?"

"Well." You smile past dry lips. "At any given time I'm thinking about polar bears."

Wasn't well.

You don't have a spouse, but you have Mom, and Dan. You don't have a newborn, but you have Sammy.

Sometimes you'll stand in front of the mirror for long quiet minutes. You don't look dangerous, you think. Maybe if you did, fewer men would scream at you from their cars. But you'll think of those ads on the bus, too. Those posters of girls, always blonde, thin, and white, tear tracks lit in sepia. MENTAL HEALTH AWARENESS, it advertises. It never says what to be aware of.

Imagine what people would see—if you wore your insides out, if they could see your thoughts projected. Imagine what they'd think. Hysterical. Paranoid. Crazy.

Mom, and Dan, and Sammy—they wouldn't look at you like that. They'd never.

They just might not look at you the way they do now.

The volunteer firefighter is doing better, you'll learn three weeks from today. He looks happier. He's gained some weight.

"But you never really know," Flora will sigh into the phone.

"Mm," you'll say to a fixed point on the wall. "I guess not."

Nineteen

THE HOME AWAY FROM HOME

THE PATH AHEAD has split into two.

In one, the alleyway entrance to the Mockingbird's office, undisturbed by the things set into motion at its core. In another, the kitchen of the Summers' condo narrows to a sharp point, Nick Lansbury standing at the center.

The image of the kitchen holds for a moment. The light mist falling over both of us belongs on Sutton Avenue, not here. But it pools on the floor. It flows down the cabinets in rivulets. Nick's hair is soaked, plastered to the sides of his face.

And closer than ever, that roar. I can make out another sound now. Something churning.

"Rose."

The images overlap as I blink. The ground rising and flattening, pavement to tile, pavement to tile. The windows of the buildings around us shrinking and narrowing into cabinets. Nick, everywhere, no matter what I'm seeing. Everywhere as always.

"Rose."

Like a screen door, the present moment slides back into place.

We're standing in Lotus Valley, Nevada: the door to the caverns behind us, faint signs of life from the street. But that cold, damp air engulfing me, the slight shift of the colors in the world like a winter day sapping the brightness of the sky—those don't fully recede.

My fear is driving the memories I see. Whatever I'm feeling, we both feel it. And if I spin out, so does the Flood.

So calm down.

Sure. Thanks, Rose. What a revolutionary concept.

"Rose."

My shoulders jerk upward. Cassie's calling me. I heard her the first time. Did I not answer her the first time?

"Y-yeah," I say. "I'm here."

Not how I meant to say it. She notices, too.

Past her shoulder, Felix is saying something to Alex in a low voice. Alex nods sharply but doesn't look up—he's holding his palms down and flat in front of him, staring kind of wonderingly at his quivering hands. I know that look That look that says you didn't realize how scared you were until just now.

Alex glances at me, over my shoulder. Which he probably can't help. If I could see what he sees, I'd be staring, too.

Felix, on the other hand, is looking right at me.

"Whatever you're thinking," Cassie says, "stop."

"I didn't say anything." Felix's mouth snaps shut briefly. "But maybe I should."

"Felix—" Cassie starts.

"It's okay." My thoughts feel fractured, the way they always do after a panic attack. "Let him say it."

Alex's hand is still shaking as he takes Felix's elbow. "This isn't her fault."

"I *know*. So you can all stop looking at me like that," he says. "I'd still like to hear what happened down there."

"Nothing that's going to happen again," I say. Nothing that *can* happen again. I could feel it that time, the full power of the Flood hanging over us. What would have happened if I hadn't calmed down?

"The Flood hasn't shown you someone else's memories before, right?" Felix says. "Hell, they've never shown *us* anything before."

"If they feel what I feel," I say, "then I won't do it again. I'll control myself better."

"Rose," Felix huffs out, "do you understand what's happening here? This thing is—"

"Dangerous?" I say faintly.

"Felix," Alex says. "Give her a minute."

"We don't *have* a minute!" he says, throwing his hands in the air. "We barely have more than a day! How are we supposed to help if she can't *talk* to us?"

"Maybe there's no helping them." There's a crackling static down my spine. I didn't mean to say that out loud.

Felix barks out a laugh. "First thing you've said that's made any sense."

"Listen to me." There's a bone-deep chill to Cassie's voice. "If I can be calm about this, so can you."

"Oh, well, if you say so," Felix says. "If you're going to tell us what you know, then tell us. Don't expect us to take your word for it."

"What I know," Cassie says in a low shiver, "would break you in half. So do yourself a favor and drop it."

There's a long stalemate, none of us quite willing to come close to eye contact. Finally, Alex clears his throat.

"I think we could use a break," he says. A little more pointedly to Felix, he adds, "*I* could use a break."

"Fine." Felix clears his throat and straightens. "I'll drive you back to the station."

Cassie's arm slides into mine. The edge in her voice hasn't quite left. "We're going to walk."

"Yeah. Sure." Felix doesn't look at me at first, as he passes. But before he turns the corner, I hear him mutter, "Sorry."

Alex doesn't say anything. But the look he gives me before he slips out of sight is—kind of soft. Scared, too, but mostly soft. I think that's what it looks like to have someone afraid for you.

Don't get lost in your own head. That was supposed to be my rule. But this isn't all in my head, is it? Not anymore.

IT'S A CLEAR, dry day outside. If this is the second to last day of Lotus Valley's life, at least it's a nice one.

We pass Paul's Pawn and Loan, and there's a line stretched around the corner; people shifting their worldly possessions in their arms as they wait to lighten their evacuation load. Across the street, Theresa leans against the side of the garage. She doesn't notice us. She's too busy watching the procession.

Cassie walks in step with me, careful not to crowd but close enough that any onlookers will know I'm with her. She takes a swig of her water bottle, then hands it to me.

"I should apologize," she says as I'm drinking. I almost choke.

"For *what*?" I sputter. There's only one harbinger of destruction in this conversation, and it's not her.

"That night at the diner. You told me about your PTSD," she says. She either doesn't notice the flinch or ignores it. "I haven't thought about how this must be affecting you. The things you must be seeing. And I'm sorry for that."

"You've been nothing but nice to me," I say slowly.

"Partially so you would help. So you'd trust me," she says with a shrug. "I'm told sometimes I can be . . . careless with people. You might have noticed by now that I can't always tell what we've talked about and what we haven't. Sometimes I don't have the patience for conversations. Where I'm concerned, we've already had them and moved on."

"You don't have to be nice," I say. "You'd have every right to blame me for this."

"That's the good thing about looking ahead," Cassie says. "I was done blaming you a long time ago, even before I knew for sure that it wasn't your fault. And if blaming you fixed anything, you'd have that covered by yourself, wouldn't you?"

I wince. "That's fair."

"It's really okay." She laughs. "The first time I saw tomorrow night—that was such a long time ago. I've seen it from every angle since then. And I've seen glimpses of your life. So many times now. So when I tell you that it's not your fault, or even the Flood's fault, that's not to make you feel better. That's because it's true. Most bad things happen without malice, y'know? They just *happen*. Storms never wish anyone harm. They just come and go."

Something about the way she says it sends a rush of goose

bumps up my arms and legs. "What did you mean before, what you told Felix?"

There's enough of a beat that I know she's scripting an answer. "I don't blame him for being scared. He has a big family. He wants them out of harm's way. But that doesn't mean he gets to forget that the rest of us are scared, too."

I nod. I don't buy for a second that that's it, not when she still hasn't told me how the prophecy ends. But she's respected my silence countless times, without question, in the past day and a half. The least I can do is return the favor.

Cassie chews on her lip for a moment. "Rose. What happened with the Mockingbird . . . you don't have to explain it if you don't want to. But maybe you should think about telling someone."

I laugh weakly. "I don't think I'm ready to hear what they'd have to say."

Cassie's eyes narrow. Not the answer she was expecting, I think. "What do you mean?"

I concentrate on my feet, shifting my weight. "Not everything 'just happens.' Sometimes it happens because someone didn't do all they could."

She looks perplexed at first. She gets this look, like she's doing math in her head. Then her eyes get wide.

"Oh no, Rose," she says. And she looks—sympathetic? "You haven't been—Oh no, no, no. It's not like that."

"What's not?" I say slowly.

Suddenly, we're not walking anymore. She's facing me, holding my shoulders. "Listen to me," she says. "What happened to that girl was an accident. Just an accident. It's not like what he did with you."

There's a pause. A long, cold moment I can't quite put my finger on. A burn of metal up my throat and across my tongue.

"What did you say?"

Cassie's eyes get wide in her pale face. "I hadn't told you yet," she whispers, her voice hoarse. "Had I?"

I saw you, she'd told me, yesterday. *Just you, standing in the middle of this empty road.* But she saw more than that.

"You saw what happened to her." My tongue feels thick. The metallic taste floods my stomach, dissolves into a rush of churning blood. "No . . . you saw *all* of it. What happened to me, too."

"I'm so sorry, Rose." She's stammering, clasping her hands together. To her, we've had this conversation, already moved on, and yet she's at a loss for words. "It wasn't supposed to go like this, I—"

"Oh my God." Laughter bubbles up, unstoppable. "I haven't told anyone. I was never going to tell anyone, and you knew. You knew before it even happened."

"Rose." Her hands hover at the edge of my space. "Why don't you sit down."

We lock eyes. I wonder what she sees in mine to make her look at me like that. I wonder if she can see threads of cause and effect as easily as she can see futures. I don't want to sit. I want her to explain.

Did you see what I agreed to, that night on the road?

Or *I didn't want him to lose his license, can you believe that?*

Or *Would she have gotten in his car if I said something? If I picked up the phone?*

Or *Did you see what happened to her?*

Did it look like it hurt?

Did they mean it when they said it was quick?

What finally comes out is "I'll meet you at the station."

"*Rose*," she says again, in a rush of air. "I don't think you should be alone."

It's like there's a break in the water, and I drag myself to the surface. I can convince her I'm okay. If there's one thing I'm good at, it's looking okay. But I can't keep talking to her—not like this.

Because next time I open my mouth, everything might come tumbling out.

"I'm fine," I say. "I am. But I need a minute."

Cassie chews on her lower lip. "If anything happens, *call me*. I mean it."

"I will," I say. I think she hears just how perfunctory that sounds.

"Listen." She drags a hand through her curls. "You don't have to talk to me. Just . . . maybe it'll be easier. That you don't have to start from the beginning."

She watches me for a long time as she walks away. The ghost of her stare lingers after I turn to the empty road.

EVEN THOUGH LOTUS Valley looks empty at first glance, there are surprisingly few places to be alone. Everywhere I try, there's always someone staring, or trying to talk to me.

I end up wandering in circles at first. Walking used to help—especially at night, when the sounds of my neighborhood were sleepy and muted. That was never Mom's favorite habit of mine.

But there were no dangers out there that I hadn't already thought through, back to front.

I should try the Flood again. I haven't seen them since I left the Mockingbird's. But my vision is still swimming, and my tongue feels heavy in my mouth.

Eventually, my aching feet decide for me. So I find the quietest place I can to sit: the back steps of the Sweet as Pie Diner.

The back door stands open, straight into the kitchen. Faint sounds filter through: the clinking of forks, the sizzling on the stove, and the murmur of the TV on the counter. Maggie Williams's inescapable voice.

The time is now, she says. *Your civic duty is clear. Vote YES ton—*

The auburn-haired waitress is by the counter, spacing out even pours of coffee. When I shift on the stairs, it gets her attention. She doesn't seem startled, though. Her mouth thins into a thoughtful line.

And then she does something I don't expect. She reaches over, turns the dial, and shuts the TV off.

"Adrienne—" someone starts to complain.

She cuts them off with a look. "You ain't watching it," she drawls.

And then leaving the mugs on the counter, she crosses the kitchen to the back steps.

"I'd bring you some of that coffee," she says. "But something tells me you don't need it."

We look at each other for a long moment. Then she giggles. And surprisingly, I laugh, too.

"Rough day?" she says, grinning.

"Nah," I say. "Living my best life."

She throws her head back and flat-out cackles. "Can I let you in on a secret? Get the Home Away from Home. Cures all ills."

"Oh . . ." I glance at the laminated menu on the back door. Sure enough, there it is: THE HOME AWAY FROM HOME SPECIAL. PLEASE INFORM YOUR WAITRESS OF ANY FOOD ALLERGIES OR UN-PLEASANT TASTE ASSOCIATIONS.

I have several follow-up questions. But what I end up saying is "Strawberries make my mouth itch?"

"Home Away from Home without strawberries, got it," she says, already half turned away.

"But I—" I crane my neck after her. "I don't have any money!"

Adrienne waves blithely as she sweeps back into the kitchen. "I'm putting it on the sheriff's tab."

She closes the door partway behind me, shielding me from the craned necks of the diner patrons. And the sound of clinking forks and sizzling oil goes quiet.

I look down at my phone, wincing. I was more distracted than I thought. My nerves have been so finely attuned to my buzzing phone this almost-year, it's not like me to miss any texts.

From Christie: *Just got back. Heard about Mockingbird's. You okay?*

From Alex: *Felix is sorry. I don't know if he'll tell you that, but he is.*

And more than a few from Cassie.

I'm so sorry I told you like that.

I really thought we'd talked about it already.

I know it doesn't compare but we can skip my next few turns in the game? You can ask me anything you want.

I smile. Not the best way we could have discussed it, yes. But it's nowhere near her fault.

For a second, I consider how easy it would be to tell her everything. The urge doesn't quite fade even after I type, *next question: five most overrated John Jonas prophecies?*

Her responses come rapid fire:

omg

Buckle up

I've been waiting all my life for this

I laugh and set my phone aside. And I let that overpowering, momentary longing fade completely.

The door creaks open, and Adrienne backs through with the plate of food, a puzzled look on her face. "Gotta tell you, this is a new one. Where you from, anyway?"

Without thinking, I start to answer her, but when she places the plate on the step next to me, I forget the question completely.

Four fat pieces of hand-rolled sushi are lined up across the plate, perfectly spaced. They're inexpertly done, uneven at the edges, not quite fully closed at the ends. Just how Gaby would have—

Mouth dry, I pick one up to get a better look. In the center of the rice, a single slice of avocado has been lined up against a slab of mango.

"Who made this?" My own voice sounds distant.

"You're looking at her." When I glance up, her smirk has settled into something softer. "It's not like I look at someone and know right away. But when I walk back to the kitchen it just happens. The taste of home, or your money back. My manager's guarantee, by the way, not mine. And sorry about the rice. Best I could do on short notice."

I absorb about half of what she says, one of the rolls still pinched between my thumb and index finger. Distantly, I hear Flora's voice: *A meal has a protein, Gabrielle.*

And Gaby, muffled, biting into a chunk of mango: *I'm a rebel, Mom.*

In my daze, I remember what she asked before. "My best friend, um—she took a class, with her stepfather," I say quietly. "How to make sushi. And since then she was a *monster*. She wanted to roll everything ever made in sushi rice. She was going to open a fusion restaurant with maki made from dishes from around the world. This was her favorite, though. She called it the avomango. She would have lived off of these, if her parents would have l—"

Abruptly, I realize I'm rambling. Adrienne is still looking at me with that soft smile.

"I should let you try it," she says. "But if it's not right, let me know, okay? Anything I've made once, I can make again."

She sweeps back toward the kitchen, and I raise one of the rolls halfway to my mouth. Gaby would kill me for not using chopsticks. But Gaby's not exactly here to complain.

My eyes close as the flavor melts across my tongue. She's right. The rice isn't perfect. It doesn't matter. It tastes like long nights in Jon and Flora's basement, watching bad movies and sneaking drinks from the lower cabinet.

It tastes like home. Or at least how home used to taste.

DECEMBER 27, THREE NIGHTS AGO

NOTE TO SELF: Maurice can be wrong.

Well, no. That's not fair. His exact words were *If you could tell one person in your life what's been happening, who would you tell?* He never said, *Tell Flora.*

And you should have known better. The second it's out of your mouth, you know it was a mistake.

"What?" she says.

This past year, you've learned the twitches and creases of Flora's face to the minute. Even after she moved, even over the phone, you know her. You see her straighten. You see her blink. You see her knuckles whiten.

"It sounds more dramatic than it actually is," you say quickly. It didn't sound that dramatic. You were so sure of that. You used that full name, clinical and straightforward. No four letters. But she heard them anyway. Loud and clear.

For a moment, you think her face is about to crumple. Then the set of her mouth thins into placid confusion.

"That doesn't sound right, Rosie," she says.

There's a weightless feeling in your stomach. Like you missed a stair, and you're falling.

"No, I'm . . ." You swallow. "Like I said, my therapist—"

"Have you told him everything?" She sounds delicate. She never sounds delicate. "I mean, you've always been so sensitive. That doesn't mean you're . . ."

It's a different story than she told every time you were allowed to do something that Gaby couldn't. If you were allowed to watch scary movies, or walk to the store by yourself, or stay at home alone, it was only because you could take care of yourself. *Rose can take care of herself. Rose can take care of herself.*

This isn't how you practiced it. If she cried, if she panicked, if by some miracle she *understood*, then you'd know what to say.

"I really think it's different," you say. You try for conviction. It doesn't stick.

"Have you thought about trying someone else?" she says. "Like a second opinion. You're grieving, sweetheart. Of course you should talk to someone. But what you're talking about— that's a serious condition. That's . . ."

Dangerous. She's not going to say it. But you're going to hear it nonetheless. And there's a long moment of hot white noise after.

It's weird to wish that your therapist was here. But right now he'd give you that side-eye, this incredible look of pure salt you never used to think he had in him. That look he gives Flora— well, the idea of Flora—more often than anyone. *She's having a hard time*, you always say. *So are you*, he always replies

If Maurice was here, you might take that unsaid word for what it is. An intrusive thought. More to do with her than with you. But here's the thing. Maurice isn't here.

"Yeah" is what you say. What you hear yourself say, without much conscious choice on your part. "Maybe."

Flora's face tightens. "Please don't be upset, Rosie."

"I'm not," you say quickly, because comforting Flora is solid ground. This, at least, you know. "I promise. I'm just . . . gonna get us more tea."

Her mouth is still slanted, unsure. You hug her on your way out the door. What else would you do?

You wait until you're in the stairwell to breathe.

Believe it or not, there are times when even your head can shut up. Doesn't mean it's quiet, though. There's electricity in your veins, a buzzing in the absence of words.

Dangerous.

It's been half a year now since you realized, standing in the hallway of your apartment, what's happening to you. It's felt like so many things these past few months. But not since that moment has it felt like a sickness again. Not until now.

You turn the corner. And there's someone else there.

It's not Jon. The figure at the end of that narrow hallway of a kitchen is taller than Gaby's stepfather, leaner. He's carrying a duffel bag, his posture as lopsided as his grin. And for the first time since the funeral, you are face-to-face with Nick Lansbury.

He keeps smiling. Because unlike you, he was expecting this.

"Hey, Colter."

Twenty

THE MISSED CONNECTIONS

THE SUN KEEPS shining, relentless, but the heat doesn't quite reach me. I lock my arms around my little takeout container of avomango rolls as I walk down Morningside Drive, but I can still feel the chill under my skin.

Cassie asked me, when I first came to Lotus Valley, if there were ever times when I couldn't get warm. Apparently there are.

She's expecting me by now. I think so, anyway. It's 3:58, which tells me nothing. If my watch could tell me when Cassie left exactly, that would be much more helpful.

But before I go to the station, there's one more thing I need to do. And I feel just steady enough to try.

"Are you there?" I say quietly.

I know they are. Sutton Avenue is swimming into shape in front of me. It shimmers, shifting when I turn my head. From one angle, it's the street that lives in my mind, flat and bare and starless. From another, it's—I haven't seen it for almost two years, but this is how it must look in reality. Buzzing with fireflies and crickets. Shrouded in trees.

Something cold brushes my ankle, and I gasp and jerk back. There's water trickling down the road, branching into little rivers across the pavement.

I turn toward the low, ever-present roar. Because I know what it is now. It's the beginning. It's the full force of an ocean, bearing down on us.

"I didn't meant to upset you," I whisper. "I did upset you, right?"

There's a hum that sounds like assent. Or it could be a distant car engine, here in the memory. But I'll take it as a yes.

"Was the Mockingbird right before?" I say. "Were you feeling what I felt?"

This time, I hear it in the air, down to the tone and texture. *Mmmhmm.* It rushes down my back like a shiver.

"I'm fine now," I say. "So you don't have to be upset."

There's a rustle in the branches that sounds distinctly like laughter. Which, frankly, is kind of uncalled for.

"Okay, okay, sure," I say. "A little less than fine."

Sutton Avenue flickers again. The air crackles with distant potential energy.

"Your friend—the Mockingbird—she told me what happened," I say. "You just wanted to watch us, right? And now here you are. What a species we must be to do this to you."

Silence this time. I venture on. "But it was me who did this to you."

This time I feel it, as clearly as words: a deepening of the chill around me. A yes, I think.

There's someone walking down the road to me. Indistinct enough, at first, that I start to get hopeful. But they're tall, skinny.

Not short with dyed black hair and a fluttering, long-gone maxi dress. And the image of Nick Lansbury settles, straight-backed and blank-faced, in the middle of Sutton Avenue.

"You saw me back in that kitchen. Right?" I breathe. This time, the Flood definitively nods. "So what exactly did we feel back then?"

He stands there, smack in the middle of my vision. The fulcrum of the memory. And undoubtedly, the answer to my question.

Unlike the Flood, I have the language to describe that moment, how it felt. But I can't do it any more than they can. The only thing that's held me together these past couple of days is that I've shoved every second of it to the back of my mind.

But they're watching. Quiet, unblinking. So maybe they need me to say it.

"Was I really going to—"

My phone buzzes, and the present snaps back into place.

I scramble for my phone, heart hammering. I really wish I could bring myself to turn it *off* already. Especially when I swipe up to find Flora Summer's name.

It figures. Gaby used to say her mom was like Beetlejuice. Say her name three times and she'll appear, asking how many carbs you've consumed today.

Can we please talk? the text says.

Maybe I should answer honestly. What's the point of a nervous breakdown if you're going to keep it to yourself?

hey! babysitting Sammy right now, I blatantly lie. *what's up?*

There's a long beat. Then she's typing.

You're not being fair, Rosie.

My chest feels tight. Hot. It's hard to believe I was shivering a second ago. *I don't understand*, I type.

Another pause. *It took time for me to forgive Nick, too. But it wasn't his fault. He still has nightmares.*

It's not the kind of thing I should laugh at. It's not, but—holy shit. According to Flora-logic, Nick fucking Lansbury gets to have trauma and I don't.

I'm trying is all I write. It's all I can get down. Even once I control my laughter, my entire body is still vibrating,

Please give him a chance, she writes back. *We could call you now.*

I know that if I did, she'd back off. If I white-knuckled it through a fifteen-minute call, it'd be over, done, back to normal. But I've done so many things I didn't want to since all of this started. Calling Nick is not going to be one of them.

not right now, I type. *I'm really sorry.*

A pause. *This is important. I thought you'd understand that.*

I shouldn't respond to that. I shouldn't be responding to *any-thing* when I'm seeing this much red. My fingers are typing before my brain can think to stop them.

if that's what you thought, why didn't you tell me you'd invited him?

There's an interminable beat, filled only by the sound of the sun sizzling on the sand. The next response comes not long after she starts typing.

I'm not having this conversation by text, Rose. Call or don't call. It's entirely up to you.

I almost fling my phone as far as it will go. The only thing that stops me is the knowledge that I'd just have to go find it again.

My breath is coming in shuddering gasps, though my eyes

are stubbornly dry. I think it'd probably feel better if I cried, like finally throwing up after hours of nausea. I used to be a crier. I cried at sad movies, and bad days at school, and the day at Astronomy Club when we brought the Thorn Brook Elementary kids to look in a telescope for the first time. But I bit it back that morning of the funeral, the morning I heard Flora's sobs and shoved my own away, and they stayed like that. I've tried going through the physical motions of crying, like it would jog my memory. But it feels clumsy and unfamiliar. Something's missing. Something's stuck.

It might be the eeriest part of this. It has some stiff competition. But nothing makes you feel sick inside like forgetting what you never had to learn.

Just down the road, I catch sight of Theresa's garage, and numbly, I walk toward it. I'll go to the station right after. But first I want to check on my car.

I pass a line of metered parking. Out of the corner of my eye, I see the keys dangling in the ignition of a sleek red sedan. Miles away, out in the desert, I see another car turn onto the access road and toward the highway. And the urge to slide into this car, to floor it until I catch up—it's unbearable.

But I'm surrounded by people who want to run as badly as I do. I can go home. They *are* home. And every one of us is in this mess because of me.

Even the Flood.

I pull my hand back. And the wide open desert closes in around me.

I jog the rest of the way to the garage.

"Theresa?" I ring the bell once, twice, and it echoes back to me.

Stanley the Sedan looks better at least. His car-guts are spilling out a little, but honestly, it's a relatable look. With everything wide open like this, maybe she won't be gone for long. It won't hurt if I kill a little time here.

Theresa's garage, upon closer inspection, is surprisingly normal. Her desk looks like anyone else's might. She has knickknacks. She has a to-do list, half crossed out. She has pictures.

I reach for one of the frames, even knowing I should leave them be. Most of them are of the same two people: a preteen girl and a middle-aged man with a potbelly and a warm smile. The girl has a gap-toothed grin and a sky-blue eye-patch over her right eye. Without that eye-patch, I may not have recognized the younger Theresa. It's not like I could say for sure, but I can't see her smiling like that, ever.

"What are you doing?"

I almost drop the picture frame. "I-I'm sorry," I say, gingerly placing it back among the others. "I . . ."

The words stick in my throat as I look up. She sounded angry, just now. But her face is blank.

I swallow. "I didn't think anyone was here."

Without looking away from me, she pops the earbuds out of her ears. "Didn't hear you," she says.

"I was coming to check on the car," I manage.

"I told you," she says. "I'll call you when it's done."

There's heat unfurling in my chest, like I'm having another panic attack. *Fight or flight*, my brain supplies numbly. *Or freeze.*

"I'll leave you alone," I mumble as I move toward the door.

She slides into my path.

"You know, Ms. Nobody," she says. "You may have been invited in, but take care that you don't make yourself too much at home here."

"I'm sorry," I say, my throat tight. "I don't—"

"Let me be clearer, then," she says. "Not everything in this town is about you."

Move, I remind myself. It doesn't work.

"If this is about your desk," I say slowly, "I'm very sorry. I didn't—It was wrong of me. I won't do it again."

She watches me for a long moment, with that hard, unblinking eye. And then smoothly, without a sound, she leans in close.

"Just messing with you," she says, her lips twitching.

Queasily, I smile back. But her grin doesn't seem to reach her eye.

"Your baby's coming along nicely," she says. "Should be ready in a day or two. Can't promise that it'll be done by showtime, but don't worry. If we have to evacuate, I'll give you a tow."

"That's kind of you," I say carefully.

"All part of the Gibson Repairs guarantee." Her gaze travels to the takeout container in my hands. "Didn't know the Sweet as Pie was selling sushi now."

My grip on the container tightens. "It's the Home Away from Home."

"Ah, Adrienne. Hell of a cook," Theresa says. "It's a shame, though."

It's odd enough that for a moment, I forget my unease. "What is?"

"The Home Away from Home," Theresa says. "She couldn't always make it, you know. Not until the day she lost her mom.

Went to work from the hospital hoping she could get her mind off things, and it just"—she snaps her fingers—"happened. But no matter how hard she tries, she just can't seem to make one for herself. Says it doesn't taste the same. Can you imagine how that'd feel? To give everyone that taste of home except yourself."

My panic is draining away. But something else fills my chest in its place.

She was so nice to me. So nice. But that means something different here in Lotus Valley.

"What do you think she would give?" I say. "To be able to make it."

I realize just how odd the question sounds when it's out of my mouth. But if Theresa's taken aback, it doesn't show. She blinks once, thoughtfully.

"If it were me," she says, "I imagine I'd kill for it."

Twenty-One

THE FOREGONE CONCLUSION

THE FIRST THING I see in the lobby of the station is Deputy Jay, pacing by the front desk. His hands keep clenching and un-clenching, and there's a sheen of sweat across his forehead. Either our impending doom at the hands of Lotus Valley's civic spirit is starting to get to him, or that's just his normal resting face.

"Oh!" He sits up so sharply, I think I hear his back crack. "Ma'am. I'll let Cassie know you're here."

Ma'am. I was *miss* to him before—when I wasn't a harbinger of destruction, I guess.

"I'll let her know myself," I say with a wobbly smile.

"Can I get you anything?" His hands are under the desk, but I can see the muscles in his arms working as he wrings them. "Water? Seltzer? I think maybe we've got some soda?"

"I'm fine," I say. As impossible as it seems, I think he's more anxious than I am. "Thank you."

He says something in response that I don't quite hear, and then I'm moving deeper into the building, down where the hallway opens. My heart is just starting to slow from my sprint across Lotus Valley, but now I'm dazed. Floating. Like on the off chance that this hallway and this building are real, I've been cut and pasted in.

I'll describe this to Maurice, if I tell him any of this. I'll bet he has a word for it.

As I round the corner, I see Alex is at his desk, working hard on his thousand-yard stare. And standing opposite him, leaning against the wall, is Sheriff Christie Jones.

She grins, though even that looks somber.

"Sorry I'm late."

"Welcome back." To Alex, I smile and ask, "You okay?"

He levels me with a long look. His face doesn't have a whole lot more color in it than when we left the caverns. But he looks calmer.

"I'm fine," he says. "It wasn't as bad as I thought it was going to be."

I narrow my eyes. "How bad did you think it was going to be, exactly?"

Christie Jones laughs. "Alex, would you mind bringing Cassie and Felix back here? I'll get Rose caught up."

She watches Alex's retreating back down the hallway, but she doesn't say anything at first. She crosses the room and sinks into Alex's chair, motioning for me to take Felix's. I glance down at her feet. And I see the shadows there warping, stretching toward me.

Rudy is struggling to get to the Flood.

She sees me looking, and she grimaces. "I've got him. Just be careful. I don't think he can control himself right now."

I nod slowly, and I let myself look away. It's not his fault, really.

Rudy's trying to protect Christie, like he always has. And I've felt the Flood all around me since we left the Mockingbird's. Right now we must be indistinguishable to Rudy.

"What happened with the Mockingbird . . ." I say slowly. "It won't happen again."

"Rose." She twists a lock of hair around her finger. "I know I've asked a lot of you. I know grown-ass adults who would've buckled under the pressure we've put on you. But I can't help you if you don't tell me anything."

The same thing Felix had said. It sounded so easy when you put it like that.

I fiddle with a Post-it note on his desk. And eventually, I start talking.

"I saw other memories besides mine," I say. "Cassie's, Alex's, Felix's. The Mockingbird says that's what it'll look like, when the Flood comes."

"I heard," Christie says.

I nod, eyes on my feet for a long moment. "She also told me that the Flood looked to me to answer a question," I say. "That I gave it the wrong answer."

Christie nods. "I heard that, too."

My voice drops to a whisper. "I think that's true."

There's a long silence. But she doesn't look surprised. "Just because it's the answer that brought you both here," she says, "doesn't mean it's the final one. Answers change."

I smile weakly. It's not like Rudy's with her for happy reasons. Maybe she'd get it.

"I think I'm different than I used to be," I say. "I don't . . . think I know myself so well anymore."

She nods slowly, her jaw working. "Well," she says softly, "I think that when we change, we carry our past selves with us, you know? For better and for worse."

My heartbeat stutters. The adrenaline is still primed from before, right at the surface. "Like I said, it . . . won't happen again."

Christie's smile eases into something rueful as she laughs. "God, you're just like Cassie. Since when did I stop understanding girls your age? I didn't think I was that old yet."

It's half to herself, like an offhand stray thought she'd happily let go. But I raise two questioning eyebrows.

"I love her like my own, you know?" she says. "My wife and I both. We're not old enough to be parents. Not to a teenager. But we always . . ." However she wanted to end that thought, she shrugs it off. "But Cassie thinks of herself as a guest in our house. Her parents send money every month, a Christmas card every year. But she never sees them. They live on the edge of town, drive out to Dead Creek to do their shopping, do everything they can to avoid us. All I know is that she had a talk with them one day, when she was thirteen, and they decided it was best that they live apart. It was the most bloodless breakup of a family I've ever seen."

She tips Alex's coffee mug in a slow circle. Round and round.

"Cassie was right, wasn't she?" I say. "Her parents didn't commission the Mockingbird."

She lets out a humorless snort. "They lost a child before Cassie. I thought that was as good a reason as any to call the Flood here. But Cassie said the only reason I was going was because I wanted to know why they sent her away." Christie grimaces. "Right as usual. The little shit."

"Do you think it was something to do with the Flood?" I say.

"Even now, they won't say. Said they *promised her*." She taps rhythmically at the edge of the mug. "Nice of them to start caring how she feels now."

I hope this Post-it wasn't anything important. It's in shreds now.

"You know what I think?" Christie says.

Nothing good. But I ask anyway. "What?"

"I think that if she tells me, she expects me to make her leave, too." A short breath, almost a laugh, punches out of her. "And who can blame her for that."

I twist the ruined paper around and around my finger, already regretting what I'm about to say. But she looks so miserable that I say it anyway.

"There's something else it could be," I say.

I wait for her to ask. But she doesn't rush me. She's raised her eyes to me, narrowed her attention. And she lets me start when I'm ready to start.

"When you tell someone something painful," I say. "Someone who loves you. You think of the worst-case scenarios first. That they won't believe you, they'll think you're overreacting, or that they'll react worse than you did. But what's the *best* case? That this person who cares about you so much, who wants so much for you to be okay, finds out how bad it's been, and that you never told them. And that you have to see that look on their face when they . . ."

I can feel my pulse in my fingertips, in my throat. But if Christie has any idea that I just danced much closer to the truth than I've gotten before, it doesn't show on her face. She mostly looks thoughtful.

"That's not the best-case scenario," she says.

My mouth curls into a tight smile. "Then what is?"

"That you tell them," she says. "And they understand."

"Understand what?"

When I turn, Felix's rueful smile greets me. He slouches against the doorway like it's holding him up. It may well be. Alex hovers behind him, and Cassie even farther. Like she doesn't want to risk eye contact with Christie.

"Sorry," I say to Felix. "I'm in your chair."

"I think after the day you've had, you deserve the chair." He shifts his weight from foot to foot. "And, uh. After how certain people here spoke to you."

"Certain people shouldn't worry about it." I smile slowly. "I can move."

"Take mine." Christie stands, hewing to the lengthening shadows as she crosses the room. "Rudy's getting restless."

I look down again. Sure enough, the shadows around her feet are still flickering. Unless it's my imagination, Rudy's stretching a little farther from her than he was before.

Felix crosses the room, but rather than sitting down himself, he rolls out the chair with a flourish. Alex shoots him a long, dubious look, but Felix's grin never wavers. To my surprise, Alex gives in, sinking into the seat.

"Jay's gone into full feeder mode," Felix sighs. "He keeps trying to offer me my own leftover tahdig. It's *my* tahdig."

"You know him," Alex says. "He gets nervous."

"Yeah," Felix says, "but doesn't he seem *more* nervous to you lately?"

"Let's let Jay deal with this his own way." Christie's tone has shifted, all business now. "I'll ask you what I've asked the others, Rose. Talking to everyone today, did you notice anything? Anything at all."

I let out a slow breath. "Well. John Jonas might've had the most positive view of the Flood that I saw. And Theresa's seen him at the pawn shop more than anyone else."

"Trust me, I'd love that," Cassie drawls. "But I don't think he'd do this."

"Let's not rule anything out," Christie says. Cassie determinedly doesn't react to that.

"Loreen Murphy's a frequent customer, too," I continue. "But . . . I don't know."

"Kinda seems like they're enjoying watching Maggie Williams squirm," Felix says.

"There must be easier ways to do that, though," Alex says.

"I don't know," Felix says. "Go big or go home."

"And . . ." I falter, not sure whether to say this out loud. "There's the waitress from the Sweet as Pie."

"Adrienne?" Felix blinks. "We didn't talk to her."

"I stopped there on my way back." I look to the floor, fiddling with the hem of my shirt. "Plenty of people here have been kind to me. I don't want to suspect anyone just for that. But . . ."

"But when you think about it," Christie says, "she gives people back what they've lost every day. And she can't give that to herself. That has to sting."

Cassie shakes her head tightly. "She's not on the customer list."

"The list was just one lead," Christie says. "Just because she wasn't *seen* there—"

"If we want to start suspecting people just for experiencing something tragic, we're back to square one." Cassie's still just looking at me, not Christie. "People don't come here for happy reasons. Why do you think it's just us here in this room? No one here has experienced that kind of loss except for you, Rose. We're not going to be tempted the way others might. We didn't even tell Sandy."

Now Christie's not looking at Cassie, either. "Sandy lost a twin sister, when she was young. She'd never do anything like this. But I didn't want her to have to make that choice."

The tension between them is palpable. I'm in no position to lecture anyone on communication, but someone needs to lock them in a room together.

"Well," Christie finally says. "Go for the sympathy vote tonight. Appeal to the Flood's right to be here. And keep an eye on those three, as well as anyone else who comes out strongly in our favor. Not to target our allies, but . . ."

"What if we told everyone about the commission?" Alex asks.

I nod. "The Mockingbird doesn't keep records. The pawn shop doesn't have cameras. But friends and neighbors are going to notice where you're going or who you've lost."

"Yeah . . ." Felix says. "But do they have any reason to believe us at this point?"

"More importantly," Cassie says. Her voice is brittle. "Does it really matter if we find them or not?"

Christie turns to her, and there's an odd, frozen silence. I fight the urge to slip under Felix's desk. "Something on your mind, Cassie?"

Another beat. And then, with a defiant raise of her chin, Cassie finally looks at her.

"What if the person who made that tape doesn't know how to stop it?" Cassie says. "What if they're just as lost as we are?"

"They know something," Christie says. "They have to."

"Why?" She laughs, high and humorless. "Because you say so?"

"Because I've tried everything else!" Christie snaps back. It hits the room like a shockwave. "It's this or give up, Cassie, and I'm going to keep trying, like you *asked* me to."

"Maybe you're trying the wrong things." Where Christie's anger is explosive, Cassie's is tight, restrained. But I can hear her voice shaking. "Maybe there's not a *person* you can blame this time."

"And what does that mean?" Christie says.

"It *means* that not everything works out like Rudy. Not everything can be *talked out*," Cassie says. "And if for one second you stopped worrying about the neighbors, maybe you'd be a little more worried about—"

What happens next is almost too quick to see. Christie barely, barely inches forward, just far enough out of the shadows. And Rudy rises up from the floor and lunges for me.

Christie is just as quick—she grabs and pulls at him, wrestling him back toward the floor, but the massive, hungry shadow trying to fight his way toward me is actually not my first concern. Because there's a fathomless chill spilling over my shoulders. Rearing up like a predator.

The office around us fades into a pale, carpeted bedroom, and distantly, I see a young woman, her hair in braids, her face cautious, her hands raised. Christie, maybe six or seven years younger. Before her, much smaller than he is now, I see Rudy, defensiveness in every line of his form.

Christie's mouth moves, forming the same two words over and over. I can't hear her. But I see what she's saying, and I wonder.

"It's okay," I breathe, timing the words with young Christie's. "It's okay, it's okay, he won't hurt you, it's okay . . ."

I come back to the present slowly. And when I do, I can faintly hear Christie, still telling Rudy the same thing.

At length, she turns back to me. She looks stricken. "Rose, I'm—"

I shake my head, try to smile, even as my stomach churns. Christie lets out a long, controlled breath. "Go ahead. I don't think I should be near you right now."

Cassie's out first, the click of her heels echoing ahead. The rest of us mumble our goodbyes and file out of the room. Alex sidles up next to me as we exit into the foyer.

"Are you okay?" he says.

I nod. I don't *feel* okay. Every nerve in my body is still trembling. But for the first time since I got to Lotus Valley, I'm hopeful.

Because for a second back there, whether consciously or not, the Flood showed me how they felt: cornered, agitated, even scared. And when I comforted them, they listened.

Twenty-Two

THE DANGEROUS GIRL

THERE'S ONLY ONE place in Lotus Valley big enough to hold the town hall. So within the hour, we're on our way to Lotus Valley High School.

Alex and I split off from the group and walk to the far classroom hall. They closed it earlier this year, he explains—ever since Cassie's prophecy, there's always a new wave of people leaving town during the summer break. They need fewer classrooms than they used to.

All around us, among the darkened doorways and lockers, I see little glimpses of Cassie's, Alex's, and Felix's lives. A cabinet of trophies: football, debate, Academic Decathlon. A small section of art projects. Class pictures from each year. The class sizes are dramatically smaller than my own back in San Diego. It doesn't take me long to find the shot from the end of last year. Felix with his arm slung around a stiff, uncomfortable-looking Alex. Cassie, standing a little off to the side, leaving an awkward gap between her and the group. And among the group, a few familiar faces from earlier today.

Next to me, Alex shifts his weight.

"This must be eerie for you," I say.

"A little." Alex attempts a smile. "But it's quiet."

"Can you try first?" I ask. Alex has more practice than I do. I want to see if it'll be any different.

He nods. And though his expression doesn't change, his face gets a little paler. "Is there anything you'd like to tell Rose?" he calls out quietly.

A stack of papers slips from the top of one of the lockers, and they slap against the tile hard enough that I flinch. They fan out, gently fluttering in the air-conditioning. At length, they shiver themselves still.

I think the living embodiment of human memory just left us on read.

"You should go to the gym," I whisper. "Maybe it will help if I'm alone."

Alex has this look like he doubts that very much. But as usual, he's too polite to say.

He steps back slowly, as if to give me time to reconsider. I won't, much as I want to. But I do finally get the courage to ask.

"Alex . . ." I chew on my lower lip. "What you can do . . . Do you ever wish it would . . . stop?"

The second the words are out, I wish I'd left it alone. But he doesn't shrink back, or ask why, or do anything else I'd do. He's quiet for a moment. Thoughtful.

"It's like part of my body now," he says. "I'd always feel where it used to be. And I—I don't just want it to go away. If I don't make anything of it, it's just something that happened *to* me."

I watch his face, shrouded in the dim light of the hall. I'm not sure what's helpful to say. But he's told me, more than once, what I need to hear. The least I can do is try.

"You're doing great, you know," I say.

His face, as always, stays closed, neutral. But something in it softens as he smiles.

"I'm not always good at hearing that," he says. "But . . . it does help."

I smile back. "Go on, I'll meet you in there."

He starts to turn and then pauses. He's silent for long enough, I think he might have reconsidered what he wants to say. But he gets there, eventually.

"I know it's a scary thing to think, Rose," he says. "But there's something that you and the Flood have in common. And if you find that . . . well. If nothing else, you can work from there."

He slips down the hall and out of sight. And I turn back to the hallway. Both feet planted frustratingly in the present.

"Is he right, do you think?" I whisper. It carries much farther than I meant it to. But still, nothing stirs. "Is there something we have in common?"

There's a *click* in the distance. Several someones just walked through the front doors of the school. I can hear low, furtive voices.

"I know you want to tell me something," I say. "But if tonight doesn't go our way, you won't have the chance. Show me something that will help. Buy us some time. *Anything.*"

There's a sharp sound. Rubber, squealing across pavement. My head whips to the side, but there's no street there beyond the window. Just a playground, still and quiet in the desert night.

There's a sharp, wet chill at my feet, and my head jerks down.

There's droplets of water blanketing the tile, sliding down the lockers. In the dark, they look thick and black.

Then seconds later, somewhere out in the street, I hear the crunch of metal and glass.

Out of the corner of my vision, the scenery shifts. And I shut my eyes tight.

"I don't need to see that," I whisper. They know that, don't they? I'm not Gaby. I didn't need to see the car. I didn't need to see the body. And I don't need to see what happens next.

"My." The voice that answers instead is one I've only heard in person once. But it's been following me around all day.

I open my eyes. Lotus Valley High has solidified, once again, before my eyes. The hallway is clean and dry. And Mayor Williams is walking toward me.

"Something wrong?" she says.

I take that tightness in my chest and exhale it out. "Communication issues."

"There's that wit," she says, almost warm. "Ace Martin said you were funny."

I can tell by the light, deliberate way she says the name: she's trying to trip me up. "I liked Mr. Martin," I say, just as deliberately. "I liked everyone."

Her face doesn't change. "I see," she hums. "You liked them so much you'll continue to put them at risk."

I hold myself straighter. "I like them," I say again, "so I'm going to do what I can to help."

"And you know for sure that you're helping," she says.

My legs still feel wobbly, like all that blood and energy is redirecting to my pounding heart. But somehow I *sound* calm.

"I'd love to," I say. "But I'm not a prophet."

She's giving me that same vague, pleasant look. But I can tell that landed. "If you've heard that," she says, very slowly, "then you've also heard I don't do that anymore."

"I have." My voice does waver, this time. "But they're not totally clear on whether you can't—or won't."

The pleasantness slides away like fabric dropping to the floor. Fluid, soundless, final.

"And you think you know?" she says quietly.

"I think that either way, you could try," I say. "And if you see something that could help, we could stop this together."

She stares at me a long moment. Unblinking.

"You know what I know for sure, Rose Colter?" she says. "That you are dangerous. That's the only information I need."

She takes a step back and settles her shoulders. Then she slides her politician's smile back into place as she sweeps past me.

"I hope you've said your goodbyes to that thing," she calls over her shoulder as she disappears into the dark. "One way or another, it's leaving tonight."

FELIX HAS SET up a line of chairs on the stage when I make my slow, unsteady way to the auditorium. I collapse between Alex and Cassie, the chair creaking from my sudden shaky weight.

"We'll start ten minutes late," Cassie says. "At least."

I blink at her. "You saw that?"

"No," she says, shrugging. "That's just a given."

I briefly meet Felix's and Alex's parents, seated in the first row.

Mr. Harper, almost as pale as his son, nods and smiles. Felix's parents, who introduce themselves as Dr. Abbasi and Dr. Sohrabi, are much more animated. Dr. Abbasi, a stylish woman with a sleek bob and a British accent, nods diligently to our pleasantries and informs me she'll look forward to my findings. Dr. Sohrabi is too busy taking video on his iPad.

"Baba," Felix hisses.

"You all look so professional," he gushes. One of Felix's three sisters swats at his arm.

Sheriff Christie Jones arrives ten minutes later on the dot, holding her parasol over her head. She nods to us but keeps a careful distance. I can see the edges of her shadow quivering.

"I want you all to clean up after yourselves this time," says a balding, exhausted-looking man into the mic. "I won't ask twice."

A cluster of teenagers in the back groan audibly. "This gym's gonna be gone by Friday, Mr. B."

"Then it will be pristine," Mr. B says tightly, "until the moment it floats away."

Mayor Williams arrives in a whirlwind moments later, like she's just rushed in, like the two of us don't know fully well that she's been here for the last fifteen minutes.

"Christie," she says, sugar-sweet.

Christie smirks. "Marge."

The pale flash of anger across Mayor Williams's face is quick enough that it's safely filed away before the audience can catch it. "Let's begin, then."

But before Christie can open her mouth, the mayor gestures to a familiar face in the front row. "Ace, you had something to say?"

"Maggie." Christie looks thrown. "We'd agreed to start with statements."

"Due respect, Sheriff, I don't think there's a need for that." Ace Martin eases himself off the seat. Maybe it's my imagination, but he looks apologetic. "Ms. Colter had the entire day to make her case. And I have no doubt that she means well. But we're unconvinced, me and mine. And we're not willing to risk this any longer. Motion to begin the vote now."

There's a flurry of whispers through the auditorium, and to my shock, someone in the crowd stands up before any of us. I catch a flash of auburn curls against a peach uniform—Adrienne from the Sweet as Pie. I try to watch her without staring. "Doesn't seem quite fair, Madam Mayor," she says evenly. "I say let them talk."

"Seconded," Sandy Alvarez calls out. She's looking straight at me, sincerity and concern in every inch of her face. I understand instantly why Christie and Cassie would never suspect her.

"One motion at a time, please," the mayor says. "Would anyone like to second Ace's proposal?"

"This is low, Maggie," Christie says tightly.

"This is democracy at work," the mayor chirps. "We've been having this conversation for years. I think we're all quite sick of it, aren't we?"

"Actually, I've foreseen several undecided votes." John Jonas, second-most accurate prophet in Lotus Valley, smiles serenely at the stage. "Your assistant, Loreen, for example."

"Thanks, John," Loreen drawls, barely glancing up from their phone. "Way to narc."

I don't think anyone misses the gaps in Mayor Williams's smile this time. "Then I'll ask that you decide quickly," she says. "I second Ace's proposal. We'll be holding the vote effective immediately."

"You'll be holding *a* vote."

Gaby's voice jolts through me, so completely out of context that I almost don't recognize it. It's only when I see the look on Christie's face and feel that ancient old chill that I understand why the back of the auditorium has gone so dark.

The Mockingbird. And she's not alone.

I catch familiar movements—the quick, hazy scurrying of the figures from the library, moving into the upper balcony seats, and the shadows at the ceiling bursting into chattering, snakelike streamers, just like at the movie theater. But they're not the only ones. I can faintly see a figure by the stage curtains, thin and unnaturally tall, peering at us through stringy hair. And though I can't tell what's under Ace Martin's seat, I see how pale he goes, how he mouths, *It's you.*

"I can't say I understand *all* of your laws, Madam Mayor," the Mockingbird says, with Gaby's voice. "But you can't just turn to the end of the book, can you? If I grasp your rules correctly, before you can vote, you'll need to vote on whether or not to proceed with a vote. Seems a bit circular to me. But if it makes you feel better."

I laugh. I can't help it. It's not how she'd say it, obviously, but it's just the way Gaby would twist it.

"Ms. Mockingbird." Mayor Williams goes stiff. "I didn't realize you'd be coming."

"Mmm," the Mockingbird says. "No. You *hoped* we wouldn't."

"Here to defend your buddy?" someone calls out, then promptly shrinks in his seat as the Mockingbird turns her focus to him.

"Here to cast our votes," she says. "As is our right. The Flood is one of ours, yes, as is the sheriff's pet. But we are here, first and foremost, as your neighbors."

Once again, I can feel her attention shift without seeing it. "Several of us lack hands to raise, Madam Sheriff," the Mockingbird says. "I'd be happy to tally on your behalf, if that's sufficient."

A bright, rueful smile spreads across Christie's face. Wondering, I think, why she didn't try this from the start. "I'll trust you."

The Mockingbird laughs. "Not always the wise choice, I'll grant you."

"All right, then." The mayor's fingers curl and uncurl. "All in favor of holding the vote immediately."

A number of hands do go up. But I'm more surprised at how many don't. Even Ace, his stare fixed on whatever's hiding under his chair, doesn't vote for his own proposal.

Rudy's limbs don't move. But Christie grimaces, sweat beading across her forehead, and glances at the parasol's shadow. "One in favor here," she manages. Whether Rudy managed to vote or just tried to lunge at me again, it's hard to say.

"Six in favor here, as well," says the Mockingbird. "Apologies, my clever one. But the confusion and chaos of my friend's return, the emotions and memories that would come pouring out of every one of you—that would be quite the feast for some of them. You understand."

There's a high, lilting laugh from the rafters. The same we heard at the hospital. "*Let us feed*," something whispers. "*Let us feed.*"

As if sensing my shoulders tense, one of the creatures from the movie theater slides around my neck and nuzzles. "Vote," it chirps. "Vote."

Christie turns back to the crowd. "And all against?"

The hands raise—the human palms high and open, the flickers at the balcony, the skeletal limb of the figure by the curtains. Alex reaches out to grip Felix's arm, as if by reflex. I know the feeling. Even without the Mockingbird's tally, it's more than half.

But I can't help but notice Theresa, directly in my line of vision, didn't vote for either option. She's too busy looking at me.

"Rose," Christie says over her shoulder, "I believe that means the floor is yours."

"Oh," I say. Yes. Right. That was the plan.

I move forward on the stage, a few steps away from Alex, Felix, and Cassie. It's like I've left them miles behind. Whoever wasn't staring before, they are now.

With a burbling giggle, a few more creatures from the theater descend, weaving in and out of my legs. "Are," one whispers.

"You," another volleys.

"Familiar."

"With."

"The."

"Entity."

"That."

"Was."

"Born."

"Here."

I'm not saying this in front of the Mockingbird, but they're my favorites.

"Yes, Ms. Colter," the mayor says through her teeth. "What insight *can* you share with us?"

I could almost thank her. The quick jolt of anger is what I need to get started.

"Not much more than you could, maybe," I say. "But I've spoken to them."

Another rush of murmurs from the crowd. "And?" Theresa speaks this time, arms still folded.

When I hesitate, a quivering hand goes up toward the back. "Are they good?" a woman asks quietly. "Or bad?"

"I don't think it's like that," I say. "I think they're too different from us to say what they are. It's like having a feeling you can't describe to begin with, and then trying to describe it in another language. They told me they would destroy this place. But I think they've been trying to tell me why. And if I can figure it out, then maybe I can convince them to stop."

Another round of murmurs. I can feel the Mockingbird nod approvingly at me.

"Why do *you* think they're doing it?" Ace says. It's not accusatory. Just curious.

"The Mockingbird said something changed them," I say. "That they believed they couldn't come back to this place without becoming the ocean they once were. I think they saw terrible things out there. And maybe now they can't see anything else. I know you're all scared. I can't imagine how it feels, knowing that you might lose your homes. But this town was built on something bigger than fear. I don't know if Rudy can stop this tomorrow. But there's something you all owe the Flood first. Something every citizen of Lotus Valley was promised."

"Which is what?" Theresa says.

"Hospitality," I say. "A home for living things that can't be home anywhere else. And more than anyone else here, this *is* the Flood's home."

There's a near-unnatural stillness. It's the mayor who finally breaks it.

"And do you think it's fair," she says, "that you're both gambling with *our* homes?"

I open my mouth to answer. But I don't get a chance. The overhead lights brighten, flooding the auditorium. And the scene changes.

Not now, I think. But then I realize that, once again, the memory we're in isn't mine.

The light lingers, spreading across the room, spilling from sconces and table lamps and floor-to-ceiling windows. There's a cabinet of fine china on one side, and on the other, a painting of boats at sea. And behind me, two blonde women, talking in heated whispers.

"Please." The older woman raises her hands placatingly. "Just one prophecy. Even a little one. They came all this way—"

"I don't *want* to." The woman opposite her is nearly identical—same sweater set, same shade of lipstick. But the outfit and the makeup create an illusion of someone older. She's my age. "I don't want any more customers. I don't want to see another future, *ever*."

"You don't mean that, Mags." The older woman smiles. Her hard, pleading eyes don't smile with her. "This is the most important thing you'll ever do."

I can see it the second it happens—the girl's spine stiffening. Calcifying.

"If I could stop it right now," she says quietly, "I would."

The lights dim, and the house dissipates back into a stage. The girl lingers in my vision, at first. And then she fades into the woman opposite me. Same sweater set. Same lipstick. Looking so much more like her mother than I think she'd want to believe.

"Well?" Maggie Williams says.

She looks confident—which means she didn't see what I did. Judging by a quick look around the auditorium, the Flood only showed it to me. But I smile. Not only because I see her, really see her now. But because back in the hallway, I asked the Flood to do anything they could to buy us some time.

And this, I can use.

"I don't know, Mags," I say. "Is it fair that you've made your childhood trauma our problem?"

Under the layer of makeup, I can see her go white. "Excuse me?"

"What's the plan?" I say. "Make this place normal, bit by bit? Hope that it'll make you normal, too? Because pretty soon you're not going to have a town to force your issues on."

"Th-this is—" Maggie rounds on Christie. "Are you just going to let her—"

Christie beams, leaning back against the wall. "Yup."

I never understood why Gaby liked picking fights. I'd asked her about it once. *I don't* really *like fighting*, Gaby had said with a shrug. *I like telling people about themselves.*

I take a step toward Maggie. She rocks back on her heels. "I heard what you told John Jonas. That you saw a future where your abilities controlled this town," I say. "That came true. You *made* it true. All these people are here tonight because what you can do scares you."

"That's *not*—" She whirls on the audience. "She knows she's got no one but herself to—"

"Trust me, I've got plenty of blame for myself." I almost waver. But I've come too far for that. "I *am* dangerous. But I'm not the only one. And if you've chosen not to help us just because you want to be normal? Whatever happens tomorrow is on you, too."

"Enough of this!" Maggie's voice breaks on the last word. Beyond her, I can see my words working their way through the crowd. "There is one reason and one reason alone why we're all here, and it's time we deal with the person responsible!"

"She's not responsible!" Deputy Jay blurts out.

The whole auditorium turns to Jay. He's been so quiet all night, I'd forgotten he was there.

"She didn't choose this," Jay says The words come slow, like they take effort. "There's something you don't know. Something I . . ."

The crowd looks baffled. Even Maggie. No one in our corner of the stage does.

"I'm sorry, Cassie." Tears pool in his eyes as, for the first time, he looks at her. "You trusted me with this. No one's ever done that before. And I . . ."

"What." Cassie doesn't sound angry. Or disappointed. Just final. "What did you do."

"I never meant to say it," he whispers. "It just happened."

Twenty-Three

THE NIGHT IN QUESTION

I HADN'T SEEN Christie Jones angry before. I'm pretty sure I could have done without it.

"And," she says, in the silence after Jay stumbles through his explanation. It's deadly calm, but I can see Rudy scrabbling at the corners of her shadow. I think if we weren't in front of a crowd, she might be tempted to let him go. "You don't remember anything."

"I'm sorry." Jay's lower lip is wobbling. He's so obviously crushed, it's hard to look at him. "They kept buying me drinks. I know it was someone I knew but—"

"You're the sheriff's deputy." Christie's voice goes thinner. Next to me, even Cassie flinches. "You know everybody."

"I didn't tell them everything." His voice drops to a whisper. "I just remember wondering what I was going to see. I was so worried I said too much, but I didn't think anyone would figure it out from *just* that—"

"I'm not sure I understand." An elderly woman in the crowd raises her hand. "You're telling us that this flood will bring back people we've lost?"

"It's not like that." I'm calm. I think I'm calm. But whatever Alex hears in my voice makes him touch my arm. "You don't get to choose what comes to you. And even when—even when it's what you *want* to see—you can see them, and you can hear them, but they're not there. It's worse, I think, than if they weren't there at all."

"But someone in this room has decided that it's worth the risk," Christie says. "That this town, and maybe even their own safety, is a worthy trade for even an echo of what they've lost. And if they won't come forward and tell us what they know, then we need to find them."

"So what do you want us to do?" Loreen says. "Or whatever."

There's a murmur of agreement. A stronger one than I expected.

"Well," the Mockingbird says. Her voice is Mom's again. "You should start by interviewing every woman in this room."

"Woman?" I echo.

There's a quick, confusing shuffling across the room—some turn to look at each other, and others turn to us. Felix, with a little triumphant laugh, gets there first. "You *do* remember what they looked like!"

The Mockingbird's laugh is a rolling sound, like thunder. "Apologies, clever one. I didn't trust before that you had my friend's best interests at heart. I'm afraid I don't have the eyesight that you humans do. But I can spot a lie from across this desert. My client identified herself as a woman. I did not detect that she was lying."

"Then I'm sorry to have to do this," Christie says. "I know you've all got packing to do, and I'll have you out of here as quickly as possible. But I'll need every woman in this room to stay behind."

Shockingly, there's another murmur of agreement. But this one isn't unanimous. "You can't know she's *here*," one man calls out.

"Oh, she's here," the Mockingbird says. "I doubt I'd recognize her, Madam Sheriff. Your scents are all so tangled now. But I can feel it in this room. That absence of fear."

She lets that sit for a moment. I sweep the auditorium. If the Mockingbird's client was a woman, that rules out John Jonas and Loreen.

"We'll cooperate," says Adrienne. I meet her eyes. She looks as scared as I feel. I'd really like to believe that she's as scared as I feel.

"Jay," Christie says. "I presume you remember where you were that night."

Jay sniffs. I know he's the reason we're here, kind of, but I feel a pang anyway. "Paco's."

"Then you'd better hope they still have the security footage," Christie says. "Because you and I are going to make a list of every person who was there that week."

"And the vote?" Ace Martin asks. But his heart's not in it.

We're still for a moment, save for Rudy. I can see him straining at the edge of the parasol's shadow. He can see what's closing around us—closing around Christie, his whole world. One slip of her hand, and the decision would be made for us.

Maggie smiles. It's tired this time.

"I think I know when I've been overruled, Ace," she says. "But all in favor of my proposal, please. Surprise me."

There's reluctance on some of those faces. A few shoulders twitch.

But not a single hand goes up. Even Ace, smiling grimly, keeps both palms flat against his lap.

"Sorry, Maggie," he says. "If one of us did bring that—that Flood here . . . then Ms. Colter's right. One more day. They didn't choose to come here. But they can choose to make this right."

"And I appreciate that," Christie says, as we walk briskly to the front of the school, "but you need to head home."

"I can help Jay," Alex says.

"Your father's starting to get worried about all these late nights," Christie says. "Felix, your father's out front, too. I'll send your mother and sisters home as soon as I can."

"They didn't do it," says Felix halfheartedly.

"Well, of *course* they didn't," Christie huffs. "But if the others see me giving out special treatment, they're not going to be cooperative."

"I guess that means I'm staying, too," Sandy says, trailing behind Christie.

Christie smiles hesitantly over her shoulder. "Glad to see you're still talking to me."

"For now," Sandy says. "We'll chat later about how you didn't think I could resist the temptation to destroy our town."

"I didn't!" Christie goes pale. "I just—"

But Sandy's already breathing out. "I *know*. And yes, it would have hurt, choosing not to see my sister again. But I'm an adult, Chris. That's a choice I can make."

Christie looks at her a moment, meek. "If it helps," she says quietly, "I also wanted to spare you the pain of keeping this hot gossip to yourself."

Sandy looks at her sideways. Her eyes are narrowed. But her lips do twitch. "I would have if it killed me," she says.

Christie grins. Her nose even crinkles. "Trust me, I know."

I don't miss Cassie's full-body eye roll next to me. As much as she insists she doesn't see them as family, it's the look of someone whose parents are flirting in public. "I'll go with Jay," she says.

They both turn to look at her. "Honey," Sandy says, "you should get some rest."

"In a bit." Cassie shrugs. "You're both here. Who's going to be looking for me?"

Christie gives her a long, searching look. And eventually she sighs. "A couple of hours. Then you're going home."

"I've still got pastelitos left," Sandy says. "And I'm not eating them all myself."

Cassie smiles thinly back. "Yes, ma'am."

Sandy heads back toward the school, and Jay and Cassie split off across the parking lot. "Give you a ride back?" Felix says to me as he opens the door for Alex.

I shake my head. "I'm going to stay."

"She'll take the ride," Christie says. To me, she adds, "Go with Felix. I'll call you tomorrow."

"I can help," I say quickly. The Flood comes tomorrow. I *have* to help.

"The biggest help to me right now would be you going back to the house," Christie says.

I laugh, though it's not funny. "I've been trying to talk to the Flood all day."

But she doesn't react to that. She speaks slower, calmer. "What you need to remember," she says, "is that they're trying to talk to you, too."

I let out a long, slow breath. "So what do I do?"

She picks my bag up from the ground and slides it onto my shoulder. She told me earlier she wasn't sure how to be a mother. But it feels like such a motherly thing to do.

"Go back to that house," she says. "And listen."

THE EARLY EVENING passes in flickers. We pick up drive-thru fast food on the way out of town and eat it on the ride to the Lethe Ridge housing development in complete silence. We pull up to the driveway and watch the houses, shrouded in darkness, for a long moment. Alex is the one who eventually asks if I want them to come in with me. I thank them but turn them down.

I glance around me, into the model house. The living room is a little island of light in the sea of dark—from my seat on the couch, I can see down the bedroom wing hallway, and little shadowy angles of the kitchen.

If there's a good time to talk, this is it.

"So," I say. "Here we are."

I don't need to feel the shift in the atmosphere anymore to know that they're hearing me. I swallow.

"I'm not sure if you were listening before," I say. "But Christie Jones, the sheriff . . . I was telling her I've been trying to talk to you. And she said—well. She kind of thinks I've talked enough."

Nothing. I take a deeper breath. "So," I say again. "If there's something *you* wanted to say . . ."

I curl deeper into the couch in the silence that follows. It's like approaching a cat, I think. I need to let them come to me.

I check my phone again. Nothing from Cassie. Nothing from Felix or Alex, or the sheriff. Nothing from Flora, as promised—presumably that conversation will wait until I give up and call her, and somehow that's less of a relief than I thought it might be.

Something else buzzes in, though. My little brother's daily composition practice.

Hi, Rosie, Sammy texted fifteen minutes ago. *Today I was very busy. We bought hats and noisemakers for the new year party. I asked Mom to buy one for you in case you came home. She said yes. I'm going to get ready for sleep now.*

I run my fingers over the edges of the cracked screen, and I feel as close to crying as I have for months. Even then, it doesn't happen.

Good night, Sammy, I text back. Closing my eyes, I slide the phone next to the cushion under my head.

I don't realize I'm falling asleep until a buzzing wakes me up.

THE PHONE WHIRRS, shrill and sharp, next to my cheek. I claw my way up, mouth dry, and for a moment, I have no idea where I am, or what's shuddering next to me. The web of cracks on my screen look deeper, more numerous, and my vision is blurry at the edges. I pick it up without seeing who the caller is.

"Hello?" I say, my voice crackling.

There's a wheezing, in and out. Then that voice. The same voice as always.

Rose . . .

I jerk the phone back away from my ear, and I see the screen clearly, now. Time: 1:05 a.m. Caller: Gaby Summer.

And when I scramble to my feet, I see what's been in front of me the whole time. Gaby—a silvery, unsteady reflection of Gaby—is standing at the door, mouthing along with the voice on the phone.

Rose, are you there?

I hear the rustling, as always, in the background of the call— the male voice, words indistinct. The Gaby in front of me starts and looks over her shoulder. Her posture doesn't quite relax, but what she sees makes her turn more fully. She didn't trust Nick, but she didn't *not* trust him. She had no reason to not trust him.

I don't see him there, over her shoulder. But all the hairs on my arms stand on end.

Gaby turns and vanishes into the dark. And even knowing that it's the Flood who just disappeared through that front door, I sprint after her.

I cross the threshold, and I stop so suddenly that I almost trip. I'm not in the model house's yard at the Lethe Ridge housing development. I'm standing in the middle of Sutton Avenue.

The next thing I hear, just to my right, is the screech of tires.

I turn away sharply. There's a *hiss* and a *crunch*, and I can smell burning rubber.

"This is cruel," I whisper, and I know the Flood can hear me. "I don't need to see this."

They don't respond to that, either. Maybe they're waiting for me to notice. And gradually, I do.

There was no splash. No sound to indicate a car going into the water. And more importantly, where I'm facing, I see the old oak tree looming in the distance, marking the corner of Sutton and Chamblys. The corner of Sutton and Chamblys should be the site of the accident. Which is behind me.

That damp, bitter air hits my lungs again. This time, I recognize it.

Slowly, I turn. I see a car spun off the road and into the grass, half-tipped into a ditch, nothing but rubber burned into pavement to indicate the trajectory the vehicle just took. I hear the whine of steam. And I see someone stumble from the passenger's seat of the car. Eyes wide.

Holding her wrist. What I looked like in that moment, over two years ago.

This is not Gaby's accident.

This is mine.

DECEMBER 14, TWO YEARS AGO

NOTE TO SELF: "Don't get into cars with strangers" is incomplete advice. Statistically speaking, it's the people you know who hurt you.

"Need a ride?"

Over the next two years, you will imagine a dozen different ways you could have said no. But this is here and now, standing outside Ariella Kaplan's grandparents' cabin at the end-of-semester party you didn't even want to go to. The light gauze of rain and fog won't let up for hours yet, and this cold snap will last another week. Gaby is home with the flu. Your ride into the woods was Kelly Townsend, currently passed out in the guesthouse bed with her sweatshirt still halfway over her head. Ariella promised to keep an eye on her. All that's left is to decide between a long walk to the bus stop or using your emergency forty dollars for a cab.

So you turn around and look up at Nick Lansbury, standing over you on the front steps. "Yeah," you say. "Please."

He laughs. He's got the kind of laugh that puts you on guard. But he's not a bad person, is the thing, and he's doing you a favor.

So you smile and you get in the car. And you don't say anything when he floors it.

Your fingers curl into the drink holder, but you keep smiling and keep not saying anything. It's an empty stretch of road, straight and quiet. He'll slow down when you get to Chamblys.

"Good party," he says at length.

"Huh?" you say. "Oh. Sure."

"Really?" You're not sure you like how he's smiling at you, like he thinks he knows you. "Didn't look like you were having a lot of fun."

You make a noncommittal sound. You promised last week that you'd come with Gaby. And by the time Gaby canceled, Kelly made you promise not to let her drink. There's not a force in the world that could keep Kelly sober, but you gave it your all.

"Next time you should sit with me," Nick says. "You'll like it more when you're not stuck with Kelly. You're not like her, you know?"

Nick isn't a bad person. But here's the thing about him: he thinks things like that are compliments.

But you don't have time to tell him Kelly is a first-chair violinist and a chemistry genius. What you have to say instead is "You're going kind of fast."

Maurice will tell you one day that you have a talent for understatement. When something crosses the point where you can let it go, there's nothing "kind of" about it.

But Nick doesn't know you as well as he thinks he does, and more importantly, he doesn't know that he is going faster than you have ever felt a car go. He snorts. "Relax. No one here but us."

As if to prove his point, he accelerates.

In the coming months, you will marvel at all the things that had to come together in these next few moments. The drizzle. The cold snap. The light layer of water and ice against the smooth, flat pavement, and Nick's foot on the accelerator.

You'll learn the word later for what the car is doing now: *hydroplaning*. All you can wrap your head around is the feeling of it, like the moment between when you slip on ice and when you hit the ground, except that would end in a second, and this *keeps going*.

You'll learn later that the best thing Nick could do in this moment would be to ease off the accelerator. He slams on the brake. Jerks the wheel. And you're spinning.

The car slides to the right, *hard*. You catch yourself against the window, and your wrist crumples under your weight, but something had to take the hit and in that moment it was your arm or the side of your head. There's a rolling, shuddering shockwave as the wheels slide from pavement to dirt and Nick is yelling, cursing, driving his full weight into the brake.

The dirt has traction, and the traction slows you down, but the first law of motion still applies. It's not until the back of the car tips up and the front hits something solid that you finally, finally stop.

There's a bang like a gunshot and a spray of searing heat across your collarbone. The kind of thing someone should flinch at, but you're frozen. You have to blink a few times to see what's in front of you: the airbags deployed, pressing you in.

The claustrophobia is sudden, sharp, immediate. By the time you think to move you're already scrambling backward out of the car. The ground is uneven, you stumble. The car rests half in a ditch. The engine lets out a low keen. You breathe in, the air sharp and wet in your chest.

Your fingers come to rest around your wrist. You finally notice how much it hurts.

"Shit." Nick throws his door open and stumbles out of the car. He's clutching at his hair, pacing in short, agitated bursts. You wish he'd stop. The reality of the situation is still hanging, precarious, somewhere beyond your reach. You want to back away from it slowly, quietly, as if too much movement will draw its attention.

"My car," he's whimpering. "Shit, shit, *shit*—"

Eventually, he seems to notice you. "Rose," he gasps out as he moves toward you, "are you okay?"

Finally, you flinch.

His hands are still hovering, halfway to your arms. "Rose?"

You hold yourself out of his reach. Your spine is so straight it hurts.

"You can't tell anyone," he says, and whether he notices it or not, he's shifted his stance, his angle. In front of you, there's Nick. Behind you, the passenger's door. You're out of the car, but you're still trapped. "Rose, please—I *just* got my license."

"I told you to slow down," you say. Your voice gets softer the closer he gets.

"*Rose.*" He all but falls to your feet. You shrink until your back brushes the car. "I was an idiot, okay? But it's not going to happen again. You're not hurt that bad, right?"

Your wrist throbs under the pressure of your grip. You can wiggle your fingers. It's probably not that bad. It's probably not that bad, but.

"Your car," you say. Even in the dark, you can see the state of the front bumper.

"I'll say I hit a deer." He shrugs. There's a sort of nonchalance to the gesture. A chill jerks through you. "My parents can pay. But you get it, right? If I tell them what happened, they will *take my car*."

There's something in the way he says it. And enough of your rational thought has come back to you that you can wrap your head around where you are: in the middle of nowhere, here with Nick Lansbury and his busted car and his huge pleading eyes, and no way ahead but through him. You wonder how he'll look at you if you say what you'd like to say right now.

"Fine," you say, with no sense of what you've just set into motion.

His arms twitch, as if he wants to hug you but thinks better of it. "And your wrist?"

"I can say I fell," you say.

"Good," he says. And he's *smiling* as finally, finally, he takes a step back, lets the damp night air hit you like a wave. "Good, that's perfect."

He gives you fifty dollars for a cab, and another fifty dollars for urgent care. He tells you to go up the road to call the taxi service so no one sees you together, to text him once you get home. You feel his eyes on your back as you walk.

Like I said before. He's not a bad person.

(He's not a good one, either.)

Note to self: Everyone will believe you when you tell them you tripped. There's rarely any reason not to believe you, at least right now. But in two weeks, Gaby will say Nick Lansbury's name, and she will notice the way your back snaps straight. She will always notice those things about you.

"*Rose*," she'll say. "*Tell me what he did.*"

Note to self: I know you can't read this. I know you can't know these things now when you need them. I know you will look at this chance to tell her, and you won't take it. I know you think he'll make your life hell if you do.

But I'm going to ask you anyway: Let him make your life hell. Be grateful for every second of it. There's a worse kind of hell waiting for you.

But you can't read this, and you can't know this. So you tell her he didn't *do* anything. That you just don't like him.

And that will be the end of it.

Twenty-Four

THE OBJECTS IN MOTION

MY SILHOUETTE IS still visible in the distance. Still slowly making her way to the old oak tree. Still holding her wrist to her chest. The road fades away before she—before *I* do.

The sounds of Sutton Avenue go quiet, leaving only my own ragged breathing. When I turn, the scene has changed again.

The walls and floor are as black as empty space. It's just me, a Rose from over a year later, curled into our living room couch. Though the TV isn't visible in this snapshot of memory, I see its reflection in the light on my face.

No. This one isn't me—when I look at her, I see it in the way she looks back.

"Why did you show me that?" I choke out.

The Flood gazes dispassionately from the couch. The angles of their face shift in the changing light of the TV, but the light never reaches the deep black pools of their eyes.

"It's not why I'm like this," I say. "I was fine. I don't have the right."

The Flood opens my mouth, and the voice of a news anchor comes out.

Another deadly accident at Sutton Avenue and Chamblys Road last night, she says. *Seventeen-year-old Nicholas Lansbury was forced into Chamblys Pond when an oncoming driver swerved to avoid Sutton's notoriously treacherous oak tree. We are sad to report that his passenger, sixteen-year-old Gabrielle Summer—*

"I know." My hands clutch at my hair. "I know, I know. Do you think I don't *know*? 'His passenger, sixteen-year-old Gabrielle Summer, was killed on impact. Mr. Lansbury is expected to recover from his injuries, and the unnamed driver of the second car is scheduled to be arraigned next week. Reports—'" My voice breaks. "'Reports allege that the driver was intoxicated.'"

The Flood is still watching me. But the light of the TV has disappeared, casting their face in shadow.

"Do you know," I finally say, "how many times I was told that he did the best he could? That it isn't his fault he survived and she didn't?

"And you know what? I'm *aware*," I spit out. "I know it was an accident. I'm not an idiot. But they don't know everything. You do."

I grab for another breath. It slips through my fingers. "Gaby had every opportunity to stay out of that car. Everyone—*everyone*—knew Nick was a disaster behind the wheel. They didn't need me to tell them. But you can't tell me that Gaby wouldn't have taken it more seriously coming from me."

The Flood is still. Completely still. And the longer they're silent, the louder I hear myself get.

"To call me like that, when it would be over an hour before I could come get her—she could have stayed with Ariella if she didn't want to go with him!" I say. "You can see exactly how many times I've thought that, right? How sick is that, expecting that of her when I did the same goddamn thing? Will you please just *say* something?"

I'm gasping by the time it's all out but still not crying—not even now. It's too dark to see the Flood's face. But I know they haven't looked away.

Their mouth moves again. Gaby's voice this time.

"Rose. Tell me what he did."

"Stop that," I gasp.

And again. Christie's voice. "Did he hurt you?"

"Stop!" My legs tremble with the word. "Please! You saw what happened in that kitchen. Do you know what Christie and Cassie would say if they knew? How they would look at me?"

"Listen," she says. "Remember. Understand."

"Understand *what*?" My voice cracks, hard. "You're showing me shit that I *already know*!"

A percussive blast of sound rattles me from the ground up, and I whirl around so fast I'm dizzy. The dark edges of my living room burst into light and color and stretch into the distance, until a suburban street snaps into place. By the end of the street, on the left, there's a house, brightly lit, shaking under the force of the music inside. Marin Levinson's house. Marin Levinson's party.

I don't need to remember how it felt, for the bass beat to hijack the rhythm of my heart. I'm feeling it now.

I stumble as I turn, and the present twists back into focus, the lights of the model home spinning. The image is still blurred as

I claw my way to the door, the knob liquid and unsteady in my hands. I grasp for something I can lock. The house shivers under the force of the music, and with every pound the walls creep tighter, closer. It's at my heels as I sprint to the bedroom farthest from the sound, it's in my ribs when I clamp a pillow over my ears. My grip is so tight, my knuckles hurt. I really don't care.

It's hard to say what ends first—the attack, or the music. Sleep comes slow, then suddenly. But the dread sinks in all the way to my dreams.

THE MORNING AFTER a bad panic attack must be what a hangover feels like. My skin feels too tight for my body. My brain feels too big.

There's a small, detached part of me that's equal parts embarrassed and impressed. I've never melted down like that before— not out loud. Always too many people around to see it. For once in my life, there's no one.

Here's what Maurice would tell me, if he knew everything I knew. What happened to Gaby was an accident. What Nick asked of me wasn't right. And if every one of us had done everything right, it might have happened anyway.

That night in his car when we hydroplaned into a ditch was over two years ago. He was young and stupid and scared. His terrible driving became an open secret at school, without my help. And he owned it. He was voted Most Likely to Total His Car by the senior class, and he accepted it, laughing. Like it was a cute fucking character quirk.

And then there was Gaby, who knew that as well as anyone. Who got in his car anyway. And here's where Maurice would remind me that Nick's driving was irrelevant. There's one person to blame, and that's the drunk asshole who killed her.

Strange that he's the one I stopped thinking about a long time ago. The one variable I could never have changed. Maybe he keeps someone else up at night, somewhere, but he would have been there no matter what I did.

Maurice could tell me all of this. But I've been telling myself those same things for the past year, and I've yet to believe a single word.

My phone buzzes, and Cassie's name pops up, fragmented by the screen. I accept the call and tuck it against my ear.

"Anything?" I ask.

"Good morning to you, too." She falters. "You sound awful."

A laugh punches out of me. I almost deny it. The relief when I realize I don't have to makes my knees a little weak. "Then we match."

She clears her throat pointedly, but she still sounds a little rough when she speaks again. "We have officially run out of civic spirit."

"That bad?" I say.

"Ms. Jones got through . . . maybe half?" she says. "And sent a big group home based on the security footage. So the people left are getting . . . antsy."

"And Adrienne?" I ask.

"Was on the tape," Cassie confirms. "Jay's with her now."

I shrug a flannel shirt over my shoulders and comb my fingers through my hair a few times. "I'll be there in half an hour."

"I know." A beat. "But I wanted to warn you first."

There's a twist low in my gut.

"Look out the window," Cassie says, even and slow. "Don't panic. But look."

I make a low sound of agreement in the back of my throat. But my hands still shake when I pull the blinds.

The sky is a dark, cloudy green. The kind you see in the moments before a tornado.

I ease open the window and stick one hand out. The air feels cool and choppy, the edge of a changing front.

"I checked the weather," Cassie says. "Eighty-five and sunny. It *still* says that."

I pull my arm back slowly, as if from a wild animal. "I'll be there as soon as I can." I pause. And then, stupidly, I add, "Don't worry."

At least, it jolts her into a firm, haughty tone—something much closer to herself. "I never worry."

"You sure?" I say. "If I saw the future, I think worry would be my entire life."

"Worry is for when you think you know," she says.

I pinch the window latch between two fingers, testing its strength. As if that'll help. "What do you call it when you know you know?"

She's quiet long enough that I think she hung up. "Dread," she says. There's another long beat. "Be careful on your way here."

White noise fills the line as she disconnects.

I toss the phone on top of the duvet, laughing softly as I wander into the master bathroom. "Good talk."

I wonder what it is *I* feel. Worry, or dread. At least for a second, all I feel is the splash and sting of cold water on my face.

I straighten up and catch a glimpse of myself in the mirror. And I freeze.

My reflection looks back at me, gray-faced, her palms riddled with scrapes. Breathless, cold water still dripping down my neck, I look down at my hands. Clean, bloodless. And when I face front, the only person waiting in the mirror is me.

"I thought I told you to stop," I gasp. But before it's fully out of my mouth, I know that's not right. I don't feel that cool mustiness is the air. The Flood isn't here.

With a shaking hand, I grip the cuff of my flannel shirt. My muscle memory does the work for me. I left this in my car before Marin Levinson's party. I slid it on while I was sitting there after, waiting to warm up. Slid it over my wrists so I could grip the wheel through my sleeves, blot the blood on my palms.

The Flood showed me this moment, too, in the police station bathroom on my first day in Lotus Valley. But this feels different. This feels physical. Like I was standing in just the right place to see something hidden. Not just watching Past Rose but standing in the same space in time, close enough to forget we aren't the same person.

I didn't see the scrapes on her palms, did I? I felt them on my own.

Almost like—

I'm dialing Maurice's number before I can think better of it.

It rings long enough for me to think close to clearly again. It's still morning. He has appointments in the morning. It's New Year's Eve, but that probably means he's busier. He always says holidays will do that.

Hello, his voicemail greeting chirps. *You have reached the confidential mailbox of Maurice Martin.*

"Calm down," I whisper. I have somewhere to be. And besides, what am I going to tell him? That I *think* I finally had a real flashback?

He'd take me seriously. He always takes it seriously. For one traitorous second, I think about how nice that'd be: to be told how strong I've been. That I can stop. That I can go home.

It's a second too long. The voicemail beeps. The story hovers, heavy, on my tongue.

If anything, he hears the gasp when I realize it's recording. And then I hang up.

SEPTEMBER 17, THREE MONTHS AGO

NOTE TO SELF: Maurice knows everything. This is not always a compliment.

Nine times out of ten, it is. But it can, on occasion, get irritating when he knows what's in your head before you do.

"And he was just like—" You affect a high, nasally voice. "I understand your frustration, but I can't let you take your car unless I'm going to let everyone."

Maurice laughs. "Do me a favor. Try saying that one more time without the voice."

Against your will, you laugh, too. "Okay, yeah. He probably didn't think like that in his head."

"Tone is hard to gauge over email," Maurice says gently. "This might be the kind of thing better suited to a phone call."

"Maurice." You grin. "Only monsters use the phone."

You found Maurice Martin, LICSW, on the internet. He had a nice bio, he was close to your apartment, his listing offered an email as well as a phone number. And when you looked at his specialties, *Grief counseling* is there, right next to *Trauma*. It's what you could point to, when Mom asked.

You told her about the appointment. It's her insurance; you couldn't not. She was so relieved it was hard to look at her.

You told Maurice Martin about Gaby first, and you expected stony, clinical acceptance. You watched it wash over his face instead. *God*, he said, *I'm so sorry.*

It's weird to see that empathy, that understanding on the face of someone you don't know. He still looks at you like that sometimes.

You're not sure how you feel about how nice it is.

"Maybe I just won't go," you say.

"You were excited for this, weren't you?" he says.

"I mean, yeah. I kind of fell out of Astronomy Club—after," you say. "But I'm not taking a bus out to the desert."

You made a choice, before that first appointment, not to use those four letters. To catalogue your basket of symptoms like you had no clue. You told yourself it was so you wouldn't bias him. But he didn't need your guesses. Looking back, he diagnosed you in ten minutes.

It's not like I was in the accident was your token protest. Though even then, you wondered.

He didn't—doesn't—know that part of it. But he still smiled sadly and said, *That doesn't matter.*

You made another appointment with him. You looked up whatever information you could with your halfhearted search terms. *Less-terrible PTSD. A casual users' guide to PTSD. PTSD for Dummies.*

And the summer went on. The worst of it isn't sudden, exactly, because it was already there. You just noticed it, that's all.

"I have to ask, Rose." He leans forward, elbows on his knees. "Did you tell him why you wanted to drive? Or just that you wanted to?"

You don't need to answer. Your tight smile tells him everything he needs to know.

"It sounds ridiculous," you say with a laugh. "Doesn't it?"

And it *is* ridiculous. It's totally fucking absurd. Nobody puts trigger warnings on passenger's seats and screeching tires and ringing phones. But he's Maurice. So he says, "Of course it doesn't."

"I guess I'm kind of like . . ." You chew on the words a long time. He waits you out. He always does. "Can't people just . . . guess?"

"That'd be easier, yes." He laughs. "But people have short memories, Rose. They're not going to know unless you tell them."

You won't go stargazing in the desert with the Astronomy Club. But you'll do your homework. You'll map the patterns of your adrenaline, you'll chart the highs and lows of your pulse, and you'll talk to yourself. You'll talk to yourself in the mirror, you'll talk to yourself in writing. You'll stop telling yourself to shut up and start telling yourself that you'll be okay.

It'll scare you a little, how normal you can look. How cheerful you can sound. How you can get text upon text of prom dress pictures and dating rants and respond to every one. How you can take call after call from Flora Summer in the middle of the night, sobbing that she needed to hear your voice. You'll keep going. You'll twist, you'll dance, you'll sidestep the panic as it comes, even when all you want to do is sleep.

But there'll be time for sleep later. You need to apply to colleges. You need to eat something. You need to stop saying *you* like you're talking to some other girl.

And if you feel like you're still spinning on that dark, wet road, well then, what's changed? A body in motion, et cetera.

Twenty-Five

THE THIRD DAY

IT'S POSSIBLE THAT hanging up on Maurice wasn't my best idea. If I left a message, I could have played it like nothing was wrong. He knows something's wrong now.

Rose? Did you call earlier?

The text stares me down much like Maurice himself would do if we were face-to-face. I start a reply. Mom always says not to text and walk, but it's not like there's anyone around to bump into. The streets are emptier today. The signs of life come from the houses: blurs of movement and suitcases in the open garages. Sometimes I catch, out of the corner of my eye, faces at the windows. But whenever I look, the curtains snap shut.

Yeah sorry, I say. I mean to expand on that, but nothing comes to me.

Is everything okay? he asks.

It should be easier to lie when he can't see my face. And yet I type, *I don't think so.*

There's a long pause before he types again. *I have appointments until five*, he says. *But I can call then. Would that help?*

I laugh quietly. It depends, Maurice. I don't know what I'll be doing at five. This disaster I started doesn't have a timeline I can follow.

But I write back, *Yes please.*

The school stands, waiting, just a few feet ahead.

Felix and Alex are collapsed on a couple chairs in the lobby when I open up the double doors. Neither of them lighten up a whole lot at my arrival. I have to imagine I'm making a similar face.

"Get ready for a lot of unhappy people," Felix says, by way of greeting.

"We're taking a break," Alex says. "But you can go on through."

I nod and do just that. As I leave them behind, I catch Alex slide his head onto Felix's shoulder.

I pass through the entryway, cast in that murky, unnatural sunlight, and turn deeper into the building. I don't need to ask where I'm going. There are plenty of voices for me to follow, for one. But the hallways ahead are shimmering, just a little. Like something is shifting under the surface.

I think the Flood is agitated. And it doesn't take me long to see why.

". . . get to my age, you know more dead folks than live ones." An elderly woman sits in the classroom to my right, her back straight and her smile taut. I pause long enough to see Loreen opposite her. "My parents. My best friend. My baby brother. Would you like me to start somewhere, Loreen, or shall I go in order?"

I know that voice. I've seen this woman before: she threw a dish at us yesterday when we tried to interview her. Maybe that's a habit of hers, because Loreen looks ready to dodge a few projectiles, too.

"I know it's hard," Loreen says. "I'm sorry. But if you could walk me through it . . ."

"You already know that," someone says in the next classroom up. "You were at the funeral."

I straighten. Adrienne's voice.

I hear Deputy Jay next, tight and strained. "If you don't mind—for the record . . ."

Adrienne's back is to me when I peer in. All I see is her auburn hair and her peach uniform. She adjusts the set of her shoulders as she speaks again. And for a second, the floor shifts to grass, dotted with gravestones.

I don't think they can see it—they don't react—but just like at the Mockingbird's, the Flood's focus has widened, taking in the torrent of memories around us. Maybe it's all these interviews, stories of things and people lost. Or maybe it's just another sign of how close the Flood is to Lotus Valley now.

"I don't know, Deputy," she says. "*Have* I suffered a notable loss? I think about it every day, every time I'm in that kitchen. Sometimes it's more than I can bear. Sometimes it's kind of comforting, like she's there, guiding my hand. But most times it's just like wallpaper. Just all around me, the rest of my life. Is that notable enough for you?"

I don't hear Jay's answer—harsh, terrified sobs from up the hall tear my attention away. I feel the cool, ancient air before I hear the voice. Maurice's. And yet definitely not Maurice.

"I understand this is difficult for you, dear," the Mockingbird soothes. "But if you don't use your words, we're not going to get anywhere."

"We might need to find the Mockingbird another job." There's a dark chuckle behind me, and I turn to find Cassie, listening, too. "People get kind of . . . flustered . . . with her."

I smile weakly. "To be fair, the others didn't seem much happier."

"They don't like being asked to relive it," Cassie says softly. "Guess I understand that."

I glance back to Adrienne and Jay's classroom. "I don't know, Cassie."

"About what?" she says.

"Adrienne." I watch her back, watch the rigid line of her shoulders. "When Theresa told me what it was like for her, I just felt . . . I don't know. Like it made sense? But look at her. That isn't someone who thinks her pain is going to end soon."

Cassie steps back, taking it in—not just Adrienne, but the whole line of classrooms. I think she gets what I mean. The only thing on display here is grief, scabbed-over and ripped-open. It's no wonder I can feel the Flood taking it all in.

I wonder what we *are* looking for. Desperation? Relief? Anticipation?

We venture a little farther down the hall. Christie's in the next classroom—she's speaking quietly, her interviewee out of our sight. Cassie's gaze unfocuses as she watches her.

"She told you about my parents," she says. It's not quite a question.

"She says they didn't say much," I say.

"Oh, I'm sure they said plenty," Cassie says. "Just not what she wanted to know."

Christie extends a hand to the woman opposite her, who instead nods curtly as she collects her purse. And as I watch her go, my mind begins to churn.

"Ms. Jones said they lost a child, before you," I say.

"It wasn't them," Cassie says.

"I know that, I was—" Thinking out loud. I stop, and I put my thoughts in order before I try again. Though by the time I do, I'm not sure I want to.

"You told me yesterday," I say slowly, "that they had a good reason to want the Flood here, but that they had a better reason not to."

Cassie looks up at me. It's the look she gave me three days ago, when she realized, for the first time, who I was. "I said that," she says, carefully.

"So," I say. "What was that reason, exactly?"

But if she was going to answer me, she doesn't get the chance. Theresa Gibson strolls into the room in a tank top and jeans, her arms swinging freely at her sides. It's different, somehow, from how she carried herself yesterday. She looks calm, almost balloon-light in her steps.

And the traces of memories all around us abruptly vanish.

"Chris," Theresa says.

"Theresa!" Christie's smile is warm, familiar. "Go ahead and sit down. This should only take a few minutes."

"Something wrong?" Cassie says, seeing the look on my face, maybe.

"I'm . . . not sure," I say slowly. I've been able to feel the Flood stirring since we got here, taking in all the grief and pain, but they're completely still now. Theresa laughs as she pulls out the chair with her foot, and I wait to see her memories flicker into view. Nothing happens. It's almost like—whatever the Flood is getting from everyone else in this school, they're not getting it here.

I don't see that grief and pain in Theresa, either. Her shoulders are relaxed. Her smile is easy. She doesn't look like someone who knows she's about to be asked about the worst day of her life.

And I think of yesterday, in the garage. When she'd told me about Adrienne. When she caught me looking at her pictures.

"You may have been invited in," I whisper.

"Rose?" Cassie asks.

I grip her arm to quiet her. "Yesterday, in the garage, that's what she said to me. 'You may have been invited in.' But she shouldn't have known about the broadcast."

Cassie's eyes widen. I wonder if she's cataloguing it, too: the comment about Adrienne, the list of pawn shop customers. From the very start, all from Theresa.

"Cassie," I say. "I think—"

"You don't think," someone else says. "You know."

We whip around. And behind us, breathing hard, her perfect clothes and perfect hair in disarray, is Mayor Maggie Williams.

We lock eyes for a long, long time. And Cassie may be the prophet, but I get there first.

"You finally looked." I smile slowly. "Didn't you?"

Maggie goes white, her jaw visibly working. But she nods.

Adrenaline surges down to my toes. "Then go," I say.

For a second, I think she'll remind me who's in charge here. But she settles her shoulders, and she does what I ask.

"Knock, knock," she trills, sailing past us and into the classroom. "Hope you don't mind if I sit in, Chris."

"I"—Christie opens her mouth, closes it—"wasn't expecting you, Maggie."

"Yes . . ." Theresa's still got that easy smile. But I can see it calcifying. "Why don't you sit down, Madam Mayor? You look out of breath."

And then, ever so slightly, her head shifts to the hall. "And who's out there?" she calls, smooth and cool as a river rock. "Cassandra? Or is it you, Ms. Nobody?"

"Something the matter?" Christie says. Her voice doesn't change. Her posture does.

"You're busy women, both of you." Though I know she can't see me, she never looks away. "We've all got important things to do today. Let's not waste time."

Christie barely flinches. But I see the shift behind her eyes. She's guessed. She knows.

Maggie perches on the edge of her chair, and for once, I'm grateful for her unflappable PTA grin. "Okay, then," she says. "Let's start with what you mean?"

"I think you know what I mean. But if you need me to say it, then yes. I'm the person I imagine you've been looking for.

"So." Theresa leans back in her chair. "Let's get this over with."

Twenty-Six

THE DUE TO THE DEAD

"YOU LOOK SURPRISED," Theresa says.

Christie's palms lie flat on her thighs, as if she's considering whether to move or stay still. "A little," she says evenly. "Seems like a lot of effort to hide what you were doing, just to tell me so easily now."

"I didn't expect our Mags here to pick up soothsaying again." Theresa shrugs. "Clearly I gotta work on *my* prophesying skills, right? Anyways, I figure I've bought enough time."

"Time to what?" Maggie says.

Theresa gazes across the table. Still smiling. But underneath that, implacably calm. "If you figured me out too quickly, you might've tried something else. Maybe you would've even figured out how to stop this. If I could keep you distracted—with the list, with Adrienne—I could keep you from looking for other solutions."

There's a beat of silence. I can feel Cassie, shifting closer. "Anyway," Theresa says. "I've taken enough of your time. You've got an evacuation to run."

"Don't you worry about the evacuation," Christie says.

"And are you worried, Maggie?" Theresa says.

I can see her trying not to bristle. "We have our differences of opinion," Maggie says. "But when it comes to the safety of this town, I trust Christie implicitly. And if she trusts her—Rudy to assist, then I defer to her judgment."

"Could've fooled me," Theresa says with a shrug. "Okay, then. *I've* got plans tonight. Few things to prepare and all that. So can we make this quick?"

"And who was it you went through all this trouble for?" says Christie.

"Ah, yeah. You didn't know him, did you?" She's bordering on chipper. She could be talking about any new year's plans. "My father would have passed when you were about this high. It's too bad. He would have liked you. I really do think you should evacuate, Chris."

"The evacuation"—I hear the edge in her voice for the first time—"is taken care of."

"Oh," Theresa says. Something in her expression shifts. "Were you hoping *I* could tell you how to stop it?"

"Theresa," Christie says. "I'm giving you the benefit of the doubt here. I'm assuming you would never bring this to our doorstep if you knew what it was capable of."

"Don't condescend to me, sweetheart." She smiles thinly. "I'm not an idiot. Of course I know."

Cassie has started gripping my arm right back. Hard enough that I might just be holding her up.

Christie leans back in her chair. "Let's start with how you know, then."

THE VALLEY AND THE FLOOD

"It was just that I started to wonder," Theresa says. "About this place. About you in particular, Chris—about how things changed after you came back to town. I used to like poking around the archives, just to read about all the weird shit that's passed through here since before we were alive. You know me. Business gets slow, I get bored. But then you come back. You become sheriff after the Harper incident. And then not long after, we get Cassandra's prophecy. Suddenly, certain pages of the archive files are always checked out. By our sheriff herself. I didn't guess why at the time. Just thought it was strange.

"But then about two months ago, talking to your wife, she said something that bugged me." Theresa leans back in her chair. "She was laughing about how upset her parents were that you'd said no to their holiday invitation *again*. Said that it wasn't your fault you were allergic to the cats." She snorts. "Funny. I remember a little Christie Jones who played with the feral cats in the high school parking lot. Don't worry, though. I didn't tell her that."

"And what was that to you, exactly?" The question drops the temperature a few degrees.

"Nothing," Theresa says. "I just started to think that you've disappeared, like clockwork, to spend the holidays doing 'charity work.' Right after Cassandra started living with you."

Cassie's gone rigid. Her grip has started to hurt.

"And I thought, if Cassandra's involved, there's only one thing it could be about. But her prophecy never said *when* this flood was meant to come. So why the same time, every year? And I guess it was then I started to connect the dots. Started wondering about that archive, what was in those missing pages."

Theresa grins. "Believe it or not, I had no idea what I was in for when I ran into Jay at Paco's. I just wanted to know what else you were hiding."

Cassie starts to shiver. "What's wrong?" I whisper, as if they can hear us as well as we can hear them.

"She knows exactly what she did." Her voice is a tight whisper. "Doesn't she?"

"So you went to the Mockingbird," Maggie says. "Knowing they were friends."

"Jeez." Theresa laughs. "I'm not a mastermind, Maggie. How could I know they knew each other? All I was thinking was I've gotten this far. Fish or cut bait. And what better bait than someone who can sound like anyone? It's not like I started anything that wouldn't have happened anyway."

"It might not have happened at all without you," Christie says.

Theresa smiles blandly. "Good thing I was proactive, then."

I look to the classroom, then back to Cassie. Her lips are starting to go white. "Cassie," I hiss. "Are you okay?"

She jerks her head, vaguely, like she changed her mind halfway between a nod and a shake.

Christie's stare is hard, watching Theresa. And at length, Theresa looks up again. "You know, Chris," she says. Her smile thins, just a little. "I've always wanted to ask you why you tried so hard to hide this. Bet Maggie here would love to know, too, right, Maggie?"

"No," Maggie says tightly. "I would say I'm starting to understand."

"Don't you two get it? This is a *good* thing," Theresa says. "Think about all the people in this town with someone they'd like to see again. Your friends? Your staff? Your partners? If you'd given us a choice—asked us which we'd rather have—I think I wouldn't be the only one willing to start over. You can rebuild a town. How often can you bring back the past?"

"You know I couldn't do that," Christie says.

"We don't know that they're going to hurt us," Theresa says. "Even Cassie couldn't tell you exactly what happens. How do we know this isn't a gift? Creating a new Lotus Valley with all the things we've lost?"

Cassie's fingers lock tighter into my arm, and I can see the bone of her knuckles. "Cassie," I say again, more firmly.

"*Nothing* is wrong," she says,

"Yeah," I say, "it looks like it."

"Who are you to talk?" she snaps. "You haven't explained a thing since you got here."

"Yeah." The word comes out in an exhale. "I haven't. But you told me yesterday that even if I didn't tell everyone, I should tell someone."

"I already did," she says. The anger is melting back, leaving something pale and unsteady. "It didn't work out, remember?"

Voices drift from the classroom, though I've lost the thread of their conversation now. Cassie told her parents. Cassie's parents sent her away.

Theresa leans back in her chair, untroubled. "I told you, I don't have anything that's going to help you. I don't know any more than you do."

"And I should, what," Christie says, "take your word for that?"

"Take it however you like," Theresa says. "I'm still waiting for you to answer *my* question. Why was it so important to keep this from everyone who might disagree with you? Why can't you trust this town you say you love so much?"

I can see the muscles working in Christie's jaw. Theresa leans slightly forward, like she's smelled blood. But Christie's eyes shift to the hallway as she exhales, long and low, and a little of the tension leaves her shoulders.

"I don't know." The admission draws a laugh out of her. "I don't know what's going to happen, either. But my kid asked me to stop it, so."

I hear Cassie breathe in next to me, but I can't look away just yet.

"She's not *your* kid," Theresa says.

"She is for as long as she'll have me," Christie says.

"You'd go this far," Theresa says, her voice flat and her stare sharp, "just on her word?"

"She made a decision," Maggie says. "Just as you did. But the difference is, Cassie is still alive. She can tell Christie what she wants. You don't know what your father would have wanted, Theresa. The only needs you're looking out for are your own."

Christie laughs. "Didn't think I'd be saying this anytime soon. But Maggie's right, Theresa. Cassie hasn't told me everything. She doesn't have to. I trust her."

There's another little gasp next to me, and Cassie's grip falls away from my arm. She's crying almost silently, her hands at her mouth.

"Cassie?" I ask.

"It's so stupid." She laughs wetly. "She's the smartest person I've ever met. I don't—Why did I think she wouldn't notice? Of course she noticed."

"Noticed what?" I say.

I reach out to touch her shoulder. The next thing I know, her arms are around me and her face is in my neck. I can feel her eyes screw shut against another sob, and tentatively, I reach up to run a hand through her hair.

"She m-must've seen the look on my face, right?" Her teeth are almost chattering with her shivers. "When I told her we had to stop the Flood. I thought I hid it. But she saw how scared I was."

"Shh," I breathe, my sleep-deprived brain shocked into auto-pilot. "It's okay. It's okay."

"It's me, Rose." Cassie's voice is muffled by my neck, but the words are clear. "I told you my parents had a better reason to hope the Flood never comes. The better reason is me."

"Cassie—" My fingers stutter, catching between strands of her hair. "I don't understand."

"Are you going to arrest me now?" Theresa's voice drifts down the hall.

"I wouldn't be opposed," Maggie says primly.

"Nothing illegal about getting a man drunk, or making a tape. Trust me, I wish there was." Christie sounds weary now. "It's time to evacuate, Theresa. And I hope you come with us. I feel for you, I truly do. But your loss isn't worth dying for."

There's a pause that leaves the room, the whole building, eerily still. Without that pause, I might never have heard Cassie's whisper.

"My prophecy," she says. "I think it ends with my death."

Faintly, over my shoulder, I hear Theresa's low laugh.

"Yeesh. No faith," she says. "The past is coming back to us, Chris. And when it does? I'm gonna be here to welcome it home."

Twenty-Seven

THE EVACUATION

"**YOU CAN'T TELL** her," Cassie informs me halfway to the lobby.

I bite my lip. "I think we should."

Cassie's eyes are still noticeably red, but her back is straight, her tone is determinedly chipper. "She has more important things to focus on."

"This is exactly what she should be focusing on!" I hiss.

"I've had a lot of time to think about this, okay?" she says. "She already suspects something's really wrong. If she knows what I've seen, it'll just make things worse."

"And if what you saw comes true—"

"If it comes true," Cassie says, each word precise, "then I've had a lot of time to think about that, too. You've got your own problems tonight. Let me deal with mine."

"You heard her, Cassie." I snag her arm, hold on until she turns to face me. Her rigid smile flickers. "She loves you. She— she wouldn't want you to be alone."

Now that Cassie's stopped, she can't seem to find the momentum to start walking again. She sinks a little, the nervous energy seeping out of her.

"You wanted to know what I saw," she says. "I saw it come. I saw it carry this town away with it. And I saw it consume me. And then I didn't *see* anything. I felt cold. I—It's never *felt* like anything before."

She takes a full, shuddering breath. "Say I tell her. What if it takes her, too, because she 'wouldn't want me to be alone'? Or if it doesn't, she lives the rest of her life knowing that I didn't trust her with this. And just for my peace of mind? It's fine, Rose. Actually, I'm tired of waiting. Part of me just wants . . ."

Her smile, inch by painful inch, twitches back into place. "Worry about yourself, not about me. Now come on."

"Cassie," I say, before she can finish turning around. I take the deepest breath I can around the vise on my throat. "I'm sorry."

The hard, tired look melts away, just a little. "You didn't make this happen." She reaches over to my hand, still on her arm, and squeezes. "It was inevitable."

Dropping her hand from mine, Cassie leads the way to the front of the school. Despite the haziness of the light through those dark green clouds, my eyes still water in the desert sun. In the time it's taken Cassie to calm down, everyone has gathered out front: Alex and Felix stand next to the door, with Christie farther away, in a huddle with Maggie Williams by the steps.

"I'll drop you off at your dad's," Felix is saying.

Alex shakes his head. "I can walk. You should get to your family."

"It's an extra five minutes," Felix says. "Just let me do this for you."

I take a step, but without quite looking at me, Christie calls out sharply, "Stay where you are."

I freeze. A rueful grin flickers across her face. "Sorry, Rose. You should stand way back."

I still can't quite see Rudy beyond the edge of the parasol. But the limb that's in view droops, like he's pouting.

Maggie Williams doesn't notice.

"Any time you'd like to let me in on this, Christie," she says tightly. "I just backed your evacuation plan in public, you know."

Christie snorts. "You backed me in front of *one person*."

She shudders like a bird resettling her plumage. "People talk."

"We're starting now?" I say.

Christie, standing on the edge of the school steps, squints at the sky and points her parasol at the hazy sun. "I was counting on more light," she mutters. "But this'll have to do."

It could easily be a non sequitur. But I've been here in Lotus Valley long enough that I assume she was answering my question.

"I'm taking a lot on faith here, Christie," Maggie says, a little louder. "Are you really sure this creature of yours will focus on the task at hand?"

"Boss," Felix says, his voice tight. "Not to agree with Williams or anything, but . . . Rudy's pretty agitated."

Christie's mouth twitches as Maggie nods emphatically. "Felix," she says. "Do you trust me?"

I expect more of a fight from Felix. But his shoulders sink grudgingly. "Of course I do."

Christie's lips curve into a full-blown smile. Then, slowly, she lowers the parasol.

Thick black tendrils spread from her feet in all directions, ahead and behind, reaching out until the ground itself looks like a massive hole in the earth. In the distance, Rudy's reach expands: I see one tendril loading a startled family's belongings into their trunk, another redirecting a passing car toward the highway, another gently prodding a reluctant man from his home.

One of Rudy's limbs makes a beeline toward me, but with a grimace, Christie wrangles him away from the building and toward town. "Not now, big guy," I hear her say through clenched teeth. "They'll be here for real soon enough."

In unison, our phones start to shiver. And then they start to *shriek*, blaring emergency broadcast tones all down the street.

IN ACCORDANCE WITH LOCAL CATACLYSM, LOTUS VALLEY RESIDENTS MUST EVACUATE EFFECTIVE IMMEDIATELY. CITIZENS SHOULD CONVENE ON THE HIGH GROUND PAST THE LETHE RIDGE HOUSING DEVELOPMENT. THIS IS NOT A TEST.

I look to Christie, who shrugs. "It's running on every station. And if they don't have a smartphone or a TV—"

There's a rush of air and a burst of sound overhead, and I look up just in time to catch the creatures from the theater, giggling and twisting through the air. "Evacuate!" they chirp. "Evacuate! Evacuate!"

"I'd been teaching Rudy to carve the PSA into walls. But this is easier," Christie says with a chuckle. "Poor guy. He's been practicing his penmanship for months."

"Well." The frozen, white-faced Maggie Williams clears her throat. "I'm sorry for doubting you."

Christie grins. "You doubted Rudy, not me. But don't worry. A few bags of fries and he'll forget all about it."

Shockingly, Maggie manages a queasy smile. "That can be arranged."

"Then we'll talk about it later," Christie says. "They listen to you, Maggie. Go help."

Maggie bristles. But there's no energy to it. "I don't take orders from you, Sheriff."

She rabbits down the steps, her heels clicking, and Christie turns back to face us. "Go get your families. I'll see you later with any luck."

"You're not coming?" I say.

Christie's face drops. There's a grim set to her shoulders. "We did the best we could, Rose. It's time to let Rudy take over."

"You're not—" I'm dizzy suddenly. I wanted the Flood gone. I wanted them gone, right? "Let me try again."

It sounds unbelievably stupid, coming out of my mouth. But sympathy floods her face.

"Rose, all I need for you to do right now is to get to somewhere safe. If the Mockingbird is right, at this point, the Flood is more focused on the town than you. But if you stay here, you're going to get caught in this fight." She turns to Cassie, next to her. "Sandy's waiting for you at home. Tell her I'll be right there."

Cassie looks a little past her, to me. She's giving me a warning look. I don't need the reminder.

"I can drive you," Felix says to me.

I shake my head hard. "I'll walk. I need to get my stuff from Lethe Ridge."

"Rose," Cassie says. Another warning. But just because she's accepted this is happening doesn't mean I need to.

I'm close. I have to be. And these stakes aren't just mine. Not anymore.

The Flood is ready to talk. Has been, this entire time.

So here I am. Ready to listen.

LOTUS VALLEY HAS exploded into a burst of activity. Families packing cars or hoisting suitcases onto bikes. Rudy's smoky tendrils corralling pets and small children. Really, Rudy's everywhere at once.

I catch a few familiar faces. Loreen loading as much as they can onto their motorcycle. Ace Martin and his friends, ushering a reluctant John Jonas into their SUV. The woman who threw a casserole at us yesterday, prodded along by Rudy as she tries to double back into her house.

But the Flood hasn't crossed the border into Lotus Valley. Not yet.

By the time I get to the Lethe Ridge model home, there's a line of headlights on the access road, driving past me and into the desert. I shut the doors to the model home tightly behind me. The Flood doesn't like an audience.

There's not much for me to pack, but I take it slow. Do I pretend I'm not waiting for them? Do I call to them myself? And what if they've already given up trying to talk to me?

My phone buzzes. Even now, already primed for something coming, it makes me flinch. But the adrenaline recedes when I catch the caller ID. Maurice.

Right. He did say he was going to call me at five, didn't he?

I reach for it, ready to reject the call and give a quick excuse via text, but I pause halfway.

I'm trying too hard to get their attention. The Flood from the start has responded the strongest to what I'm *feeling*. And if anyone knows anything about what I'm feeling, it's Maurice.

I need to see what happens if I tell him more.

I sweep the phone into my hand and say, "Hey. You never had to get a late pass, did you?"

Even when I'm trying to open up, I lead with a dumb joke. Luckily—unluckily—he doesn't take the bait. "I didn't want to keep you waiting. What's on your mind, Rose?"

I wonder if that's something you have to perfect when you're a therapist. How to tell someone, gently, with acceptance, to get to the point.

"So," I say. My throat feels tight. "Happy early New Year, first of all."

He doesn't wish me one back. Any other day, I'd pretend to be offended. He makes a low, thoughtful sound. *I'm listening.*

"I'm not with my family," I say.

"You still have time to go home, if you want," he says. "You did a very kind thing, visiting Gaby's parents, but that doesn't mean you can't—"

"No, Maurice, that's . . . that's the thing." Breathe. Inhale for seven. Hold for two. Exhale for eleven. "I left the Summers'. I left three days ago."

There's a brief, telling silence. "And you didn't go home."

"I didn't." For lack of anything better to do, I start pacing the length of the house.

"Where—" He stops himself from finishing that thought. I think he's trying not to scare me. That, in itself, makes my stomach clench. "Are you somewhere safe?"

I start to laugh, before I realize that makes it look worse. I'm not, really, but I'm safe in the way he means. So I say, "Yes. I'm going home soon." Reaching the end of the bedroom wing, I turn, make my way back to the front entryway. "But my parents don't know where I am and . . ."

And then I trail off. Rather than the reds, oranges, and sharp corners of the model house, I see cool blues and grays, a bookshelf. Two armchairs facing each other. I'm in one. Maurice is in the other.

"I thought maybe someone should know," I finish distantly.

"Thank you for telling me," Maurice says. At least, that's what I think he says. My ears are ringing, watching the Past Me and Past Maurice consider each other from their respective ends of the room. I'm sitting straight, balanced at the edge of the chair. The first thing I do when I get to his office is usually to move the cushion into the curve of my back, so I can sit without being swallowed into the leather.

I catch the paperwork in my lap and realize: this is my first appointment with him.

"My mom's my emergency contact," I'm saying. My voice is high, formal. Not at all how I talk to him now. "And I'm on her insurance, but that doesn't mean she can ask how it's going, right? I'm not eighteen until January but—"

"That won't matter." He smiles, warm even back then. I didn't expect warmth that first time. It caught me off guard. "These sessions are confidential, Rose. There are very few circumstances where I can share what you tell me here. *Very* few."

Standing here, outside myself and outside my own head, I can tell that I know he's trying to reassure me. And I can see where I've snagged onto those last few words. "What circumstances?"

"Ah, well," he says. "If you could just turn the page—"

"Rose?"

That one was in the present. Present Maurice, who says my name like it's not the first time he's had to in the last few seconds. "Sorry," I say. "What?"

"Do you want to talk about why you left the Summers'?" he asks.

"I . . ." My mouth is dry. My throat is dry, all the way down. I remember now. I remember what was on the next page. I see the flicker of it on Past Rose's face.

"I can disclose the contents of our sessions," Past Maurice says, "if in my professional opinion, you pose a danger to yourself or others."

Past Rose laughs. It's a sharp little sound. "Oh, yeah," she says. "I think I saw that on *Law and Order*." She signs the form, indicating that she understands, and the session moves on. I can't quite hear it anymore.

What you're talking about, Flora had said, just four nights ago. *That's a serious condition. That's . . .*

Dangerous. And I knew she was right, didn't I? I knew what has been waiting, all these months, to claw its way out. What I couldn't contain anymore, back in that kitchen.

What the Flood saw in me.

"Rose," Maurice says again. "Are you there?"

"I can't," I say. The hand holding the phone shakes so hard, I wonder if he can hear me. "I don't—"

"Okay," he says. His voice has changed again, like he's soothing a skittish animal. "We don't have to talk about it."

"This wasn't a good idea," I say. "I shouldn't—I—"

"*Rose.*" Distantly, I realize that for all of our sessions, this is the first time he's heard me lose it. "Are you okay?"

"I have to go," I whisper. "I'm sorry."

"Rose, wait—"

I hang up before he can finish. It's not long before my phone buzzes again—Maurice, calling me back. I finally do what I should have done from the start: I throw it as hard as I can, like an insect, like a poisonous snake. I can hear it on the other side of the living room, still vibrating. I didn't break it. Even with all my strength I didn't *break* it.

Behind me, there's a clatter. I don't want to turn. I don't want to see what it is. But my body twists on its own.

The blues and grays, the armchairs, the Past Me and Past Maurice are all gone. The living room is the way it should be. But beyond it, in the kitchen, I see something on the empty countertop. Shivering, like someone just put it down. A paring knife, just barely balanced on the edge of the tile.

"The Mockingbird said," I say quietly. I can still hear my phone, buzzing behind me. "That you came to me looking for an answer. Is this the answer I gave you?"

My only response is the knife, still shivering.

I cross the living room and gingerly move across the kitchen floor. Nothing changes. This is the model house kitchen, not the Summers'. I don't see myself, the Rose from four nights ago. And I don't see him.

But the knife keeps wobbling, balancing. And I think I know what I'm meant to try.

I walk past the knife a little ways and to the other end of the kitchen. There's no way to be exact, but I think this is just about the distance I would have been standing. And I swear, when I hit the right spot, I feel a shiver. Like I'm walking over my own grave.

And when I turn, there I am, standing in the Summers' kitchen. Straight down the barrel of Nick Lansbury's stare.

He grins. Close-lipped, crooked. "Hey, Colter."

And I'm afraid. More than I've ever been.

But he's not the one I'm afraid of anymore.

Not for a while now.

DECEMBER 27, FOUR NIGHTS AGO

NOTE TO SELF: They were right when they said he looks different. Not that you doubted it. It's just not something you liked to think about. Nick Lansbury is the reason you're here. You don't want him to have the decency to look ashamed about it. Less complicated if he doesn't.

But one thing hasn't changed. There he is again, just like that night. Standing squarely in front of your exit.

He stares at you. You stare back. The dark circles under his eyes make him look older. He looks every bit the haunted soul people think he is now. It doesn't make you feel better. It makes something in your throat *burn*.

"What are you doing here?" you manage to say.

The corner of his mouth twitches. "I was invited," he says. And suddenly you're very sure that he hasn't changed that much after all.

You must look—you're not sure how you look, but something must be clear to him, because he adds, "Flora asked me here. For the anniversary. For Gaby."

The heat inside you pools into your chest and pumps out into your blood, out to your limbs and your fingers and your toes. It's not like you haven't seen him since the funeral. He's in your grade now, repeating his senior year. But in the back of your mind you're always aware of his movements, his schedule, the halls that will take you past him without ever locking eyes, and when you have to see him, you have time to brace for it.

This is how it feels when you don't brace for it. This is, you think, how you've always felt. What you have been able to swallow.

It wasn't his fault, you think, a last-ditch urge to stop feeling whatever you're feeling. *It was an accident. It wasn't his fault.*

A delicate wobble in the corner of your eye catches your attention. There's a paring knife to your right, just barely balanced on the edge of the counter, as if set down in the middle of a task.

He's smiling at you now. He should stop.

"Colter," he says. "What happened with us—obviously I shouldn't have done that. But you know that Gaby—that was different, okay? It's been nice talking to Flora. It's been really, really nice. So if you could just—not say anything."

You are miles away from home in the Summers' kitchen, cool tile under your feet, a simmering, humid night beyond the windows. But right now, in this moment, you might as well be back in that night. On the road, in the dark, breathing airbag powder and misty air.

You can't tell anyone, please.

You go silent. It can't have lasted all that long in reality, but in the moment, it is an infinite stretch of time. The acid in your chest burns. The knife on the counter bobbles. Your next thought comes so fully formed, it's like a voice in your ear.

This is what it feels like to want to hurt someone.

The handle of the knife shivers to a halt. And you—*I*—imagine sliding it into my hand. Using it. I imagine it so vividly that it feels inevitable.

"Oh!"

Flora's come up behind me. She slides past my shoulder, pushing the knife safely onto the counter as she gathers Nick into her arms. "I thought you couldn't make it until Monday!"

"Got off work early," he's saying, somewhere far away.

They're both looking at me now. They're looking and they're not looking. They're looking at the me who would be here normally: silently asking me to be okay with this, even in their absolute confidence that I will be. They don't see me as I am now, with pins and needles from head to toe like all the skin is trying to crawl off my body.

What was that just now? is all I can think. *What* was *that?*

"Rose?" Flora says slowly. *Please don't say anything*, her smile begs. *Please just be okay with this.*

I don't say anything. I don't trust myself to. I smile, and I leave the room.

And I pack my bag.

THE LOCAL TIME is 11:46 p.m., and there are three hundred and thirty-two miles between Las Vegas, Nevada, and San Diego, California.

The GPS sits on the hood, a bright pop against the night.

It calculates four hours and thirty-one minutes for the drive home.

I want this to be over. I want this to be over. I want this to be over. Please just let this be over.

Twenty-Eight

THE ANSWER

WE RETURN TO the present in bursts:

The reds and oranges of the model house kitchen.

The paring knife, still balanced on the counter next to my hand.

The Flood, opposite me, wearing my face, my clothes from that night. The handle of Flora Summer's paring knife rests in her upturned palm.

"Listen," the Flood says. "Remember. Understand."

"I am. I do." I cross my arms, like it'll stop something. Like it'll hold this all in. "You saw that happen, didn't you? Was this where you found me?"

The Flood nods once. Their face, my face, is a careful blank.

"And did you know what I was thinking," I say, "standing in that kitchen?"

I could swear, for a second, that a shadow crosses the whites of their eyes. But they nod again, impassive as ever.

A little, painful sound escapes my throat and clapping my hands over my mouth doesn't smother it. "Earlier that night,"

I whisper, through my fingers, "I told Flora what was—what's going on with me. She said that it was—She didn't finish, but—she was going to say 'dangerous.' Wasn't she?"

Their face does darken this time.

"And is that what you think?" I say. "That I'm dangerous?"

Their gaze shifts to the knife, still balanced delicately on their palm. Their head inclines, just slightly, almost like a bird's.

"Please"—the words come out in a rush, a torrent—"please, you don't have to do this."

"Understand," the Flood says softly.

"I don't," I say. "I didn't—I've been trying not to think about it. I haven't tried to understand it. Please, this doesn't have to be the answer—"

They open their mouth again. But not for words this time. A torrent of water spills out, more than any human could ever contain, splashing onto the floors, against the walls. Their edges blur, like a dam opening, until they no longer look like me. They are dark, churning liquid, rushing toward me.

The foundations of the house tremble. The windows rattle. Slowly at first, then steadily, water begins to pour down through the roof, through the cracks in the windowsills. The wallpaper starts to lift from the walls, like the house is tearing itself to pieces strip by strip.

And the distant roar of that ancient ocean—it builds like a train, bearing down on me.

I was supposed to get my things. Right now, I couldn't remember where they were if someone held a gun to my head. Nothing I own is as important as running, and running *now*.

The blast of sound as I hit the front steps rattles like a physical blow. My vision tunnels, I barely recognize Marin Levinson's front porch under my feet. I need to focus, I need to *focus*, but my blood is clawing at my skin and my lungs are inching up my throat and I know I'm not dying but right now that's impossible to remember. I get down the stairs and to the cul-de-sac, and I stay on my feet, but—

The world flips on its axis as I turn the corner. I'm not headed away from the Levinson house anymore, I'm headed *back toward it*. The houses and streetlights, barely more than sketches against the vibrant center of my memory, shivering with every bass beat.

I scramble into a turn and sprint for the cul-de-sac. This time, I dart down a different street, but again, the world flips, again it sets me on a track for that bright shivering house. It happens again, and again, and even at the farthest I can get, the volume never fades.

There are other flashes, too. Felix's family, loading up the car. Alex's father, sweeping a table of meds into a backpack. Cassie, moving silently across a lawn under that eerie green sky. Mom, sitting by the window in our apartment, just watching.

My foot catches on an edge in the sidewalk, throwing me on hands and knees to the pavement, and I let out a sound I didn't realize could come from my mouth. I don't feel the pain as I push myself up. There's no space in my body for it.

I double back to the house, I climb the steps, and I pound on the door.

"Shut up!" I start in with one fist, then two, then with every bit of my weight. The wood bows inward with the force of me. I throw myself against it. "Shut up, shut up, *shut up*, SHUT UP!"

It doesn't shut up, it doesn't *stop*, even when my words become howls, and I sink to the side of the house and clamp my hands over my ears. My fingernails dig into my scalp. The house pounds against my back.

I drag air in through my nose and out through my mouth, rapidly at first, and then timed in the way I've been taught, in for seven, hold for two, out for eleven. *In—you're okay. Hold—you're okay. Out—you're okay.*

After a while, I can whisper to myself on the exhales. "Shh. You're okay. You're okay. It's okay."

I'm gradually aware that the shuddering of the house has slowed. The music has stopped. The only beats against my back are my own heart. I don't recognize the front door I'm leaning against, but I know I'm back in Lethe Ridge.

Dazed, I take stock. There are beads of blood against my jeans from where I tripped, bits of pavement in my palms. My throat feels ripped and raw. I can't help but feel a distant sense of wonder at how thoroughly I just lost my shit.

I'm not sure what me "letting it out" looks like, I confessed to Maurice once.

Like that, apparently.

The air stings my skin as the sweat starts to cool, and little by little, my breathing evens out. Lethe Ridge shivers, as if bracing for the impact we can both feel coming. And that presence all around me, that overwhelming feeling I've come to recognize as the Flood—it doesn't leave me altogether, but it diffuses, as if spreading to every corner of town. And that tornado-dark sky saps the last of the color out of Lotus Valley.

I feel for sure now that the Flood's attention isn't on me

anymore. That they've set their sights, permanently, on the town ahead.

But I don't think they've crossed the borders yet. Lethe Ridge, and everything beyond it, lies undisturbed for now. I'd felt the world crumbling at the edges during the attack. But here it still is.

I squeeze my eyes shut and run my still-shaking hand through my hair. Nothing's harder than trying to think post-panic, with my thoughts blasted apart and scattered. I raise myself onto un-steady legs and turn to the distant sound of cars. If I can't think, then I'm going to follow the one concrete plan I had: find the exit.

It takes time. Every house looks the same as the others. But I've got the distant sounds of the evacuation to guide me and a clumsy-but-sure urge to run. Higher brain functions can follow. I'm shivering still. I miss my sweatshirt. It's probably still behind the couch at Flora's.

Don't get lost in your head. The thought is automatic. That's why we're all here right now, isn't it? Because I couldn't follow my own rule?

But there's a second thought, a little stronger than the first. All I've done since I got to Lotus Valley was keep myself from thinking about Flora's. And I think that made it worse. I haven't tried to understand what I felt, looking at Nick. I haven't tried to figure out what answer I gave *myself*, let alone the conclusion that the Flood came to.

It hits me with enough force for a moment that my footsteps slow. And again, I take stock of what the Flood has shown me so far. Sutton Avenue, Flora's kitchen, the thrift shop, Maurice's office, Marin's party, the morning of Gaby's funeral. All con-nected to something I felt in that present moment, as concrete as the cul-de-sac on the TV or as vague as a shirt, a window, a similar emotion. But all connected to how I feel about my diagnosis, too.

Except for the morning of Gaby's funeral. That was months before my diagnosis.

Unless that one was meant to be about Flora and me.

Think, I tell myself. The Flood showed me that after our first real conversation. What were we talking about?

This is your home. You're really going to destroy it?

Can you tell me why?

That was their answer. Flora and me, on that floor, on that morning. Why was that their answer?

The faraway rumble of voices grows stronger, distracting me for a moment, and when I cut through the next backyard, I find the fence I scaled that first morning. As I hoist myself over, the crowd briefly swings into view, clustered on a high hill half a mile out. My legs quiver a little harder just looking at the climb. But I've barely taken a step when a car pulls up next to me.

A back door swings open. And John Jonas flashes that implacable smile. "I foresaw that you needed a ride."

With a shaky laugh, I get in.

We park near a cluster of cars on the far side of the hill, and I mumble a thank-you as I let myself out. I don't think he hears me. He, like the gathered crowd up ahead, only has eyes for the town below.

There are two people watching for me, though: Felix and Alex, standing a little apart from the crowd. And when they catch me coming, they break into a run.

"Rose," Alex gasps out. His face is bloodless. "She's not with you?"

Just over their shoulders, I can see Sandy, her hands twisted, her eyes red. There's a rush through my ears. I hardly hear my answer over it. "No one's with me," I say. "What happened?"

"Cassie's—Cassie's gone," Felix says. "You were taking so long, we thought maybe she'd gone to get you, but—she never met up with Sandy at all. She's not here."

I turn back to the faint outline of Lethe Ridge. Maybe I missed her, back there in that labyrinth of houses, but—

It's fine, Rose, Cassie said, before. *Actually, I'm tired of waiting.* And I think of that glimpse of her in the Flood. Walking alone.

"She never left town," I say.

"Why the hell would she—"

The rush of blood to my ears drowns out the rest of the sentence. I have to go back. I have to get her. But I can feel it—the full force of the Flood, almost here. There's not going to be enough time. Not if I can't convince them to stop this.

I screw my eyes shut. *Think, Rose. Try one more time.*

And this once, I let myself think about the morning of Gaby's funeral. Fully think about it. And I remember exactly what went through my mind, standing in that doorway. When she asked me to take that reading. When I took on her grief, and then I never put it down.

"I don't want to," I gasp, "but I have to."

"What?" Alex says.

"That first night I spoke to the Flood," I say. "I asked them why they were doing this. That's what they were trying to tell me. I don't want to, but I have to." I take a steadying breath. "I have to go back."

"I'm coming with you," Alex says.

"Allie—" Felix starts. He gets *just* that far when Alex rounds on him.

"I'm going," Alex grits out, "to town. And if you think you're going to talk me out of it—"

"*Alex.*" Felix squeezes a sigh through his teeth. "I know."

Alex, who's halfway through a retort, all but freezes on the spot. "You do?"

"Wait here," Felix says. As he turns and sprints to the blur of a police car, Alex watches him go, still tensed for the argument that didn't come. I think he's forgotten that I'm here.

Felix comes back with three long cylinders tucked under his arm. "Signal flares. We split up, cover more ground. Whoever finds Cassie fires one of these, and then we *all* get out."

Something not quite readable passes across Alex's face, but in the course of a moment, it hardens into resolve. He steps forward, raises himself onto his toes, and reaches out—past the flares and up to Felix's collar, which he grabs and pulls. And then he kisses him.

It's not a *long* kiss—we don't have much time, after all. He draws back after a moment, smiling as Felix's lips chase him a ways.

"Thank you," Alex says. Then, sliding a flare out of Felix's now-loose arm, he ducks into the passenger's seat of Felix's car.

I take my own flare as Felix stares slack-jawed after him. "Congratulations," I say.

He tightens his grip on the last flare and turns, but not before I catch the rush of blood to his face.

I let them go ahead for a moment—just long enough to catch my breath, to hold the flare a little tighter in my hand. Behind me, the desert opens, long and vast and somehow as narrow as Flora's doorway. Full of innumerable exits that I can't—won't—take.

I'm not sure I can do this.

But I have to. And this time, I want to.

So one more time, we climb into Felix's car. And unnoticed by the crowd, we drive down the hill and toward the town. Back to Lotus Valley. And back to the Flood.

Twenty-Nine

THE FLOOD

WE SPLIT UP at the gates of Lethe Ridge, leaving the car parked on the shoulder. I kiss both of them on the cheek before I go. Felix doubles back into the housing development, and Alex veers west, in the direction of city hall. And I head the other way, straight down Morningside Drive.

I don't need to guess where I'm going. I've been able to feel it since we crossed into town. A tug at my ankles, like an undertow.

The sick green tinge of the sky has turned dark gray and unsettled, and it's only getting darker as I go. No longer the color of an oncoming storm—the look, instead, of a storm that's already here.

And I'm heading right into the middle of it.

Once I'm sure Felix and Alex are far behind me, I stop holding my shoulders so tightly together, stop clenching my fists into the fabric of my shirt. There's no one else around. And I don't particularly care if the Flood sees me shaking.

I pass empty houses and their scattered signs of recently departed life: doors open, luggage forgotten on curbs and driveways. I pass Theresa Gibson's garage, still lit in a sea of shuttered storefronts. She's in there probably. Waiting.

And as I pass, head farther down Morningside Drive, I see another sign of life. A massive, tangled web of shadows, stretched so wide and so far, I don't even see Christie. Rudy's just waiting. Ready for the fight we've been holding him back from these past three days.

He's not rushing at me this time. The Flood isn't following me anymore, after all. But I can feel him watching as I approach. Like he's . . . considering me.

I take a long, slow breath. We've been operating, all this time, on the assumption that if given the opportunity to fight the Flood, he wouldn't be able to resist. That he only knows one way to protect Christie.

But I think of their long drive back to Lotus Valley, of how she came to want for him to be something good. She said she didn't know if they wanted the same things. Maybe it's time to ask.

"Hey, big guy." I manage a queasy smile. "I think I can handle this on my own. But Cassie's still in town somewhere. Can you help Christie find her?"

For a long moment, he's still. My back is so rigid, it hurts. But at length, there's a low, pensive growl. And he recedes back into the heart of the town.

I exhale hard. "Good boy."

The beats of my heart feel like fists at a door. Weeks' worth of lost sleep throbs at the backs of my eyelids. But it's a little easier to think than it was before. At a time like this, I should be thinking of Mom, or Dan, or Sammy. Or Gaby. Always Gaby.

And I'm thinking of Maurice instead. Of a day months and

months ago, reading an email from the Astronomy Club advisor. Of the tone I'd affected, reciting it out loud.

Read it again without the voice, he'd laughed.

Someone's shouting in the distance. I can't discern the distance in the whipping of the wind, but I can make out the voice. Christie Jones, calling out something to Rudy. Without any idea, I think, that the girl she considers a daughter might be close enough to hear her, too.

It's impossible to tune her out. But that's just what I have to do. There's only one way to help now.

"Can you hear me?" I call.

At first, I think they're beyond hearing me, until I see a flicker of movement by a dark, shuttered ice-cream shop. The Flood stands against the glass facade, wearing my face again.

I freeze, and in response, they're nearly as still. Then they nod.

I let out a long, slow breath. "I didn't understand," I say, "what you were trying to tell me before. And I'm so sorry for that. I know you must be tired of holding this back. But if you really don't want to do this, then let's talk one more time. I want to be sure I give you the right answer."

It's quiet long enough that I don't think they heard me. But, imperceptibly at first, the world begins to spin.

The first scenes I see, in flashbulb-quick bursts, aren't mine. Some are as sweeping as war or famine or disaster, some as intimate as small, barely attended funerals, or the last devastating blow of an argument. They never linger long enough for me to see the details of anyone's face beyond the despair written in their features, front and center, but the final image wavers for a long moment. Cassie, tucked into the corner of two buildings. I hear

Christie's voice again—whether that's in the Flood's projection or here in reality, it's hard to tell, but Cassie's fingers curl into her hair as they clamp over her ears, like she can hear it, too.

The Flood doesn't think like I do. But I know racing thoughts when I see them.

"Focus." The word's punched out of me, shorter and harsher than I meant it. It gets the Flood's attention. Cassie's face fades back into mine, implacable and waiting. "If I'm going to understand you, we need to use my memories. Okay?"

The scene begins to waver again. But this time it darkens at the edges, narrows into a point, and solidifies into a single, white-and-glass front door.

All at once, the silence shatters into a low, vibrating beat, and the shadows shift into Marin Levinson's neighborhood, Marin Levinson's party. I'm standing on the porch, and toward the end of the cul-de-sac, I see movement. There's a girl on her hands and knees, her breath coming in shuddering gasps as she rides out the end of her first panic attack.

That first night in Lotus Valley, May 24 Rose Colter looked normal to me, digging through her back seat and wrapping herself into her overshirt. But I'm no longer afraid to look into the car—I step to the driver's side window, my face just inches from hers. I can see the fine tremor running through her, the blank, dazed stare. I can see shock that's about to tip into fear.

But when I look for something perceptibly different—something wrong in the way she looks, the way she holds herself—I don't see that.

"Show me another one," I say, and the scene whirls.

There's a quick glimpse of a familiar sight—a road, the long shadow of a tree—before we settle into my own darkened apartment. The windows are open, the sounds of our street drift in like the walls are no barrier at all. I can't feel the temperature through the Flood's projection, but I can imagine the lingering summer heat in the air.

I stand opposite another Rose, halfway down the hall, silhouetted in the low light from her room behind her. Visibly, she's more pulled-together than her May 24 counterpart. But as she lifts a hand to her mouth, I see the same fear at the back of her gaze.

"Oh," she whispers. "Oh, shit."

In the next moment, there's grass under my feet, and in front of me, the bright corona of light through the edges of a door. Out of the corner of my eye, I see the shadow of branches. I turn my head away as I reach for the door. I'm not there yet. That can wait.

I cross the threshold, and step right into the thrift shop that July afternoon, wedged in that narrow aisle between a baby carriage and a group of women. I look at myself closely this time. But that clawing, desperate panic I felt—that's not there, not visibly. I look pale, instead. Sick.

"Honey? You okay?" the woman with the carriage asks.

Here in the present, I flinch. I—don't remember that. I didn't notice, or I didn't hear.

Next: Me again, on the floor of the Summers' master bedroom, holding Flora Summer in my arms. "Shhh, shh, shh," she breathes, not loud enough to be a whisper, as Flora buries her wail in Rose's neck. "It's okay. It's okay. It's okay."

Something in my chest clenches, tight enough to make me dizzy.

She—I—I talk to Flora, to us both, like my fingers are locked at the end of a ledge, like my words might keep us from falling.

I don't know why I expected to sound insincere. Like I was faking that empathy, or that I wasn't capable of it anymore. Even after everything that's happened with Flora, I still feel it now.

The Flood doesn't wait for my prompt this time—we move to the next scene on their own, from one Summer bedroom to the next. To a moment just four nights ago.

Except this time, the scene flips. I'm not watching myself do it. I'm sitting here, on the bed with Flora, right here in the memory.

At first, I freeze. She watches me, curious and intent. And I realize I need to say my lines.

"I, um," I say. I don't have to think back to the words. They're right there waiting for me. "We. My therapist and I, I guess. We think it's something like . . . post-traumatic stress disorder."

Flora's face freezes. That, at least, is like I remember. What I don't remember is hedging so much, circling those four letters, trying to soften the blow. In my memory, I just said it.

"What?" Flora's breathless, like I've punched her.

"It's really not that bad," I say, quickly. I'm not sure if it's me feeling this or me from four nights ago feeling this, or if we're both on the same page here, just desperate to make her hear us. "It sounds more dramatic than it actually is."

I said it to make her feel better. But it wasn't completely untrue. That's what Maurice kept trying to say. That I could go through hell and it didn't mean I was broken.

"Why did I tell you?" I whisper to the image of Flora. The memory doesn't react. "When Maurice told me to tell someone, why did I decide it had to be you?"

My little brother, Sammy, is the one who texts me composition practice every day, trying to turn the sound of my phone into something good again. My stepfather, Dan, is the one who tries to make sure I drive alone as little as possible, who rests his hand on my shoulder on tight curves. Mom is the one who smoothed her hand over my cheek just two weeks ago and asked, *Rosie, you know if there's ever anything . . .*

"All this," I say, ending my thought out loud, "and I told *you*? You were always going to react like this. You always did with Gaby. Did I think you'd understand because you lost her, too? Or did I—"

I choke on the next words. But I know what I was going to say. *Did I hope you'd set aside your own feelings and just comfort me? Just like I did for you, that morning we buried her?* Probably that. Probably both.

"You're grieving, sweetheart," Flora says, the memory uninterrupted. "Of course you should talk to someone if you need it. But what you're talking about—that's a serious condition. That's . . ."

This time, I don't just finish her sentence in my head. I say it out loud, faintly. "Dangerous."

And then the memory goes off script.

"Oh—" Flora's face freezes. The way it would have, I think, had we done this in reality. "No—no, sweetheart, that's not what I meant."

She smiles, anxiously, down at me. Looking at her, I'm reasonably sure of two things. That it was exactly what she meant. And that the way she's looking at me isn't fear. More like how she looked at me later that evening, standing side by side with Nick. *Please just be okay with this.*

THE VALLEY AND THE FLOOD

And I think I'm finally sure of the answer I gave the Flood that night. That the two of us had this danger, this damage that needed to be contained. For me, that answer meant that the PTSD had changed me in ways that I couldn't take back. For the Flood, it meant that all the fear and pain they'd taken in had changed them, too. That they needed to hold it all in, or it would overtake everything, just like the ocean they once were overtook this desert. That they were destruction once, and they might be destruction again. And if we couldn't control the things that brought us here, or how we felt about them, then maybe we couldn't control ourselves.

It might have been the wrong answer.

"Keep going." I breathe. There's only one memory that'll tell us, one way or the other.

And when the world twists into that familiar shape, I don't look at the road, or the tree—I look across the ditch, across the battered car, and lock eyes with Nick Lansbury. "Not here," I say. "I've spent enough time here."

Nick's gaze is so blank, so measured, that I know it has to be the Flood looking at me through his eyes. Nick's head tilts, politely curious.

"Go on. It's okay," I say. "You know where I want to go."

I hold the Flood's stare as Sutton Avenue brightens and fades. The yellow light of the Summers' kitchen pops against the evening dark through the line of windows on our right side. It's like the world beyond has ceased to exist.

The only way I can make myself reach toward the counter is if I don't look at it. I don't close my fingers until the handle fits against my flat palm. I don't lift the knife until I gently map out the blade with the pad of my index finger, my touch too light to break skin.

Nick's eyes get a little brighter as, for the first time, I see the Flood's gaze light up with interest.

My arm shakes, almost too hard to keep my grip as I lift the knife.

This isn't the Summers' kitchen, and the figure opposite me isn't Nick Lansbury. What I do here changes nothing. But those facts fall away, bit by bit, the longer I look at him. The reason Gaby no longer exists. The reason for everything.

I could do whatever I want, couldn't I? I could do whatever I want, and I'd be the only one to know.

And even here, where it doesn't count? I put the knife down.

Then I start to *laugh*. I press one hand over my face, wrap one arm around my stomach, and I laugh so hard my face hurts. "I wouldn't have done it," I gasp. "I never would have done it."

I turn, addressing the walls this time. "I never would have done it!"

The trappings of the memory fall away like a curtain, and I can see where we really are: back in Lotus Valley, standing in the pitch-black of Morningside Drive.

That's when I see little white crests forming in the edges of the shadows, and I realize: that distant roar is here now. Dark, gathering water, the full force of the Flood, blocking my view on every side.

I smile. And slowly, I unfold my arm and extend my hand.

"I want to change my answer," I say, breathless. "Will you listen?"

There's a low rumble from deep within the earth, and a damp

chill against the tips of my fingers, which flinch back against the feeling. I hold them where they are. I can't pull away. No matter what.

"You've seen so much," I say softly. "And then to meet me like you did, in that kitchen? Poor thing. You must have been so scared."

There's a stillness, at first. I keep my hand where it is.

"I don't know if this will help, but . . ." I take a slow, deep breath. The air tastes like sharp points. "God, I never thought I'd be the kind of person quoting my therapist, but he told me that we don't just talk about terrible things to purge them from ourselves. We talk about them so that the people who love us can tell us when we're wrong. That we're being unkind to ourselves, or unfair, or that the things that have happened to us are not our fault. Because fear turns the world a different color, and we don't always see clearly through it.

"It wasn't like I thought he was wrong. But I've always known myself so well. And then it was like there was this new person where I used to be, and I wasn't sure I knew what she was capable of." I take a long, slow breath. "But I hate Nick Lansbury as much as someone can hate *anyone,* and I was still never going to pick up that knife. The worst thing that was ever going to happen was that they were going to know I wasn't okay with it. Or, you know, okay in general. That they were going to know what I'd become, but I . . ."

My fingers quiver against the bristling of the wind. "But I haven't *become* anything. I am exactly as dangerous as I've always been, because I am exactly the person I've always been."

The Flood's gone still. The chop of the water, the silent white peaks of the waves have smoothed out. It's like a breath being held.

"Do you think that maybe it's the same for you?" I ask. "Because I don't think this is who you've been for a long time. Are you really dangerous? Or did you start to believe that witnessing terrible things makes you capable of them, too?"

The water towers high above my head. I take a step toward it. "I know you've been fighting this for a long time," I say. "I know you can always hear that water coming, because I've been hearing it, too. But I don't think that's real. I think that's a memory. And I think you can let that memory come."

The waters actually recede from my feet, just a few inches. Still trying to protect me.

"Hey. It's okay. It's going to be okay." I lower the pitch of my voice. The hard edges of the words drop to a soft, gentle swish. I don't know how much they understand. But knowing what to say, even now, is easy. Think of what you want to hear most in this world, and tell them.

The words aren't easy to get out. But if I don't believe this will work, neither will the Flood. So I believe it down to my toes instead.

"This is not what you are anymore," I whisper. "And I'm going to stay with you until this is over, because I know you're not going to hurt me. You don't have to keep holding this back. All that pain you've taken in, all these years—you can let it go."

A fine tremble runs through the water, the last vestiges of the dam. There's still some unconscious force drawing away, holding it back.

"Shhh," I breathe. "It's okay. Everything's okay."

I hear the *snap* right before it happens, like the last fiber of a fraying rope. And then I'm surrounded by damp, cold air.

I don't see anything this time—just darkness, just water.

But the water doesn't touch me.

What I feel instead are decades of emotions: some recognizable, others abstract, not quite human. They rush past, too quickly to discern, not long enough to grasp. It's like listening to a sad story. It's like holding Flora Summer in my arms on her carpeted floor, feeling her tears on my shirt. It's like all of that in seconds, or maybe longer.

And through it all, I think I see someone next to me. A short figure with black-dyed hair and a flowing, long-gone maxi dress, holding my hand.

The water passes. My right side clears, then my left, then the sky over my head. Dawn has started to creep into the spiderweb of clouds. And when I look behind me, all I see is the sweep of something passing through town like a gust of wind.

I take a long breath. It tastes like the first hint of a hot, hazy day.

The last fading tendrils of the Flood slip out of the clouds. They slip over the edge of the horizon, leaving only the empty, slightly disheveled stillness of Morningside Drive.

It's not quite empty, though. Small and in the distance, nearly out of sight, I see someone stumble from the alcove of a building, her blonde curls rumpled, blinking at the sky. I see another, dwarfed by the swirling shadows around her. And when they see each other, they meet in the middle.

I'm too far away to hear them. I don't need to. The way Christie grabs near-frantic at Cassie's face, her hair, the way Cassie nods, her lips forming the same words over and over, the way they fall into the hug, inevitable as gravity—that's everything I need to know.

It's a while before they notice me.

I think I'm smiling as I wave them over. And even from a distance, I can see their mouths hanging open.

The sun is rising on another new year. One full year since I lost Gaby.

And somehow, here I am.

Thirty

THE RETURN

"IT'S NORMAL."

For the first time since I've met him—but possibly not the last—I'd like to take Maurice by his thoughtful, empathetic shoulders and shake him, just a little. "Seriously," I say.

"Seriously," he says. "Completely normal."

"I wanted—" I have just enough sense left that I remember where I am, turn my head a little away from the street where the crowds have started to mill back into Lotus Valley. "I wanted to *kill* him."

"Of course you did," he says. "From what you've told me, I'd be surprised if you *didn't* want to kill him just a little."

"Maurice," I say, plaintive.

His laughter echoes through the phone speaker. It's making my head spin, just a little. But also, I think I really worried him. So I can deal with him laughing at me a little. "I don't mean to tease you. But, Rose—having the thought doesn't make it more likely to happen."

I let out a long, slow breath. It's what I know now—intellectually, at least—to be true. Hearing him say it knocks something out of me.

"I can't stop thinking about it," I say, softer.

"Imagining hurting someone—that's not the same thing as wanting to," he says gently. "Intrusive thoughts feed off each other, especially when they're distressing. Remember what I said before? If you told yourself not to think about polar bears, the first thing you'd do is think about a polar bear."

"Yeah, you said that," I shoot back. "And yet I'm still thinking about gutting Nick Lansbury in Flora Summer's kitchen. Where's this polar bear I was promised?"

I think better of that about two seconds later. "Um," I say. "That was—"

"Joking about it is good, Rose," he says. And I hear the smile there. "You can't control your own thoughts. But you can find ways to neutralize them, or turn them on their head. That's something we can work on together."

"Oh," I say. It sounds—not simple, exactly. But more straight-forward than I imagined. "That would be nice."

"And . . ." He hesitates. "It sounds like you've been worrying quite a lot about how you might have changed, this past year."

There's a silence. I don't realize he's waiting for me to speak until he says my name again.

"Yeah," I say faintly. I was distracted for a moment. Because in the little alcove between the two shops across the street, the scenery has slowly but surely begun to change.

"I can see you sooner than Thursday, if you like," he says. "When will you be home?"

In the alcove, shimmering like the surface of water, is a glimpse into a bedroom. Mine. I'm sitting on my bed, my knees pulled up to my chest, my shoulders shivering. And across from me, concern and love and a hint of Biblical anger written into her face, is Gaby.

Not anger at me, of course. Anger at whoever it was who made me cry. I can't tell, looking at it, who that might've been, when this might've been. All I can look at is her face.

"No, it's—Thursday's good," I say, in a voice outside of myself. "I'm going to have a lot to say, so. I need to think of the best way to say it."

"You *are* heading home, though," he says. His tone suggested I *better* be heading home.

I laugh again, around that concave feeling in my gut. In the alcove, Gaby scoots closer to me, takes my face in both her hands.

Oh, Rosie, I hear her whisper. She presses a kiss to my hair. *Oh, honey. It's okay. It's okay.*

"In a couple of hours," I say faintly.

"Drive safely," he says. And then, after a pause: "Thank you for telling me, Rose."

I blink. And my bedroom, and me, and Gaby—we're all gone.

I wrap my free arm around the curve of my waist. There's something inside of my throat, something jagged and stuck that hurts worse than I could have imagined. But I can still feel her hands on my arms, my cheeks, my forehead. And they're warm.

"Thank you for listening, Maurice," I say. And I hang up.

I cross the street, maneuvering around the steady stream of people making their way back into town. The first few don't notice me. I wonder if to most of them, I'll be this distant, cryptic thing, the strange girl who brought upheaval and a brush with disaster to their sleepy town. But then fingers brush my arm.

"I saw her," someone whispers. "Thank you."

I turn. And Adrienne, her eyes wet and smiling, winks at me.

"Your next coffee's on me," she says. And then she keeps walking.

A few more call to me as they walk past. *"Be well, kid,"* says Ace Martin. *"Thanks, or whatever,"* says Loreen. *"Goodbye, goodbye, goodbye,"* whisper the creatures from the theater as they sail overhead, drifting back home.

And looking around, in the maze of confused and weary faces, I see the awe and gratitude and overwhelming pain. All across Lotus Valley, even up to the high ground of the hills, the past became the present for one night. And for them, it was gone.

I step out of the way and leave the street clear for everyone to pass, to carry everything they've seen over the past several hours back to their homes. I move, instead, into the alcove, where Gaby and I were sitting just a second ago.

This is a hole I'll never fill. But I don't want to. I want to preserve this spot where she stood until time and erosion wear it away.

"Thank you," I say as I feel the Flood's chill around my shoulders. Because we finally, finally understand each other.

I'm not sure how long we stay like that. Eventually, I feel a hand against my arm, and when I turn, Cassie's there. Her face looks puffy and red, and her eyes are still brimming.

And yet when she hugs me, she cradles the back of my head, runs her hand through my hair, like I'm the one being comforted.

I understand that better when I go to speak and I can't get the words out.

I don't cry, though. Not yet. Crying, I think, is going to take time, unwrapping those layers of performances and straight faces. But I was the one who wrapped them. So I think I must know where the knots are tied.

"So," I whisper. "I don't think you have a shot at second-most accurate now."

She pulls back, her mouth a perfect O. "*Wow.*"

I let out a choked laugh. "What do you think changed?"

"Well. I'm guessing." Her shoulders twitch, like she's too tired to shrug properly. "But I think they were just so convinced they were going to hurt us, that that's what I saw. I've never seen a vision of anyone's *fears* before. But I'll think long and hard about what that means once I've slept for eight years."

"Might boost your status in the prophet world," I say.

"I mean. It might." Cassie's still scowling. But she looks thoughtful, too. "But I think we can all agree that I still get to be mad as hell, right?"

"Oh God, yeah," I say, so quickly that she snorts. "You lost family. Years of your life."

"It's a lot to think about," she says softly. "But. Well. I suddenly have a lot of time I wasn't planning on."

She's smiling. I don't understand why until I see Christie Jones making her way through the crowd, Maggie Williams trailing behind her. Her parasol is by her side, and Rudy's tendrils spread from her feet, whipping all around her.

"And," Cassie says, "I didn't lose everything."

Over my shoulder, I smile back at her, even as I stand a little straighter at Christie's approach. There's something rigid in the way she's walking. It occurs to me too late that she's still holding Rudy back.

"I spoke to Theresa," she says, by way of greeting. "And your car is ready whenever you are. She fixed it within a day, apparently. But, well. Didn't tell you, for obvious reasons." Her gaze darts over my shoulder and then softens—I think maybe Cassie just shot her a look. "I don't want to rush you," she says. "You're welcome here as long as you like, though I'm sure you want to be back with your family."

"And . . . ?" I say, mildly. Because she's still looking over my shoulder, but not at Cassie.

Finally, she looks at me properly. Rudy's many arms stretch, just a little, toward me. "And," she says, resigned, "the Flood is following you again, aren't they?"

Next to me, Cassie doesn't flinch. If I wasn't watching Rudy's slow approach across the pavement, I would have been touched that she's still holding my hand.

"Please don't hurt them," I say. I'm not sure if I'm talking to Christie or the shadow at her feet.

"Rose, look at me." Christie's dark brown eyes hold mine for a long beat. "We don't want to hurt them."

Maggie, who'd been letting her take the lead, blinks. "We don't?"

"This was a misunderstanding," Christie says. "We know that. But you need to be at home, where you can heal. And you don't have to bring them back with you. We can figure something out."

I hold her stare. She looks so concerned. For the first time all week, she doesn't have to be.

"I don't think," I say slowly, "that they'll be with me forever. That's not what either of us wants. But if they're around a little while longer—we're okay with that. If that makes sense."

THE VALLEY AND THE FLOOD

"Still." Christie's lips are pursed, tight. "This is living memory itself. Their concept of 'a little while' might be very different than yours."

There's a light stir of air at my back. I reach up to touch my shoulder, as if they have a hand to hold. Just hours ago, the worst thing you could have said to me was that I would never be able to shake the Flood. And now, with them standing as close to me as it's possible to get, I know that I won't. We'll drift gradually, maybe, like plates beneath the earth: shift by minuscule shift. I don't know how long it's going to take. And that doesn't scare me.

"They're safe with me," I say. "And I'm safe with them."

The crease on Christie's brow melts away. And gently, Rudy's limbs loosen and recede. One slides into my palm and, laughing, I scratch it until I hear a low purr.

"Well," she says, a little rueful. "That sound good to you, Maggie? I think she knows better than we do."

Maggie's lips thin, and for a moment, it looks like she's going to object. "It's all the same to me, Christie." She sighs. "That's not what I came here for, anyway."

"You didn't?" Christie says. But Maggie's attention is now, fully, on me.

"Rose," she says. "You're going to be all right. I wanted you to know."

I meet her solemn, steady gaze. I've heard a lot of grand pronouncements from Maggie Williams these past few days. But Cassie was right. It sounds different when you're sure.

And I'm grateful. It's nice to be reminded. But I mean it when I tell her, "I know."

———

CASSIE, FELIX, AND Alex walk me to Theresa's garage. Or rather, Cassie walks me to the garage, and Felix and Alex gaze into the other's eyes.

"You guys are gonna crash into a pole," I say, with all the love in my heart.

Alex pulls Felix into another short but emphatic kiss, and Felix reels back, grinning. "Gonna be worth it," he says dreamily.

"I've been waiting on this for the better part of a year," Alex says. "So I'm collecting. With interest."

"You've been—a year?" Felix says. "So you didn't realize—"

"Oh, no," Alex says, "I knew you were interested, too."

"And you didn't ever say *anything*?" Felix says.

"Felix," Alex says, with a slow, fond smile. "I really, really like you. But if you didn't stop treating me like fine china, I would have had to kill you."

Felix frowns. Then nods. He's still got the look of a guy who thinks he's dreaming and isn't going to question it. "That's fair."

Satisfied, Alex settles back into the arm Felix wraps around his shoulders. Theresa's garage slowly settles into view ahead, shimmering in the desert afternoon.

"You're not headed out right away, right?" Felix calls up to me.

I shake my head. Freshly fixed or not, my car isn't going to do well in the heat of the day. "Tonight, when the sun goes down. I was actually hoping that once we pick up the car, you'd all let me get you a slice of pie? It's the least I can do to make up for all this."

"You don't have to make up for anything," Felix says, to

which Alex nods fervently. "I'll buy my own slice."

"I'm in more of a strawberry milk shake mood?" Cassie doesn't have to look back at Felix and Alex to add, after a beat, "Which I will of course pay for myself."

I do my best to look preoccupied with straightening the sign on Theresa's door. It gives me a couple of seconds to swallow the lump in my throat. "Wait out here?" I ask. "I'll be right back."

No one fights me on that. They are, at least, willing to leave this last little bit of awkwardness to me.

I open the door to find Theresa Gibson pressing the hood of my car back into place.

She doesn't turn to look, and I think, for a second, she didn't hear me come in. But a beat later she calls, "There you are. I've been waiting all morning."

There's no trace of that usual ease in her tone, but somehow I smile at her anyway. "Kind of a mixed message," I say. "You wanted me here and now you want me gone?"

"Not exactly fair, maybe," she grunts. "But I'd just as soon—"

She cuts herself off. Her gaze has shifted to the desk. The wall's blocking where she's looking. But that picture must still be there.

"You didn't see your father?" I ask quietly.

"Oh, I saw him. Something that looked like him, anyway." The brisk clip of her tone fades into something bitter. "But that wasn't him, was it? It was an echo, just like you said."

Slowly, I take a step closer. "You've been researching the Flood for months," I say. "You had to know already that they weren't going to bring back the dead."

"That's not what I was—" I can see her teeth press down against her bottom lip, hard enough to draw blood. She squeezes her eyes shut. Then she lets the breath she's holding go. "I knew it wasn't going to bring him *back*. But I thought it would—I don't know. Stay, until I stopped caring about the difference. All those months of my life. I thought he would at least *see* me."

I'm as close to her as I'm willing to get. And I feel—not forgiveness, exactly. But something close to understanding.

"There's a bright side, at least," I say. "If you're willing to hear it."

Her gaze sharpens enough that I'm sure the answer is going to be no. But she inclines her head into a nod.

"It's that the Flood doesn't show you anything that you don't already have," I say. "For better or worse, your past is a living thing. And if you take pieces of the people you lost, make them your own—nothing ever really ends. Not completely."

If that sinks in, it's hard to tell. Her face seems to shroud, close in. She pops the earbuds out of her ears, sets them on the edge of her workbench, and gestures vaguely to a switch on the wall.

"To open the garage," she says. "When you're ready to go."

"I haven't paid you," I say.

"I've done enough. I'm not taking your money. Don't worry about closing up behind you. I'll be in the back." She turns away, as if to leave, but then she hesitates. "Thanks. For saying all that."

And she vanishes behind the back curtain.

It's quiet long enough that I know I'm alone now. The garage windows are too tall for me to see out, but Cassie and the others must still be out there, wondering.

I'll make this call quick.

Slowly, I slide my phone out of my pocket. My fingers are shaking too hard to dial, so I hold down the button instead. "Call Mom," I say.

She picks up quickly.

"Rosie!" Her voice is heavy and sleep-rough, like I caught her in the middle of her post-holiday afternoon nap. "Happy New Year! I thought you were going to call last night?"

I tuck the phone under my hair, cradling it to my ear. "Sorry, Mom."

"No, no, don't worry," she says. "We missed you, that's all! Dan and your brother are out back—should I bring the phone to them?"

"No, that's okay, I-I'm actually packing up here," I say. "I'm heading home tonight. So I'm going to see you all soon."

I thought I said it normally. But she pauses. "Rosie," she says. "Did something happen?"

"When I get back," I say slowly to make sure I'm heard, "can we talk? I—I mean, it can be tomorrow. I'm not leaving until tonight. It's going to be late."

I hear a shuddering breath over the line. But when she speaks next, her smile is audible. "I'll wait up for you, baby. As long as it takes. Just come home."

It takes effort to loosen my grip on the phone. If I hold it any tighter, I'm going to finally break it.

"I love you," I say, in a rush of breath. "I'll be home soon."

"I love you so much, Rosie," she whispers. "You'll be back before you know it."

I wonder if she hears it, before she hangs up, when I press the phone to my chest and hold it there—the rustle of fabric, the sound of those choked almost-sobs. I see the seconds keep ticking on my phone for a full beat before the call ends, so I think she heard it. I'm okay with that.

I keep holding it there. I take a breath. And I let it go.

JANUARY 1, NOW

LISTEN: IT HAS been two hours, twenty-five minutes, and thirty-eight seconds since you said your goodbyes and left Lotus Valley behind you.

You are long past the California border, and in the distance, you see city lights. This is where you will pull onto the shoulder and switch on your hazards. This is where you will climb out of the car and wander a little down the road, far enough that those city lights disappear into the edge of your periphery. Just far enough that you move past the path of your headlights and into black, reaching distance.

Even here, outside your car, outside the cities, with only the stars for light, you should be able to make out glimpses of the desert through the dark. But what you are looking at is not desert.

It looks infinite from here, this ocean of recorded time.

"Not much farther now," you whisper. It's anyone's guess whether this wine-dark sea can hear you. But you don't go through what the two of you did without sharing a language. You both know that, if nothing else.

It's so quiet now. You have to hold very, very still, and breathe very, very gently to hear that little cry from the churning water. *Rose, are you there? Rose, are you there?* That same sentence: looping, calling, unanswered forever.

But listen: Today it is as far away as it has ever been. It is an echo, a receding footstep, the last syllable of a dying sound. It is an alarm defending a still and empty house, long after the intruder has gone.

Keep listening. It gets quieter and quieter every day.

Resources

Post-traumatic stress disorder, or PTSD, affects about eight million people in the United States alone.

In the media and pop culture, PTSD is most commonly connected to first responders and military veterans. *But PTSD can affect anyone after any kind of traumatic event.* If you relate to any of Rose's symptoms, or if you are otherwise struggling in the wake of a traumatic experience, you don't have to struggle alone.

The National Alliance on Mental Illness (NAMI) has a comprehensive overview of PTSD symptoms and treatments, which you can access here: nami.org/About-Mental-Illness/Mental-Health-Conditions/Posttraumatic-Stress-Disorder/Overview. For information, referrals, and support, you can call 800-950-NAMI, or for crisis counseling, you can text *HOME* to 741741 if you are in the US or Canada. Text options for the UK and Ireland may be found at crisistextline.org.

If you are experiencing suicidal thoughts, please consider reaching out to the National Suicide Prevention Lifeline at 800-273-8255, or accessing their live chat at suicidepreventionlifeline.org. You can also find a directory of international suicide prevention hotlines here: suicide.org/international-suicide-hotlines.html.

Sharing your experiences with PTSD can be intimidating. You may worry that your trauma is "not bad enough" to justify your struggles. Please don't forget: Your pain is real. You deserve support. And you deserve to be heard.

Acknowledgments

Thank you, first and foremost, to my incomparable agent, Hannah Fergesen, without whom this book would not exist in its current form. I am grateful every day for your humor, patience, honesty, and editorial brilliance. I'm so lucky to have you in my corner and I'm so lucky to know you.

I am equally lucky to know Alex Sanchez, editor extraordinaire, who has been a champion for this book beyond anything I could have imagined. Thank you for your insight, your creativity, your trust, and your always impeccable style—it is such a joy to work with you and this story is so much richer for it. Thank you as well to the wonderful Razorbill team, including publisher Casey McIntyre, copyeditors Marinda Valenti and Jody Corbett, proofreaders Krista Ahlberg and Maddy Newquist, cover artist Matt Saunders, cover designer Maggie Edkins, and everyone who put their time, energy, and enthusiasm into making this book so beautiful. Thank you as well to Dr. Jennifer L. Hartstein for her careful read-through and advice.

Thank you to the Writers Room of Boston, where I wrote and revised the majority of this book, and to Debka, Alexander, and the fantastic community there. Thank you as well to the crew at Futurescapes for your invaluable feedback on the first chapter, for showing me the desert sky, and for all of your I-15 fact-checking.

The Valley and the Flood could not have been written without the brilliant, hilarious, boundlessly talented communities surrounding me. There are so many people who have given me advice, support, and hope over the years, and it would be impossible to name them all, but I'm going to try anyway. Thank you to the writers of the Mr. Crepe group (with thanks to Rachel for bringing us together), the Kidlit Alliance, and the Roaring Twenties, and thank you to my friends of the 198 (with special thanks to Kendra for being my first ARC reader), the Bridge Podcast crew, and the Forest of Mutual Pining. Thank you especially to my fellow KT Literary clients, especially my fellow Hannah clients. I don't know what I'd do without you.

I especially want to thank: Susan and Kate, two of the kindest and most generous people on this planet and the best writing crew I could ask for; Christine, my fabulous Salt Friend, whose words and excellent company sustain me in equal measure; Shannon, the funniest person I know and the best dinner companion I could ask for; the e l e g a n t Alex, the best podcast partner in crime I could ask for; my roommates Lynne and Erin, for their enthusiasm and their boundless patience with my mid-drafting memory lapses; and Miranda and Sarah, my sisters in every way that matters, for being there from the very beginning.

Thank you to Rob, who honestly deserves a cowriting credit at this point, but would definitely never accept it. I've tried so many times to tell you how much you've helped me, but words never seem to cover it. Thank you for everything.

Thank you to my incredible extended family, who would fill an entire new book if I tried to name them in their entirety, but who have offered their love, excitement, and expertise at every turn. Having your support has kept me afloat this past decade. Thank you in particular to my godmother, Katie, who always let me check my email when she took me out to dinner.

And finally, to my family, who never seemed to doubt that I would find my way here: Dad, Keenan, Sara, and especially Mom, my first editor. I love you all so much.